MISSIONS FROM
THE EXTINCTION CYCLE
VOLUME 1

MARK TUFO - ANTHONY MELCHIORRI
JEFF OLAH - RUSSELL BLAKE - RACHEL AUKES

FOREWORD FROM EXTINCTION CYCLE AUTHOR
NICHOLAS SANSBURY SMITH

GREAT WAVE INK
PUBLISHING

To the Extinction Cycle fans that have propelled the story and characters to a level I never thought possible.

Thank you for your support and encouragement.

#TeamGhost

"All it takes, is all you got…"

Foreword
by
Nicholas Sansbury Smith

Dear Reader,

Thank you for picking up a copy of Missions from the Extinction Cycle. These aren't just any missions. I hand selected these reader favorites because I believe they play homage to Team Ghost and the Extinction Cycle storyline I've created.

Please note, all of these stories were previously featured in Amazon's Extinction Cycle Kindle World. As you may know, Amazon ended the Kindle Worlds program in July of 2018. Authors were given a chance to republish or retire their stories, and I jumped at the chance to republish them and share them with you under my small press, Great Wave Ink.

For those of you that are new to the storyline, the Extinction Cycle is the award winning, Amazon top-rated, and half a million copy best-selling seven book saga. There are over six *thousand* five-star reviews on Amazon alone. Critics have called it, "World War Z and The Walking Dead meets the Hot Zone." Publishers weekly added, "Smith has realized that the way to rekindle interest in zombie apocalypse fiction is to make it louder, longer, and bloodier... Smith intensifies the disaster efficiently as the pages flip by, and readers who enjoy juicy blood-and-guts action will find a lot of it here."

In creating the Extinction Cycle, my goal was to use authentic military action and real science to take the zombie and post-apocalyptic genres in an exciting new direction. Forget everything you know about zombies. In the Extinction Cycle, they aren't created by black magic or other supernatural means. The ones found in the Extinction Cycle are created by a military bio-weapon called VX-99, first used in Vietnam. The chemicals reactivate the proteins encoded by the genes that separate humans from wild animals—in other words, the experiment turned men into monsters. For the first time, zombies are explained using real science—science so real there is every possibility of something like the Extinction Cycle actually happening. But these creatures aren't the unthinking, slow-minded, shuffling monsters we've all grown accustomed to in other shows, books, and movies. These "variants" are more monster than human. Through the series, the variants become the hunters as they evolve from the epigenetic changes. Scrambling to find a cure and defeat the monsters, humanity is brought to the brink of extinction.

We hope you enjoy each of the five Extinction Cycle missions and will continue to the main series.

Best wishes,
Nicholas Sansbury Smith,
NYT Bestselling Author of the Extinction Cycle

Contents

Darkness Evolved

by

Anthony J Melchiorri

— 1 —

Marine Staff Sergeant Jose Garcia did not flinch when the tattoo gun needle jabbed into his skin at a rate of almost one thousand times per minute. He sat on the edge of his berth aboard the USS *George Washington*, steadying his arm as he took the tattoo gun to himself. The gentle waves of the Atlantic rocked the massive carrier ever so slightly, and the buzz of the gun drowned out the metallic creaking of the ship.

Each time the needle pierced his skin, it left another black mark in the stylized cross tattooed on the inside of his right forearm. And each time it stabbed in, he hated that he had grown used to it. Hated that the pain of the needle was nothing compared to the pain of what had driven him to take his tattoo gun to his own arm once again. Hate had become almost as familiar to him as the tattoo gun. He had lost far more than brothers to the Variants; he had lost his family too.

Yes, hate for the Variants and for the men who created them came easy to him.

When he was satisfied with the new addition to his artwork, he pulled the gun away and took his foot off the pedal. The gun fell silent. After stowing it back under his berth, he rotated his arm. He pulled his hand over his short-cropped hair and admired his work. With a long exhalation, he dabbed at the spots of crimson pushing themselves up through the black ink and olive skin.

Ray Stanford.

He would never forget that name, and it was not just because the name was now tattooed on his forearm.

Stanford had been one of Garcia's men, a brother in arms serving in the six-man Force Recon group he led. He did not need a tattoo to remind him of Stanford's valiant attempt to hold back a swarm of Variants when they had been on a mission outside New York City. The images of Stanford being ripped apart, his ribs torn from his chest, his femur bursting from his flesh, hot scarlet liquid splashing out of his neck when the Variants sank their fangs into him, were more than enough to ensure Garcia never forgot his fallen brother.

In twenty years of service, Garcia had memorialized too many of his comrades within the cross on his arm. It had taken almost two decades of fighting overseas, largely against terrorist and insurgent threats in the Middle East, to add the first half-dozen names. There had been plenty of raw skin still ready to use as fresh canvas. It had only taken a few weeks after the spread of the Hemorrhage Virus to fill the cross to the point where he only had room for seven, maybe eight more names.

A shiver snuck through his freshly inked arm. He wondered how long it would take before he needed another cross. Letting out a deep breath, he closed his eyes.

Please, God, don't make me write another name.

He crossed himself and said the Lord's Prayer, praying for strength, for deliverance from the heavy weight of loss and death weighing on his mind. But he worried God was not going to solve his problems. God was not going to save his men. It was the damned US Army that had performed the perverted medical research resulting in the Hemorrhage Virus, then VX-99, which swept through the United States, turning men into monsters. It was mortal men who developed the bioweapons that had created the Variants. Humans had gotten themselves into this mess, and now they would have to get themselves out.

A knock at his hatch broke his dark reverie. Garcia stood. His boots slapped against the metal deck. He puffed out his chest, willing himself to appear strong while taping a strip of gauze over the tattoo to soak up the blood.

When he opened the hatch, a man with a mustache and hair to match Garcia's gave him a nod.

"You okay, brother?" Rick Thomas, a sergeant in Garcia's team, asked.

"Once we rid the earth of all those damn Variants, then I'll be okay," he said through gritted teeth. He was lying, though. He knew he would never truly be okay. Not with everything he had already seen and lost.

"You and me both. Lt. Davis sent for us. Wants us to meet her in CIC."

"When?"

"Now," Thomas said. "Said it's urgent."

"When isn't it?"

Garcia closed the hatch and strode through the passage toward the CIC. Thomas fell in step beside him as men and women rushed past. Each shared the same bags under the eyes, the same weary looks.

Thomas eyed the fresh gauze on Garcia's arm. "Stanford hasn't even been laid to rest. What do you want to bet Davis is sending us out again?"

"Our work's never done. Not until the geeks in the lab come up with a cure or we meet our maker." A new bioweapon that could eradicate the Variants could not come soon enough. With every passing day, Garcia worried there were not enough bullets or soldiers in the world to eradicate the monsters.

"I'm starting to think meeting our maker will come first," Thomas said, dodging past a group of SEALs jogging down the corridor in full battle regalia.

Garcia stopped himself before he said the words floating in his mind. He wanted to tell Thomas he was ready to meet his Lord, ready to be reunited with his six-month-old daughter, Leslie, and his wife, Ashley. Regret hung heavy on him with each passing day spent in their absence. His thoughts often turned toward the "what ifs." What if he had stayed behind with them when his orders had come in? What if he had gone AWOL, running to the hills or mountains with his family instead? What if he had known the outbreak would end only in destruction, death, apocalypse? Sorrow filled him as much as exhaustion these days. Instead of staying behind and abandoning his duty, he had reported for duty and was whisked away to the *George Washington* strike group while his family had been stranded in their home in North Carolina and undoubtedly fallen to the Variants.

He hated to admit it, but getting a fast-pass ticket to Heaven would be a welcome reprieve if it meant he could hold Leslie in his arms once more and share a loving embrace with Ashley. Then again, at this point in his life, he was not sure Heaven was where he would go if he died. Ashley had been a saint, volunteering at women's shelters and cooking for soup kitchens. She had run a nonprofit community health center. All Garcia knew how to do was take lives. Better he stay on Earth and do his part to serve humanity, prove to himself and the guy in the sky he was worth something.

Thomas stopped in the passageway and held a hatch open. Garcia rolled his sleeve down over the gauze and entered the CIC. A wave of noise overwhelmed him as people leaned over monitors, watching the movements of dozens of different spec ops teams, mechanized units, and airborne forces on missions all across the United States.

A lean woman with eyes as blue as the Atlantic and a jawline sharper than a knife approached him.

Garcia and Thomas straightened at the sight of Lt. Rachel Davis and offered a salute. "Ma'am," they said in unison.

"At ease," she replied, gesturing toward a table where a group of marines huddled. "I know your team just returned. I promise we'll take the time to properly honor Stanford later, but I need you guys now."

"Yes, ma'am," Garcia said. He willed the weight on his eyelids to subside as he and Thomas followed Lt. Davis to the chart table. There he joined the rest of his now five-man team. Steve "Stevo" Holmes stood with his arms crossed, his Dumbo ears sticking out against his boyish face. Next to him was the massive form of Ryan "Tank" Talon with the team's radio still strapped over his shoulders. Beside him stood Jeremy "Mulder" Weaver. The man was a natural-born sprinter with a runner's lean form. When news of VX-99 spreading like wildfire first got to Garcia's team, Weaver had offered a lame guess that the virus had extraterrestrial origins. The men never let him live it down. In fact, it was Stanford who had given him the name Mulder after the famous extraterrestrial believer from *The X-Files*.

Another unfamiliar marine with straight black hair sauntered over to them, an MK11 slung across his back.

"This is Lance Corporal Howard Kuang," Lt. Davis said. "He'll be your sixth man."

"Sarge," Lance Corporal Kuang started, nodding at Garcia, "I know I can't replace Stanford, but I'll give it my all. Whatever the hell I can do for the team, I will."

The tattoo with Stanford's name still stung. The skinny marine seemed confident enough, but confidence in the CIC often did not translate to confidence in the face of Variants with maws of daggerlike fangs and claws long enough to gut an elephant. "Understood, Marine," Garcia said. "How many Variants have you killed?"

Kuang's expression dropped. "More than I can keep track of. Not enough to make me happy."

No amount of dead Variants would make Garcia happy.

"I'm not unfamiliar with the monsters' ferocity, if that's what you're implying." Kuang pulled his shirt up, revealing a scar stretching from hip to sternum.

"Fair enough." Garcia held out a hand. "Kuang, is it?"

Kuang gripped Garcia's hand in a firm handshake. "My team called me Kong. I ain't royalty, so don't call me King."

Garcia could not help but smirk. It sounded as though the marine had delivered that line more than once. "Very well, Kong. Welcome to the team."

The group turned their attention to Lt. Davis. She gestured to a monitor set up on the chart table.

Garcia's stomach twisted into a painful knot as he stared at the map. Adrenaline pumped through his vessels, churned on by unadulterated anger. Ashley's face appeared in his mind, at first her beaming smile as she bent to kiss him. Then the look of horror he imagined she wore when the first Variant found her and Leslie. Sweat dripped down his spine. His fingers trembled, and his jaw went slack as he tried to work the muscles in it. The snarl of emotions forcing themselves through him felt like a dagger ravaging his intestines and cutting apart his organs in slow, savage strokes. "Pardon me, ma'am, but seriously?"

Lt. Davis sighed. She knew where he came from, where his family had lived. "It's why I picked your team, Garcia."

The monitor displayed the lengthy stretch of beaches and parks that comprised North Carolina's Outer Banks. It was a place etched into his mind. He had spent many long weekends with Ashley, basking in the sun on the gentle sands of the beach. In fact, he had proposed to her in a lighthouse on one of the Outer Banks barrier islands, and it had been the site of their first and only family vacation with Leslie.

"I don't know another person who knows the banks as well as you, Garcia," Davis continued. "And that's why I need your team to do something that no one else has been able to."

— 2 —

Garcia did not look forward to the mission to the Outer Banks, and he could not help the sigh he let out. One tinged with grief and sadness.

"President Mitchell ordered the reestablishment of Naval Station Norfolk in Virginia," Davis said. "We've had the chance to salvage most of the base, and we're on track to making it functional again. It's the largest naval station in the world, and we absolutely need it as a resource to keep the *GW* strike group afloat."

"That would be a tremendous boon to the navy," Garcia said. Anything to relieve the strike group's constant worry about how and when they would refuel, resupply, and make repairs would drastically improve the ships' chances at making it through the apocalypse, not to mention bolster the crew's morale. But Garcia had long since learned all great gains came with great costs. "So what's the hitch?"

"Perimeter defenses were holding until a new influx of Variants threatened the naval station's restoration. Variant attacks have been increasing both in size and frequency. The Variants started coming once or twice a day in small groups, almost like they were probing the defenses. Now the attacks are occurring every two to three hours, and the monsters are finding their way into the base. Casualties are mounting, and President Mitchell is considering abandoning the station entirely."

"Christ," Thomas said. "Can't catch a break in the apocalypse, huh?"

"If the military can barely hang on to the station, how do we fit into this?" Garcia asked. "Don't see what good we'll be at holding a large-scale attack off."

"Good question," Davis said. She tapped on a keyboard, and the map displayed on the monitor zoomed in to a satellite image of a small town near the north end of the islands. Garcia recognized it: Corolla, located just south of the Currituck National Wildlife Refuge. "We've been using drone surveillance to track the Variant movements toward Norfolk. Most of the Variant movement has been traced from somewhere on this island."

"Why not bomb the whole place and call it a day?" Mulder asked.

Deep creases formed in Tank's forehead. "Sounds a bit overkill."

"Truth is," Davis said, "we simply don't have the ordnance to waste haphazardly bombing up and down the length of a two-hundred-mile island, hoping we hit a Variant hive."

"But if we can locate the actual hive, then it's a go?" Garcia asked, guiltily hopeful of the Variants' lair exploding in a hail of fire and brimstone. Served the devils right. If he could help make that happen, he would oblige.

"Exactly," Davis said. "So that's where you all come in. As much time as our eyes in the sky have spent above the area, we can't seem to actually find where these things are coming from. We need boots on the ground to figure out what the hell is going on."

"Sounds right up our alley," Garcia said, rubbing the fresh tattoo on his arm. He noticed a slight frown in Davis's expression. "What's the catch?"

"You all aren't the first team we ordered to investigate the area." Davis indicated a spot in the middle of the refuge. "An eight-man team of SEALs made landfall at approximately 1600 hours. They traveled only three klicks south from their insertion point before we lost radio contact. I've highlighted their last known location for your reference. This is Objective A." She passed a paper map across the table to Garcia. "We need you to locate them then pick up where they left off. Objective B is Corolla, a small town on the Outer Banks. This is a prime candidate for Variant hive activity."

"Locate a missing SEAL team and a possible hive of Variants," Kong said. "Doesn't exactly sound like a cakewalk."

"I don't give easy missions to my best teams," Davis said. "And this is no exception." Garcia wanted to feel pride at the compliment. But worry wormed itself through his nerves as Davis unveiled each new detail of the mission. She placed a cell-phone-sized device with an LCD screen on the table.

"New toys?" Garcia asked.

"Very new." Davis pushed it toward Garcia, and he examined it. "This is a locator. It tracks other soldiers on the ground through what's called the Warfighter Integrated Navigation System. Works even when GPS doesn't by using inertial sensors to calculate motion and trajectory. Gives us something to see through terrain and obstacles unfriendly to GPS."

Garcia appreciated anything that would give them another tool to navigate through the unknown. Especially when that unknown and darkness Davis referred to was filled with hungry Variants. "WINS devices." Garcia stuffed the locator in his pocket. "Isn't that experimental tech? Not even approved for field use yet?"

"No one gives a rat's ass about regulatory approval right now," Davis said. "The SEALs were equipped with WINS chips. Should help you find them." She deposited six plastic devices, each the size of a credit card and three times as thick, in front of the marines. "Each of you will have one on this mission." Davis placed her palms flat on the table as she leaned over the map. "And that's not all. Reports from Norfolk indicate the Variants that have been attacking them have been demonstrating progressive adaptations over time. We're talking gills, scales, fangs, and all kinds of other strange mutations." She pressed her lips together. Garcia knew the look. It was the same one the doctor had given him before telling him his mother had passed away on the surgical table, or when his old CO had told him he was shipping out to fight the Variants. "The team in the labs wants samples to see if they can figure out how these changes are taking place."

"Samples?" Stevo said, his eyes wide. "It's going to be a real pain in the ass bringing back bits of 'em. Pardon the language, ma'am."

Davis raised an eyebrow.

"We'll bring whatever the hell you want," Garcia said. "Blood, tissue, limbs. Consider us your Variant delivery service."

The others enthusiastically voiced their assent to Garcia's promise.

"That's what I like to hear," she said. "I know we're asking a lot. But I've got faith in you, Garcia. Faith in all of you."

"We won't fail." Garcia's chest swelled as he stood straighter. But he knew they would need more than faith if they were to survive what the night would have in store for them. Once the sun settled over the horizon and Variants stalked the land in full force, all bets of faith and hope were off. Valor and bullets spoke louder.

Davis forced a smile. "I know." She regained a stern look. "You've got thirty minutes to load up and ship out."

"You heard her, brothers," Garcia said. "Ammo, armor, and chow if you've got time. Let's move."

The men started filing out of the CIC. Garcia followed.

"Sergeant," Davis said, and Garcia turned. "I appreciate what you've done for us. One mission after another, virtually no sleep. I'm asking the impossible, but it seems like every damn mission, the odds are getting worse."

"You don't need to tell me." Garcia wrapped his fingers around his tattooed forearm. As the odds got worse, so did the snakes of guilt constricting his mind tighter and tighter with each new death. "Rest assured, we can handle this."

"All it takes is all you got, Marine."

"Yes, ma'am," Garcia said.

"But just in case that isn't enough, I've briefed another team. They'll be joining you on the Osprey. You'll have command in the field."

***

Garcia adjusted the chin strap on his helmet as he marched down the corridor to the boat bay. Tank reached the hatch to the top deck first and opened it. The din of idling aircraft and the thrum of the aircraft carrier pushing through the ocean overwhelmed them. A warm, seaborne wind blasted into the corridor. The smell of brine swirled around them. Three gulls dove toward the deck. One cocked its head, eyeing Garcia, then caught an updraft. He watched the bird, wondering if the animals had noticed what had happened to their world.

A blue-shirted flight-deck crew member waved them through the churning air and cacophony on deck. He gestured to a V22 Osprey. The tiltrotor aircraft's props were spinning up, and the rear door lay open, welcoming Garcia's team into the fuselage.

As Tank, Stevo, Kong, and the others strapped themselves in, Garcia eyed the other marines Garcia would be leading. The group had already secured their harnesses, with their equipment at their feet. A flight-deck crew member shut the rear door of the Osprey, drowning out the cacophony enough to give Garcia's eardrums a rest.

"Monster Hunters, prepare for takeoff," a pilot called back.

One of the marines that had been waiting on Garcia's group answered, "Ready. And we're not the goddamned Monster Hunters." The words came out laced in venom. "Sounds like some pansy-ass group out of a B-rated sci-fi flick. Variant Hunters, man. Variant Hunters." The marine, Staff Sergeant Wesley Rollins, leader of a fellow Force Recon team, gave Garcia a shit-eating grin. Most of the time, Garcia's group and Rollins's operated independently. But now was one of those rare times when

Command deemed the mission dangerous enough to send both teams.

"Finally something we can agree on," Garcia said. "Monster Hunters sounds like we're going to end up in some bullshit zombie-tornado movie. Never been a fan of things with teeth in my tornados."

"That's goddamned right," Rollins said, cracking his knuckles. "Variant Hunters. We hunt goddamn Variants. Should be pretty simple." His eyes narrowed. "Can't wait to shoot up some of those oily bastards again."

The aircraft lifted off the deck, and the marines wrapped their fingers around their harnesses as the rotor blades chewed into the air.

"So you're leading us tonight, Garcia?" Anton "Russian" Gorbachev said with a plain Midwestern accent that seemed to contradict his name. The son of Russian immigrants, Russian had joined the Marines at the age of eighteen, vowing to defend his parents' adopted country.

Garcia nodded, scanning the rest of Rollins's team. Jeff Morgan sat stoic and silent beside Russian, with one hand gripping his MK11. Beside him, Jimmy Daniels checked the magazines for his M4. His short-cropped hair, mustache, and olive skin made him appear like a slightly younger version of Garcia. Brad "Chewy" Olsen, tall and lanky, appeared every bit his namesake, with a thick coat of hair covering his arms like Han's sidekick and, when prompted, was willing to make the half-growl, half-gurgling call of a Wookie.

Garcia noted they were missing a sixth member.

Rollins seemed to notice him surveying his team, and he scrunched his brow. "Lost Williams on our last recon." He spit at his boots. "Fucking Variants."

"Damn," Garcia said. He had heard the rumors of the

group's surveillance mission outside Boston. What was supposed to have been a covert observation mission had turned into an all-out slugfest with the Variants. Garcia wished his team could have been there to help them instead of being stuck near NYC. "Sorry to hear it, brother." He found himself saying another silent prayer for yet another marine who had paid the ultimate price.

"Same with you by the looks of it," Rollins said. "Who's the new guy?"

"I'm Kong. And don't call—"

Before he could finish, Rollins started laughing. "Man, who the hell started calling you Kong? You're skinnier than a goddamned scarecrow. More like a shitty little capuchin. You probably wouldn't even be an appetizer to the Variants."

"That's my team member you're talking about," Garcia said. "If Davis says he's capable, he's capable. Plus, he's a marine like us. You know as well as I do what that means."

Rollins held his hands up in a supplicating gesture. "Hey, hey, no need to get so defensive. I'm just trying to lighten the mood."

"Lighten the mood?" Tank said with a slight snarl. "There's no such thing as lightening the mood when you're about to face Variants."

The pilot's voice came over the speakers, interrupting the marines. "Insertion point ETA in five."

Any purported attempts of Rollins to cut the tension evaporated like a puddle in the desert with those words.

Rollins popped a magazine out of his TAC vest. He took several rounds out, scratching something into the casings. His face seemed stuck in a permanent scowl as he did.

"What's that about?" Stevo whispered, leaning over to Garcia.

"Does it for every mission. Etches the names of his wife, mother, father, and sister into them," Garcia replied. Every soldier had their way of coping with the mounting deaths. And good God, they needed those methods now more than ever. Garcia scratched at the gauze taped over his tattoo.

"Lost them to the Variants?"

"Lost them to the Variants. He talked Davis into letting his family onto a ship in the *GW* strike group."

"Variants got on the ship?"

"No," Garcia said. "Family never made it on the ship. Things tore his sister from his arms before they could load an escape boat." Images of his own wife and daughter flashed through his mind. "Took his wife, parents. Horrible."

"Horrible," Stevo agreed.

Garcia twisted to stare out a window. The last rays of the sinking sun cast an orange glow over the barrier islands along the coast, giving them the appearance of dying embers.

"Them the Outer Banks?" Mulder asked.

"That's right," Garcia said.

The islands themselves appeared strangely peaceful. Sun-glinted waves lapped the expansive beaches, and trees populated the marshy lands Garcia knew contained a wild-horse population roaming the wildlife refuges—if they had survived the Variants. But just past the islands, all along the main coastline of North Carolina, columns of smoke stretched into the darkening sky. Beyond that coast lay his home, ravaged no doubt by the Variants, where his daughter and wife had been taken from him.

Someone kicked Garcia's boot, and he jolted away from the window.

"Hey, man, you look like you're going to puke," Rollins said, one eyebrow arched. "You sure you can take the lead here? If not…"

Garcia straightened. Rollins was known to be brash. Bullheaded even. But suggesting he would assume command took it to a new level. He narrowed his eyes, meeting Rollins's gaze. His voice came out in a low growl. "I got this."

All it takes is all you got, he thought. He was about to confront monsters that had not only once been human, but also ones that haunted his memories and nightmares. But he had no choice. This was his duty, his penance, to serve those still left in this world. He started to mutter the Lord's Prayer under his breath, instilling himself with the strength of a higher power—hoping that a higher power was still up there listening to him.

"You praying again, Garcia?" Rollins asked. He forced a curt laugh. He glanced out the window, past the Outer Banks and toward the fires still raging across the coastal towns where Variants roamed, hunting the remaining humans. "Maybe you need to pray harder, because I don't think those goddamned prayers have helped anyone."

— 3 —

The Osprey's rotors tilted as the aircraft began its descent. Dark beaches rose toward the craft. Gritty sand kicked up under the rotor wash, tossed from the insertion point.

Garcia crossed himself then pressed two fingers to his helmet, touching the spot outside of where he had the photo of Ashley and Leslie taped. "Variant Hunters, this is it. Mulder, you're on point."

The thin marine locked a magazine into place on his M4. "You got it, Sarge."

"Russian, Tank, you're on rear guard."

The two hulking marines nodded.

"Everyone else, eyes open, keep your firing lanes clear."

The Osprey jolted as its tires hit the shifting sands, and the rear door opened. The Variant Hunters sprinted from their seats, boots stomping across the metal deck, and fanned out of the rear of the aircraft.

"Victor Hotel Alpha, clear," Garcia said, chinning his mic.

"Victor Hotel, Griffin One out. Headed back to the *GW*."

The air swirled around the team. Wet sand sucked at Garcia's boots. He shouldered his M4 and scanned the rapidly darkening landscape as the sun sank. The other Variant Hunters circled up, bristling with weapons, searching the encroaching shadows for the monsters they knew were out there. A lone, shrill screech broke through the night air, echoing over the island.

Garcia tensed, adrenaline already barreling through his vessels. His finger hovered near the trigger guard while he stared down the optics of his rifle. He sniffed the air, anticipating the fermenting-fruit-and-rotten-meat odor characteristic of the Variants. The distinct smell usually wafted on the air ahead of the beasts. "Contacts?"

He waited for the chorus of other shrieks and the clicking joints that would precipitate a raucous assault, but none came. No odor reminiscent of death and rot, either.

"Negative," each of the Variant Hunters reported in turn.

The hair on the back of Garcia's neck stood straight as he signaled the team forward over the beach, toward the snarls of trees in the wildlife refuge. Somewhere in those thickets, the SEAL team had ceased contact with the *GW*. No amount of moonlight would permeate the dense canopy shrouding the forest, and Garcia imagined the demonic eyes watching them from those shadows. Darkness and the unknown. That was all the Variant Hunters faced. The final columns of dark blue and purple succumbed to the blackness of night.

"NVGs on," Garcia said. His command was met with a flurry of clicks as the others flipped their NVGs down. "Radio discipline."

They crossed the beach toward a cracked asphalt road.

Mulder stayed on point, swiveling left then right. Leaves rustled, and at first, Garcia could not tell if it was the wind or Variants lying in wait, ready to ambush their unsuspecting prey.

But the steady drone of cicadas and low chirps of hidden frogs and birds grew louder. Approaching the road gave Garcia some comfort. At least, the animals of the refuge seemed not to have noticed any genetically engineered super predators lurking among the trees.

They reached the sandbank leading up to the road. Garcia held a hand up. Cars lined the roadway, stuck forever behind an overturned SUV only a dozen meters from their position. Glass shards from busted windows sparkled in the moonlight, like a thousand glittering stars fallen to Earth. A warm breeze picked up. Garcia's nerves lit up in excitement. This time, the wind carried the distinct rotten smell of death.

Out of his periphery, Garcia saw Russian cringe at the scent before the man regained his composure. The odor of decaying flesh and meat continued drifting around them, and Garcia searched for the source.

He expected to find the shredded bodies of humans scattered along the road, with Variants creeping among them. But as they weaved between the wrecked and abandoned vehicles, he could not see any human corpses. Instead, all they discovered were suitcases torn open and spilled clothes across the ground like a wounded animal with its guts splayed over the road. Soggy boxes of food and bottles of water lay half-buried in the sand. All signs indicated people had attempted a desperate escape from the Outer Banks, but no signs indicated where those people had gone.

Tank seemed to be reading Garcia's mind and shot

him a questioning look. Garcia lifted his shoulders in a noncommittal gesture. They pushed past the roadway and reached the tree line. Snarled roots broke the surface of the ground like sea serpents, and thickets of brown and green grass pressed up through the marshy landscape. Trees jutted up before them, dense and thickly packed like a phalanx marching toward them. Even with his NVGs, Garcia could not see more than a dozen yards into the forested area with all the branches and foliage blocking their view.

Mulder paused at the tree line and looked back at Garcia for his next order. Garcia scanned his men. They wore varied expressions ranging from stoic determination to hints of unease and fear, evident by widening eyes and tense muscles. He did not blame them. After everything they had been through, their most dangerous enemy was the unknown. The Variants had drastically changed since the start of the outbreak. They had evolved from zombielike beings with a thirst for flesh to creatures with beastly features that rendered them more monster than human. Evolution seemed to have been expedited in their ranks. Garcia had learned not to be surprised when a Variant showed up with claws the size of kitchen knives, chameleonlike color-changing flesh, or joints that bent like a spider's. Not knowing exactly what lurked in the forest, not knowing whose eyes watched them or what had become of the SEAL team, was no doubt eating at each Variant Hunter's mind.

But their directive was not to cower in fear or turn back at the first hint of danger. They were the chosen few, those selected to complete missions just like this.

Still, nervous sweat beaded across Garcia's forehead as he signaled Mulder to surge forward into the forest. The man disappeared into the shadows of the trees, with Chewy, Stevo, and Thomas close behind. Garcia went in next beside Rollins.

Even though I walk through the valley of the shadow of death…

The words came almost unconsciously to Garcia, echoing in the recesses of his mind. Gnarled roots and seeping puddles threatened each step he took. He directed his men down the path he had memorized from the map Lt. Davis had given him, trusting his instincts and internal compass. While the buzz of insects and croaks of frogs accompanied their journey, the stench of rotten meat grew stronger. Nausea almost sabotaged Garcia's fierce demeanor, endangering the meager meal he had managed to scarf down on the *GW*.

He could hear the labored breaths of the others over their comms. Their rifles probed the darkness, roving side to side in response to every creaking branch and lizard scuttling up the tree trunks. Garcia tried to maintain visual contact with the team of eleven, but the men constantly shifted in and out of his sight as the trees grew closer together, threatening to become an almost impenetrable obstacle. He diligently avoided the tangles of dried branches and leaves. With each step, small fiddler crabs scattered and dove into burrows.

The passage into the wildlife refuge became hypnotic as they trudged past the same plants and leaves and trees. The only thing that seemed to change was the burgeoning stink of decay.

Then Garcia heard a sickening crunch like breaking bone. His heart climbed into his throat, and he swiveled to his right, his M4 seeking a target.

Instead of a monster careening out of the darkness, he saw Kong frozen, his nose scrunched in disgust. He made an apologetic face at Garcia. The man had stepped onto what looked like a broken rib.

As Garcia gazed at the rib, he knew it had not come from any human. The bone itself was larger than his arm. His eyes widened as he spotted the trail of other bones intersecting the Variant Hunters' paths. Large femurs and long, misshapen skulls lay scattered among the puddles and roots.

At first he feared the bones belonged to the Variants and the creatures were evolving faster than even the science teams back on Plum Island and in the *GW* strike group had guessed. But his fears were slightly allayed when he realized that the bones and mostly eaten corpses had belonged to the wild-horse population. The poor beautiful creatures had met the Variants. A shudder snuck down Garcia's spine. He wondered whether the horde that had devoured the horses still lurked nearby.

Even as the eleven-man team moved past the horses-turned-carrion, the intense smell of death never abated as Garcia had expected. Instead, it followed them, stubbornly lingering even when a salty breeze twisted between the dense trees. They continued to put distance between themselves and the deceased horses.

Garcia held up a hand, signaling Mulder to hold. The group paused. Something was not right.

Then Garcia realized the bugs had gone silent. The only sounds he heard were the shallow breathing of the Variant Hunters and his thundering heart. He shot the others a quick hand signal to stay alert and keep an eye out for contacts.

He reached into one of the pockets on his TAC vest and pulled out a small device with an LCD screen. It blinked, displaying a single arrow pointing in the direction of the WINS device that was supposed to be on the SEAL team's squad leader. The blinking grew rapider as they drew closer to the purported location of the WINS device, and Garcia's pulse accelerated in response. They were close. So damn close.

His eyes scanned the muddled green and black shapes through his NVGs, seeking out any sign of life, any sign the SEAL team was nearby. Faster and faster the locator blinked until it reported that they were almost on top of the WINS signal and, Garcia prayed, the SEAL team.

Suddenly, the locator displayed a single black circle, signifying that they were in the immediate vicinity of the WINS device. Garcia gestured to the others to fan out. Chewy nudged a thicket with his rifle muzzle, and Kong peered around a particularly knotted mass of roots. Stevo sifted through the edge of a creek with his hand, breaking the surface of the stagnant water. His fingers left a tiny wake, and he peered into the shallow water.

The SEALs had to be around here somewhere. Whether they were dead or alive, Garcia was determined to find them—or at least learn what had happened to them. He sucked down gasps of humid air, his eyes scanning back and forth.

Then he saw it. A pair of legs in black fatigues sticking out from a gap under a fallen tree trunk.

One of the SEALs!

Garcia nudged Rollins and Russian, and the duo sprinted with him to the trunk. They leapt over the rotten log to the trapped SEAL beneath it. Garcia's boots landed hard in the mud, kicking up flecks of soil and broken twigs. The other Variant Hunters swarmed around, setting up a perimeter. But Garcia's guts twisted painfully when he saw the rest of the SEAL—or rather, the lack of the poor SEAL.

The entire top half of the man was gone.

— 4 —

Garcia knelt next to the torn torso of the SEAL. His eyes followed a trail of blood and shredded organs spread across the broad leaves and vines. His nerves burned hot, and his jaw clenched tight enough he risked grinding his teeth to stubs. The brutality of the beasts astounded him. The monster must have killed the SEAL out of pure bloodlust. It had not even bothered to stop to finish the man off and make a meal out of its prey. Then again, Garcia wondered if the Variant had left these SEAL carcasses to rot for a reason. He tried to shrug off the thought, unwilling to believe the monsters were intelligent enough to apply rhyme or reason to their actions. Still, he shouldered his rifle and searched for the monster that had done this. Maybe the Variant Hunters' arrival had scared off the Variants from their kill or at least distracted them from their meal.

A smattering of nearby deformed footsteps contained puddles, but the patterns led in all directions. Tracking down the Variants those footsteps belonged to would be an arduous, if not almost impossible, task.

"Stevo, Kong, Daniels, Morgan, check for survivors," Garcia said. "The rest of you, watch our backs."

Six other SEAL bodies lay among the weeds. Judging by the dark stains splashed on the tree trunks and soaking into the ground, Garcia guessed he would not find a pulse in any of them.

But damn it, he had to try. He threw himself down near a SEAL sprawled on his back with limbs outstretched. Deep lacerations crisscrossed the SEAL's flesh, and his fatigues hung off him in ragged strips. Dark bruises covered the man's face, and dried blood crusted over his eyelids.

Garcia grabbed the man's wrist and pressed his fingers against his skin, praying for a pulse. "Come on, buddy. We're here to help you."

He did not expect the man to acknowledge him, much less be alive. And matching his expectations, only the coldness of death crept from the man's flesh into Garcia's fingers.

"Any survivors?" Garcia asked.

"Negative," Rollins replied. The others confirmed Garcia's dark suspicions. He looked up, surveying the mangled bodies of the other SEALs. Besides the one missing the top half of his body, he saw another whose spine had been ripped out next to a corpse with no head. The other two were no better, their bodies nothing more than disemboweled sacks of ragged flesh.

"Found a dead Variant," Stevo said. "Not much of him left. Usual gray flesh and claws and shit. Got some weird growths on his back."

"Grab a sample like the scientists ordered," Garcia said, glancing at the abominable corpse Stevo stood over. The marine bent next to the body and tore off several pieces of flesh he stuffed into plastic tubes. Bullet holes riddled what little was left of the Variant's body, and just as Stevo had said, dark plates covered its back and parts of its arms. Its fingers had fused together, forming a pincerlike appendage rather than a hand. Most of its muscle and flesh had been torn off its bones. Garcia guessed its fellow Variants did not want the dead body to go to waste and made a meal of it. He took his eyes off the creature's remains and surveyed the scene once more.

Then something struck him. He counted the SEALs again. There were only seven of them. Davis had told him the SEAL team had consisted of eight men. Where was the other?

"Command," Garcia started. "We found the SEALs. We've got seven confirmed KIA. One MIA."

"Copy, Hotel Victor," a specialist called back. "Are there any indications as to where the missing SEAL may have gone?"

Garcia looked to his men, all of whom shook their heads. The WINS locator displayed no eighth signal. Maybe the SEAL's device had been torn from his fatigues or malfunctioned. Either way, it was of no help now. "Negative."

"Then you're to proceed to Objective B."

"What happened to never leaving a man behind?" Rollins asked, one eyebrow arched. "They want us to just abandon the last guy? He's probably wandering around, looking for us."

"Then pray he finds us. We have our orders," Garcia said, hating every word he spoke. Never in his two decades of service with the Marines did he dream of leaving a US serviceman or woman behind, even after death. "We don't have the luxury of time to perform a man search."

Stevo gawked at the dead soldiers. The man had a

terrible poker face, which made it easy for the others to fleece him whenever the group had a card night. It also meant Garcia saw the look of pain cross the man's face when he realized they would be leaving the decimated SEAL team behind.

The missing man was probably dead like his comrades. He prayed their souls had at least found solace in Heaven, far from this hell on Earth. Tension hung thick in the air as Rollins scowled, shaking his head and trudging away from the deceased. Russian's eyes lingered over the tangled roots of a twisting tree, and Thomas looked away, unable to meet Garcia's gaze. Garcia had served with most of these men long enough to read their thoughts, even if their faces were as stoic as gargoyles on a cathedral.

They were not happy. Not one bit. They did not want to leave the missing SEAL behind, but Garcia had his orders.

"I don't like it," Rollins said, almost spitting. "I'm not about to act like a chickenshit little boy scared of those goddamned monsters. We need to bring that boy home."

With one hand, Garcia took the dog tags glistening on the ground next to the SEAL pinned under the tree. He looked at the bloodied man for a moment then looked back at his men and stood.

"If you asked him what he'd want us to do, do you think he'd want us to risk our asses for his remains? Or do you think he'd want us to go on with the mission—the one he might already have sacrificed his life for?" Garcia stared hard at Rollins. The fellow marine's eyes narrowed, and his nose scrunched into a snarl. If the man were a dog, Garcia would expect to hear him growling and snapping with his ears pressed flat against his skull.

"Fine. I want to kill some damn Variants and find our guy," Rollins said. "But do what you want. It's on your goddamn conscience."

A final prayer whispered through Garcia's mind. He turned away from the remains of the SEAL team. Rollins was right. This would weigh on his conscience, adding to the already-overflowing deposit of dark memories and devastating choices, and he would pray to God every day for these men he had left to rot in this marsh filled with unseen monsters.

But his corporeal obligations were to the men still standing beside him, the men who had trusted him with their lives, and he was not about to fail them or Lt. Davis.

"Mulder, take point. Chewy, Morgan, on his flank," Garcia ordered. "South toward Objective B. Let's find out where in the hell these Variants are coming from."

The trio converged ahead of the group, their rifles shouldered and probing the darkness. They moved forward like panthers lurking through the shadows. Muck and mud sucked at boots, and the ground gave way to shallow, salty water made opaque with silt. They marched between the trees again, ducking under vines and low-hanging limbs, making their way out of the refuge and toward Corolla. Soon they would be out of the grasp of the marsh.

But something still felt wrong. Garcia's nerves tingled.

He peered through the forest. Out of his periphery, he thought he saw movement. He whipped his rifle around. His pulse thumped like war drums in his ears, and his finger slid forward, ready to meet the trigger.

Nothing.

Maybe it was just the wind causing the tree branches to dance. Still, the explanation did not satisfy him. He could practically sense eyes on him as they distanced themselves from the sight of the SEALs' massacre.

But the rotten odor of death never disappeared. Even as they approached fifty yards out from the SEAL team, the smell of moldy fruit and maggot-filled meat never left his nostrils. At first, he had attributed the odor to the SEALs' corpses, but now he warranted that they were too far away to smell the bodies.

Adrenaline started to surge. The sounds of the forest had not returned either. No bird songs. No croaking frogs or chirping insects.

No, no, this was not right at all.

He opened his mouth to warn his men, but as soon as he did, something burst from the shallow water before him. Muddy droplets sprayed up, blinding him momentarily. Gritty sand scratched his face. Clawlike fingers wrapped around his ankle, dragging him to the ground. His elbow hit a tree trunk on his fall. Pain throbbed through his bones, and he lost his grip on his rifle. The back of his head hit a rock buried under the sandy mud. Something towered above him, hissing. Its eyes burned like budding volcanoes through his NVGs, and saliva sprayed from its pursed lips. Muscles coursed under sickly gray flesh. Hair hung off the creature's head in ragged clumps. Hard plates covered its body, and its fingers had grown together into pincers not unlike a crab's.

Variant.

The strange Variant opened its mouth wide. It lunged at Garcia with all the darkness and ferocity of a horseman of the apocalypse. Garcia stared past the serrated teeth of the monster, into the recesses of its throat, where he was sure he could see a tunnel straight to hell as the Variant bore down on him, ready to destroy him as it had done the SEAL team.

— 5 —

Garcia knew he would meet his maker someday. His time on this Earth would not be for eternity, and he welcomed his reunion with Leslie and Ashley beyond the pearly gates. He would embrace their heavenly spirits readily.

But today was not that day.

He still had a duty to humanity on Earth and a deep-seated anger that needed to be satiated. He rolled to the left. Water soaked into his fatigues, and he recovered his dropped rifle. The crablike Variant crashed into the muddy water where he had been a moment before. Its claws stabbed into the sand, and its teeth gnashed together in a sickening chorus of clicks and hisses. Twisting to face him, it snarled and bared its pointed fangs. Sinew tensed under the plates and almost-translucent gray flesh covering its demonic limbs.

The sounds of more clicking joints, yells from other marines, and Variant hunting cries echoed between the trees in a cacophony grating on Garcia's eardrums. Gunfire flashed. Rifles barked. Bullets riddled Variant bodies.

The fight around Garcia had become a messy, bloody blur. But where the hell had these monsters come from?

He knew the goddamn island was infested with them, but he had not even seen these creatures on their approach. It was as if they had simply teleported like ghostly apparitions at their feet.

He did not have long to consider the mystery of their origins as the creature bent to tackle him. It charged forward, flat webbed feet slapping into the muck, splashing. Claws glistened in the wan moonlight, and Garcia brought his rifle up.

But he could not fire on the Variant. Not while his men were scattered in the darkness around him. Not when he could not be sure he would not hit one of them embroiled in hand-to-hand combat with the creatures. And by God, he was not about to help these abominations finish the job they had started.

As he stood his ground, Garcia's muscles tensed. The creature leapt through the air. Claws slashed like so many menacing daggers. Garcia juked to his left and hammered the back of the Variant's skull with his rifle. He was rewarded with the hot spray of flesh and gore.

Such a wound would have debilitated a normal human but not a hungry Variant with one thing on its mind: kill.

Spinning on its heels, the Variant reared back and came at Garcia again. An agonized human scream burst out somewhere to Garcia's left, momentarily drawing his attention away from his attacker.

Rookie mistake for a Variant Hunter.

The creature took advantage of Garcia's surprise and rammed into his chest. Air whooshed from Garcia's lungs. The creature's shoulder dug hard into his sternum and knocked him on his ass. Garcia swung out with the rifle. He attempted to bash the creature's mutated snout with the gun's stock.

But the Variant was ready. It wrapped one repulsive claw around the barrel of the gun and tore it from Garcia's grip then flung it away.

"Son of a bitch!" Garcia yelled as the creature whaled on him with both pincerlike claws.

He tried to block blow after blow, but the Variant drove a knee into his chest. He gasped for breath as the monster's claws hammered into his arms. The violent shock of bone slamming against bone sent waves of pain shuddering through Garcia. He constantly twisted, still pressed flat on his back, to avoid the snapping jaws of the furious monster.

Maybe he had been wrong. Maybe this *was* it.

Ashley…Leslie…

Another bloodcurdling human yell rent the night air, filled with panic and pain. Even through the animalistic intensity of the wail, Garcia recognized the marine to whom the voice belonged: Mulder.

The thought of Mulder ending up like one of the SEALs galvanized what little strength remained in Garcia's battered limbs. As the Variant drew its club-like appendages back for another round of pummeling, Garcia grabbed both of the monster's wrists, fueled by a mix of rage and adrenaline.

The Variant almost seemed surprised. Its mouth opened in an expression that appeared simultaneously shocked and angry. Garcia surged up from the ground, every muscle in his body quaking, and he shoved the monster backward, pushing it toward a tree trunk. The creature fought in his grasp, twisting and screaming. Spittle sprayed across Garcia's face.

He would not let this beast win. Not now. Not when others' lives depended on him.

The Variant's spine slammed against the tree trunk, and Garcia dropped one of the creature's wrists. He pressed his palm flat against the creature's forehead and summoned all the power he had, thrusting his hand forward. A cry of pain escaped the Variant's lips. The back of its head was bleeding, devastated by Garcia's early attack with the rifle.

Garcia slammed the monster's head against the tree again, smearing bits of flesh and bone against the hard bark. Each time he bashed the creature's head, the monster's eyes seemed to lose a bit of the spark that had made the beast appear so fearsome and hellish. Its thrashing and bucking grew sluggish and its limbs listless. Then its eyes glazed over. Its tongue lolled out. Garcia let the monster fall into the water at his feet.

"Bastard," Garcia spat.

His chest heaved as he scoured the darkness for the rest of the Variant Hunters. It did not take him long to spot them through his NVGs. Their green bodies lit up in flashes as they struggled against the sinewy forms of the Variants. All of them seemed to be shifting and moving rapidly, each marine engaged in a deadly dance with a mutant partner.

Garcia scooped up his rifle and sprinted at the nearest Variant. Like the one that had attacked him, it had pincerlike claws and crustacean-inspired plates bumping up along its flesh. But none of that armor did it any good as Garcia pummeled the back of its head. The monster dropped, and Garcia plugged a couple of rounds into its skull for good measure.

When the monster's twitching ceased and a death rattle signaled its demise, Garcia offered a gloved hand to the marine who had been at the receiving end of the monster's hammering claws.

Kong took it and hoisted himself up. "Thanks."

Garcia simply nodded then pointed to the next group of embattled monsters and men. Together they killed a Variant pushing Stevo's head into the sand and making him suck down mouthfuls of muddy water. Near them, Rollins kicked another Variant into a tree then slung a blade from his sheath and stabbed it through the monster's eye socket. He dug the knife around, rotating it until he turned the creature's brain to mush.

One by one, the Variant Hunters finished off the creatures that had ambushed them. The clicking of joints and claws finally abated. Garcia gathered the men on his position, and they circled around each other, their rifles diligently sweeping the trees and shrubs as they searched for new targets. Each gasped, recovering from the brief but brutal skirmish.

"Contacts?" Garcia asked.

No response.

"Head count. Now!" he said. Stevo piped up first, followed by Thomas, then Tank. Then a beat of silence. "Where the fuck is Mulder?"

— 6 —

Garcia scanned the group. *No, no, no.* The lanky Variant Hunter could not be gone. He searched the corpses but saw only the twisted forms of the slaughtered Variants bleeding into the filthy water around their ankles.

"Chewy's missing, too," Russian said.

"And Morgan," Rollins added. "Son of a bitch!"

Thomas surveyed the Variants' bodies with his rifle. "Where the fuck did those monsters come from?"

"I don't see Mulder anywhere," Stevo said.

"Jesus," Tank said. "Did they take Mulder?"

"Where the fuck would they take them?" Daniels asked. "Can't see any goddamned footprints in this marsh." The man started to wander toward one of the bullet-riddled Variants leaning against a tree.

"Stick close, and stay together," Garcia said. The Variants had outwitted them, performed an ambush that neither he nor his men saw coming. He wanted to run after his men, but no good would come from rushing into the darkness. That was what the Variants wanted. The damn things wanted them to panic, wanted them to let rage and anger and feral instinct drive them into their clutches. As much as Garcia wanted to tear the monsters apart with bullets and knives, seeking revenge for what they had done to his men, the SEALs, and for that matter, the rest of humanity, he knew it would be foolish. "I don't want anyone else going missing." He wracked his mind for what to do next and looked to the sky. The stars were blotted out by the thick blanket of tree branches. There were no answers from above. God was not about to intervene. "Command, this is Victor Hotel. We encountered hostiles. Three men are MIA. Orders?"

"Victor Hotel, Command. Continue as planned."

Garcia nodded to the others. "Keep your eyes peeled. I—"

"Fuck that," Rollins burst out. "I'm not walking around here with our thumbs up our asses while those things eat our men. We're going after them."

Garcia's brow pinched into a furrow. He fought to control the heat washing into his face. "We have our orders."

"Goddamned Command doesn't know shit about this marsh," Rollins said. "You saw those SEALs. You saw how those Variants came from the ground like some ass-ugly crabs in the sand."

Rollins's volume was ranging dangerously high. Garcia did not want to add fuel to the fire and call more Variants to their position by engaging in a noisy argument. But he needed to quench this insurrection before it threatened their mission—and the lives of everyone else still with them.

"Rollins, our orders are to carry on. We don't know where those bastards took Mulder, Chewy, or Daniels. Running off into the darkness won't help them or us. We stick together and find out where these assholes are coming from. If we can do that, maybe we find where they took our boys."

"Maybe?" Rollins held his hands out in a disbelieving gesture. "Maybe? I don't work well with fucking maybes." He shook his head, his NVGs clicking as they jostled. "No way. Russian, Daniels, on me. We're getting our men back."

Russian sidled up to Rollins. His expression was wrought in fierce determination. Daniels looked between Rollins and Garcia like a dog choosing between two masters.

"Come on, Daniels," Rollins growled, studying the screen on his locator synced up with his men's WINS devices. "I've got a read on Morgan. He's headed south."

"Don't do this," Garcia said, his voice rising sharply. Heat flushed across his cheeks, and his nostrils flared. Rollins was proving Garcia's deepest fears of the man's bullheadedness right at the worst possible time. The man had an understandable chip on his shoulder against the Variants, but now was not the time to go full Rambo on their gray asses. "You'll be court-martialed. This is suicide. For you, for us, and for them." He waved one hand into the darkness.

"This was already a suicide mission when Davis sent us here," Rollins said then charged off into the underbrush with Russian at his tail.

Daniels gave a final glance back at Garcia. "Sorry, Sarge." He took off after the duo. They smashed through branches and stomped over the foliage, disappearing beyond Garcia's line of sight in seconds.

"Damn it," Garcia muttered as Tank, Kong, Thomas, and Stevo stared at him, awaiting their orders. This mission had already been derailed. By Variants and by

Rollins. Garcia knew Mulder, Morgan, and Chewy's lives depended on him, but so did the thousands of others at Norfolk Naval Station. And if the United States stood any chance of wiping out the Variant threat, he had to succeed. Had to control the anger that Rollins could not. He had to find the Variant hive where all these monsters were staging their attacks.

He knew his men could not fathom the loss of their brothers. Truthfully, neither could he. But he had to deal with that on his own later when he added their names to the cross on his forearm. Because his men and Lt. Davis needed a leader that could be trusted. A leader to complete this mission.

"What now, Sarge?" Thomas said softly, almost weakly.

All it takes is all you got, Davis had said. In that moment, he knew she was right.

Garcia clenched his jaw and wrapped his fingers around his M4. "We finish what we started."

"And Rollins?" Kong asked, adjusting his MK11.

"We finish what we started with or without him."

***

They continued south for what seemed like hours, surrounded by the chorus of animals calling throughout the marshland. A couple of gulls squawked overhead, hidden by the dense tree canopy, and Garcia sucked down breath after breath of humid air. It felt as if he were breathing in water.

"Rollins, do you read?" Garcia asked over his mic.

Once again, Rollins ignored him. He had already reported to Command that Rollins had gone AWOL, taking his squad with him, and the man had refused radio contact. Davis had promised she would deal with him later.

If there was a later for him, Garcia thought morosely.

They continued slinking between the trees like ghosts wandering the woods. Garcia checked his locator. Three icons blinked, representing Mulder, Morgan, and Chewy. They were spread out, carried away by the Variants, but they were all generally south of the Variant Hunters' current position.

A snapping branch caused Garcia to spin to his right. He searched for the source of the noise with his rifle pointed at the trees. A silhouette moved into his vision, limping. His muzzle never wavered off the center of the target, but he did not pull his trigger. Out of his periphery, he saw Tank follow his lead, while the others covered their backs.

At any moment, they expected the calls of Variants to shatter their eardrums as the monsters ignited another attack. But no gargling yells or howls called out into the darkness.

Just this single shape.

"Help…" the limping thing said. Or at least, Garcia thought that was what it had said. He still could not be sure, not with the Variants demonstrating varying degrees of intelligence and evolution. It was impossible to discern what was a trick and what was truth anymore.

But as the limping thing came nearer, Garcia realized what it was. Half the person's face was torn, shredded to the bone. It left no mystery as to the physiological workings of his jaw. One eye was gone, as was most of his right forearm. Dried blood and mud covered his fatigues. Claw marks stretched down his torso and over his legs. An ankle bent inward at an unnatural position, and Garcia lifted one hand, signaling for his men to hold their fire. He dropped his rifle to his side. Its strap caught his shoulder, and he sprinted to meet the injured man.

The missing SEAL!

"Thank…you…" The man slumped into Garcia's arms.

A thunderbolt of worry cut through Garcia. They had to save this man. Had to bring him back. He would not let him die, not when everything else in this mission was unraveling around him.

"Morphine, now!" Garcia barked. Tank dug into his pack, immediately complying. He readied the emergency syringe as Garcia lowered the man against a tree trunk. It was all too much like déjà vu. Was this another trap set by the goddamned Variants? Were they using this SEAL too as bait, lying in wait, ready to attack and carry away more of his men?

Tank handed Garcia the morphine, and he wasted no time in injecting the painkillers. The SEAL looked as if he could use more painkillers than the Variant Hunters had with them in all their medical supplies. But he feared a more-permanent painkiller was fast approaching this man.

Death.

Garcia chinned his mic, once again ready to call a med evac.

The SEAL waved him off. "Don't. You know…you know they'll just come for us…come to the chopper… Don't waste your lives on me. I'm already gone."

The man was lucid, brave even in the face of an agonizing death. Garcia hoped he could carry just a quarter of that man's courage with him for the rest of this mission. "I can't let you die out here."

"I can't let you all die out here," the man countered as bloody saliva dripped from the corner of his mouth where the skin of his cheek had been shorn. "Those monsters. They ambushed us. From the ground."

Garcia shuddered. An hour ago, he would have thought the man meant the Variants had simply sprinted at them, dodging between tree trunks and using the shadows as cover. Now he knew the man quite literally meant the Variants had burst from the ground. It fit with the speed at which the monsters had surprised the Variant Hunters.

Trying to guard against the Variants was getting increasingly difficult.

"Do they burrow? Do they use a tunnel system or something?" Garcia asked.

"Don't know." The SEAL's remaining eye closed as the morphine washed through him, assuaging the fires that Garcia knew must be burning throughout his body. "Didn't have time to investigate. They came out like goddamned dead men escaping their graves, plowing right into us. We didn't stand a chance. We weren't ready."

Neither were we, Garcia thought. "Brother, do you have any idea where their hive is?"

The man shook his head slowly, his movements fast becoming more and more lethargic. "No, no. We never found it." He let out a sardonic laugh. "No wonder the drones couldn't track these bastards, huh? Digging their tunnels underground like ants or something. No wonder…"

The SEAL's chin slumped to meet his chest, and Garcia thought that was the last of him. He started to stand, but the SEAL opened his single eye and stared intensely at Garcia.

"You've...you've got to find them. All of them," he said.

"We will, and then Command will bomb the living shit out of them."

The SEAL's head shook slightly. "No, no, not the Variants. The...the..."

His voice faded, and his chin drooped again.

Garcia crossed himself then muttered a quick prayer for the man.

"Who was he talking about, Sarge?" Tank asked. "He saw his team die, right? He couldn't have meant them."

"No, and he couldn't have known about Mulder and the others," Stevo added, peering around nervously into the dark.

"Then who the hell are we supposed to find?" Tank asked.

"God only knows," Garcia said, "and we better figure it out."

Stevo eyed Kong. "Hey, man, you good? You look like you saw a ghost."

"Might be we all saw a goddamned ghost," Tank said. "That SEAL shouldn't have even been alive when we got here."

Kong nodded sullenly as they crept forward toward the edge of the forest. "You know, when I was a kid, I used to be afraid of the dark."

Garcia shrugged. "Everyone was."

"I know. I outgrew it like everyone else, too." Kong's eyes roved between the pockets of shadow and murk around them. "But goddammit, I'm not too proud to admit I'm afraid again...now that the darkness has evolved."

Normally such chatter would have drawn the chuckles

of more seasoned marines. But not here. Kong was right. Garcia, too, was afraid of the darkness and everything that grew and lurked in it now. The Variants were an almost-unknowable and unpredictable force, attacking more furiously than a hurricane and constantly changing, both biologically and mentally, as the war against them raged on.

Kong was right.

The darkness had evolved.

— 7 —

The group trudged onward, still with no sign of Rollins or the Variants. Garcia glanced at his locator to determine Rollins's location. The WINS devices were new technology. They had barely transitioned from the research labs to deployment with the armed forces. Now, Garcia stared at a symptom of their newness. Or at least, that was what he hoped he was looking at.

According to his locator, Rollins, Daniels, and Russian were scattered over the small town of Corolla. The WINS devices relied on inertial sensors when it was not receiving proper GPS signals due to jamming or interference of some kind. A myriad of possible explanations for the marines' varied locations rattled through Garcia's head. Maybe the trio had found the Variants' tunnels and the sensors were only able to report their location intermittently and inaccurately while underground. Maybe they really had spread out in their search for Mulder, Chewy, and Morgan, all three of whom now had disappeared off the locator device completely.

Or worse yet, maybe Rollins's group had fallen victim to the Variants.

"Rollins, Garcia here. Do you read?"

As he had expected, Rollins offered no response. The group exited the woods. Garcia cursed at the man's insolence and signaled for his squad to pause at the edge of a treeless expanse. Waves lapped a sandy shore, and short, verdant bushes lined a roadway leading to Corolla. Several beached boats, hulls rotting and torn open like decaying whale carcasses, lay along the beach. One sailboat lolled side to side. Its sails hung off its masts in long tatters.

Like the roadway they had seen approaching the refuge, burned-out husks of cars and trucks littered the asphalt. The wind tickled remnants of soiled clothing seeping out of torn luggage, and an empty water bottle rolled back and forth as the seaward breeze cut across the wide space. Beyond the beach, the first few roofs of buildings stuck up, marking a place where humanity once lived and thrived. A lighthouse towered above the restaurants, motels, and vacation homes like a morbid beacon inviting ghost ships and nothing more.

"Anybody see any bodies?" Garcia asked as the Variant Hunters scanned the landscape.

"Nothing," Thomas said.

"Nada," Tank agreed.

"Doesn't seem right," Stevo said. "Those things leave a wake of destruction wherever they go. But what happened to the people? They didn't all just escape."

"No, I'm afraid they didn't," Garcia said as they started over the beach. "Something's not right, and I think we're going to find out what it is."

The men grunted their agreement as their rifles roved across the barren world they had found themselves in.

Garcia took his first tentative step on the sand, waiting

at any moment for a bloodied claw to shoot up from beneath his feet. He considered the long walk over the beach toward the town with increasing dread. There was a time when walking on the beach would have brought him comfort. The salty air would have swirled around him as he held Ashley's hand in his. Now, the only thing reaching to grab hold of his limbs would be creatures desperate to sink their fangs into his flesh.

With a swift hand gesture, he guided his men toward the line of wrecked and rusting vehicles. Thomas took point, slipping between a sedan and SUV. Each step on the cracked but sturdy asphalt gave Garcia a fleeting sense of relief knowing that even burrowing, crablike Variants should not be able to break through the road beneath their boots.

"Sarge!" Tank whispered trenchantly.

Garcia whipped his head around. He peered over the beach to where Tank had aimed his SAW. Sand seemed to shift at a specific point as if it was being syphoned into a small whirlpool. It soon stopped, but Garcia watched in horror as another spot started to cave in as a hungry sinkhole formed.

Then another and another.

"What in the hell?" Stevo asked no one in particular.

"Stay low and keep going," Garcia said. "Tank, watch our flank. Kong, stay vigilant on rear guard. If those things are moving about under there, we've got to move on."

Onward they snuck between the cars as other sinkholes, no more than a couple of yards wide, gaped on the beach. Garcia's heart climbed into his throat as he stole the occasional glance at the undulating beach, but he forced himself to continue, reminding himself that their objective was in Corolla—as were Rollins and his team. Gawking at whatever the hell was going on now would not be helpful to any of them, and if the Variants started pouring out of those sinkholes, he did not want to be here when they crawled across the landscape like ants in search of food.

A few gulls circled overhead. One dove to rummage through the refuse along the road. Garcia hoped the gull's brazenness was a sign that the sinkholes were nothing to worry about.

Slowly, they made their way through the vehicles, carefully avoiding the glass shards strewn about from broken windows and busted bottles of food and drink. Garcia checked his locator. One of the blips began pulsing on the LCD screen, signaling that its source was close. It belonged to Russian.

Garcia silently showed the screen to Tank, and the two of them peered around, searching for the large marine. The signal seemed to be coming from a school bus with its emergency doors and front door cranked open. Several passenger windows had been broken, leaving only shards of glass around their perimeter like the teeth of some laughing monster.

With a couple of hand gestures, Garcia commanded Thomas, Tank, and Stevo to guard him and Kong. The duo climbed up the steps into the bus slowly. Every creaking step caused Garcia to pause. He tried to control his breathing and listen for the telltale scrapes and scratching of a Variant. Once positioned by the driver's seat, Garcia looked over the vinyl seats. Several sported long gashes where stuffing spilled out. Dark stains covered the floor, and more emergency food supplies and clothes were strewn over the seats.

But no bodies.

He crept forward between the seats. His rifle and Kong's swiveled back and forth. He did not dare whisper Russian's name, but he listened intently for sounds of the man's breathing. Anything to let him know the man was still alive.

The sound of something scraping against metal caught his attention. Maybe something jostled by the wind cutting through the bus. Kong straightened, acknowledging the noise with a nod. They crept forward. Before they reached the source of the scraping, a shining piece of plastic glinted from the space under a vinyl seat. Garcia dropped to his knees and bent to retrieve the plastic. He picked it up between his thumb and forefinger. It was sticky, wet with blood. Rotating the plastic object he had picked up, Garcia recognized the small device. It was one of the WINS devices.

Russian's.

Moonlight reflected on several cylindrical objects at his feet. Bullet casings. Pieces of black fabric from fatigues not unlike those Garcia was wearing were draped over the seat. A holster and handgun, slide locked back as if its magazine had been spent, lay under another seat.

The scraping sound near the back of the bus grew louder, and Kong started to prowl toward it. A pit formed in Garcia's stomach, threatening to swallow him whole. He shot up, shouldering his rifle, and swung it to aim at the spot where Kong was headed.

"No, Kong! Stop!"

But it was too late.

A Variant exploded over the seat, its claws outstretched. Reptilian scales covered its body, and its yellow eyes glowed in the darkness. Its legs looked as though they had been borrowed from a Komodo dragon as it clambered toward Kong. The marine managed to fire a couple of quick shots that lanced into the monster's body, plunging through scales. Squirming, the Variant absorbed the blows and screamed, baring all its curved teeth as it tackled Kong.

The marine's rifle flew from his hands, and Garcia sprinted toward him. Marine and monster disappeared behind one of the seats. Only their feet were visible, sticking out into the walkway. Desperation spread through him on the back of wild wrath. He would not let this monster take another Variant Hunter. Garcia lunged over a suitcase and a box filled with canned food. Another muffled gunshot rang out, but Kong did not yell, either in anger or pain. The Variant growled, and Garcia heard the sickening sound of tearing flesh, sending his heart pounding anew.

He rounded the seat where the Variant and Kong struggled. They intertwined in a tangle of limbs. Blood was smeared across Kong's face, and Garcia could not tell to whom it belonged. The Variant seemed to have its body wrapped around Kong, almost as if it were more snake than human, crushing Kong's ribs with its grip. Kong's mouth gaped like a fish sucking for breath on dry land, and his fingers splayed, quaking slightly. The man's condition stoked the fires of Garcia's rage.

He bashed the Variant's head with his rifle. The creature turned, growling at him, and whipped one hand laced with daggerlike claws at Garcia's face. Still, the creature did not lose its grip around Kong. It let out a resonating war cry, spraying saliva over Garcia. Pallor seeped into Kong's face as the Variant tightened its hold. There was no time to lose. Garcia leveled his gun at the monster and started to squeeze the trigger.

But the Variant seemed to understand what was about to happen. It rolled, using Kong like a human shield, and Garcia was forced to lower his weapon. His chest heaved as he stared the creature down, anger building in him like a boiler ready to explode. Writhing in the monster's grip, Kong tried to free himself, but the thin man was no match for the reptilian Variant and its unquenchable hunger.

"Stay strong, brother!" Garcia barked. He shed his rifle and tore out his knife. The Variant growled, squeezing Kong harder. Kong's eyeballs bulged, and Garcia lunged. He dug the blade under the creature's scales. The knife bit into flesh and muscle, sawing through one of the creature's arms. Enough sinew tore for Kong to shake himself loose from the monster's arm. He crumpled at Garcia's feet, on his hands and knees, gasping for breath.

Garcia stepped past him and drove the knife down at the Variant again. The creature tried to dodge but had nowhere to go in the bus seat. The blade cut into the beast's neck, and the Variant's growling came out intermingled with gurgling. Blood bubbled from its mouth.

Garcia twisted the knife, drawing more blood. One of the Variant's flailing arms caught the side of his head, knocking him backward. Pain flooded through his head, and his vision turned red for a moment as snowflakes appeared.

The Variant towered above him. Long ropes of saliva dripped from its sucker lips and dangled over its scaled chest. It lifted its good arm, ready to strike again. Its tongue danced over its teeth, and it dove at Garcia. He was not going to let this bastard win.

He kicked a boot up, landing it square in the middle of the creature's chest. Air hissed from between the Variant's teeth, and Garcia kicked with his other foot, catching the monster behind one of its ankles. The beast tumbled forward, straight onto Garcia. Garcia's arm lashed out, but not to catch it. The Variant landed on the blade, and the knife stabbed through its neck. Hot liquid poured over Garcia's fingers, and the Variant's muscles spasmed in its death throes. Its clicking joints tremored for the last time.

Catching his breath, Garcia kicked the beast over and pulled out his knife. He recovered his rifle. Kong still had not moved from where he had crawled from the Variant. Garcia bent toward the marine. Kong twisted his neck and looked at Garcia with a pained expression. Bullets of sweat coursed over his forehead.

Garcia offered a hand, but Kong refused to take it.

"Don't think…don't think I'm getting up again, Sarge," Kong said. He clutched his belly with one hand and waved Garcia off with the other. It was covered in blood.

"You'll be okay, brother," Garcia said, already worried the words rang untrue. But what should he say to the man? That he looked as if Death's skeletal fingers were wrapping their icy grip around his dying heart? "Let's get you out of here."

Kong fought against Garcia's attempt to help him. Wet liquid glistened across his belly. A painful knot twisted in Garcia's gut. Kong had been split open from his groin to his sternum. If the man moved his hand, he would lose his innards.

Pounding footsteps echoed in the bus. Tank's hulking

form sped down the aisle. "Sarge! We got company!"

"Shit," Garcia said. "What is it? How many?"

"Those sinkholes…" Tank's words lingered in the air as he pointed out the bus's windows.

Garcia stood tentatively and peered out a broken window. Beyond the glass shards jutting from the window frame, he saw movement all over the beach. Dark, mutated shapes pushed out of the sand, like nocturnal creatures crawling out of their burrows to embark on their midnight haunts. Dozens upon dozens of them appeared, shaking the sand off their bodies. Their eyes glowed like hot embers as they surveyed the roadway. They studied the vehicles and seemed to be searching for the Variant Hunters.

"We need to leave," Garcia said. "Kong, come on. I'm not giving up on you."

Kong groaned in pain when Tank tried helping him. "No, Sarge, I'm not going anywhere."

A rush of guilt thrashed through Garcia. This man had been on his team for a matter of hours, serving as well as any other man before him. He did not want to see Kong's name added to the tattooed cross on his arm. Despite all the evidence pointing to Kong's certain death, a deeper desire burned in Garcia. He could not give up on a fellow marine. He could not bear to be responsible for another death.

"I'm not letting you do this to yourself," he said. Chinning his mic, he called out to Thomas and Stevo. "I need you guys in here now."

His order was soon met with the clatter of feet on the bus floor as the two Variant Hunters joined the group. Every one of the Variant Hunters he had left was here. A dying man and three other marines who would follow him to the ends of the earth, through the deepest hells the Variants had to offer.

The howls of the creatures on the beach grew louder and rolled across them like thunder from a summer storm. Their noses pointed up to the breeze, sniffing for signs of life, no doubt attracted by the ferrous scent of blood dousing the bus now. The monsters began filtering between the wrecked boats and refuse littering the beach, headed to the roadway.

"I'm not going anywhere, Sarge," Kong repeated. "And you're not going anywhere if you don't move soon. I can hear those things. They're hungry, they're thirsty for blood. They won't dig their way back to the burrows they came from without meat." Kong's eyelids quivered as his gaze met Garcia's. A devilish grin broke across the marine's blood-covered face. "Let me give it to them."

Garcia gritted his teeth, pushing all emotions to the back of his mind. He would give his life for his men, and he knew they would return the gesture. This man he barely knew was ready to give his. If he did, Garcia had a duty to fulfill, to carry out this mission and pay full respects to Kong's impending sacrifice. He owed the marine that much.

Kong ripped off his dog tags and held them, dangling between his fingers, for Garcia. Garcia took them.

"I got one request," Kong said. "Don't let me go out like a fucking wuss."

"You got it," Garcia said reluctantly, his heart climbing into his throat as the howls outside became louder.

Kong snatched one of the grenades from his vest and held it out. Garcia nodded, understanding immediately what Kong had in mind.

"Screw you, Kong," Tank said as he relinquished two

of his M67 grenades to the thin marine. "Never wanted to see a brother go out like this. It's not right."

Kong forced a painful laugh. Blood streamed in rivulets out the corners of his mouth. "I'll make this worth it."

Stevo said nothing as he offered the downed marine another grenade.

"That'll do," Kong said. "Don't have too many hands. Now, go, get the hell out of here." He caught Garcia's eyes. "Honored to serve with you, Sarge. Remember me when you tell stories about your victory here, okay?"

"I won't ever forget," Garcia said. He already felt the itching on his arm where he would add Kong's name. His heart hung heavy in his chest. The clicking of joints increased in volume. It sounded as though hail pounded around them as the Variants descended on the roadway. They seemed to know the earlier gunfire and brief skirmish had taken place somewhere among the broken and debilitated vehicles, but they did not seem to be focused on the bus yet. He looked at Thomas, Tank, and Stevo. "Out the back, now. Guard it."

The trio complied with his orders, jumping out of the emergency exit.

Kong's fingers wrapped around Garcia's wrist. "Never thought it'd end like this, Sarge." His face seemed to go even paler than Garcia realized possible. "Didn't want Rollins to be right. Thought I'd live…" He stopped as his face distorted in a wave of pain. Shock and adrenaline were wearing off, leaving him to fend off the full brunt of agony undoubtedly pulsing through his mangled body now. "Didn't think it'd come to this."

His lips quivered, and his right arm twitched, fingering one of the grenades. Garcia had seen this look before. It meant Kong would say nothing more. Could say nothing more. He had minutes to live, if that.

"Thank you, brother," Garcia said. "Thank you." He started to slip toward the rear of the bus, ready to jump out the emergency exit and join the other three.

Kong watched him warily, his eyelids sagging and his hair matted down, sticking out from under his helmet, soaked in sweat.

"All it takes is all you got, Marine," Garcia said. He thought he saw Kong offer a subtle nod before he leapt onto the roadway and ducked behind a nearby sedan where Tank, Thomas, and Stevo were hiding.

They crept between the vehicles, winding toward Corolla, toward the lighthouse, toward their last objective. Variants scuttled over the beach, and their claws tapped on the asphalt and crunched over broken glass.

A loud, animalistic yell echoed from the bus. Kong. His voice was filled with primal anger, hatred for the Variants, and topped with the agony clutching his body. It was his final call, an invitation to the monsters that were responsible for his death, entreating them to come aboard the bus with the promise of fresh meat. And equally so, it was a cry of anger and rage at the Variants responsible for so many other lost lives, responsible for the impending extinction of the human race. But Garcia imagined the Variants did not hear all of that in his yell, as he did. All they heard was dinner being served. They scuttled over cars and SUVs, jostling and shoving each other as they crammed onto the bus.

For a moment, Garcia thought that was it. The monsters piled into the bus until it was full of the scaled, pincer-clawed abominations, and dozens were left outside, trying to squeeze into windows or claw their way into the emergency hatch on the roof.

Had Kong been killed too quickly? Had his final courageous effort gone unrewarded?

Garcia offered a silent prayer for the marine. He was brave enough to at least draw the creatures away from the other Variant Hunters, blessing them with a chance to live, to finish their mission. Before Garcia could even say an Amen to himself, great plumes of orange and red shot from the bus's window in a series of explosions. The entire vehicle leapt a foot or so off the ground, and all the remaining windows burst in a spray of deadly shards. Glass pinged off other cars and trucks and pierced Variants like shrapnel. Those beasts caught in the blasts dissipated in the rolling fire and smoke. Their limbs tore from their bodies, and their heads shattered like gore-filled light bulbs. The sound of the detonations echoed over the beach, nearly deafening Garcia. A heat wave followed soon after. Nearby, a car alarm began wailing, at first sounding muddled through Garcia's ringing hearing.

Variants writhed on the road, their bodies broken and battered. The few still walking ambled confusedly around, searching for new prey that had not yet erupted into a ball of fire.

Garcia would not give them the opportunity. He signaled his men onward, away from the macabre bonfire, and he slunk away with the Variant Hunters toward Corolla. Kong had given them another chance, and he was not about to dishonor the man by not taking it.

— 8 —

Dark pillars of smoke billowed up from the inferno devouring the bus, blotting out the lights of the stars jeweling the obsidian sky. A few Variants called out to reassemble their remaining forces.

As a member of a Force Recon team, Garcia's missions were supposed to be silent get-in-and-get-out types. Leave no trace behind. Draw as little attention as possible.

They had already blown that.

Engaging with this many hostiles was not what he had intended, and he was afraid this was just a taste of things to come. They had struggled to handle the monsters that had attacked them in the marshland and on the beach, but they had escaped both times. If the Variants here could muster attacks that threatened the stability of Norfolk Naval Station, then Garcia feared the Variant Hunters had barely scratched the surface on the hordes of creatures that must be lying in wait on this island.

It was precisely those hordes they needed to find.

The Variant Hunters ducked behind a series of hedges tracing the perimeter of a Corolla house. Garcia checked his locator. The locations of Rollins and Daniels had not changed. Neither had Russian's WINS device, but Garcia at least had an answer as to why that one had not moved. Now he feared the stories told by Rollins and Daniels's lack of movement were the same as Russian's.

He imagined the Variants attacking them, disarming them, and carrying them away to whatever den they had crawled out of. Cursing inwardly, he clenched his fists as he thought about Rollins rushing away again in a blinding rage, headstrong and determined to save the others.

Rollins had failed and had probably caused his death, Russian's, and Daniels's while doing so. *Damn fool.*

But the mission was not over. So long as Garcia could still walk and hold his M4, he intended to finish what Lt. Davis had entrusted him to do.

"Sarge," Stevo said, on point. He was peering over another bush and pointing toward something beside a vacation home.

The house brought back painful memories of Ashley and Leslie. It was in a similar place, just several dozen miles south of here, that Garcia had spent part of his leave with his family in a house with a tiled roof and vibrant stucco walls. Stevo pointed past a column of flamingos and a dilapidated porch. Garcia's gaze followed the man's finger to the beach. Another hole in the ground appeared near the base of a palm tree. Its diameter stretched to that of a manhole cover's.

And it was not alone. At a neighboring home, two more similarly sized holes breached the ground. Fresh piles of sandy dirt encircled them. Garcia stood slowly and pressed a pair of night-vision binoculars to his eyes. He did not have a great vantage point given the flat landscape. But even so, he could see several more holes poking up from various lawns. The holes pockmarked a small park with a broken water fountain and fallen trees, and the gravel parking lot of a seafood restaurant had devolved into a cratered mess like a lunar landscape from the underground burrows.

"Davis will want to hear about this," Garcia said, scanning the land with his helmet-mounted cam, ensuring the specialists back on the *GW* got a full view of what they were looking at. He chinned his mic. "Command, Victor Hotel Alpha. Do you read?"

"Copy, Victor Hotel."

"Are you seeing what we're seeing?"

"Vid feed is clear," a specialist's voice drawled back. "We see those holes all over, too."

"Good. Those look to be the Variants' burrows, judging from their earlier attacks."

"Understood. Hold on one second, Victor Hotel. I've got an incoming request from the science team. They've gotten reports of Variants using the subways in the cities and sewage systems. Can you confirm these burrows lead to somewhere similar?"

"I can't confirm anything yet," Garcia said. "But I'm going to guess that's a negative. There are no subways on the Outer Banks and definitely no sewage systems under the beach or in the marsh."

"That's what the science boys and girls feared. They're running around with a hypothesis that the Variants on those islands evolved some kind of capabilities to dig their own tunnels. Might be individual burrows, or you might be facing a widespread network under your feet. They say to be careful out there."

"Got anything for us we don't already know?"

"One other thing. Lt. Davis wants you to find out

where all those tunnels lead, if they do indeed exist. Over."

"Copy," Garcia said. "Victor Hotel out."

Stevo looked at Garcia with a slightly worried expression. "We just going to drop in those holes?"

"That's what it sounds like," Thomas said.

"I don't like it," Stevo said. "Whenever I stuck my hands in holes like that as a kid, my fingers would get pinched by whatever crawdad or crab was hiding in 'em. I don't much like getting pinched by a Variant."

"Agreed. Poking about in those holes would be as dangerous as it is stupid right now," Garcia said. "We'll snoop around town a bit. See if we can't find any clue as to where these bastards are really living. Their central hive has to be here somewhere."

Tank gave a noncommittal shrug. "Who the hell knows?"

Stevo appeared more ready to agree. "Kind of like an ant colony. Got the queen's chamber and the place where she lays all the eggs. Plus, there are separate chambers for food storage and waste."

"You an entomologist and you didn't tell us?" Thomas asked.

"I like Animal Planet. So sue me."

"Let's just hope we don't find a queen or any eggs," Garcia said. "That's the last thing we need, but I'm guessing a food chamber isn't so far fetched of an idea."

"Think that's where they took Mulder and the others?" Stevo asked.

"Could be. If so, we'll get them the hell out of there," Garcia said.

Before he got too far ahead of himself, he needed to figure out where the hell they should start looking.

Standing in the backyard of someone's beach house was not going to help, and wandering through this neighborhood seemed to be a good way to attract Variant attention. He wanted to be somewhere he could survey the landscape and get a better idea of what surrounded them. Maybe they could see a pattern to the burrows, something the drones had missed flying so high above the island on their resource-limited passes around the whole of the Outer Banks.

At least, now, Garcia felt certain they were narrowing down on where these Variants slept, where they called home between attacks on civilization. If he were a gambling man, he would bet that the central hive—or at least the food stores—were somewhere within the town of Corolla. During the initial outbreak of the Hemorrhage Virus and the results of the VX-99 bioweapon, more Variants and human prey would have been concentrated in the town than on the beaches and parks. It made sense to Garcia that the creatures would start hoarding their food nearby rather than drag it miles to some other random location without good reason.

Garcia surveyed the town again, looking for higher ground. Somewhere with sweeping views of the town and surrounding beach. Somewhere like the lighthouse standing near the middle of Corolla. The lighthouse where he had proposed to Ashley. Where he had started the life that the Variants had ripped away from him. Fresh anger threatened to upheave his concentration on the task ahead.

"There," he said, pointing to the lighthouse. "We go there. See what we can from the lighthouse then make our next move."

"You got it, Sarge," Stevo said, with Tank and Thomas

nodding their agreement.

Stevo pushed through the hedge first and dashed to the nearest house. He paused at the corner, scanning the yard and beach before signaling that the coast was clear. Garcia and Thomas came next, with Tank guarding the rear. They moved like this between houses and vehicles, tediously making their way to the part of the town where the lighthouse stood. Tropical trees and neglected flowers wilted in what had once been beautifully manicured lawns and planters along the quaint streets. The smell of rot permeated the air, reminiscent of the odor of Dumpsters behind seafood restaurants that played loose with food-regulation standards. It provided a constant reminder that the Variants were all around them, invisible and lurking underground.

They approached a store with a sign hanging by a single chain and touting cheap souvenirs. Cages for hermit crabs with brightly painted shells sat in the window. All the crabs had since died off, stuck in their prisons once the humans abandoned them, and beyond their habitats lay a wasteland of towels, T-shirts, and flimsy snorkel masks emblazoned with various beachside images or the words Outer Banks, North Carolina.

Stevo ducked into the shop and took shelter behind the front counter. He signaled the others to follow. Thomas went first, with Stevo covering his approach. He sprinted across the street. Garcia leaned out from around a parked SUV, ready to lunge across the street, when he heard a distinct clicking echo down the road.

He curled around the bumper of the SUV and peered through the optics on his M4. He could not yet see the Variant, but he recognized the sound of the monster moving on its spidery, bent appendages. It let out no howl, no cry to let others know it had spotted prey, and for that, Garcia thanked God.

But he would not feel relief until the creature was either dead or gone. The clicking grew louder as the creature approached. It did not take long for Garcia to spot the Variant moving between vehicles. Its skin stretched over elongated, lean muscles, and its glowing yellow orb-like eyes twitched left and right. The monster's head cranked as it searched under and around vehicles as if it were probing for something it lost. Tension worked its way through Garcia's muscles as he held his position. The monster would never find what it was looking for. Garcia would see to that.

Clicking echoed off the sides of buildings from somewhere behind them. More sounded to the north. The Variants were closing in. Whether the strange creatures were actively scouting for the Variant Hunters or not, Garcia did not want to be here to find out.

But by now, the nearest Variant, the one ambling along the road, was too close for Garcia to scamper across the street unnoticed. Gunfire, even suppressed, might be too much. He did not need the muffled shots to career into cars or trees and let the other Variants know where they should be searching.

Garcia slung his M4 over his back and turned to Tank. "Cover me if things go south. No matter what, we make it to that lighthouse."

"Yes, Sarge," Tank said, clenching his jaw and shouldering his rifle, prepared to take the Variant down should Garcia fail.

Garcia's fingers tingled in preparation as he slipped his knife from its sheath. He tensed his muscles, crouching at the bumper of the SUV with one hand on the hood, ready to pounce. His nerves coursed with energy. Like a tiger in the grass, he coiled when the Variant scratched at a nearby car. The monster's nostrils twitched and flared as it sniffed the street under the vehicle. Its eyes swept the ground.

Just a few more seconds, and Garcia would dig his knife into the skin under the creature's chin, his blade biting into vessels and flesh, ending the monster's putrid existence. He would make the creature pay for the sins of its brethren, for being part of the mob of abominations killing those he loved and those he served beside. Then he and Tank would sprint to Stevo's position unseen and unheard.

But the monster had other plans.

Its hissing growl sounded like a grizzly announcing its presence to a hapless rival. The Variant stood, stretching to its six-and-a-half-foot height. It had twisted around the SUV before Garcia could react. The creature let out a howl then careened toward Garcia.

So much for a sneak attack.

Garcia stuffed his knife back into its sheath and flipped his M4 up, immediately sighting the Variant within his optics. A swift squeeze of the trigger sent a flurry of bullets plunging through the Variant's chest. Bone and scales popped. The monster tumbled forward, sprawling over the asphalt, its claws outstretched.

It was dead.

But it had already done enough damage. A storm of clicking and scratching echoed everywhere. The other monsters prowling the streets descended on their position, attracted by the attack cry of the Variant.

There was no more time for crouching, crawling, and creeping.

"Go, go, go!" Garcia yelled. He and Tank sprinted to the souvenir store where Stevo and Thomas covered them. His shoulder slammed into a rack, spilling plastic snorkeling fins and inflatable inner tubes. The group charged through aisles of snow globes and picture frames.

A low growl caused Garcia to spin and face the front of the store. A window shattered, breaking into shards of glass like so many pieces of deadly hail spewing over the Variant Hunters' bodies. A monster landed on the floor, hunching its back and wielding its claws. The Variant did not even have a chance to set its sight on any of the marines before bullets chewed into its gray flesh. Its body slumped to the floor, bleeding.

It was soon replaced by two more creatures. The men dispatched them with swift lead justice, and more Variants poured into the broken window.

"Changing!" Stevo yelled.

Tank's SAW barked, chattering with the guttural roar of 5.56mm rounds ripping the air. Garcia did his best to bring down the creatures as he slowly retreated to the back of the store. A wall of Variant corpses clotted the entryway to the shop. The macabre barricade gave way as writhing limbs spiked with talons forced themselves through the mess.

Then a new sight evoked a fresh wave of adrenaline to surge through Garcia's vessels. The floor tiles cracked and crumbled underneath a fallen clothes rack. A pincerlike claw pierced the devastated flooring. Tiles and the rack tumbled into a gaping sinkhole. Two Variants crawled out, dragging themselves into the shop.

"Good God," Thomas said as he swiveled to aim at the mutants.

"Back door! Now!" Garcia yelled. Panic threatened to

overwhelm his mind, flooding him, and subvert their escape.

Tank leveled a huge boot at the door and kicked it down with a single blow. It flew off its hinges and clattered onto the broken asphalt of a parking lot. But the exit offered no better escape from the masses of Variants accumulating to make good on the promise of a new hunt. Creatures stampeded over an RV and Volkswagen Beetle sitting in a puddle of oil. The herd swarmed over the vehicles as if they formed a single, fluid organism. Tank sprayed bullets into their numbers, but Garcia knew the four of them stood no chance against the oncoming tide.

With monsters crashing at the front of the store and avalanching toward the back, Garcia saw only one way out of this mess.

He did not like it one bit.

— 9 —

"You're shitting me, Sarge!" Thomas yelled over the roar of Tank's M249.

"'Fraid not!" Garcia leapt into the sinkhole left by the Variants. His boots hit something hard, almost like concrete. His NVGs gave him a view into the pervasive darkness. A tunnel stretched far in front and behind him. The ground beneath him looked to be constructed of hardened mud. Stevo dropped down next to him, followed by Thomas. The trio leveled their rifles down the tunnels, but no Variants appeared.

At least, not yet.

Tank's light machine gun continued to bark from above.

"Tank! Now!" Garcia yelled through the mic.

The huge man jumped in, his boots smacking against the floor. He flung out a hand to brace himself against the tunnel wall. His head swiveled as if he was questioning which direction they planned to travel.

Garcia knew exactly which way to go. The world above might have erupted into a fang-filled hell, but they still had a mission to fulfill.

"South! That way!" He pointed in a direction that

should take them to the lighthouse.

His team sprinted ahead, and he lingered for a moment. With his rifle slung, he snatched an incendiary grenade from his TAC vest and tossed it up through the sinkhole. It clattered on the floor of the souvenir shop. Normally, Garcia would not dare close off their only sure way of retreat out of an enclosed space. But the souvenir shop was no longer an option for them. The Variants would force themselves forward, churning after the Variant Hunters in hot pursuit if he did not do something to stop them.

Waves of heat and red-and-yellow light rushed overhead, quickly igniting the T-shirts and sweatshirts strewn about the shop. The glow of the fire flickered as Garcia hurried after his men. Agonized howls of Variants caught in the fiery blast echoed after them, but Garcia thanked God for every second that it was only their voices and not their clawed feet chasing them through the tunnels.

They sprinted through the tunnel, the slap of their boots echoing around them. The orange glow flickered, growing more distant. A shriek sounded out, and Garcia twisted to face the sinkhole again. Three Variants plunged into the tunnel. They barreled forward. Flames still danced across their skin and fanned behind them like demonic capes.

Tank paused beside Garcia, and the two of them sent a wall of lead into the creatures, ending their pursuit. Fire consumed their bodies as other creatures dropped into the hole, riled up by pain and the thrill of the hunt. Again, Tank and Garcia knocked the monsters off their feet with a spray of bullets, but they could not sit here all night, trying to take them out one by one.

"Let's go!" Garcia yelled.

Tank and Garcia dashed after Stevo and Thomas. They caught up in a couple of seconds as more creatures spilled into the tunnels. It was as though the faucet had been turned on, and the monsters dropped faster than they could dispatch them. On they ran. Garcia and his team had trained their bodies to remain in peak physical condition, but the apocalypse had been hard on them. Garcia's lungs burned, and he felt the stinging buildup of lactic acid in his leg muscles with each loping step. The frantic breaths of the Variant Hunters sounded around him as they carried on.

A three-way intersection appeared, forking off to the left and right. Shrill, bloodcurdling screams pierced Garcia's eardrums, and he swiveled to the right. A trio of Variants rushed them. One galloped along the bottom of the tunnel as another dug its claws into the side. The third followed the ceiling like an oversized lizard, scuttling toward them with its tongue swatting over its wet lips.

Stevo swung his rifle up and put a bullet through the first creature's head. The monster slid over the wet dirt floor, skidding to a stop. Thomas sprayed a three-round burst into the monster on the wall, and it stumbled before recovering and continuing its warpath. Tank's SAW chewed through the monster's chest, riddling it with 5.56 mm rounds, and Garcia fired at the Variant closing in on the ceiling.

Bullets slammed into the Variant's arm and knocked it off balance. More rounds plunged into the dirt walls as the Variant deftly leapt to the ground and pounced. Its pincerlike claws grabbed Garcia's shoulder, biting into flesh. Pain lit up his shoulder in agonizing lightning strikes. He tumbled backward under the weight of the creature. Its maw opened, ready to tear a chunk out of his neck. Right as its teeth snapped together, the Variant was lifted from his body and thrown into the wall. Tank battered the Variant with a debilitating elbow strike to its jaw then delivered a teeth-rattling uppercut to its chin.

More cries echoed from the other two corridors.

Garcia peered behind him to see the tunnel they had come from filled with Variants. The other must have been littered with other sinkholes and intersections, because creatures churned through them like raging rapids, trampling each other as they raced toward the Variant Hunters' position.

Garcia's fingers toyed with one of the remaining M67 grenades on his TAC vest. Maybe he could collapse a tunnel—or better yet, the intersection. Stevo's rifle barked as he took precise, powerful shots. Tank sprayed rounds into the creatures, batting back the oncoming forces. Thomas gave Garcia a sideways glance, waiting for an order. He eyed the grenade Garcia was examining. Such a blast in an enclosed space like this was practically suicide.

But Garcia decided the chance of suicide was better than guaranteed death at the hands of the Variants.

"Fire in the hole!" he boomed over the rattle of gunfire and howls of the Variants. He lobbed the grenade toward the intersection and signaled for his men to resume their flight away from the roiling masses.

A Variant poked its head in from an intersecting path before them, and Garcia ended its life with a trigger pull. A couple of other creatures peered in from other paths that spiderwebbed in front of them, and the Variant Hunters plastered them against the walls with gunfire as they ran.

Then the ground rumbled beneath their feet. A deafening blast overwhelmed them. Garcia's ears rang before silence enveloped him. Sheets of heat scorched his body, and pebbles and rocks pelted his back. He risked a glance behind them. The ceiling had collapsed. Variants trapped under the rock, sand, and mud stuck their claws out of the debris, trying to shovel themselves out before they suffocated. Garcia's gamble had paid off.

Then the earth trembled. Dust and rocks shifted from the ceiling, and fissures formed all along the tunnel, cracking above and around Garcia and his men. More sand and rubble fell behind them. Garcia heard the debris clattering to the ground through his muddled senses. His pulse thumped in his ears, and he urged his body onward, relying on every reserve of strength he could muster. The others rushed beside him, sweat and dust covering their faces. Chunks of earth crashed, walloping the floor. Variants crawled out of other intersecting tunnels before them, threatening to cut them off.

The Variant Hunters used elbows, rifle stocks, and gunfire to keep the Variants at bay, demolishing the creatures almost as soon as they appeared. Pure instinct kicked in, fueling their progress. Garcia guided them down another tunnel to escape the collapsing underground networks. Holes above them flickered past, revealing momentary glimpses of a star-studded sky. Creatures leapt in as they passed, attracted to the hellish cacophony.

Garcia wished he could get an idea of where they were now under Corolla, but the tunnels filling in behind them and the Variants crashing into their escape path dashed any hopes of finding a chance to reorient himself.

Stevo juked to his left, narrowly avoiding another

snapping creature, and Tank clocked the monster with the stock of his M249, smearing its skull and brains against the wall. Another tried to jump at Tank, its claws outstretched and muscles undulating. Garcia sent three precise shots lancing through the monster, knocking it off its trajectory. Its crippled body tripped two other Variants chasing the group.

A half-dozen other creatures trampled the monsters, narrowing their distance to the Variant Hunters. Howls echoed, warning Garcia of the hordes that had survived the collapse and doggedly pursued the marines. Before them, somewhere in the slew of intersecting tunnels, more calls cried out.

Pain still fired through Garcia's shoulder. Soon these tunnels would become like catacombs, entombing men and monsters alike. It would not be long before the Variants sank their teeth into Garcia and his men. He could already feel their spittle on the back of his neck, their claws digging through his muscle. Adrenaline surged through his vessels, fighting to keep those nightmares from becoming reality. A claw stretched out, threatening to tear at Tank, and Garcia put a flurry of bullets into the offending creature. The marines' strength was flagging. Their ammunition would not last forever, and the Variants grew more numerous and hungry by the second.

"Up!" Garcia yelled. It was their only salvation.

Stevo hopped up the first hole they ran under. He made it to the top, his fingers barely gripping the edge as dirt crumbled around him. Once he pulled himself through, he bent back down and helped Thomas. Tank and Garcia covered the duo, knocking down the leading ranks of Variants crawling across the floors, walls, and ceilings. Their corpses crumpled, quickly crushed by the feet and claws of their relentless brethren. Tank gestured to help Garcia next, but Garcia shook his head, refusing and making the big man go first.

Thomas and Stevo were forced to work together to hoist the heavy man out of the hellish lair and into the night air. Garcia leapt up next as the first Variant closed in, its claws just missing his ankle. He scrambled up the side of the hole, his hands fighting for purchase, digging into the earth as he clawed himself out.

Sharp pain radiated up his leg, and he turned to see one of the monsters with its pincers around his calf. He kicked at the monster with his free leg as other creatures leapt, jostling with each other for position. A heavy blow in the face did nothing to perturb the Variant with a death grip on Garcia.

"Come on, you ugly bastard!" Garcia boomed.

Hands wrapped around his wrists. Tank grunted as he fought against the Variant's weight, desperate to pull Garcia from the tunnel. Another Variant climbed the one holding onto Garcia, followed by a second. As strong as Tank was, he could not lift Garcia and three Variants.

Garcia slipped one hand from Tank's, gritting his teeth, and reached for his holster. Tank's fingers started to lose their hold, and Garcia slid six more inches into the hole, dangerously close to the Variants fighting with each other to get at him. Another began climbing up the sidewall.

Garcia's fingers found what they were looking for, and he pulled out his M9 Beretta. The pistol barked in quick succession. Bullets could not miss in such short range, cutting through bone and flesh. The pincers around Garcia's legs let go, and he flew up, aided by Tank. The night air welcomed him into its warmth, and he tumbled over soft grass jutting through sandy soil.

"Fire in the hole!" Thomas yelled, dropping a grenade into the hole.

A blast soon sounded afterward. Bits of Variants flew out like a geyser. Chunks of flesh and blood and dirt rained around them. Garcia quickly took stock of their surroundings. They were in the middle of Corolla, in the lawn near the tourist center. A few feet away lay a road packed with vehicles. Garcia's eyes locked onto a twelve-foot-long moving truck, and he sprinted to the vehicle. After bashing in the window, he reached in and unlocked the door then hopped into the driver's seat. He did not expect the engine to start, but he twisted the keys dangling in the ignition anyway. The starter clicked uselessly, so he put the truck into neutral. Tank and Stevo seemed to understand Garcia's plans without a word. They had served long enough beside him to create a sort of instinctual, nonverbal communication within the group.

And their work together paid off in dividends.

The duo threw their backs into the rear of the truck. They shoved it forward until momentum carried the heavy vehicle. It thumped over the curb and rolled straight to the sinkhole, still surrounded by chunks of Variant appendages and broken bones. A Variant emerged from the hole, its plated torso singed and bleeding. Garcia leapt out of the truck and tumbled onto the ground. The vehicle crashed into the hole, teetering over the edge, and smashed the Variant. While it could not fit down the burrow, it clogged the entrance enough to satisfy Garcia. The scratch of frustrated claws against metal rang out from the undercarriage of the vehicle. Garcia's maneuver had bought them some time, but he had no idea how much and did not want to stick around to find out.

After wiping his forehead with the back of his hand, he pointed toward the lighthouse once more. They seemed to have made it about a half mile closer, with only another half mile or so to go. That half mile had been hard fought, and Garcia feared what that foretold for the rest of their undoubtedly tumultuous journey.

Thomas patted his back, his white teeth shining out through the grit and dirt covering his face. "All it takes is all you got. And you got a hell of a lot, Sarge."

"Let's hope we have more of it," Garcia said, guiding them past the tourist center and around a burned-out ice cream stand. They crouched for a moment by the melted plastic and scorched wood, taking sips of water as they took turns covering the group's momentary reprieve.

That reprieve seemed as if it would be short lived. Variant calls echoed around the island like the howls of wolves announcing an impending hunt. Garcia had heard the same sounds too many times to count tonight, but they never failed to send a wave of shivers through his flesh.

He looked at each of his men. The three that remained from the ten he had started with. "Time to move."

— 10 —

The lighthouse loomed against the night sky. It beckoned to Garcia as Stevo led the marines to a restaurant with a wooden sign hanging by one chain, announcing Robby's Crab Shack. They snuck into the Crab Shack, and the odor of seafood left to bake in the heat hit them with an almost palpable force. As they crept over soiled napkins and tablecloths and past overturned tables and broken chairs, Garcia felt the tug of the lighthouse. It was almost as if he had left a piece of his soul there and someone from above was telling him to return to it, to retrieve it from this wasteland.

Hell, he was certain he *had* left a piece of himself there. His memories of embracing Ashley up there, of holding her close to his chest, feeling her celebratory tears drip onto his shoulder, were almost too much, threatening to distract him from the mission at hand. The Variants' unyielding cries made sure his mind did not stray too far. His face grew hot with his anger, and his fingers clenched tightly around his M4. If he could just kill every one of those goddamned creatures…

His team crept through the kitchen. Water pinged as it dripped from the ceiling and landed on metal pots and pans. A layer of brown liquid covered the tile floor, and claw marks cast long gouges in the metal door of the walk-in cooler. The door was stuck open. A wooden crate prevented it from shutting. The smells wafting out of the room evoked colorful images of what the steel and stain-covered glass hid. None of them inspired Garcia to investigate.

Scratching claws and clicking joints sounded somewhere toward the front of the restaurant. Garcia signaled the others to duck, and they crouched behind the stainless-steel appliances and counters. The scuffling continued onward, growing quieter. The Variants had not spotted them yet.

Once the clicking and scraping quieted, Garcia motioned to the marines again. They squeezed through a door in the kitchen leading to a fenced-in area with a Dumpster. Dark stains marred the gray concrete, and overhead palm trees cast derisive silhouettes against the starry sky, almost mocking them, reminding the Variant Hunters that this once had been paradise.

But no more.

Spent bullet casings rolled underfoot. Garcia bent to examine one, thinking it might be a sign of Rollins or Russian or Daniels. But the golden case was encrusted in mud and much too small to be from their M4s. He examined the etchings along the case. He did not need to read them to know these casings had come from a .22.

He doubted such a weapon would be powerful enough to puncture the armor-encased bodies of the crablike Variants they had seen roaming this island. Hell, even if it were a fleshier Variant, a .22 would be like throwing sewing needles at a charging rhino. Likely whoever had made their last stand here had perished under the slicing claws and pointed teeth of the monsters.

Garcia scanned the fenced-in enclosure, even peeking into the Dumpster. He found no sign of a body other than the bloodstains in the concrete. Had the person actually escaped whatever slaughter had taken place here?

He seriously doubted it. More likely, the Variants had done something with the body, bones and all. Everywhere they had been on the Outer Banks, there had been a severe lack of human remains. Except for the SEAL team, there had been no signs actual humans had traipsed on these grounds.

What in God's name was happening here?

Garcia feared Davis had unwittingly landed them in a winding rabbit's hole of a mission that would ultimately yield more questions than answers. His men seemed to sense their leader's burgeoning worry, eyeing him furtively as they snuck through a tall patch of grass toward another ramshackle motel. Though they could not see it, Garcia knew from memory that beyond the motel lay the museum leading to the lighthouse.

He prayed the lighthouse would offer some answers or at least allow them a vantage point to tell them something, anything to help them forge a path forward. After losing the rest of the Variant Hunters, he could not imagine simply abandoning the mission and ignoring their sacrifice. As he waited for Stevo to give them the all clear, his tattooed skin under the gauze itched.

"No contacts," Stevo whispered over the mic. Thomas flew across the street, followed by Garcia. Tank continued on rear guard, ensuring no Variants stalked them. They made their way around the motel, passing rooms with doors hanging open. Many had simply fallen forward, lying useless on the wooden walkways as if the whole building were some giant discarded Advent calendar.

Garcia imagined what it would have been like when this motel still shone with its bright lime-green and yellow paint. In his mind's eye, he saw Leslie, no longer an infant, but a girl of six or seven, long dark hair and olive skin like his, running out of one of those rooms and leaping into his outstretched hands. He would envelop her in a hug as she wrapped her thin arms around his neck and Ashley joined them, folding chairs and towels in tow, ready for a day of digging their toes into the wet sand and building sandcastles, searching for sea stars and jumping into the gentle, breaking waves. That day would only ever exist in his dreams. He touched the place on his helmet where, inside, the photograph of his daughter and wife was taped. Fresh rage flowed through him again. The Variants would pay. He would see to that.

Violent light flashed suddenly over the Variant Hunters. The landscape lit up as if the heavens had parted, as if God Himself was sending Garcia a message. Darkness soon returned, followed by the rumbling bellow of thunder. The storm churned off the coast, ready to devour the island just as the Variants had, bringing more darkness, more destruction.

Maybe that was His message. That this was all hopeless. That Garcia would not have a chance to see those he loved again. Not here. Not in Heaven. Not ever.

"Sarge?" Thomas whispered quietly, peeking over the hood of a sedan in their path.

Garcia shook himself back to reality, back to one-hundred-percent focus, and stared over the pavement with Thomas.

"Good God," Stevo muttered.

Tank said nothing, watching their backs, sweeping his M249 back and forth. Garcia tended to agree with Stevo. "Good God."

A Variant dragged something behind it. It looked to Garcia like a huge garbage bag stuffed with a damned wooden barrel. It was not until he saw the broken legs and hooves that he realized it was one of the horses.

"Guess that explains what happened to the refuge," Stevo said.

Tank merely huffed.

"Poor animals," Garcia said, spotting another couple of Variants lugging a horse carcass. The corpse left a wet trail behind it as the monsters pulled it over a parking lot toward the museum at the lighthouse's base. From other directions, Variants scuttled across the landscape, pulling other things. A few looked like human shapes, and Garcia's heart skipped a beat. He wondered if he was seeing Rollins and company again for the first time.

Rain began pattering on the broad leaves of a palm tree. Drops soaked into the Variant Hunters' fatigues, and rainwater started to wash the trails of blood and flesh the Variants' prey left behind. Some of the Variants vanished into holes along the ground, tugging their loads beneath the earth. As Variants crawled underground and disappeared with their war spoils, more filtered out of other burrows, presumably setting out on some other mission.

"Maybe this is it, Sarge," Thomas said.

Garcia nodded, chinning his mic. "Command, Victor Hotel. Think we may have found one of the Variant strongholds on the island."

"Copy, Victor Hotel. Reading your coordinates via WINS now. We have you at the Currituck Beach lighthouse. Can you confirm my coordinates are correct?"

"Roger, Command. That is right. We followed a network of tunnels leading here."

"If what we're seeing through your feed is correct, you've presumably got Variants bringing food back to a hive. Do you have any evidence if the actual hive core is beneath that lighthouse or museum?"

A pit formed in Garcia's stomach. "No, but—"

"We need solid intel. This is good, but we can't order a blind bombing on what may very well be nothing but another entrance to that tunnel network."

"You want us to go in there?" Garcia asked.

"That would be correct. We need proof we're hitting the right target. We might only get one chance at this, and we need every one of those goddamn Variants in whatever hive is out there obliterated."

"Copy that," Garcia replied.

Judging by the monsters constantly ebbing and flowing from the museum and around the lighthouse, this mission was nowhere near over. He prayed the epicenter of the Variants' hive was not far from this complex. The monsters slunk under the cover of the trees that protected the lawns and their tunnels from the prying eyes of drones. It was no wonder they had operated here almost completely undisturbed. Between the dense, marshy forests up and down various parts of the long barrier island and the extensive tunnel networks, these creatures had built themselves a home almost impermeable to what little technology remained available to the US armed forces.

But even though the drones and satellite imagery had failed to locate the center of Variant activity here, technology was not the only thing the US had to offer.

The country still had its marines, and Garcia vowed to prove they were still America's most valuable asset. And by God, fear and Variants could not keep a marine from fulfilling his duty, no matter the cost. He pressed his binos to his eyes once more, studying the Variants' movements.

"We going back underground, Sarge?" Stevo asked, trepidation etching his tone.

Garcia looked up between the trees, spying the full moon peeking out from the rain clouds. "As long as we can help it, I want to stay aboveground. I don't think we need to hike up the lighthouse anymore, but something's going on at the museum."

"Doesn't seem like a school field trip, either," Thomas added dryly.

"Wait a second, Sarge," Stevo said, his eye looking through his MK11's scope. "Take a look at that mansion."

More lightning flashed in the distance, accompanied by cracking thunder. A wide, open lawn, devoid of trees, rolled toward a white-painted mansion with a black roof and shutters. The ground rippled around the house as though huge moles shoveled their way through the dirt just beneath the grass to the mansion. Grooves in the ground from all directions spiderwebbed to the building as if they were the vessels and it was the heart.

Garcia scanned the mansion's windows, spotting movement behind the cracked and broken panes. Grime obscured any hope of getting a clear picture of what lay beyond the glass, but the sight of activity there was enough to pique his interest.

"If I was a betting man…" Tank said, staring at the mansion, water dripping down his face.

Garcia nodded, bringing himself up to his knees. "Prepare to move out. I want to get a closer—"

Something crunched in the grass behind him, and he spun, aiming his rifle. Silhouetted by the moonlight, four dark shapes appeared, stalking toward them, rain sluicing off their humanoid forms.

— 11 —

"Hold your fire!" a voice snapped.

It was no Variant. It was a human voice.

Rollins.

Garcia lowered his M4 tentatively, unable to believe what his senses told him. The other Staff Sergeant strode toward him. He wore no helmet, and his fatigues hung off him in rags. Half his body appeared haphazardly covered by bandages. Daniels trudged next to him, a mirror image of scrapes and gouged skin. Lacerations marred the third marine's hulking form. *Russian.* One of the man's pant legs had been torn off, and he walked with a pronounced limp.

A gasp almost escaped Garcia when he saw the fourth man: Morgan.

"You're alive," Garcia said. Then he imagined Rollins dashing away with his team again, disobeying Garcia's orders. "What the fuck were you thinking?"

Rollins's blood-covered brow creased in thick crevices. "I was thinking I'd save our brothers."

Morgan wiped a swathe of dirt from his face as he crouched near the other Variant Hunters. "He about did, too."

"Fought the Variants in the street. Almost lost my life." Russian's eyes narrowed. "But then those damn things dove into some tunnels. We lost 'em down there."

"Got away with Mulder and Chewy," Rollins said, spitting on the wet ground. "But maybe they wouldn't have if you came with."

The words were like a knife twisting in Garcia's gut. He forced himself to ignore the jibe. Maybe they still had a chance of saving Mulder and Chewy.

"Where the fuck is Kong?" Rollins said, looking around at the haggard group.

The other Variant Hunters' eyes seemed to convey the message before Garcia even said a word.

"Gone," he said simply.

"Should've gone with us," Rollins said again. "We could've avoided—"

"Shut the fuck up," Garcia snapped, his nostrils flaring. This was not the brotherhood and respect he had been accustomed to while serving. Something was wrong with Rollins. Maybe the apocalypse had gotten to him. Maybe it was the fact that his family had been killed by the Variants. Maybe the deadly combination of PTSD and depression were inking his brain black, subverting years of professionalism and dedication. There would be time to deal with Rollins's insurrection later and time to mourn for Kong. Mulder and Chewy might still be out there, so everything else would have to wait.

"Let's get one thing straight," Garcia said. "This is my mission. Davis didn't put you in charge. If you fuck this up, if you get us all killed, that'll be blood on your hands. I don't know what the fuck is going on with you, but I need you to shut up and do as I say right now. That's the only way we're finding the Variant hive and getting out of here alive. Got it?"

Rollins glared at him, his face turning red under the grime. His lips straightened until they turned white, but he said nothing.

"Good," Garcia said. The others stood still, their eyes wide, filled with a sense of almost palpable shock. Garcia's superiors had always praised him for his calm demeanor and his coolness under pressure. He was well practiced at hiding the fury that flowed through him. His men knew him well enough to recognize that if the Sarge was pissed, he had a damn good reason.

"We came here to hunt Variants, and that's exactly what I want to do." Garcia pointed to the mansion. "I want to get in there, find out if that place leads to these monsters' shitty hive, and get the hell out of here. We're almost done, but this is the part that counts. These are the last few yards before the shit storm, and I need every one of you on your A game. We are no longer individuals. We are a team, a machine. Forget about everything else outside the mission, outside your lane of fire, outside your brothers right here on the ground. All that matters right now is what's in front of us. No more distractions."

"You got it, Sarge," Tank said without hesitation. The others, barring Rollins, voiced their agreement in soft murmurs, careful not to attract undue attention to their position.

"We're the Variant Hunters," Garcia said, his chest puffing out slightly. "Let's hunt some fucking Variants."

***

In a matter of minutes, Garcia found himself huddled behind a thick hedge near the rear entrance of the white mansion. Sheets of rain slapped against the mansion and across the lawn. Tank, Stevo, and Rollins were positioned along the hedge several yards apart. He no longer trusted Rollins to lead his team, so Thomas crouched near a shed with Daniels, Russian, and Morgan, ready to cover Garcia's team's entrance into the building. Garcia crossed himself. The words of the Lord's Prayer whispered through his head as he traversed the lawn, drawing on whatever strength he could muster to face the inevitable evils ahead.

With each step, he avoided the holes and bumps in the ground demarcating the tunnels. He did not want to fall belowground or let his thumping footsteps notify the Variants that intruders approached their gates. When he reached the porch and pressed his body flat against the wood siding, he signaled for his team to follow, one by one. They flitted over the lawn, their rifles scanning for any sign of danger. A Variant dragging a horse carcass lurched from a nearby patch of trees, and the group threw themselves to the ground, taking refuge behind the furrows. The Variant shuffled onward, lugging its cargo, too focused on its mindless task to notice the humans lurking in its midst. It vanished around the front of the mansion, and the others army-crawled the rest of the way to Garcia, soon joining him at the back door.

Thomas peered at Garcia from behind a cluster of bushes. Garcia gave a single hand signal to ensure the marine was ready. As soon as Garcia disappeared into the mansion, Thomas's team would follow across the lawn, posting up along the porch.

Stevo wrapped his fingers around the handle of the door and nudged it softly to test the lock. The door came away from the frame, opening an inch and creaking slightly. Garcia cringed, and they all froze, waiting for the howls or clicking joints to come.

When twenty seconds of only the pounding rain sounded, Garcia signaled Stevo to enter. The marine pushed the door open gently. The hinges groaned the entire way. Rustling sounds and the splat of dripping water met Garcia's ears as Stevo slipped inside. Tank followed immediately after, with Rollins being goaded onward by Garcia.

Garcia entered last. His eyes blinked to adjust to the sight before him. An intense smell like that of moldy cheese and body odor surrounded them, evoking pangs of nausea. But even more startling was the mansion itself.

In his mind's eye, Garcia recalled the early-twentieth-century furniture that had once filled the dining room, library, smoking room, and entryway with antique decadence. He had toured the place with Ashley, admiring how the old mansion had stood up to the salt-bearing winds of the ocean, a true testament to humanity's stubborn inclination to preserve the past.

Now, the mansion was nothing like he remembered. He and the others ducked behind a pile of furniture—moved by Variants or humans, he could not be sure. He peeked out from behind the mess of torn sofas and cracked tables and fought to keep himself from gawking. The innards of the mansion had been gutted like a pumpkin ready to carve. A few walls still stood, riddled with massive holes. Support beams jutted up, straining to hold the building together. But it was not the destruction of the building's interior that startled Garcia.

Rather, it was what had been constructed there.

— 12 —

A thick, weblike substance coated every inch of remaining wall, ceiling, and support beams. A few Variants scuttled across the netting like spiders and tucked things into various large pouches. The pouches—most of them, at least—contained the corpses of humans and animals. Some had evidently been eaten, and only bones remained. Horses, humans, birds. Anything and everything the Variants had apparently gotten their claws on. At least a dozen of the pouches nearest the Variant Hunters harbored writhing shapes. Humans still clinging to life, barely conscious.

One man was missing an entire arm. The same webby substance holding him to the wall was plastered over his wounds, presumably to staunch the bleeding. His jaw worked back and forth as if he was grinding his teeth. Crusty tears dripped out of his eye sockets, his eyelids yanked open. Garcia's stomach dropped, and the iron grip of nausea wrapped around him. The man had no eyes left. Just gaping wounds. Another woman cocooned nearby seemed barely more than a torso with a head. Her chin drooped against her chest, which moved in shallow, slow breaths. Garcia could practically hear the thoughts running through his team's heads.

My God. These poor souls.

Clicking and snapping sounded from holes in the rotten and torn floorboards, and Garcia leaned forward slightly to confirm what he already suspected. The massive holes revealed another terrifying tableau.

Hordes of Variants squirmed over and around each other, blankets of them so thick, it was impossible to see the ground beneath their feet. Dozens of tunnels stretched beyond this central hub, no doubt leading to various points around the island. The deep chamber below this mansion seemed to host hundreds if not thousands of the creatures. It took Garcia several moments to find one corner of the massive chamber devoid of the crablike Variants. A single Variant the size of a rhinoceros sat there with a swollen belly. Eight legs stuck out from its abdomen, and its back was protected by a crustacean carapace. Garcia shuddered at the sight of the monstrosity as a pair of normal, human-sized Variants brought it the carcass of a horse.

The monster devoured the dead animal, its talons ripping into the hide, tearing through bone and flesh with ease. It stuffed the bones into its mouth, crunching madly, as the two servant Variants retreated into the crowd. This place truly was like an ant colony. If Stevo's earlier guess was correct, that must be some sort of queen. But if that abomination was the queen, that meant...

Garcia shivered uncontrollably. He had heard rumors that the Variants might be breeding, might be repopulating even as humans desperately vied to quell their numbers.

Please, God, don't let that be true.

A voice sounded over his comm link, about causing him to jump. "Victor Hotel, this is Command. We see what you're seeing through vid link. Science team confirms this is likely the hive's core."

A hand tugged his sleeve. Thomas's group had sidled up beside Garcia's after making it into the mansion stealthily. With wide eyes, Thomas silently gestured to another two Variants dragging a human behind them deep in the chamber. The man was barely clinging to consciousness. His head lolled back and forth. Variants cleared a path for the duo as they dragged the man to the queen.

Garcia's index finger sought his trigger, his arm shaking. It was not just some hapless tourist or Outer Banks citizen the Variants were dragging. Garcia recognized the lanky man's shaved head and square nose: Mulder.

He wanted to save the man, to decimate the Variants down there, to send a storm of bullets into the queen's bulbous body. He would take pleasure in those monsters' agonized deaths.

But to do so would be to condemn himself and his men to death. All he could do was stand by helplessly. The Variants served their queen Mulder as if he were nothing more than a Big Mac. Garcia had to turn away when the queen tore the man's body in half. His voice called out, long and shrill, until Garcia heard more slurping and tearing, and the agonizing screams silenced.

No, no, no, no. Garcia's arm burned as he pictured the new name that would be added to the cross. Heat scorched his face. He wanted to yell, to curse, to rip the Variants apart piece by piece as the queen had done to Mulder. His fingers reflexively clenched until it felt as if they would punch through his palms.

"That's good enough, Victor Hotel," the specialist's voice droned through his earpiece. "You all are to head to your extraction point immediately."

Garcia started to shift back on his feet, ready to retreat. But another sight caused him to freeze. There was a woman with long dark hair plastered to the wall next to a skeleton. She was alive, intact. In her arms was a baby, younger than a year old, clinging to its mother. Both seemed asleep, draped in the mysterious webbing. A fire burned in his belly, a grim determination inching through his mind. He recalled the SEAL's last words: "You've got to find them. All of them."

He *had* found them.

And as Garcia gazed around the room, spotting the other humans still alive, still squirming or unconscious in the web pouches, he realized there was no way he could leave without trying to save them. To bomb this place was to eradicate the hive beneath their feet, but it would also sentence these people to death. Command already had what they wanted. Garcia had served his purpose for them. He crossed himself. Now he had a higher purpose to serve.

***

"We can't abandon these people," Garcia said to the group as they mustered outside the mansion. Rain flushed through the bent and broken gutters along the porch's roof. "You saw what those things did to Mulder. We leave them here, they die."

"The strike group can send a rescue team," Rollins said. "We need to go. You might think I'm an idiot, but there's no chance in hell we're putting up a fight against the Variants in those huge chambers. No fucking way."

"Sarge told you to shut up," Tank said. "Something you're pretty bad at."

Rollins narrowed his eyes. Garcia had half a mind to sit the guy on the porch and have him watch their backs to keep him out of their hair. But he was not sure if he could trust him to do even that.

"Daniels, Morgan, Thomas, you take the south wall. Tank, Stevo, and Russian, take the east side." Garcia pictured the mother and child again. "Rollins and I will take the north. Anybody that looks like they're in decent health, cut 'em down and bring them with us."

Stevo scratched behind one of his ears, his tell that he was worried. "And what about the ones in rougher shape?"

Garcia gulped. "Can't take everyone, I'm afraid. You saw the state of those people. If you think you can walk 'em out, if they'll live after we take them down, great. If not, we'll try to save as many lives as possible without getting ourselves and everyone else killed." He peered around the group, meeting each of their eyes. Everyone except Rollins. "Ready, brothers?"

Their voices whispered up in a chorus of affirmatives. A wave of thunder exploded around them.

"Remember, all it takes is all you got, Marines," Garcia said. "Reload, and take stock of everything we've got left. I don't want this to come down to a fight, but if it does, let's be ready."

The others clicked fresh magazines into place as Garcia opened a comm channel back to the *GW* strike group.

"Command, Victor Hotel Alpha," Garcia said. "Do

you read?"

"We read, Victor Hotel."

"Change of plans. We're bringing civilians to the extraction point."

"Victor Hotel, those were not your orders. You are to proceed to extraction point as planned."

"Negative, Command." A brief thought flashed through Garcia's mind, and he wondered if he was being as stubborn and foolhardy as Rollins had been. But he quashed the notion. These civilians were the ones they had been sworn to protect, the ones they fought for, the ones they sacrificed their lives for. They had already completed the objectives Davis had given them. "We're saving these people. You saw 'em. They won't last much longer here."

"No can do. We—"

"Clear it with Davis."

There was silence at the end of the line. Garcia listened to the increasingly violent wash of waves over the beaches dozens of yards away. A cold, storm-borne breeze tickled at his skin.

"Victor Hotel," the specialist began slowly. "Davis has cleared a detachment of choppers to aid in civilian extraction. Where do you want 'em?"

Garcia gave him a set of coordinates, and a wave of relief trickled through him, quenching the unending rage he had felt before. It was a small victory for him. Now, he was more certain than ever fate had brought him to Corolla, and this was what was intended for him. He needed to save these people.

With a nod from Garcia, Stevo nudged the door open to the mansion. The Variant Hunters dispersed along what remained of the floor overlooking the huge crevice full of wriggling creatures. Garcia pressed his back against the wall as he skirted over a thin strip of flooring. Risking a short glance down, he guessed that if the fall did not kill him, it would take only seconds before his body was turned into macabre confetti. The noise of the monsters growling and clicking and eating below drowned out the footsteps of the Variant Hunters, rivaling the smack of rain against the roof. The marines positioned themselves under the webbed cocoons where people still lived, if only by the threads of their life. A Variant scuttled along the wall above them, and Garcia signaled for Rollins to hide under a pouch. Garcia crouched beside one with the remains of a man's torso. Rib bones protruded from the lacerated skin, and he tried to ignore the odor until the Variant passed along to another wall.

Rollins reached to the pouch he had been hiding behind and withdrew his blade. With several precise slices, the webbing fell away, and a man slumped into his waiting arms. The man's head rolled back for a second until his eyes fluttered open. His mouth wrenched open, ready to scream. Rollins clamped his hand over the man's lips and held a single finger to his own. Pallor overcame the rescued man's face, but he nodded in understanding, and Rollins slowly released his grasp. The man crouched behind Rollins, shaking but remaining quiet as he studied his surroundings with wide eyes.

Next, Garcia cut loose a woman covered with scratches. She jolted awake, looking as if she was ready to fight, before Garcia signaled her to remain quiet, too. One by one, they made their way through the cocoons, releasing those that seemed to have a fighting chance at life. Rollins and Garcia had a group of five in tow. The others seemed to have found similar rates of success, with a group around a half dozen deep following each Variant Hunter team.

Rollins grabbed Garcia's shoulder, pointing across the wide pit toward the group Thomas led. His heart beat wildly when he spotted them taking a man with broad muscles and a trimmed beard off the wall. *Chewy.* They continued onward, one Variant Hunter stronger, releasing civilians from the Variants' prison, stopping occasionally only to hide as a creature climbed across the walls.

Finally, Garcia reached the cocoon with the woman and baby. He gingerly cut away the silky strands of webbing imprisoning the duo. The baby came loose first, and Garcia carefully took the infant out, holding the sleeping child to his chest to keep it from waking. He gently roused the mother, clasping his hand over her mouth until she saw her child was safe. Even as he helped her wobble down from her roost, the stabbing bite of bittersweet pain rocked through his heart. He had saved this woman, but he could not help wishing this were Ashley and Leslie he escorted away from the damn cocoon.

"I'm Beth," she whispered.

Garcia nodded but held a finger to his lips then pointed to the name tape on his fatigues before continuing on. When it looked as though he and Rollins had freed all those who could be saved, he signaled for the man to guide the remaining civilians to the porch. Tank and Thomas's teams were also heading to the exit, dodging between cocoons and avoiding the few Variants lurking on this level of the hive. They were almost outside, where they could begin their journey to the extraction point, escorting these poor souls to safety, out of the hell from which they had come.

Then it happened all too fast.

A Variant unwrapping a web around a horse carcass worked above Tank. One of the horse's legs flopped out of the pouch, then its torso and remaining legs slipped out. The corpse slid down the wall, headed straight toward a civilian. Tank dove to push the man out of the carcass's way, and the man yelped in surprise when his head hit the wall.

The Variant noticed immediately. Its eyes locked on Tank. It reared back, feet still clamped on the wall, pincers clicking. Garcia wasted no time in sighting the monster up and squeezing the trigger. His suppressed M4 barely let out a sound as the bullets cut through the Variant's flesh and ended its life. The monster rolled down the wall and bounced off the floor. Its corpse fell into the pit below. The dead monster crashed into a few Variants down there.

One by one, the creatures looked up, trying to figure out what had caused the disturbance. It took them less than a second to spot one of the free civilians. A single Variant cried out, its shrill voice exploding from the pit and rattling Garcia's eardrums. More voices picked up around it, causing the manor to quake. The unholy chorus roared loud enough for the sound to resonate in Garcia's chest and shake through his bones.

"Run!" he yelled above the din. He doubted the others could hear him, but it did not matter. They all sprinted for the back door, herding the civilians along.

Variants scrambled up the sides of the pit. Their joints snapped, and their claws dug into the earthen walls as they ascended, allured by the sight of fresh meat and their escaping meals. The Variant Hunters and the civilians rushed to the back lawn as the first Variant crested the side of the pit. Garcia gestured in the direction of the beach where the choppers and Ospreys were supposed to meet them.

But he soon realized they would never make it that far. All over the rain-covered landscape, through the woods and across the parks and lawns, Variants burst from the ground like exploding landmines. The demons of hell had escaped, and they had invaded the Outer Banks.

Garcia chinned his mic. "Command, we're going to need those choppers a lot closer than anticipated."

— 13 —

Human screams soon joined the throaty bellows and roars of the Variants. Civilians started to scatter, until Garcia and the Variant Hunters grabbed their arms and guided them to stay with the group. There would be no hope for any that decided to sprint into the darkness alone.

A few of the Variant Hunters looked to Garcia for guidance. Others shot into the surging ranks of Variants. The monsters were closing in on the group, with talons flashing and teeth snapping. Garcia shouldered his rifle and took down a Variant galloping toward Beth and her baby. The monster flopped forward, leaving a trail of blood in the wet grass. There would be no running from these monsters. No fighting them in the open. Going underground would be just as deadly. There was only one option.

"To the lighthouse," Garcia yelled over his mic. He pointed toward the structure in case anyone could not hear him.

His words galvanized the marines, and they encircled the civilians, rushing them to the redbrick walled museum leading to the towering lighthouse. Tank's M249 opened up, scattering a group of Variants hurtling toward them. He barreled into the front door of the museum with his shoulder, and the doors cracked backward, leveled by the huge man. The others filed in, with Russian, Chewy, and Daniels taking rear guard, covering the group's escape. Periodic gunfire lit up the museum as the Variant Hunters ushered the civilians past overturned displays of historic lighthouses as well as paintings and photographs with broken frames scattered along the waterlogged floor.

The Variants slammed against the front of the museum like a landslide. They struggled past one another into the building, breaking through other doors and bursting through windows. Their bodies bounced against each other, scales and armor plates clacking. Russian spewed curses at them as quickly as the automatic fire leaving his rifle. Chewy limped along, barely keeping pace with the group, still weak from his earlier attack. Daniels tried helping the man, but a Variant pounced forward, dodging past Russian's gunfire. Its pincers closed around Chewy's injured leg, and the marine stumbled. Daniels fired at the Variant. Bullets lanced through the creature's body, but two more Variants tackled Chewy. They bit into his flesh before anyone could stop them. Chewy disappeared under their numbers, and a dark hatred for the monsters swelled in Garcia once more.

"Goddammit!" Russian yelled. His M249 sprayed into the creatures' ranks, sending them toppling over each other. But it still was not enough to keep them from trampling over the museum's displays, glass and wood crunching.

They churned past a ticketing counter, and Tank busted down the gates to the lighthouse. Civilians and

Variant Hunters stomped up the spiral metal staircase to the top. Garcia paused at a landing, ushering them through until he spotted Russian guarding the back of the group. A couple of civilians limped in front of him along with Beth.

Garcia picked off three Variants leading the pack as Russian tried to slide the entrance gate to the lighthouse shut with Daniels's help. They had the gate an inch away from being shut when a tangle of claws belonging to sinewy gray arms reached through, scraping at the two men. Garcia tried to help pick the creatures off, his heart pounding, but one of them caught Russian by his neck. Rivulets of crimson streamed down Russian's skin. His neck split open from the gashing claws, and his face started turning pale. The man threw his body against the gate, shutting it with his last dying efforts. His body went slack as the gate locked into place, and he signaled for Garcia and Daniels to move on.

"Go!" he called. "Go, go, go…"

His voice grew weaker.

"No!" Garcia yelled. His rifle shuddered against his shoulder. Shot after shot flew between the metal bars of the grate, slamming into the Variants threatening to tear it down.

Russian dragged himself away from the gate. His bloodied fingers wrapped around the M249, and he blasted a final spray of rounds into the twisted creatures. Their corpses piled up, only to be discarded by more of their living brethren desperate to reach the humans. Daniels bent over Russian. He tried to staunch the man's bleeding by pressing his hands against the wounds. But soon Russian's eyes rolled back, and his fingers loosened around his gun. The weapon dropped.

"Daniels! Russian's gone!" Garcia yelled. "Let's move!"

Another name for the cross.

Daniels lunged up the steps. They made it up to the next landing, when the scream and screech of protesting metal sounded below. The gate gave way, and Variants poured into the stairwell. Their claws clattered against the steel steps, their voices bouncing off the cylindrical insides of the lighthouse. Garcia glanced up to see that the first few Variant Hunters and civilians had made it to the top. He prayed to God to grant him one more blessing, one more wish he did not deserve.

"Command, where are those choppers?" Garcia asked.

"Should be there any minute," the voice called back over the comm link, immeasurably calm compared to the panic of the civilians and Variant Hunters' escape.

The Variants rounded up the landing that Daniels and Garcia had just been around. Garcia fired down on them. His lancing rounds sent the first wave tumbling backward, knocking over their comrades. It provided only a brief reprieve. Variants climbed over each other and the stairs, unperturbed by the dead monsters falling to waves of bullets around them.

A yelp caught Garcia's attention. Beth caught her foot on a stair and fell. Her ankle twisted violently, and she landed hard on the steps while protecting her child. Garcia lunged, heart hammering, adrenaline pulsing through his vessels, and wrapped an arm around her. He helped her to her feet, and she stood, gingerly favoring one foot.

"Come on! You can do this!" he yelled, straining to be heard over the monsters clamoring below.

"They're gaining, Sarge!" Daniels barked. He turned

and levied another burst of rounds into the nearest creatures.

Garcia let Beth wrap an arm around his shoulder and glanced at her leg. "You going to be able to make it up?"

She grimaced but gave him a firm nod.

Rollins paused above them in the midst of a pack of civilians. He shouldered his rifle and fired into the Variants churning up the winding stairs nearest Daniels. One of them tumbled over the railing and plummeted. Its limbs flailed, and a violent wail spewed from its lips the entire drop. The wail only silenced when its body smacked against the floor. Armor plates and bones cracked. The Variant disappeared as more and more of the vile beasts filled the lighthouse. The metal stairs quaked under their thunderous footsteps. Dust shook free from the bolts holding the staircase to the brick insides of the lighthouse. It sounded as if the Variants might bring the whole damn tower down through sheer numbers.

Beth's baby cried. Its shrill sobs and shrieks pierced through the growls of the pursuing Variants. Garcia wished he could offer some comfort, some promise that they would be safe soon. But he feared their safety and survival was now out of his hands. Even if they made it to the top of the lighthouse, how long could they hold out against the horde?

Another raucous yell carried up the lighthouse. One of the Variants leapt from rail to rail, bypassing the stairs entirely. Garcia whipped his rifle around and fired on the creature. Bullets clanged against metal. Sparks flew. A few Variants crumpled, but not the one that had been jumping between handrails.

The monster's muscles coiled and tensed under its

scaly flesh. Its mouth broke into what looked to Garcia like a demonic grin, and its tongue whipped as it let out a long howl. Garcia fired. The monster flew. Its claws slammed against his shoulder. Pain rocketed through Garcia's flesh, reigniting missions-full of injuries. His helmet crashed against the wall, and he slumped onto the stairs. Beth fell, and the Variant bore down on Garcia. Spittle flew across his face as he dodged the creature's snapping jaws.

He tried to swing at the monster, but it held his arms down. Daniels bashed the Variant with the stock of his rifle. Weapon collided with skull. A sickening thud rang out. The creature never turned its attention off Garcia.

Glowing yellow eyes locked with Garcia's. They drilled straight through to his core. He could practically feel the hot pangs of anger and hunger pulsing through the genetically altered monster. If he squinted, he could almost see the man the creature once had been. Bits of green flecked its irises, and strands of hair hung over its scalp. Veins throbbed along its forehead and bulged in its neck. When its mouth opened again, teeth inches from his face, Garcia felt its rancid breath wash over him.

Deliver us from evil.

The words whispered through Garcia's mind, but he knew no divine intervention would save him now.

He slammed his head forward. His helmet crashed against the Variant's open mouth. Teeth cracked, and the monster's lips split. Surging upward, Garcia forced the monster backward. It was dazed by its cranial injury, and its legs caught the handrail. Garcia fought through his own pain and shoved the creature's chest hard. The Variant's pincer claws snapped open and closed. Garcia jumped back and delivered another kick into the monster's torso. Daniels smashed the stock of his rifle into the side of its head. It fell over the rail, disappearing into the mass of other creatures.

Daniels gave Garcia a knowing nod, and they continued upward. They were almost there. Already, civilians and Variant Hunters filled the platform around the lantern panes. The injured civilians, including Beth, were still lagging behind. The nearest Variants narrowed the gap between themselves and Garcia, now only a half-dozen yards away. Another Variant pounced across the space in the center of the lighthouse, but its claws came up short, scraping against the metal handrail. It plummeted.

The baby continued to scream, and Garcia dashed to catch up. He helped Beth along. The pain in her leg appeared to be worsening, and she winced with each step. Garcia motioned to take the infant so she could focus on herself. At first she seemed reluctant, holding the wailing baby closer to her breast. But a shriek from a Variant clattering up the stairs convinced her otherwise.

Beth handed over the infant, and Garcia tucked the young girl against his chest. The child's small fingers grasped at one of his pockets, balling into tiny, delicate fists. Daniels emptied his magazine into a couple of gaining Variants. They somersaulted forward then crashed onto the steps. Others trampled their bodies, each more desperate than the last to retake the civilians that the Variant Hunters had absconded with. Garcia's quads burned, and his lungs strained. Pain stitched itself up his sides as he finished climbing the final few steps, joining others in the light room. With the babe still secure in one arm, he reached back with his free hand to help Daniels onto the platform, where the civilians and other

Variant Hunters milled about.

Someone else grabbed Daniels's other arm and lugged him clear of the hatch to the stairs. *Rollins*. The marine slammed the hatch shut, locked it, then slid a heavy iron bar in place to keep it closed.

Frustrated clanging sounded from the other side. Scraping and scratching against the metal rang out. Muffled roars drifted from under the small gap between floor and hatch.

They had made it, and as long as that door held, they might actually survive.

"Garcia!" Beth yelled. She pointed over the side of the lighthouse. Garcia ran to her. He looked to where her index finger indicated. All along the base of the lighthouse, reptilian Variants sank their claws into the mortar between bricks. They forced themselves up the side of the tower, slinking up like so many determined spiders. The door to the platform might keep the Variants trapped inside the lighthouse.

But from those on the outside, the Variant Hunters and civilians had no such protection.

— 14 —

Garcia handed Beth's baby back to her. The woman held her infant closer to her chest, and she shrank into the others, screaming and crying. Garcia would not let these people die up here. Not after he and the Variant Hunters had promised them salvation. Not after their terrifying flight out of that hive.

Shouldering his rifle, Garcia aimed at the climbing monsters. He picked them off, one by one. The others joined him, emptying their magazines into the clamoring ranks at the base of the lighthouse. Rain pelted them in torrents. Lightning crackled. It illuminated a swarm of Variants pushing past the downpour of lead and water. Another rumbling blast of thunder rocked the lighthouse.

Please, God.

The rumble faded, and another noise pierced the night. This one did not belong to the frightened civilians, the determined Variant Hunters, or even the ferocious creatures themselves. This familiar sound inspired an emotion Garcia had almost forgotten during his time on the Outer Banks. Hope.

The heavy thwack of helicopter blades fanned the dying flame of confidence in Garcia's mind. He saw spotlights shine from the choppers. The lights swept over the lighthouse, casting their intense glow over the monsters. Then another sound, even sweeter than the beating rotors, sounded out. The heavy bark of M240s. Tracer rounds cut through the sky from the choppers like sprinting fireflies. Bullets pierced Variant shells and plates. The machine-gun fire brought death to the creatures' numbers. The Variants fell from the lighthouse as if the tower were a snake shedding its dead skin.

A Seahawk hovered above the tower. It swayed slightly while the pilot fought to control the craft against the stormy winds buffeting it. A ladder unrolled from an open side door, and a fabric rescue basket dropped from the other.

"Victor Hotel, this is Delta One," a voice sounded in Garcia's earpiece. "We don't have time to do this safely, so let's do this fast. Those who can, climb the ladders. Those who can't, take the baskets."

"Understood," Garcia yelled into his mic. A navy combat search-and-rescue sailor from the chopper slid down the ladder. The CSAR sailor fixed harnesses onto the first round of civilians, showing them how to hook their carabiners to the ladder to secure themselves in case they slipped. He led the first civilian group up. Tank and Stevo loaded a woman with a broken leg into the rescue basket. The winch whined, and it started upward.

They repeated the process. Variant Hunters guarded the rails and picked off Variants that the side-door gunners missed. After the second load of civilians, the chopper pulled back, making room for a new Seahawk. Another ladder reached to the platform. More lights swarmed over it, and civilians began the arduous climb up to safety.

A third Seahawk followed. Thunder rolled over them again, and the chopper swayed. Several of the civilians on the ladder screamed. One lost his grip, falling four feet until the safety harness caught him. He yelped, swung, snatched a rung, then returned to climbing.

When a fourth Seahawk emerged from the darkness, Garcia thought they finally had a chance at ensuring all the civilians made it. He spotted Beth across the platform.

He ran to her, heat flaring in his cheeks. "Why weren't you on the first chopper?"

"My baby is, but I couldn't climb. I was scared. I couldn't do it." Tears streaked down her face, mixing with streams of raindrops.

"Delta One, I have an injured woman down here. Her baby's on the first Seahawk. Why isn't she there?" Garcia asked, his voice quaking in anger.

"Rescue team reported a few civilians too frightened to take the baskets or ladders. Didn't have time to fight 'em."

Garcia looked at the remaining civilians. He did not have time to play psychologist and comfort these people's irrational thoughts. "This is your last chance. I need you to listen to me. Now! If you do not climb, if you do not let my men help you into these baskets, you will die."

"But the choppers!" a rotund man wailed. He did not look as if he could handle the physical exertion of climbing a ladder like this, even on the best of days. "Look at the winds. I'll fall!"

"Falling is a better goddamned fate than being torn apart by those beasts!" Rollins countered, somewhat unhelpfully.

The man shivered, rain pushing the remnants of a comb-over across his forehead.

"What he's saying is you don't have a choice," Stevo said, buckling a harness on the man and prodding him to the ladder. A CSAR sailor reached for the man and yanked his arm up. Reluctantly, the man followed. The last couple of frightened survivors finally began their ascent.

"Morgan, Daniels, Tank, Stevo, and Thomas, get your asses up there with them. Rollins and I will cover you," Garcia said. They were close. So damn close to being back on the ship.

Rollins offered a curt nod, swinging his rifle over the rail of the platform. He shot a Variant who had avoided the strafing fire of the choppers.

Only one survivor remained on the platform with Rollins and Garcia. Beth. She wrapped her arms around herself. With her twisted ankle, it would be difficult for her to climb the ladder. Garcia helped lower her into the rescue basket. The winch started, beginning to whisk her away.

A low howl sounded, chilling Garcia to his bones. The chopper shuddered when a strong wind slammed into its side. The ladder swayed and tossed the civilians about. The large man who had protested before fell. His voice echoed over the pounding rain and growling Variants. His harness started to slip, and Garcia feared his worries would soon be proved correct. One of the CSAR sailors leaped down a rung and guided the man back to the ladder.

But while the man survived, the rescue basket swung perilously close to the railing. Protruding bolts snagged the fabric and tore the basket.

Garcia sprinted toward it. "Beth!"

He grasped the basket. The tear ripped down the side,

and Beth started slipping out. Garcia grabbed her wrist, holding her as the basket whipped away, flapping in the wind. Every muscle in his arms seemed on fire. Rain dripped over his forearm and between his fingers, threatening to loosen his grip on Beth. He clenched his jaw and pulled her up with a heave. She toppled into him as they rolled back onto the platform.

More lightning and thunder belched out of the night sky. More Variants clawed at the tower. Metal rang out loudly, and a loud snapping sound echoed from the hatch.

The metal bar Rollins had placed to lock the door had bent enough to break. Claws squeezed between the hatch and lip of the platform. Variant eyes peered through the cracks, and their voices roared louder, incensed by the sight of prey. The locking mechanism failed on the hatch and broke, flinging a metal bolt that pinged over the deck and tumbled off the side.

"Go! Now!" Rollins yelled, throwing himself atop the hatch. He pushed down the hatch and batted at the claws reaching for him through the cracks around it.

Garcia rushed to help Rollins, but the marine waved him off.

"You need to go now! They'll get through soon!"

"I'm not leaving—"

"Don't be a fool!" Rollins said. "Save the woman!"

Beth cowered at the edge of the platform, her eyes entranced by the hatch as it bucked when the Variants threw themselves against it.

The tattoo on Garcia's forearm burned. The white gauze around it had bled through. A CSAR sailor dangled at the end of the ladder. The other civilians had already made it up. The sailor reached out with a harness, and

Garcia secured it around Beth. He helped Beth onto the ladder and clipped her first carabiner in place.

"You'll be okay!" Garcia said. "Just climb!"

She nodded. Her bottom lip quivered.

"Your daughter's waiting," he said. "She needs her mother."

With a new fire raging behind her eyes, she turned and started the ascent. The operator handed another harness to Garcia, and he strapped it to himself then slung his M4 over his back. His fingers grasped the first rung. His boots almost slipped when he stepped up, climbing toward the hovering chopper as it swayed in the wind. He stole a glance at Rollins. The marine had his legs propped against the short wall under the light panes, giving himself much-needed leverage to hold back the Variants. Above Garcia, Beth reached into the fuselage of the chopper.

Made it, Garcia thought, thanking God for her safety.

A loud pop sounded from the lighthouse. The hatch burst open, and Rollins was flung forward.

"Rollins!" Garcia yelled. He stretched a hand out, willing the marine to stand back up, to run and jump for the ladder. He could still make it. He could still survive.

Rollins did stand, and he swiveled at the Variants bounding from the open hatch. His M4 let out suppressed whoomphs. Bullets lanced through the first few monsters.

"Come on, Rollins!" Garcia yelled again.

The marine turned and started sprinting over the platform to the ladder. He reached the railing, his outstretched hand inches from Garcia's. So close. But Garcia was not the only one reaching for Rollins. A Variant sank its claws into Rollins's shoulder and spun him back. The monster cocked back its other hand. Claws glistened with blood and rain. Its cheekbones jutted from its thin face as its jaw wrenched open. Fangs met flesh in a flurry of crimson spray.

Rollins went down.

Before Garcia could so much as unholster his sidearm, four more Variants rushed around Rollins. They dug into his body. Flesh tore from bone. An agonized yell quickly devolved into a gurgle. Garcia wanted to rip into the monsters, to kill every one of them with his own hands, bring them the death they so deserved. But it was already too late. Rage would do nothing to save Rollins now. A bitter pang of sorrow crossed through Garcia as he considered the new name he would soon add to his arm.

The chopper lifted higher, taking the ladder and Garcia away. A Variant turned its head from Rollins's corpse. Blood dripped down its chest in a long crimson beard. The monster roared and rushed at Garcia. Its feet pounded the platform, and it threw itself off, over the rail, soaring toward the ladder. Garcia twisted, and the chopper continued upward. The Variant's claws grazed the bottom of the ladder. It plunged to the earth, returning to its brethren.

Bastard, Garcia thought as he watched it crack against the ground.

As more and more of the creatures overwhelmed the lighthouse, the chopper flew from Corolla. Lightning flashed. Thunder rolled in, slightly quieter now. Garcia climbed into the fuselage and watched the Outer Banks fade in the distance. Memories and blood washed away with the pouring rain. Low voices murmured around him. Hands clasped his shoulder as people congratulated him on rescuing the civilians, on finding the hive.

He did not deserve congratulations. He did not

deserve any of it. He collapsed to his knees near a window and crossed himself, murmuring a prayer of mercy for himself, for Rollins. A prayer of thanks for those hearts still beating in the Seahawks. For Beth. Her baby.

A prayer of love for Ashley. Leslie.

And one of forgiveness for the men he had lost.

***

Garcia put the tattoo gun to his skin again. It was a ritual that had become all too familiar.

Kong. Mulder. Russian. Chewy.

Rollins.

He dabbed the beads of blood seeping through the fresh ink. His eyes traced solemnly over the cross. Too many names. Too many damn names. There was room for three, maybe four more. He feared it would not take long to fill those spots of bare skin. This war was unlike any he had ever served in. The costs more demanding. The stakes higher. The enemy more ruthless.

At least the sacrifices had been worth something this time. A hive bombed. Civilians rescued. More scientific intelligence gathered. A child and mother delivered from the edge of darkness, of death. That had to mean something.

Garcia let out a long exhalation. He rolled his shoulders in an attempt to ease the tension that had built up in his muscles.

Kong had been right. The darkness was evolving. Every time the science junkies developed a new weapon against the Variants or unveiled a new change in the beasts' biology, the Variants introduced fresh surprises like pincers or tunnel networks.

The darkness, the Variants were evolving.

But they were not the only ones adapting and changing to this new world. The Variant Hunters were, too. They would follow the monsters into whatever hellhole they buried themselves in during the search for new clues, new intelligence on their morphing physiology. There would be no obstacle, no challenge the Variants threw at them that would stop Garcia from achieving that goal. He promised to himself, to Ashley's memory, and to all those who had fallen, he would do anything he could to restore the light of hope and optimism that had once existed on this earth. Anything to shatter the burgeoning darkness.

As Garcia examined the names on his arm, he realized the Variants were not the only source of darkness in this world. Rollins had gone AWOL, had disobeyed his orders because of his rage and vindictive nature. He had let himself lose control over his dark emotions. Garcia had been just as close to losing it. He could not let himself succumb to the nagging, pulsing seed of guilt threatening to take root. It would be all too easy to let the anger and frustration fill him, rotting his mind from the inside.

That was the real darkness. The real evil. Variants were monsters and always would be. But humans had a choice. A choice between darkness and light. He would follow the light.

A knock at the hatch caused him to turn on his bed. He padded over the deck and opened the hatch. Thomas stood before him. Scabs and bruises covered his face. Dark bags hung under his eyes. He traced a hand over his freshly shaved scalp.

"Davis wants to see us. Again."

Garcia nodded. "Variants never sleep, do they?"

"Not until we put 'em to rest."

They continued past the others rushing through the corridors. All doing their part to keep humanity chugging along in a desperate fight to prevent the ever-looming threat of extinction.

When they made it to the CIC, Lt. Davis greeted them with a solemn nod. "At ease." Her dark eyes cast a sorrowful look. "We'll pay your brothers the proper respects."

"They'd appreciate that," Garcia said. "But I take it that's not what you brought us down here for."

She shook her head then turned to a nearby monitor showing a chain of islands at the southern tip of Florida. "I've got a new mission for you. How do you feel about the Florida Keys?"

Extinction: Thailand

by

Russell Blake

An Extinction Cycle Novella

— 1 —

Pattaya, Thailand, 1972

Music blared from a jukebox in the far corner of a dark bar. A haze of cigarette smoke lingered over the crowd as the Rolling Stones' "Brown Sugar" thumped out its hypnotic rhythm. A sign announcing Hot Paris Nights hung over the watering hole entry, featuring an exaggerated depiction of an Asian nymph wearing a French maid's outfit and an expression that promised endless delight. A half dozen scantily clad working girls barely out of their teens in stiletto heels and bikinis so skimpy they were little more than afterthoughts stood awkwardly by the entrance, gazing out into the muggy night with eyes dulled by ten-hour shifts and obligatory shots of local rotgut, their slim hips swaying and bumping to the beat.

The Vietnam War had transformed Pattaya from a sleepy beach town favored by locals as a seaside getaway into an anything-goes den of iniquity where no vice was too depraved and virtually any craving could be satisfied for a price. Narcotics and prostitutes of every age and gender were plentiful in the large cities, as well as near the airfields where the U.S. Air Force housed its squadrons under the deniable hospitality of the Thai military. Pattaya was no exception: the nearby U-Tapao Royal Thai Navy Airfield provided plentiful traffic for the bars that had sprung up like green shoots since the start of the war.

The song changed to "Me and Bobby McGee," Janis Joplin's whiskey croon as thick as syrup. The lament was interrupted by the sharp crack of a ball jumping the pool table in the rear of the bar and smacking against the stained cement floor. Three American servicemen in civilian clothes laughed drunkenly as the largest of their number, a man with coal black skin and broad shoulders, leaned unsteadily to retrieve the ball, his stick in one hand and a sweating bottle of Singha beer resting on a nearby table beside an overflowing ashtray.

"You're drunk, Kyle. I mean Sergeant Kyle," declared one of his companions, a redhead named Nick. The observation drew hoots of laughter from all three, as though the idea was the funniest they'd ever heard.

"Hell no, I'm not, Nick. You ain't seen nothing yet," Kyle said, scooping up the ball and slamming it back onto the table before raising one foot and holding his arms straight out to the sides for balance. "See? Sober as a judge."

Nick clapped him on the back. "Bartender! Another round!"

His companion leaned into him and shook his head. "Not for me. Still got half mine left."

"Down the hatch. It's gonna be warm as Satan's piss in no time, Cody."

Cody shrugged and chugged his beer. The barkeep, a slim man in his forties with an almond complexion and a permanent smirk, loaded up one of the waitress's trays with beer and shots of high-octane rum. The slim woman carried the drinks to the men, and Cody tossed some of the local currency at her as she deposited the bottles and glasses on the table. She knelt to pick up the bills, her face unreadable, and then hurried away, catching the eye of several tough-looking locals who'd watched the performance from across the room.

Kyle held his shot aloft, polished it off in a single gulp, and washed it down with a frothy pull of beer. His companions matched his move and let out a whoop before resuming their pool game.

Kyle bought the next round and Nick the next as the crowd began to thin with the late hour. The waitress served them with the same blank expression and merely winced when Kyle smacked her hard on her tan buttock, leaving a red handprint as clear as a tattoo.

The toughs who'd been loitering at the other end of the bar approached the Americans, and the largest of them spit on the floor next to Kyle's boot.

"You leave now," he snapped. Kyle looked at him unbelievingly before his brow furrowed with inebriated anger.

"The hell I will," he slurred. "You gonna make me?"

Cody stepped beside his friend and regarded the Thais, pool cue in hand. "There a problem?" he asked, the words jumbled from the alcohol.

The bartender called out over the music, and one of the Thais looked over at him and growled a few dismissive words. The bartender shook his head and motioned to his bouncers, who made their way to where the standoff was taking place.

The nearest Thai looked Kyle up and down and spit again before muttering a curse. That drew a laugh from the big American, and the atmosphere grew tenser as the two faced off. The bartender yelled something to his men, and they spoke in hushed tones with the Thais, clearly trying to talk them down and avoid a fight. The discussion lasted several moments, and then the toughs backed away, clearly unhappy.

The head bouncer nodded to Kyle, his expression neutral. "Might want to finish drink and leave. Plenty more bar open."

Kyle bristled, but Nick's hand on his arm stopped him from taking a swing.

"What's wrong? Our money no good anymore?" Kyle spat.

The bouncer didn't respond, his eyes flat as lead, threads of scar tissue across his nose and forehead evidence he'd earned his position the hard way. Nick pulled on Kyle's arm as Cody swayed to the pool table.

"Come on. I'm bored with this shit hole," he said. "Time to pack it in."

Kyle scowled at the thugs, who were leaving the bar. "I'm not done with my drink," he snarled.

"Yeah. Okay. No rush. But no point in staying where we aren't welcome."

"I don't like being told what to do," Kyle protested.

"In the wrong line of work, then, buddy," Nick countered. They laughed heartily, and the tension evaporated. Kyle finished his beer and Nick glanced at Cody, who was looking slightly green as he drained his bottle. "You gonna make it, wild man?"

Cody nodded and burped. "Shouldn't have eaten that crap off the street."

"I'm sure they hose off the dog before they cook it."

Cody blanched. "Funny."

"You about ready?" Nick asked.

"Let me get my cigs and we're out of here."

They trooped to the door. Most of the patrons averted their eyes, uninterested in drawing unwelcome attention from the drunken servicemen. In any conflict with Americans, the Thai authorities would come down hard on the locals, assuming that they could have prevented an altercation if they'd chosen to. It wasn't fair, but it was the way things were, and nobody wanted to spend the weekend in jail, or worse.

The street was muddy from a recent shower, the air sticky and hot. Food carts hawked their wares as the men made their way down the lane, trailed by come-on calls from girls in the club entrances along the road. Near the intersection, a pair of scantily clad dancers shimmied on stripper poles affixed to the top of a large horseshoe-shaped bar at a club called the Pink Pony, cowboy hats and professional smiles firmly in place as they bumped and wiggled.

Cody stumbled at the corner, and Nick took his arm to steady him.

"You okay?" Nick asked. Cody gave him an alarmed look and, without warning, vomited into the gutter, retching out a splatter of booze and street food.

Kyle shook his head. "You white boys can't hold your water, can you?" he muttered, feeling for a pack of cigarettes in his shirt pocket.

Cody answered with another surge of vomit, and Kyle grimaced. "I'm gonna head down there and pee. I'll be back in a few." He paused, eyeing his friend. "God, Cody. That's disgusting."

Nick nodded as he stood by Cody, the stink from the effluvia pungent in the humid night air. Down the street, a pair of bar girls laughed as they picked their way past the puddles, hands over their mouths at the sight of the compromised American, ebony hair bouncing in a light breeze that afforded no relief from the swelter. Nick breathed through his mouth as he waited for the spell to pass, the din from nightclubs blaring along the road, Cody gasping as his stomach spasmed, the evening's excess abruptly over. He managed a few breaths and wiped his face with his arm. Nick stepped back with a look of revulsion.

"Dude, come on. You're just making it worse."

Cody grunted unintelligibly and waited to see if the spell was done, hands on his thighs for support, his body trembling. Nick slid his cigarettes from his pocket, hoping the smoke would overwhelm the stink from his companion's sick. He lit it with a dented Zippo, flipped the cover closed to extinguish the flame, and took a deep drag. When Cody didn't vomit any more, Nick checked the time and shook his head.

"Crap, Cody. It's already damn near two. Pull yourself together. We have to get back to base," he said, his voice low, eyes roving over to where some of the locals were loitering, their merriment obvious as they enjoyed the show. A shadow appeared from out of one of the clubs, and a shapely Asian approached in a miniskirt and halter top.

"Hey, boys, you wanna good time?"

Nick regarded the hooker and his eyes narrowed. "We're not into ladyboys."

The ladyboy looked him up and down and smiled. "Don't knock till you try."

"Get out of here. Scram."

The ladyboy shrugged. "Two-for-one discount…finest

kind." Seeing the expression in the men's eyes, the young man elected for a strategic retreat and returned to the bar with an exaggerated swing of his hips.

"I…I think it's over," Cody said, and spit into the gutter with a pained look at Nick.

"I think that's your liver there," Nick said, gesturing at the gutter with his smoke. Cody managed a humorless laugh.

"Wouldn't surprise me." He hesitated, looking around. "Where's Kyle?"

"Went to drain the weasel."

They waited for several minutes and, when Kyle didn't return, tottered around the corner onto the darkened dirt street. Gone were the bright lights and music, the endless party and willing bodies, replaced by the stark poverty of clapboard buildings and shanties, some little more than lean-tos with patchworks of pilfered corrugated metal for roofs.

The mud sucked at their boots as they negotiated the muddy road, and Cody pointed at Kyle's footprints trailing away in the muck.

"Least we know he's around here somewhere."

They followed the tracks as the area quickly degraded, and then Nick froze as they neared another dark road. Cody nearly ran into him and was voicing a complaint when Nick's voice stopped him cold.

"What the fu—" Nick blurted, pointing at one of Kyle's boots protruding from the mouth of a narrow alley.

Cody swallowed a mouthful of stomach acid and squinted in the darkness, trying to make out what lay just out of sight in the gloom. Nick's Zippo flipped open with a snick and flame leapt from the lighter, momentarily blinding Cody. Nick drew in a sharp hiss of breath.

"Jesus…" he whispered.

Cody peered into the alley. A rat tore by, its coat slick and wet, and raced into the night. Cody caught a glimpse of what had moments before been their friend, and fell into the mud on his hands and knees, gagging. Nick slowly backed away, the lighter shaking in his hand, his teeth clenched so hard he saw stars. The muddy sluice beneath his feet ran black with Kyle's blood, the thing on the ground hardly recognizable as human much less the strong, capable air force master sergeant who'd survived three tours in the ass-end of the world.

— 2 —

Chief Inspector Sunan eyed a cow by the side of the road as his battered police truck bounced along the ruts; his assistant, Panit, gripped the steering wheel with white knuckles. It was early on Saturday morning and they were headed from Pattaya to Bang Sare, a small beach village fifteen kilometers south of the larger town, to investigate a nuisance complaint from a farmer who'd reported that several of his cows had gone missing.

Sunan scowled at the rising sun burning off the light mist over the freshly planted fields, where a few laborers in peaked straw hats were already at work with hoes and shovels. The younger Panit glanced at Sunan and returned to watching the road. His boss was clearly in one of his moods—understandable given his assignment in Pattaya, a huge step down from his prior position in Bangkok, where he'd been one of the senior homicide inspectors in that city's police department.

"So the case of the missing cows draws us deeper into the wilds," Sunan said, as though reading his subordinate's mind.

"Well, the farmer seemed pretty upset when I took the call."

"These people let their livestock wander off and expect us to go hunt them down. If we had anything better to do—"

Sunan was interrupted by the crackle of the radio. Panit reached for the mic clipped to the dashboard and keyed it.

"Yes?"

"Is Inspector Sunan with you?" the dispatcher asked.

"Yes, he is."

"Let me speak to him, please."

Panit handed his boss the mic. Sunan depressed the transmit button. "This is Sunan."

"We've been trying to reach you for the last few hours. We tried at your home, but there was no answer."

Sunan frowned. He'd spent his evening in the company of a friend and didn't feel any need to explain himself.

"Yes, well, you've reached me now."

"We have another homicide. A block off the main drag."

Sunan exhaled loudly. "That was fast. Same M.O. as the others?"

"Yes. At least, it looks that way."

"Where exactly? Who's the first responder?"

The dispatcher mentioned two uniformed cops who were competent, but not much else—that was why they worked the night shift, which typically involved breaking up fights and arresting drunks. Sunan's scowl deepened.

"Any witnesses?"

"They took two Americans into custody."

"What?"

"You heard me. They're at the station."

The dispatcher waited for Sunan to respond.

"Is the victim still in place?" Sunan asked.

"Yes. As per your instructions."

Sunan had indoctrinated the local police not to disturb a homicide crime scene until he'd personally had a chance to go over it. When he'd first arrived in Pattaya a year earlier, the scenes had been contaminated within minutes by officers with no experience and even less education on the finer points of forensics and evidence collection. Sunan had changed all that, bringing the force into the twenty-first century, but even so he knew he was fighting a losing battle with the country bumpkins who worked the beach beat.

"We're on our way," Sunan said, his words clipped, and replaced the mic in the dash mount before looking askance at Panit. "Turn it around. We've got another one. You heard."

Panit nodded and slowed to perform a three-point turn and retrace their route to Pattaya. "That's the third one," he said.

"Yes. Assuming it's the same perp, it's a troubling trend."

"I wonder why he's targeting Americans?"

Sunan shrugged. "We don't know that he is. The Americans stick out, so if one goes missing, it's a crisis. We both know that countless peasants disappear every year without a word."

"Sure, but many are just escaping the farm. Kids running away to try their luck in the city."

"Which is accepted, so if some kid goes missing in the hills, nobody thinks anything of it."

Panit's eyes narrowed. "You really think he's killing Thais, too?"

"I don't have an opinion. I'm simply saying we can't

assume we know more than we do. This is too new."

The first body had washed up on the beach a week and a half earlier, badly decomposed and covered with crabs who'd been feasting on the remains when a local fisherman had stumbled across it. The second had been found three days ago, on a deserted back road leading from town. That corpse had been in better shape, and it had been obvious that it had been mutilated—but by whom and for what reason, Sunan didn't know.

Homicides were not unknown in Pattaya, most linked to the thriving drug trade and some to robberies gone wrong, but still they were a rarity, and the singular fact that both victims had been Americans stationed at the U-Tapao Royal Thai Navy Airfield had created a stir when the papers had gotten ahold of the news.

The American military police had demanded to be kept in the loop, but so far that had meant conveying a paucity of results rather than anything meaningful. Sunan was frustrated by the open cases, but not surprised—most homicides were crimes of passion or criminal disputes where the perp was well known to the victim. It was rare that apparently random attacks took place in sequence, and Sunan had worked homicide long enough to know that when a serial was involved, discovering the perpetrator was orders of magnitude more difficult than a normal murder.

Panit frowned at the possibilities his boss had raised. This was the first time they'd discussed the likelihood that it wasn't a lone killer responsible for the atrocities.

"My money's still on one guy. Probably hates Americans."

"Could be. Could also be anything from a rear column Vietnamese terror scheme to one of our criminal gangs having a beef with some of their customers. Although why they'd kill the men they've worked hard to get hooked on junk escapes me." Sunan paused. "Best not to speculate until we know more."

They rode in silence, with the protest of the four-cylinder motor and the grinding of gears for company, lost in their thoughts as they returned to Pattaya, leaving the farmer's missing cows for another day.

When they reached the crime scene, Sunan was pleased to see yellow tape holding back a small crowd. Three other police vehicles were there along with the coroner's khaki van, and Panit coasted to a stop near the alley. When they stepped out, the heat slammed into them like an oven after the slim relief of the vehicle's truculent AC. Sunan led his assistant to where three uniformed police stood smoking and eyed them disapprovingly.

"That it?" Sunan asked, pointing at where a black tarp was spread over a man-sized lump at the alley mouth.

"Yes," one of the men said. "It's ugly. Hope you didn't eat breakfast."

Sunan nodded and ducked beneath the tape. Panit made to follow, but Sunan stopped him. "Give me a second alone."

Panit nodded, puzzled. "Sure."

Sunan took hesitant steps toward the body, noting the hundreds of shoe prints in the drying mud from the police and coroner, as well as any of the curious who'd stopped to look before the cops had arrived. Isolating the killer's prints now would be virtually impossible, any positive that the mud might have created in memorializing his steps outweighed by the sloppy crowd work and lackadaisical approach to the scene. His eyes roamed over the rotting wood walls of the buildings that framed the alley and then settled on the tarp, which was covered with flies.

The swarm rose into the air when he raised a corner of the material and gazed down at the victim, his face impassive. He was accustomed to the distended bloat that accompanied death in the tropics, but even so, the defensive wounds on the man's arms were obvious, as was the ultimate cause of death: his throat had been ripped out.

Sunan studied the cadaver, holding his breath so the stench of putrescence wouldn't overwhelm him, and then dropped the tarp back into place and slowly continued down the alley, eyeing the sides of the buildings for any evidence the rain and the passersby hadn't obliterated. Five minutes later, finding nothing, he returned to where Panit was chatting with a squat chubby man with a bad comb-over who'd sweated through his shirt. The coroner nodded as Sunan approached and offered a gap-toothed smile.

"Another customer, eh?" the coroner asked, his jocular tone a constant no matter how heinous the crime.

Sunan frowned. "Have you gone over him yet?"

"I did a basic, but they said you were on your way, so I figured I might as well wait."

"You note the wounds?"

"Of course. Looks like he got hacked to pieces with something blunt." The coroner paused. "Maybe a pipe with an edge?"

"Just like the last two," Sunan said.

"No question. Maybe we'll find some residue to clue us in about the weapon this time."

"Hope springs eternal."

"You done with him?" the coroner asked.

"Not much else I can do now." Sunan approached the uniforms. "You question everyone around here?"

"Yes. We're still doing a door-to-door."

"Anything promising?"

The lead officer shook his head. "Not really. Nobody saw anything. You know the drill."

"Lot of drugs being dealt in this area," Panit observed.

"Doubt this was drug related," Sunan snapped. "Unless the local gangs are target—"

He was interrupted by a cackle behind him. He turned and found himself facing an ancient woman with wild white hair and a face like a catcher's mitt, burnished the color of tobacco by generations beneath an unrelenting sun. Sunan glared at the old woman, and then his expression softened when he saw the tremor in her hands. "What's so funny, Mother?" he asked.

"You'll never catch him," she said, her voice sandpaper rough.

"Who?"

"The monster."

"You mean the killer? What do you know about him?"

"He's not human. He's a devil—a demon walking the earth."

"You speak in riddles, old one."

The woman shook her head and waved a gnarled hand. "The streets are buzzing if you know how to listen. They say the same thing: it's a devil among us."

"Why haven't I heard this?" Sunan asked, humoring the crone.

"Nobody will talk to the police. You should know that. Bunch of thieves."

"Thank you for the kind words, Mother."

"Word is it's a demon. A white devil. You can no

more stop a devil than you can hold the wind in your hand."

Panit and Sunan exchanged a glance. "White?" Sunan repeated.

The woman began shuffling away, finished with the discussion. Panit rolled his eyes. "Crazy hag."

Sunan pulled away from the younger man and followed the woman. "You say he's a white devil? What do you mean white? Caucasian? An American?"

She kept walking. Sunan grabbed her arm to stop her, and she spun with surprising agility for as old as she was. "Leave me be. I've done nothing wrong."

"Why do you say he's white?"

"It's just what people are saying. I don't know. I haven't seen anything." She glanced at his face and then averted her eyes. "Leave me alone. I can't help you."

"Who's saying this? That he's white?" Sunan pressed.

"Just people. You know how it works. Someone tells someone else. I hear it over the laundry." She shrugged. "You're the only ones who don't know."

She resumed walking away, and this time Sunan allowed her to leave, his face clouded as he slowly turned, his mind churning at the implications of the old woman's words.

— 3 —

Bangkok, Thailand

Pounding at the door echoed through the cheap hotel room. A man peered from beneath the covers, hair awry, and glared at his watch. The caramel leg of a woman slid from under the sheets, and a brunette head peeked over the edge of the pillow next to him.

"What that?" she asked, her voice sleepy.

"I...I don't know," he said, sitting up and blinking away sleep. He forced himself to his feet, pulled on his underwear, and then wrapped one of the paper-thin towels around his waist and moved to the door. "Go away," he called, his tone annoyed.

"Chief Warrant Officer Four Shaw?" a muffled voice asked. "CWO4 Hal Shaw?"

Hal rubbed his eyes with the back of his hand and glanced at a half-empty bottle of rum on the table by the bathroom. "Who wants to know?" he demanded, in his pronounced West Texas drawl.

"Military police, sir."

"Barking up the wrong tree, boy," he said, and opened the door.

A pair of MPs stood at attention, seemingly unfazed by the half-naked apparition before them. "Sir? Sorry to bother you, sir."

"I'm on leave. This better be good."

"I'm afraid your leave's been canceled, sir. We were sent to give you a ride to Pattaya."

"Pattaya? Are you nuts?"

"I was told to give you this cable, sir," one of the MPs said, and handed him a yellow sheet of paper folded in half.

Hal opened it and scanned the contents. He reread it and sighed, and then handed it back to the MP. "I'll be ready to rumble in five. You boys wait downstairs. I've got company."

"Yes, sir. Sorry. Wasn't our first choice."

"Yeah. Sure."

Hal swung the door closed and padded to the bathroom. The woman tried a smile, but it looked more pained and confused than inviting. "You go now?"

Hal nodded. "Come on and shower off. We have to clear out."

Fifteen minutes later Hal made it to the lobby, where the men were sitting, their expressions blank as Hal's young companion pushed out the front door and onto the busy Bangkok street. Hal strode toward them, his bearing ramrod straight, his face tanned, eyes cobalt blue, his uniform crisp, a bag slung over his shoulder.

"Lead the way, gentlemen," he said, and followed them to a waiting Jeep parked in the red at the curb.

"You take shotgun, sir," one of the men said, and climbed into the back. Hal tossed his bag beside the man

142

and slid into the passenger seat while the driver eased behind the wheel and started the engine. Soon they were zigzagging through Bangkok morning traffic—a byzantine maze of tuk-tuks, racing motorcycles, honking cars, and bicycles, all apparently suicidal and hell-bent on meeting their maker before lunch.

Once clear of the city, Hal relaxed and considered the message he'd received. His friend and mentor at the Pentagon, General Reynold Scott, had requested that he investigate the death of Senior Airman Samuel Scott—his grandson, who'd been gruesomely murdered in Pattaya three days earlier.

While it was highly irregular for a marine to investigate an air force murder, General Scott had considerable pull and was obviously taking a personal interest in the case. His telegram had indicated in a few sentences that he felt he was being stonewalled by the commanding officer and the air force investigator and had arranged for Hal to take over. Hal was one of the corps' best, a criminal investigation division specialist who'd ascended through the ranks over the prior ten years to become an expert in every aspect of military criminality.

The general had offered precious little in the way of background—his grandson was the fourth generation of Scotts in the military and had started at the bottom, determined to work his way up. He'd been stationed at U-Tapao Royal Thai Navy Airfield for over a year when he'd met his untimely death—but beyond that, the general had no further information and had instructed him to meet the commanding officer for a full briefing: one Colonel Alexander Hedges.

The trip south took three hours, the roads clogged with tired vehicles on their last legs. By the time the Jeep rolled up to the air base gates, the sun had climbed directly overhead and the heat was broiling, the humidity adding to the discomfort as a pair of Thai guards approached them.

Clearing security took five minutes, which Hal was accustomed to from prior forays at other bases. Because of the nature of the American presence in Thailand, the Thai military was chartered with operating the bases and securing them, and the U.S. forces were technically guests who occupied a section of the airfield and kept to themselves. The Jeep cruised past rows of fighter jets until it reached the headquarters building, from which the Stars and Stripes flew.

The MPs escorted Hal to the front administrative offices, where a young man with a stern expression looked up from his work at Hal's arrival. He took Hal's information and instructed him to sit on a bank of chairs along the wall, which radiated heat like a furnace, making the ten-minute wait miserable.

Eventually the young man called Hal's name and motioned to the door at the end of the hall. Hal passed through it and found himself in air-conditioned comfort, where another young man sat behind a metal government-issue desk.

"The colonel will see you now," the man announced, and indicated another door. Hal entered the colonel's office and found himself facing a trim man in his late forties, his hair buzz cut, his face all angles, his eyes steel-gray and hard.

After introductions were complete, the colonel invited Hal to take a seat while he told him what he knew.

"We've lost three good men so far," he began.

Hal's raised eyebrows stopped him. "Three?"

"Ah. Right. We had another one last night. Sergeant Kyle Walkins. We were just notified a couple of hours ago."

"Where did it happen?"

"In town. That's all I know so far. I'll tell you what we've gathered on the first two murders, and then you can get to work," the colonel said. He read from a file and gave a five-minute briefing on the two prior murders, and then sat back as though exhausted. "Questions?"

"Did the three men have anything in common?" Hal asked.

"They were all living on base and were air force. Other than that, not that I've been able to gather. Walkins was a logistics specialist. Scott was assigned to the medical clinic. Baxter, the first death, was in the security force."

"Security?"

"Yes, he was part of our military police group."

"He was a cop?"

Hedges frowned. "I just said that."

"What specialty?"

"He was working base security, so nothing dramatic."

"No investigatory work?"

The colonel shook his head. "Negative."

"Did they know each other?"

"Other than having seen each other on base, we haven't turned up any connections."

Hal didn't blink at the carefully worded answer, but filed it away for future reference. "You mentioned in your report that your own investigators were working the case?"

"That's correct. I told them to stand down when we got the…request…from the Pentagon. They're available for you to interview if you'd find that helpful."

Hal nodded. "I would. Could you arrange it?"

"Of course. I'll have my secretary schedule something today."

"Do you know if they were working with the local police?"

That drew a laugh from Hedges. "The locals aren't exactly of the highest caliber." He paused. "That said, I've requested that you liaison with the lead investigator on the Pattaya police force. They've agreed."

Hal half rose from his seat. "That's not necessary…"

"Perhaps not, but we have a delicate balance we have to strike here, and part of it is political. The Thais have jurisdiction since the murders occurred off base. So I'm afraid it's not optional."

"I typically work alone."

The colonel regarded him dispassionately. "Not this time." Hedges stood. "Now, if you'll step outside, I'll have my man set up a meeting with our security team so you can debrief them, and then you'll have full run of the base. Anything you need, just ask."

Hal took the hint and stood as well. "Thank you, Colonel. Where should I throw my bag?"

"We've arranged for a bunk in the officers' quarters. I hope that will meet your needs."

"When am I supposed to meet with the local police?"

"Later this afternoon. I committed to going over there with you as a goodwill gesture, to show our solidarity with our gracious hosts, and to retrieve two of our men who were out with the victim last night."

"So there were witnesses?" Hal asked.

The colonel shook his head. "Not from what I can tell. The Thais are pretty closed-mouthed about things, but it seems as though our men found their buddy dead."

"Then why are the police holding them?"

"Material witnesses. Who knows? But I'm going to get them out of there. I already told Ratana to expect me."

"Ratana?"

"The police captain overseeing things. They don't want to cause an international incident, and I don't think he wants me going over his head, so they'll play ball in the end. I show up, bow and scrape a little, and they save face by doing me a gracious favor. Everyone wins."

Hal left the meeting with mixed feelings about the commanding officer. He obviously resented having an outsider—a marine, no less—foisted off on him to handle an investigation on his base, and he'd made little effort to hide the joy he felt when he ordered Hal to liaison with the Thai police. But he'd also seemed on edge and had spent considerable time underscoring that he wanted daily progress reports, which indicated that he was troubled by the murders—more in line with what Hal would have expected.

He waited as the colonel's assistant placed calls and arranged a meeting for one hour later with the air force security investigators, and then an airman arrived to show Hal to his quarters. He stowed his gear, washed his face, and sat down to jot his impressions in a notebook that would be his constant companion during the investigation, a habit he'd developed on the police force in Dallas before he'd abruptly quit and joined the marines after a scandal with the chief's daughter.

The memory of the girl brought a smile to his lips, and he whistled softly in the muggy air. Had it really been a decade ago since he'd been a civilian cop? It seemed a lifetime, if true.

He finished his notes and slipped the notebook into

his shirt pocket before exiting and making for the mess building. He hoped to grab a quick bite to counter the pounding in his head before interviewing the air force team and continuing into town to meet his counterpart on the Thai police force, who Hal hoped at least spoke some English. He shook his head at the thought as he pushed through a pair of double doors and made for the cafeteria line. Maybe it would be better if the man didn't. Then Hal wouldn't have to go through the pretense of cooperating, and could get to the serious business of catching a killer before he struck again.

— 4 —

Inspector Sunan wiped his brow with a handkerchief and replaced it in his trouser pocket as he entered police headquarters in Pattaya, a charmless cinderblock rectangle whose robin's egg blue paint was in desperate need of repair, as was the sorry collection of police trucks and cruisers parked in front. In the administrative office lobby, a creaking overhead fan orbited slowly, only slightly improving the efficiency of an air-conditioning unit that was leaking a stream of water down the wall, ignored by the receptionist and two officers at the front desk.

After being buzzed in, Sunan shouldered through the security door and approached Captain Ratana's office, from which a draft of cool air flowed. He knocked politely on the door jamb and Ratana looked up from the stack of paperwork on his desk and beckoned Sunan to enter.

"Ah, Inspector, the man of the hour. Tell me you've solved the case and we can all go out and celebrate," the captain said, his tone jocular.

"I'm afraid not, Captain. So far the only lead we have is from a crazy woman," Sunan said, taking a seat where indicated, a manila folder in hand.

"Not one of my wives, I hope," Ratana joked, and they both laughed humorlessly.

"No. A woman who lives in one of the shacks near where the latest victim was found. She claims that the murderer is a white devil." Sunan shrugged. "Or a white demon. Same difference."

Ratana frowned. "Great. So all we have to do is put out an APB on a white devil, and we're done."

"It's obviously not the result we'd hoped for," Sunan conceded.

"Well, I have some good news. You're going to get some assistance from the Americans."

Sunan's eyes narrowed. "Why is it I feel like those are the most dangerous words you could have said?"

"Because you're a racist pig, of course. It's okay. I forgive you. But try to be nice to our guests when they arrive."

Sunan held the captain's stare. "You're serious?"

"Yes. It comes from the very top. You're to work with their man. A specialist, they say."

"A specialist at what?"

"That wasn't clear. But he's your new partner until you solve this or he gets bored and goes home, so extend some of our famous Thai hospitality and wipe that look off your face. Your English is good, I hope?"

Sunan's frown deepened. "If I'm forced to babysit an American, it will just hamper the investigation."

Ratana sat forward, an eager expression in place. "Are you making such progress that you're afraid to slow your momentum? Tell me what you've accomplished. I'm all ears."

"You should know things don't work that way in these

types of cases."

Ratana nodded. "As I suspected. And for the record, I'm not the hotshot homicide detective from Bangkok, so I'm not sure how a serial killer case works. I was under the impression you investigated until you turned up leads that led you to the killer. Am I mistaken?"

"I've only had the case for a little over a week. He's left no real clues. Nobody sees anything. I'm not a magician," Sunan snapped.

Ratana's expression softened. "So would it be fair to say that other than bodies piling up, we've made no headway?"

Sunan changed the subject. "I was advised that you have two Americans here you're holding?"

"That's right. Sergeant Prasert brought them in, and Detective Tran questioned them."

Sunan's face fell. "Tran? He barely speaks Thai, much less English."

Ratana shrugged. "He did the best he could. He's filling out a report for you."

Both knew that Tran was a buffoon—the cousin of the mayor and a blowhard nobody could stand. Only in a backwater like Pattaya could he have had a career; he'd have been drummed off the force within a week in Bangkok.

"A report. Well, there's some good news." Sunan hesitated. "Why are you still holding them? Did they see something?"

"No. I told Tran to keep them here until you arrived and read his summary, just in case."

The captain's phone trilled, and he answered it, spoke a few words, and hung up. "They're here. The Americans."

"Oh good," Sunan muttered, earning a dark look from the captain.

Colonel Hedges and Hal followed the receptionist into the office and took seats after introductions had been made, the colonel in full uniform, Hal in civvies. After a few niceties and an obligatory complaint about the weather, Hal turned to study Sunan.

"Inspector, thanks for cooperating. Seems like you've got a live one by the tail," he said.

"That is one way of putting it," Sunan agreed, his English from his school years surprisingly good.

"Three dead within a week. Do you have any theories?" Hedges asked.

Sunan resisted the urge to reply with a glib "someone's killing them" and instead settled for a small frown. "The killer appears to be targeting American servicemen. That's the only commonality so far. That, and the way he's doing it."

"Which is?" Hal asked.

"They're being torn apart. We're convinced he's using some sort of blunt instrument that has an edge of some kind. But I'm waiting for the analysis to come back from forensics. The skin is torn in multiple spots, the flesh beneath it brutalized...and this latest victim had his throat torn out."

"Good Lord..." Hedges blurted.

Sunan nodded. "Yes. I've never seen anything like it."

Hal eyed him. "Have you worked many homicide cases?"

"Fifteen years in Bangkok on that desk, so enough," he said. "I presume you have some relevant experience?"

Hal grunted. "Some."

A pause settled over the room. Ratana cleared his

throat and offered an insincere smile. "We have your men in a holding cell. They were quite drunk."

The colonel nodded. "That's been known to happen on a Friday night."

"I want to see them," Hal said.

"They have already been questioned," Ratana said.

"Not by me, they haven't," Hal answered.

Ratana shifted his attention to the colonel. "I have their release paperwork here. It will take several minutes to complete. I have no problem with your man here speaking to them, if you don't."

Hedges looked uncomfortable, but nodded. "Can't see any harm in it."

Sunan placed the folder he'd been holding on the captain's desk. "Polaroids from the crime scene." He gestured to Hal. "If you want a look at what you're dealing with before you talk to your men."

Hal opened the folder and went through the photos slowly, the colonel looking over his shoulder, noting the lacerations and the throat wound. When he was done, the colonel's face had lost three shades of tone. Hal's expression conveyed nothing. He nodded. "It's an ugly one. You have shots of the others?"

"Of course. Same thing. Wasn't much left of the first one, but the second was in decent shape."

"I'd like to see those as well, when you have a chance." Hal stood. "Can someone show me to the prisoners?"

Ratana glanced at Sunan. "You can take him back, Inspector. They're in the first holding cell."

Hal followed the Thai inspector down a corridor that reeked of urine and body odor, and stopped at a cell where two conspicuously hungover young men were seated on a filthy concrete bench. They looked up in unison when Sunan called to a guard, who approached with a ring of keys as the men glared at the Thais and snuck curious peeks at Hal. The guard opened the barred door and Hal entered with Sunan. The guard stood just out of earshot, a look of boredom on his face as he fingered his truncheon.

"Gentlemen, I'm Chief Warrant Officer Four Hal Shaw. I'm an investigator with the CID. We're looking into the death of your friend Sergeant Kyle Walkins." Hal paused and sniffed the air. "Bet you're about ready to get out of here."

"You can say that again," Nick agreed.

"We're working on it, but in the meantime I want you to tell me what happened last night. Just start from the beginning, and I'll ask any questions once you're done, okay?"

Cody darted his eyes to Nick and nodded. "We were at this bar, hanging out, playing pool, you know? It was getting late, so we decided to hit the road. I was...I must have gotten some bad food, because I got sick outside the bar, and Nick stayed with me while I...recovered." Cody paused. "Kyle went to take a leak, and when he didn't come back, we went looking for him. We spotted him in the alley and then went back to the main street and had someone call the cops. The rest you know."

Hal nodded. "Did you hear anything?"

"No. It's kind of loud on the main drag from all the music, but still...I mean, somebody really messed him up. And Kyle wasn't a pussy. He could fight with the best of them."

"He looked like he was pretty powerfully built," Hal agreed. "Is that everything?"

"Nothing else to tell," Nick chimed in.

"There were two other men murdered in the last week. Did you know them?" Hal asked.

Nick and Cody exchanged a quick look. "Not really."

"Is that a yes or a no?" Hal asked, his smile in place.

"I mean, we might have said hello or something in the mess. But we worked in different areas. There are a lot of guys on base."

Hal nodded. "It's a big place." He waved a fly away. "Was Kyle into anything that might have gotten him killed?"

Cody shifted nervously. "What do you mean?"

"I don't know. These are routine questions. Anything—a fight with some locals, a woman, drugs, black market stuff...?"

Nick gave Cody a sidelong glance. "No. Nothing like that. I mean, he could get rowdy, and sometimes the locals could take it the wrong way, but nothing serious."

"So he was squeaky clean?"

"We didn't know him that well," Cody said with a slight stammer. "I mean, we'd go drink and shoot pool, but it wasn't like we were best buds or anything."

"So he might not have been all that clean?" Hal corrected.

"I didn't say that."

"It's either one or the other," Hal said agreeably. "It's okay to tell me if he was maybe just a little dirty. Everyone's human, right?"

Nick shook his head. "I don't know anything. He liked to drink beer and shoot pool. That's about as much as I knew about him, other than he was from Arkansas."

"Guess you boys didn't spend much time talking, huh?" Hal asked.

Noise sounded from down the hall, and the captain approached with the colonel, a sheaf of papers in hand. Hedges nodded at the men as the guard opened the door. They rose and saluted, and the colonel returned the salute. "Gentlemen, sorry to hear about your friend. But now it's time to head back to base and get cleaned up— your work isn't going to do itself." He looked at Sunan and Ratana. "I'll see that they're available if you have any further questions. Within reason."

Sunan nodded. "Of course."

The colonel eyed Hal. "You going to ride back with us?"

"I'm thinking I'll head over to the crime scene, Colonel."

"Very well. You'll find your own way back?"

"With your permission."

Hal and Sunan watched the men troop down the hall with Ratana and the colonel. When they'd disappeared through the door, Hal turned to Sunan. "You have a car?"

Sunan nodded. "What did you think of their answers?"

Hal chose his words carefully. "Didn't knock me out as being complete or truthful. You?"

"I thought maybe it was my English."

Hal studied Sunan with new appreciation. "We're not hearing the full story."

"I'm used to it. Everyone lies to the police."

Hal smiled sadly. "That doesn't change wherever you go, does it?"

Sunan shrugged. "Not that I've seen."

— 5 —

Sunan directed Hal to a dented police truck with balding tires and a cracked windshield. Hal eyed the vehicle without comment and waited until the inspector slid behind the wheel and twisted the ignition key before climbing in. Sunan revved the motor and backed out of the slot, narrowly missing a tuk-tuk zipping along like the devil was on its tail.

"So crime scene first, then talk to the workers at the bar?" Hal asked.

Sunan checked the time. "We need to wait for later. Night shift won't be there for hours."

"That's okay. We can walk the scene, and you can tell me what you've put together so far in terms of theories."

"Not much for theories," Sunan said.

Hal nodded. "You don't have any ideas?"

"An old lady said it was a white devil."

Hal blinked once. "What does that mean?"

Sunan shrugged. "Don't know. But that's what she said."

"You think it's another American killing them?"

"Anything's possible. But I don't have an opinion yet. Or a motive."

157

"Most of the time it's either money or a woman."

"Except when it isn't," Sunan said, his voice flat.

They arrived at the dirt road and the inspector parked the truck. Hal tailed him to the alley, which had been cleaned of human remains, leaving only a coagulated rust-colored stain in the mud that was crawling with beetles and ants. Sunan walked Hal through the scene, describing how the body had been positioned, but after studying the alley from one side to the other, they had nothing to show for their time but sopping shirts.

"You say this woman lives around here?" Hal asked, taking in the shanties with a sweep of his head.

"Somewhere. I don't know where."

"Your men went door-to-door?"

"They were supposed to. I assume they did." Sunan spit into a clump of bushes. "Nobody will talk, though. They don't trust us."

"Why?"

"Because often we're worse than the criminals."

Hal absorbed the frank statement. "How?"

"Many are corrupt. They abuse their power. Extort. Demand sex for protection. Take bribes."

"Why aren't they fired?"

"Corruption goes all the way to the top. Everyone makes money." Sunan shrugged. "The system isn't a good one."

"Obviously not everyone's a crook."

"Some of us are too stupid."

Hal chuckled. "So what now?"

"We get out of the sun and wait for dark. Maybe go to the second crime scene."

"Worth doing," Hal agreed.

Four hours later, a bruised sky was fading from

salmon to lavender as they sipped sodas on the main street. The visit to the second scene had been worse than useless. Local girls barely old enough to wear makeup padded in twos and threes to work, laughing and joking as they dodged puddles from a late afternoon cloudburst. Sunan watched as pimps and low-level pushers skulked into position in the shadows, the light having gone out of the sky like the flipping of a switch. The volume of the music that blared from every bar notched up with the arrival of the first of the American soldiers in civvies, the men standing a foot taller than the average Thai.

"You from Pattaya?" Hal asked, making conversation.

Sunan shook his head. "Bangkok born and raised."

"What brought you here?"

"Bad judgment. The universe. Glutton for punishment. Take your pick."

Hal let the subject drop, sensing the older man's reluctance, and was surprised when Sunan asked him where he was from.

"Texas," Hal answered.

Sunan nodded. "That's why you talk funny."

"Didn't realize I did."

"Sure. Like John Wayne."

Hal smiled. "Not hardly, pardner."

Sunan chuckled. Hal tossed back the remainder of his soft drink and stretched his arms over his head.

"So we go in and talk to the bartender?"

Sunan shook his head. "Won't work. That bar's protected."

"What do you mean?"

"Owner's connected to the government. Bartender won't tell us anything."

"Then how do we handle this?"

"We talk to the bar girls. They know everything."

"Ah. Of course."

Sunan signaled for a waitress and gestured for the check. The woman, wearing go-go boots and shorts so tight they could have been a tattoo, strode over and named a figure in Thai and then in English to Hal. Hal extracted a small wad of baht and handed her a few bills. She smiled and clomped away, bottom wiggling. Sunan caught Hal's interest and raised an eyebrow, but said nothing.

The inspector led Hal across the street to the bar and murmured to him as they reached the curb, "Let me do the talking."

Hal nodded. "I'm just here to see how it's done."

"The girls will know I'm police in two seconds. But a little money goes a long way."

"Maybe I should do the questioning?"

Sunan shook his head. "Only if you want fairy tales."

Speakers on either side of the door pulsed "I Can See Clearly Now" as they neared, the six girls on shift undulating unenthusiastically as they sized up Hal and Sunan. The inspector grinned wolfishly and offered a greeting and the girls tittered replies, though several of them appeared guarded. One moved closer to Hal and slipped her arm around his waist.

"Hey, soldier boy. You look for love?" she purred.

"Maybe later," Hal said, returning her smile.

"Special for you, big man."

"Every day," Hal replied with a wink.

Sunan asked a question in Thai, and the libidinous smirks changed to blank expressions. Two of the girls shook their heads and made for the bar door. The remaining four exchanged glances and then returned to eyeing the street for more promising fare.

Sunan was undeterred and pressed the girls, with no success that Hal could see. Hal was preparing to intercede when Sunan removed several large-denomination baht notes from his pocket and showed them to the bar girls. The one still holding onto Hal like he was going to make a break for it stood on her tippy toes and whispered in his ear.

"You pay my bar fine, maybe I tell you what happened."

Hal looked her up and down, trying to tell whether she was lying, but couldn't read her. "Maybe doesn't cut it."

"Okay. I tell you."

Sunan had caught the exchange and frowned. The girl whispered a number in Hal's ear, laughably cheap by American standards for the fine, which was payment to the bar for the hours of profit they would lose by letting the girl leave with him.

"Let me think about it," Hal said, and she pouted.

"I worth it."

He nodded, eyes roving over her toffee skin. "I'm sure you are, little lady."

She giggled. "I like how you talk."

"I've been getting a lot of that," Hal said.

Sunan didn't seem to be having much luck and, after a few more minutes, motioned to Hal to accompany him to the next bar. Hal detached himself from the bar girl and gave her a final smile, and then joined the inspector at the doorway of the next watering hole, this one featuring a borderline pornographic depiction of a tiny Thai girl riding a stampeding bull.

"How'd it go?" Hal asked as another group of bar girls descended on them.

"They won't talk. A couple said to come back later. I get the feeling they're afraid to say anything."

"Why?"

"Habit."

Hal nodded and told him about the girl's offer. Sunan's eyes glittered in the blinking neon from the club.

"You feel like throwing money away, that's one way," he said.

"What if she's on the level?"

"Anything's possible," Sunan said, his expression doubtful.

"Why don't you give me a half hour, and I'll see what I can get out of her?"

Sunan smirked. "Only half an hour?"

"I'll know by then whether she's making things up." He paused. "I can't believe you didn't get statements from them last night."

"Welcome to Pattaya. I wasn't on the case until this morning."

"If one of them saw something…"

"Then your new friend might be worth the price."

"Only one way to find out."

"It's your money." Sunan glanced at his watch. "Meet you at the corner in an hour? Just in case you decide to get your money's worth?"

"Split the difference—forty-five minutes."

Hal returned to the bar and the girl's face lit up. He took her hand and walked inside with her, where an older woman shaped like a fire plug was sitting on a stool. The girl rattled something off in Thai and the woman held out her hand. Hal paid her, and then the girl disappeared into the back of the club. Two minutes later she reappeared wearing shorts and a black top, and then they were back outside, the other girls trying to coax him into buying one or two more of them.

"Come on, Yankee Doodle! We make party time!"

Hal waved them off and allowed the bar girl to lead him down the street. "Where can we talk?" he asked.

"Uncle own a hotel. Super cheap for all night."

Hal slowed. "That's not what I paid for."

"Not for you. For me. He know the mama-san. She think something up, she ask, he say I there with you."

Hal tried to see a way out of the girl's trap, but couldn't, and realized that there might have been more going on behind her eyes than he'd first thought. He was used to the hustle, having been in-country for a year, but he thought he was smarter than that and grudgingly had to consider he might have overestimated his acumen.

They rounded a corner and fifty yards down reached a single-story motel built around a courtyard.

"What's your name?" Hal asked as they neared the office.

"Lucy. But my real name Pui."

The man behind the desk was no more than five feet tall. His teeth were yellowed from smoking, and the small reception area reeked of stale cigarettes. Hal forked over more baht and the clerk handed him a key, never saying a word. Hal nodded and left with Pui, who directed him to one of the doors.

The interior was everything he'd expected from the grounds—a peeling linoleum floor, a window fan instead of air conditioning, a bed that looked like it had been there longer than Hal had been alive. Pui threw herself down on the bed and bounced on the end, grinning from ear to ear. Hal moved to the bed and sat beside her, and she immediately moved to rub his shoulders. He stopped her, trying not to show his irritation.

"No, Pui. We need to talk."

"We talk while I massage?"

"Better if we just talk."

She pouted. "You no like me?"

"I need information."

She frowned at the word. He tried again. "Tell me about last night. At the bar. Three Americans were in there, playing pool?"

Pui nodded. "That's right. Drink a lot. Same as always."

"You've seen them before?"

"Oh, yeah. Lots of times."

"Were they with anyone? Any of the girls?"

She shook her head. "No. They just play pool and drink."

"Did anything happen? Unusual?"

"The black one—he the one die?"

Hal nodded. "That's right."

"He almost get into fight."

Hal's pulse quickened. "A fight? With who?"

Her eyes darted to the side. "You sure you no want massage? I very good."

"Who did he almost fight, Pui?"

"Couple guys."

"American?"

She shook her head again. "No. Thai. Bad men."

"Bad?"

"Gang."

"Which one?"

Pui pulled away from him, suddenly less friendly. "They leave. No problem."

"That's great. But which gang?"

"Cobra Boys."

Hal didn't recognize the name, but it didn't mean anything that he didn't. There were hundreds of Thai gangs involved in human trafficking, drugs, weapons, extortion, robberies, even murder for hire.

"So they left, and then the Americans left?"

"Not for while." Her face told him that she was unwilling to continue that line of questioning. He shifted gears.

"You said you'd seen them before. But they never bought girls?"

"No. Just drink. And the one die, he bring a girl couple times. I think he like her lots."

"You recognize her?"

Pui shrugged. "Maybe."

Hal intuited that she knew more. "No games, Pui."

"Maybe I know her name." She yawned. "Want to lie down?"

"No. I want you to tell me who she is."

Pui smiled. "My mother need operation."

Hal decided to play along for the further extortion. "Most of Thailand needs an operation."

She mentioned a number. The equivalent of twenty dollars—double what he would have had to pay to sleep with her. She sensed his reluctance and slid closer. "I tell you name and then we play some?"

"How much do you know besides her name?"

"I know some."

Hal fished his money from his pocket and counted off the cash. Pui snatched it away as though he was going to reconsider, and slipped it into the pocket of her shorts.

"Girl name Aranya. She used to dance, but now too good for it."

"Aranya. That's it?"

"She friend of plenty people. Soldier boy. Bad men."

"The same bad men who wanted to fight?"

Pui shook her head. "No. Just bad men."

"Where can I find her?"

"She used to dance at Poodle Club."

"But not anymore?"

"No."

Ten more minutes of questions didn't yield any further information, and Hal rose, his patience exhausted, the remnants of his hangover thudding in his temples. Pui looked up at him from the bed and smiled, the expression far more knowing than her years. Hal leaned down and kissed her forehead.

"How do I get out of here without the clerk seeing me?"

She winked. "No way. You stay while."

He exhaled loudly. "No. I can't."

"Have to."

"Pui, it's not me that gets into trouble if he sees me. Either way, I have to go."

The pout returned. "Maybe you quiet, you sneak by."

Hal nodded. "I'll be extra quiet. Probably best if you don't try to go back to work tonight, Pui. You made your money."

"I no go nowhere."

He believed her. "I'm going to turn the lights out now so he doesn't see the door open. Be good, Pui."

"I real good. You come back, I show. You want me long time."

Same story Hal had heard hundreds of times before in Thailand. Peasant girls from the north wound up in the big cities as prostitutes, there being no money at home, and their families starving. Most turned hard by the time they were really adults, but Pui had probably only been in the game for a short time, judging by her demeanor and eagerness to connect with him. All the girls dreamed of the same thing: a rich American deciding they liked their Asian friend and taking them across the ocean to the land of plenty.

Hal switched off the lights and waited for his eyes to adjust, and then cracked the door open and peered out. The courtyard was in shadows, the only light by the office, and with a little luck he might just make it out without catching the clerk's eye. Music drifted from the open doorway of the office, which would help mask the sound of his footsteps. Hal stepped outside and pulled the door closed, wincing at the snap of the lock.

He edged along in the gloom and, when he was across from the office, slowed further, eyes locked on the reception counter. The clerk was sitting behind it, staring up at something to the right of the door—probably a television.

Hal stood in the darkness, the minutes creeping by, and then the man's face changed, stretching and contorting...and he sneezed, hard.

Hal bolted for the front gate and was through in moments, his boots silent on the moist dirt as he trotted toward the main drag, where he hoped Sunan would still be waiting.

— 6 —

Nick elbowed Cody in the dark as they walked toward the rear gate of the air base. Both were still dressed in civilian clothes, with an overnight bag over their shoulder, Nick with a baseball cap pulled low over his brow. They reached the guard post, where four Thai soldiers sat listening to the radio. One of them looked up as the pair of airmen approached, and nodded when he saw who it was.

Nick returned the gesture and they continued past the guards without comment, boots crunching on the gravel. The air was still sweltering even at night, the scent of jungle intermingled with jet fuel and exhaust. Nick lit a cigarette and blew a stream of smoke at the moon, and then offered Cody one. Cody shook his head.

"No, thanks, man. I'm still rough from last night."

"First thing we do tonight is fix that right up," Nick said.

"Maybe buy a bottle…but we're not to go out, remember?"

"That's what I meant, man. Ease up. We grab some frosties and some rum, kick back, and groove."

Cody nodded. "No reason we can't enjoy ourselves."

"You aren't worried about going AWOL?"

"Nah. We just have to stay out of sight until the cops move on to whatever."

"What do you think happened with Kyle? You think it was related to…our thing?"

"I don't know what to think. That's some freaky shit, though. I've never seen anything like it. I mean, Kyle could deal, you know? Must have been a bunch of them to be able to take him down so fast."

"Think it was the dudes from the bar?"

Cody frowned. "I don't see that, do you?"

Nick drew another long drag. "Not really. I just hope it isn't…doesn't involve us."

"Why would it? Think about it. We haven't pissed anyone off. Everybody's happy—we're all getting paid, right? No, this is something different. Besides, the other two victims were torn up the same way. They got nothing to do with us."

"Not completely true. You know that."

Cody shook his head. "He was just a grunion. He didn't know squat. You need to relax some, bro. Maybe we should get some Thai stick to go with the brews. Settle your nerves right down, right?"

"Twist my arm."

They continued down the road until they arrived at a rusting sedan behind a grove of trees. Nick felt under the front fender and straightened with a key in hand, and Cody swung the passenger door open. Five minutes later they were putting along the road to Pattaya, the headlights dim, the jungle stretching toward the sky on both sides. Cody fiddled with the radio and found a station that was playing Neil Young's "Heart of Gold."

"Can you believe this guy's got a career? I can strangle

a cat and make it sound better than that," Nick complained.

"I dig it. It's got soul."

Nick threw him a doubtful look. "Maybe the Thai stick isn't a great idea. You're going soft in the brain if you think that whining's good."

Cody shrugged. "I don't give you shit over the ugly-ass broads you chase." Cody paused. "Probably ladyboys anyway."

They continued on in silence, the radio playing the American Top 40 interspersed with rapid-fire Thai from a disk jockey who sounded like he was after a job in Motown. When they arrived at the outskirts of Pattaya, Nick fished a scrap of paper from his pocket. He squinted at the numbers on the exteriors of the run-down houses and then ground to a halt in front of a dark brown single-story that was falling to pieces. Cody grimaced and shook his head.

"Let's find a market. We can drink it pretty," he suggested.

"Doubt there's enough hooch in all Thailand for that," Nick said.

"Home sweet home. Cockroaches are probably bigger than my foot."

"Get some extra cigarettes in case some want to smoke. Don't want to piss them off."

Cody sighed. "I hope this isn't going to take weeks."

Nick threw a final glance at the house and put the car back into gear. "Me too. Bad enough being stationed in this backwater, but having to stay in this dump...almost makes me want to put in for a transfer to the line."

Cody laughed harshly. "Not me. At least we don't have to worry about Charlie coming out of the brush while we sleep."

"Not that I'm going to get much, the way you snore."

"Come on. I'll buy the first round of hundred-proof earplugs."

Nick gave the old car gas and they rolled away from the house. "You're on."

***

Colonel Hedges bounced along the road to town in the passenger seat of an olive green Jeep, his driver with his eyes glued to the treacherous ribbon of asphalt, the darkness around them complete. They arrived at a village, little more than a scattering of shacks along the road, and the colonel leaned into the driver.

"Pull over up by the market," he said.

The driver nodded. "Yes, sir."

The vehicle drifted to a stop in front of the dimly lit entrance, and the colonel stepped from the Jeep and walked into the store. Several minutes later he emerged with a bottle of Coke, and after taking a long swig, walked to a pay phone mounted on the wall, deposited a coin, and dialed a number.

"Hello?" a voice answered in Thai.

"I need to speak to your boss," Hedges replied in English.

The voice called out to someone in the background, and Hedges listened as footsteps approached on a hard floor.

"Yes?" a different voice said in English.

"I have a problem."

"How can I help?"

"The police questioned two of my men. I got them off

the base so they couldn't continue the interrogation, but I don't like the direction it's going. I overheard the last of it, and I have reservations."

"Who on the force? We know just about everyone."

"It wasn't one of the Thai police. An American."

There was a long pause. "I don't understand."

Hedges offered a short summary of Hal's assignment. When he was finished, the voice on the phone sounded troubled.

"This murder. I read about it. Did it involve…"

"No."

Another pause. "What do you need us to do?"

"Keep an eye on the men. I can't afford to have them surface while this investigator is still here."

"But if it's not related to our business, why are you worried?"

"I don't need that can of worms opened as a by-product of the investigation."

"Can of worms?"

"Situation. A euphemism."

"Ah. Well, if you think the risk is significant, perhaps a more permanent solution is prudent?"

The colonel hesitated. "We can't have any complications."

"I understand. But there might be a way that eliminates any further digging." The voice spoke for a minute, laying out an option. When it finished, Hedges sighed.

"It's tempting; however, it could cause more problems."

"What is your saying? Dead men tell no stories?"

"Tales. Tell no tales."

"Where are they located?"

Hedges was silent, his mind churning over the implications of the call. Eventually he answered, and when he mentioned the address, his voice was barely a whisper.

The voice matched his tone. "Do not worry, my friend. We shall solve your problem. You can demonstrate your gratitude however you like when we are successful."

"It absolutely can't lead back to us."

"It won't."

Hedges hung up and returned to the Jeep. His driver was staring straight ahead, awaiting instructions. Hedges checked the time and shook his head. "Change of plans. Back to the base."

— 7 —

Hal awoke to a persistent rapping on his door. He groaned as he forced himself to his feet, his hair matted on one side, sleep crusting his eyes, insect repellant slicked on every visible area of his skin.

"Yes?" he called out.

"Sir, there's a phone call for you."

Hal checked his watch. Eight a.m. He'd been asleep for five hours, after a long night with Sunan that had yielded nothing but sore feet and fatigue.

"Okay. Give me a minute."

Hal donned civvies and made for the door. A uniformed airman was waiting outside and led him down the hall to an administrative area, where he indicated a desk with a phone. "We'll transfer the call there," he said. Hal took a seat, and the phone jangled thirty seconds later.

He raised the headset to his ear. "Yes?"

"He struck again late last night," Sunan said. "I got a call this morning at home."

Hal absorbed the news. "That's a manic cycle."

Sunan grunted assent. "Can you get a ride to Pattaya?"

"I'll find a way."

"Write this down. I'm heading to the scene now." Sunan gave him a street and number and then hung up. Hal stood and approached the airman, who was waiting a discreet distance away.

"I need a ride to Pattaya," he said.

The airman nodded. "The colonel said you get whatever you need. When do you want to leave?"

"Five minutes ago."

The ride to the crime scene took too long for Hal, who shifted impatiently in the passenger seat of the Jeep as another airman drove. When they arrived, they found themselves facing a row of police vehicles, roof lights strobing off the surrounding home façades, the area as run-down as any in Pattaya.

Sunan was standing by a van, writing in a notebook, a dour expression in place, when Hal walked up to him. He looked up at Hal and shook his head.

"It's ugly. Looks like the pair didn't stand a chance."

"Pair?"

Sunan nodded. "It's the two men you interviewed at the jail."

The blood drained from Hal's face. "What?"

"That's right."

"What were they doing here?"

"I have no idea." He glanced at his watch. "Let's go in and take a look."

"You've already been, obviously."

"That's right. But I want to hear your impressions."

"Any witnesses?"

Sunan barked a harsh laugh. "Of course not. Nobody knows anything, and everyone's blind, deaf, and dumb."

"At least they're consistent."

The inspector led Hal past a group of uniformed officers and through the door of the house, where a forensics technician hovered around two corpses on the floor. The tech looked up at the new arrivals and hastily made way for them.

Sunan and Hal stood over the victims, who were bloated and swollen in the rising heat, their skin discolored and shredded from defensive wounds on their arms.

"What do you make of it?" Sunan asked.

"Looks like the photos of the ones you showed me." Hal paused, squinting at the corpses. "Except...their throats."

Sunan nodded. "Exactly. They were slit, not torn out. An important observation, because we never allowed that detail to be published."

"But the other wounds match..."

"To a point." He gestured at a nearby table. "See the drug paraphernalia? Looks like they scored."

"I still don't understand why they were off base. It doesn't make any sense."

"Someone wanted this to look like the same killer. We can start there."

"But why?"

"Because they wanted them dead and wanted to stick the blame on the serial killer. That's my working assumption."

"And you're sure it isn't just a change in the MO?"

Sunan shook his head. "I doubt it. The other three victims all had their throats torn out. That was one of the most unusual aspects of the killings. These had them cut—you can see a blade was used. And given the amount of blood and the condition of the defensive wounds, I'd guess those were inflicted after they were already dead, not before. Forensics will be able to tell us for sure, but it looks to me like this is a copycat. I'd also bet that they were killed elsewhere and moved to the floor."

Hal sighed. "Great. An already complicated case getting worse by the minute." He scanned the room. "Where do you think they were killed? You mean a different location?"

Sunan frowned. "No. Sitting down over there by the table with the drugs is my guess." He slowly turned toward the entry and then back to the rear door by the kitchen. "The killers came in through there. You can see the latch is broken. They probably had guns, which is why the victims didn't run."

"Or maybe they knew them?"

"Also possible. But even if so, they wouldn't have sat still while they had their throats cut. That's why I'm guessing guns. There are also some faint bruises on their wrists that are consistent with having been tied up. So my take is the killers entered, one of them bound them while the other held a gun on them, and then slit their throats."

"But there's no blood on the chairs."

"Could have been wiped clean. Or they could have been dragged to the floor before they were killed. Again, forensics will be able to confirm. But this is a totally different type of crime than the others." He paused. "So now the question is why someone wanted them dead, and why cover it up in such an elaborate fashion versus tossing them into the ocean for the sharks to feed on?"

Hal frowned. "They weren't telling us everything yesterday. We could both tell."

"Agreed. But we can't assume that they were killed to

keep them from talking, although that's the most likely reason."

"Let's follow that logic, though. If they were, to keep them from talking about what? What's worth killing two men over?"

Sunan eyed the drugs on the table. "Most murders are about money or passion, as you said. This was an execution. That's never passion—which leaves money."

"And making it look like the killer instead of dropping them into the sea?"

"Obviously, if they'd just disappeared and turned up floating, it would raise questions about why. This way, it's a crazy serial killer. Convenient, and would have probably worked except for the detail about the throat wounds." Sunan walked over to the table and turned to the forensic technician. "Did you already dust these for prints?" he asked in Thai.

The tech nodded.

Sunan picked up a yellow cellophane-wrapped Thai stick and sniffed it. "Good quality. Maybe we can start with this."

"Weed?"

"We find who sold them the drugs. This packaging is distinctive. I'll ask my colleagues on the force about who wrapped it, and that will at least give us a direction to follow."

"What about the woman the bar girl told us about? Aranya?"

Sunan rubbed his face with weary fingers. "That will take time. I can't be everywhere at once. The call on this one came in first thing this morning, and I have to finish with it before I can begin putting out feelers for the woman."

"Pattaya isn't that big a town. If this is about money, it's got to have something to do with drugs. What else is there worth killing over?"

They moved to the bedroom and went through the men's belongings. "Looks like they were planning to stay for a while," Hal commented. "So this wasn't just a crash pad they used to get high."

"Which again points to them wanting to avoid further questioning, doesn't it?" Sunan asked, his voice soft.

Hal nodded. "Yes, it does." He walked to the bedroom door, and Sunan cleared his throat.

"Where are you going?"

"I think it's time I have a chat with the colonel. Nothing about this is adding up, and I have a feeling I haven't been told the whole story about anything."

"If you wait until I'm done, I can go with you."

"How long?"

"As long as it takes. Maybe an hour. Why—do you have something pressing?"

"Not really."

"Then pull up a chair and see what I do with every day of my life. A far cry from what you're used to in the States, I'm sure."

"Seems like you do a pretty thorough job. Good catch on the throat wounds."

"In spite of anything I have to work with, not because of it. If this was Bangkok, it would be a different story." Sunan frowned again. "Let's hope I can get this over with before it starts raining again. The road south is hell in a storm."

— 8 —

Hal and Sunan arrived at the base and encountered a contingent of Thai guards at the main gate who flat out refused to allow Sunan in. Hal explained why he needed the inspector with him, but they wouldn't budge, even after Sunan threatened to call their superior and have them censured for insubordination.

"It's a federal government installation," Sunan explained as they faced off against the Thais. "Technically they're right. I have no jurisdiction on base, and they know it. I told you they hated the police here—this is their chance to get even."

"It's stupid," Hal griped.

"No question. Welcome to Thailand."

"We can go around to the other gate."

Sunan shook his head. "No point. They'll just radio these guys, and then it will go even worse—they'll start viewing you as the enemy too and make your life difficult in petty ways when you try to come and go. Not worth it. Go do what you need to do, and I'll find a telephone and make some calls about the girl."

Sunan climbed back into his vehicle, leaving Hal to

find his way onto the base.

At the colonel's office, his aide gave Hal the stink eye when he showed up and asked to see Hedges immediately.

"I'm afraid the colonel is otherwise occupied. I can see if I can fit you in…after lunch, if that works for you," the man offered, his tone disapproving.

"It doesn't. I need to speak with him now. It's an emergency."

The aide looked Hal up and down. "I see. What is the nature of the emergency?"

Hal's face flushed with color and he was preparing to unload on the unctuous staffer when the colonel's voice called from down the hall.

"It's okay. Send him back. I need a break, anyway."

Hal's eyes narrowed and he glared at the aide and then followed the colonel's voice to his office. He swept past the male secretary, entered the office, and shut the door behind him.

"Well? What's the emergency?" Hedges boomed.

"The two men who were with the murder victim? You got them out of jail yesterday."

"Yes? What is it?"

"They're dead."

"What! How?" Hedges said, half standing behind his desk.

"Murdered. Same way that the victim got it," Hal said, holding back the discrepancy in the killing, wary of the colonel and unsettled by his composure—especially given that he hadn't asked where the men had been killed.

"I don't understand."

"I'm trying to fit together how this is all connected, but I'm drawing a blank, Colonel," Hal said. "And I'm getting the feeling there may be more to the story than I've pieced together so far."

The colonel's face could have been cast in bronze. "Explain yourself."

"They were found with drug paraphernalia in a shack on the outskirts of Pattaya. Which brings up the questions of why they were off base and how they got there."

"That's no mystery. They probably bribed the guards. It's not unheard of."

"Why would they risk being arrested for desertion? It doesn't make any sense."

"I can't answer that for you. But you said they were murdered the same way as the others?" He paused. "Good God."

"The Thais believe it's a white man who's doing the killing, Colonel. Someone with a grudge against the military, by the looks of it." Hal eyed Hedges, his stare hard. "Do you know anyone who might fit that bill?"

Hedges swallowed and returned Hal's look. "I'm not sure I like your tone."

"No disrespect intended, but if there's anything you haven't told me, now would be a good time."

They held each other's gaze, and the colonel looked away first. "You mentioned drugs? What does that have to do with any of this?"

"We're not sure."

Hedges sighed. "What I'm about to tell you is classified."

Hal nodded. "I have a security clearance."

"Fine. Almost four years ago, the military conducted a medical experiment in Vietnam—it was an effort to boost stamina and endurance in our troops. An agent had been developed that the brass thought would give our boys an edge—much like amphetamines during the Second World War, which were given to pilots so they could fly around the clock for days at a time."

"I've heard that a lot of our men use it here, too."

Hedges waved the comment away. "Anyway, the first field trial of the agent was a disaster. It…it turned the men into monsters. The Pentagon decided to end the trials and shelved the project."

Hal waited for more. Hedges glanced at his window and then returned his eyes to Hal.

"There were…rumors…that some of the men in the trial went missing."

"I'd think that was knowable."

"Not as easy as you might imagine. From what I gather, a pitched battle with Charlie took place during the trial, and with all the pandemonium it was impossible to account for everyone."

Hal's eyes narrowed. "What do you mean when you say it turned them into monsters?"

"They became killing machines. I mean completely crazy, unconcerned about being wounded, and some of them turned on each other when there were no more enemies standing. It was a bloodbath. Enough so the DOD destroyed the files."

"How do you know about it, then?"

"Shortly after the first victim washed ashore here, a member of military intelligence showed up and gave me a briefing."

"I don't understand. Vietnam's a long way away, and that was four years ago," Hal said.

"They think there's a possibility one of the trial subjects might have worked his way from Vietnam and is now in Thailand."

Hal absorbed that. "A white devil," he murmured.

"The agent was called VX-99. It was a nightmare drug. But if this is one of the test group committing these crimes, you could be up against something superhuman."

"What exactly did the drug do? And why would it still be doing it four years later?"

"It stimulated the area of the brain that's responsible for the fight-or-flight response and increased both aggression and stamina. But it also caused vivid hallucinations. Murderous impulses. Apparently the changes were permanent."

"Did the trial participants know what they were getting into?"

Hedges' expression hardened. "That's none of your concern. What matters now is that if it *is* one of them, we need to find him and stop him before this gets any worse."

"Do you have any idea who it is?" Hal asked.

"There were two men that are still unaccounted for. One wasn't white, so that excludes him. Which leaves the other—a marine scout who was a tracking specialist from Louisiana. Corporal James Kendrick."

"Why would he be killing military here in Thailand?"

"I have no idea."

Something about the colonel's tone rang false, and Hal sat forward. "Could he have been involved in anything with these men?"

Hedges shook his head. "By all accounts, we're talking a madman, Shaw. A killing machine. Not someone who would be functioning at a very high level. I don't see how he could be connected to the victims, other than the military angle. Who knows? He's crazy, if it's him. That should be obvious."

"Back to the drugs. Do you have a big problem with them on base?"

Hedges looked away. "We're in the middle of the opium production capital of the world. But we do the best we can, and nobody I know of is using. What did they find them with, anyway?"

"Some opium and Thai stick."

Hedges waved a hand. "Don't get sidetracked with that. It's not uncommon for the men to take a little chemical vacation in their off hours. We frown on it, but you can't stop everything."

Hal switched gears. "The victim who was their buddy. Sergeant Kyle Walkins. What do you know about him?"

"Just what I told you."

"Did he have a girlfriend?" Hal watched the colonel's eyes, which flitted to the papers on his desk before returning to Hal's face.

"How the hell would I know? Pattaya's a frigging cathouse, Shaw. For God's sake, if the man had a local squeeze, what does that have to do with anything?"

"So you don't know if he had someone he saw regularly?"

The colonel exhaled forcefully and his face darkened. "You're wasting time we don't have with these tangents. If it's our man out there killing, he's not going to stop until you find him. Obviously if it's him, this is beyond sensitive. We can't allow the locals to capture him—an American serial killer would be a public relations disaster, and with the way the war is going, we can't afford that. So stay on topic, Shaw. This isn't an investigation you have weeks to conduct, running down every idiotic lead that comes up. Girlfriends, a little weed...those didn't get anyone killed. If they did, half our force would be in coffins."

"It was just a question."

"Maybe I'm not being clear enough. You were sent here by a general who pulled strings. I accept that. You're supposed to be the best. Fine. We need the best, and we need this resolved yesterday. We cannot have more murders linked to a white devil, as you called him. I've already said you can have anything you need. So go do your job and stop messing around with distractions. There's a monster loose, and damn it, he's going to strike again."

"Assuming you're correct it's him. Do you have any evidence?"

"Military intelligence sends a guy halfway around the world to tell me a story they can't put in writing. Seems like they're pretty sure one got away from them. That's good enough for me."

"That's not how it works, Colonel. That's a guess on their part. I deal with facts and evidence, not hypotheses and hunches, no matter what the source."

Hedges' face darkened. "Then go find some, and stop bothering me with tangents. I've told you what you need to know. Do your job. Dismissed."

Hal didn't allow his expression to react to the curt termination of the discussion. Instead, he offered a salute and showed himself to the door. The colonel called out to him as he was reaching for the knob. "I'm sorry if I snapped at you, but this is a crisis in the making, Shaw, and I need you giving it a hundred percent. Don't take my concern the wrong way. I want this behind us before it blows up in our faces, and the clock's ticking." He hesitated. "You can't breathe a word about the VX-99 to the Thais. That's top secret, you understand?"

"Of course, sir. But it's going to be hard to do my job saddled with a counterpart who's missing a big part of the story."

"Figure out a way to deal with it, because what you've been told is classified, and that's not negotiable."

Hal forced the bitter retort that sprang to his lips away and nodded without looking back at the colonel. "Yes, sir."

When Hal returned to the gate, Sunan was waiting for him, standing well away from the guard post, leaning against the fender of his truck. He offered a small smile as Hal approached.

"You don't look happy," he observed.

"Occupational hazard," Hal agreed.

"Well, I have some news that might cheer you up."

Hal's eyebrows rose. "Oh?"

"We have a lead on the woman. Aranya."

"That's great," Hal said, recalling the colonel's admonishment to stay focused on the murderer.

"You still sound unhappy."

"You know where she is?" Hal asked.

"I believe so." He cocked his head and regarded Hal. "You learn anything new?"

"Nothing that can help us catch a killer," Hal said— technically the truth. Understanding that the murderer might be a crazed ex-serviceman didn't open any doors; they already suspected it was an American based on the white devil description, and the chemical reason why he might be killing was immaterial to locating him. Still, Hal felt uneasy as he climbed into the vehicle, the small dishonesty of withholding information from Sunan not sitting well.

Sunan seemed to intuit his discomfiture and said nothing as he started the engine and pulled away, leaving a cloud of dust for the guards in his wake.

— 9 —

Hal eyed the three-story apartment building on one of the dirt-surfaced main roads that ran to the beach, muddy pools of water pocking the surface; the neighborhood was still one of the nicest he'd seen in the beachside city. The façade had been recently painted, and a café that occupied the ground floor retail area appeared more expensive than most in the area, with wooden tables and leather chairs instead of the ubiquitous cheap white plastic furniture. Hal followed Sunan, who was walking toward the entry at a moderate pace under the broiling heat of the direct afternoon sun.

"Pretty nice digs for an ex bar-girl," Hal murmured.

"Nicer than my place. She must be talented," Sunan agreed.

The building had a doorman, a reed-thin character in a burgundy T-shirt and ratty shorts. He was sitting behind a table with an ashtray on one corner and a water bottle in the center, a small transistor radio keening from the floor. Sunan introduced himself and had a short discussion with the man, who limited his responses to monosyllables, eyes darting from Hal to the inspector and back like he was expecting an attack.

Sunan motioned to the stairs. "Second floor."

They set off toward the steps. "Wasn't very talkative," Hal observed.

"He confirmed she's there. Hasn't left today. So that's something."

They mounted the stairs, and Sunan made for the last apartment at the end of a short hall. When they arrived, Hal cocked his head at the rock music seeping through the door—Three Dog Night.

Sunan knocked and, after a lengthy wait, knocked again. A female voice called out from inside, and then the music volume diminished and the door cracked open.

"Yes?" a slight young woman asked, peering through the gap. Hal could see that she was a stunner, her skin flawless, eyes a rich chocolate, her hair gleaming ebony.

Sunan announced himself and held up his badge holder. The woman's gaze flicked to Hal, who nodded to her but remained silent. She asked Sunan something and seemed satisfied by his answer. The door closed and the sound of a chain rattled against it, and then she swung it wide and stepped aside so the men could enter.

Hal took in her emerald green silk sheath, which clung to her curves like a second skin, noting that she couldn't have been more than five feet tall. He followed Sunan past her, the faint aroma of jasmine rising from her hair intoxicating in the confined space. She closed the door and joined them in the living room, which was appointed with contemporary, expensive-looking furniture and a late model television and stereo. Hal looked through the sliding glass doors and saw a sliver of blue—the apartment had an ocean view, which had to command a premium, as did the air conditioning, which was welcome relief after the swelter of the street.

Sunan confirmed her name and that she lived there, and then switched from Thai to English.

"Let's use English so my associate here can understand us," he said.

She nodded. "What can I do for you?" she asked. Her pronunciation was excellent.

"We're following up on the murder of Sergeant Kyle Walkins," Sunan said.

She nodded, and her eyes moistened. "I was wondering how long it would take you to find me."

"Why didn't you come into the station and save us the trouble?"

She shrugged and her cascade of raven hair shimmered in the sunlight. "What's the point? Nothing's going to bring him back."

"We need to ask you some questions," Sunan said.

She tilted her head and studied him. "Then ask."

"How long did you know Kyle, Aranya?" Hal tried.

She searched his face, and Hal felt his throat tighten at the frank assessment. She was breathtakingly beautiful, her features those of a porcelain doll, refined and delicate, unlike many of the women working the bars, their impoverished hill tribe backgrounds showing in their darker complexions and coarser looks. Her eyes held his, and then she looked away.

"Almost a year."

"He was your boyfriend?"

She nodded.

Sunan grunted. "Did he pay for this place?"

Her eyes flashed anger. "What does it matter how I pay for where I live?"

Hal tried a smile. "It's just a question. We're trying to get a picture of who Kyle was. Any help you can offer us would be appreciated."

"He helped with the rent," she said, her voice soft.

"It's a nice place," Sunan said. "Expensive?"

"It's not cheap."

"What do you do for a living?" Hal asked.

Her face was a blank. "I'm between jobs."

"When you're not?"

"I was a hostess at a restaurant."

Sunan didn't press the point that she'd been a bar girl—a sex worker at a nightclub, not a greeter at a dining establishment.

"Must have paid well," he said.

"It paid enough."

"Tell us about Kyle. Did he have any enemies you know of? Maybe an ex-boyfriend of yours?" Hal asked.

The scorn in her response was obvious. "Really? That's the best you can do? That whoever killed him was connected to me? Am I a suspect?"

"No, that's not what I meant," Hal backpedaled. "We're trying to establish a motive, that's all."

"I'm wondering if I made a mistake letting you in," she said.

Sunan cut in. "Nice stereo. And the furniture too."

"I like nice things."

Sunan nodded. "Did you buy them, or did Kyle? Or someone else?"

"What does that have to do with anything?" she demanded.

Hal gave Sunan a warning look. "An air force sergeant doesn't make that much money, Aranya," he said.

"We never talked about where he got his money from. Maybe he was well off. Did you ever think of that?"

"I did. But I've read his file. He was from a modest

background," Hal countered.

"If you say so."

"Help us out here, Aranya. Anything you can tell us might help catch his killer."

"You should talk to his buddies, not me," she snapped, and then immediately looked as though she regretted it.

"What do you mean?" Sunan asked.

"I...nothing. They were with him. Maybe they saw who did it," she parried.

"Were they involved with Kyle in something?"

"I don't know. We didn't talk about Kyle's business. It wasn't like that between us."

"He was in the air force. What business didn't you talk about, exactly?" Sunan asked.

"It's a figure of speech," she said, but looked uncertain.

"Aranya, I don't want to have to take you downtown and interrogate you," Sunan said. "We both know that can be unpleasant. So spare us both the pain and tell us whatever you know. If Kyle was into something illegal, we only care because it might provide a clue we can follow to find his killer. You want him caught, don't you?"

"Of course."

"Then tell us about Kyle's business."

She sighed and sat down, revealing a long tan leg, the slit on the dress reaching nearly to her hip. She gestured to Hal and Sunan to sit on the sofa opposite her, her brow creased in a slight frown. When she spoke, her voice was softer.

"All I know is that he had some sort of thing going with the two he was with that night. Something involving the base. It must have paid well, because money was never a problem."

"He never hinted what it might be?" Hal asked, matching her quiet tone.

"I gathered it was smuggling of some kind. But it was none of my business what he was into. That wasn't why I was with him."

"There aren't a lot of things you can smuggle onto an air base that would make good money," Sunan observed.

"I didn't ask questions." Her eyes widened. "You can't tell his friends who you heard this from. Promise me it will stay confidential."

Hal saw no reason not to, considering that the men were dead. "We won't breathe a word of it. But you need to tell us everything."

"I don't know anything more. I swear. I'm telling the truth. He did what he had to do, and I…we made each other happy. Maybe he wasn't perfect or was making money on the side doing this or that. It didn't matter to me. Lots of people here make ends meet however they can."

Sunan nodded. "True. Did he ever mention anyone he was afraid of or worried about?"

She laughed, the sound like the musical tinkling of wind chimes. "Kyle wasn't afraid of anything."

"So that's a no?"

"Right. He never expressed anything like that to me, and he wasn't looking over his shoulder."

"Did he ever get into fights?"

She looked away. "I don't know anything about that."

Sunan let out an exasperated sigh. "Seems like you don't know much besides his name and that he paid for everything."

Aranya's lips were a thin line. "Is there anything else?"

"Not unless you're going to be honest with us and tell us what Kyle was involved in."

"I've told you all I know." She paused. "I hope you find the killers."

Sunan raised an eyebrow. "Killers? Why multiples?"

"Kyle was strong as a bull. There was no way one person was able to do that to him. I read the papers. That was more than one attacker. I'd have thought that was obvious."

Hal's eyes narrowed. "Your English is very good."

"Thank you. I took classes."

Outside on the sidewalk, Sunan wiped away sweat and looked to Hal. "She knows more than she's letting on."

"She seemed genuinely worried about Kyle's buddies. That tells me that they were into something criminal enough for a street hustler to be afraid of."

"The obvious being drugs."

"It would make a lot of sense. Maybe Kyle and his friends were smuggling dope onto the base and selling it. That would explain the plentiful cash."

"True. But it's easy enough to buy anything you want without having to pay a middleman like them."

"If you're on base and don't have any leave time, you pay for the convenience. Wouldn't be the first time something like that happened. Our soldiers in the rice paddies are walking pharmacies, so no question the demand's there."

Sunan nodded. "A smoking gun. But something tells me that the drug angle isn't going to explain why all these men have been killed in such a short time."

Hal badly wanted to tell him about the colonel's revelation, but bit his tongue and instead settled for a shake of his head. "Probably not. But we don't have a lot else to go on, do we?"

"No." Sunan hesitated. "Remarkable looking young lady, isn't she? And she obviously enjoys her luxuries. Hard to believe she'd have limited her moneymaking opportunities to one master sergeant, isn't it?"

"You think she's involved somehow?"

Sunan shrugged. "I'm just considering all possibilities. She didn't strike me as guilty of anything; but then again, I'm not going to theorize until we have more to go on."

"She didn't know the two airmen are dead. She wasn't faking that."

"Agreed. I'm going to find a phone and see if our anti-drug task force has turned up anything on whose Thai stick and opium was at their place. Right now that's the only thing we have to go on."

Hal followed Sunan into the café and sat down beneath a ceiling fan while the inspector went to the rear of the restaurant to use the telephone, a vision of Aranya's mesmerizing eyes and breathtaking features at the forefront of his thoughts, which he grudgingly admitted weren't entirely limited to her role in the case.

— 10 —

"I want to go back to talk to the colonel, Sunan," Hal said when the Thai inspector returned from the back of the café.

"Not yet. We have a lead on the drugs from the murder scene. They were packaged by the Red Hands," Sunan said.

"Never heard of them."

"No reason you should. They're a midsized outfit in Pattaya. But they control a lot of the street activity and move weight."

Hal rose. "What's the plan?"

"One of their top people agreed to talk to me."

"I thought all Thais distrusted the police."

"The criminals tend to have a better understanding of our position in the food chain."

Hal frowned. "Why would he meet with us?"

"We're a land of favors. Next time he gets caught in a bind, I might be able to do him one in exchange. It's the art of compromise."

Sunan and Hal walked to the inspector's vehicle. Hal pulled his door open, and moments later the engine roared to life and they were wending along the dirt road toward the sea, tuk-tuks and bicycles parting at the whoop of Sunan's siren.

After a ten-minute drive, they parked by a large seafood restaurant a block from the beach. Its palm frond roof and stucco walls stood in typical disrepair, but the adjacent parking lot was filled with late model sedans and motorcycles. Sunan led the way into the dining room, where a pair of heavily muscled thugs stood by a door at the rear, arms folded, the bulge of weapons obvious at their waistlines beneath the thin fabric of oversized shirts.

Sunan nodded at the two guards, and the nearest one said something in a low voice. Sunan snapped a harsh response, and the other guard glared at Hal like he'd drowned the man's puppy. The standoff lasted a few uncomfortable moments, and then the first guard knocked on the door twice and a voice called from beyond it.

They entered the office and spied a squat man behind a desk in his late thirties with a Fu Manchu mustache and an elaborate tattoo running from his right ear to the collar of his T-shirt. The man motioned to them to take seats, and once they had, Sunan leaned forward and spoke in rapid Thai.

Hal's command of the language was rudimentary, but he grasped that the discussion was contentious at first. After several minutes of back and forth, Sunan sat back and turned to Hal.

"He says that the two men were known to him and that one of his street dealers sold them the drugs."

"He admitted that?"

"I'm not interested in interfering with his business. We both know that. He has no reason not to speak honestly. I promised him that anything he says will remain confidential. But he doesn't like that I brought you."

"Tough. Ask him whether the men, or Kyle, were involved in anything criminal."

The gangster laughed. "They running drugs, soldier boy," he said in broken English.

"How do you know?" Hal demanded.

"Not my drugs. Other gang. Seven Heart triad."

"What kind of drugs?"

"We try do deal, but they want to pay too little. Heroin," the gangster said.

Hal and Sunan exchanged a glance. Sunan resumed speaking Thai, and after another long interaction, Hal waited for the summary.

"He says they wanted kilos of heroin at a time. Said it was for export to the States. And needed some uncut in smaller quantities—the export had some cut, but they couldn't accept that for the other."

"How many kilos?"

"Twenty. That's one of the reasons he decided not to play—too big, might draw attention. He said a couple of times they bought some of the smaller quantity pure stuff, but they couldn't come to an agreement on the big shipments."

"And he's sure they were shipping it home?"

"That's what he said.

"Does he know how they were doing it?"

"No. Just that it was his competitor who wound up doing the deal and supplying them for the last six months."

"Who was involved? Just Kyle and the other two, or were there more?"

Sunan returned his attention to the gangster and raised one eyebrow when the man responded.

"He says there was a doctor on the base who the pure stuff was for, but he's no longer there. He offered to see if he can locate him, but it will cost."

"What does he mean no longer there? Was he Thai or American?"

"American."

Hal sat forward. "Why is he not on the base anymore?" he asked the gang boss.

The man smirked. "He like chase dragon. Maybe got kick out." He shrugged. "I find if still in Pattaya. You pay, I find."

Sunan negotiated a price, and then the meeting was over with a wai from the dealer. They returned to the dining area, and Hal spoke to the inspector in a low voice.

"What was the argument with the goons about?"

"They wanted me to give them my gun. I told them no. They didn't like that."

"You think he's on the level?"

"I don't understand."

"Is he telling the truth? If so, this could be huge. Twenty kilos a week is a lot of heroin."

Sunan shook his head. "No."

"What do you mean no?"

"Not a week. Each trip. Sometimes two or three a week."

Hal's jaw clenched as they made their way back to the parking lot. When they reached the vehicle, Sunan regarded Hal with a neutral expression. "Hungry?"

"I could eat," he allowed.

"Let's find a place with a breeze. I know a few." Sunan paused. "You can't tell your colonel about the heroin until we find the doctor and learn what he knows."

"Is it that obvious?"

Sunan smiled. "I would want to. But not yet."

"Mind telling me why not?"

"Nothing stays a secret long in Thailand."

"He's the commanding officer of the entire base, Sunan. If there's a drug ring operating out of there, he's the one who needs to know."

"I understand. But not yet. You don't know how he'll react, and once he knows, it's going to cause big problems if the investigation leads back to some of his men. Let's get our job done; then you can fill him in."

Hal remained silent for several long beats and then nodded. "I can do that. For now. But there's a limit."

Sunan checked the time and eyed Hal. "If the drugs aren't related, then they are a distraction. If they are, we need to know more before you can say anything. Either way, we don't talk." He fumbled in his pocket for the keys. "You in the mood for seafood or seafood?"

Hal squinted at the sun and mopped his brow. "A nice rib eye sounds good right about now."

Sunan looked puzzled. "Is that a fish?"

"Close enough."

— 11 —

Rain pelted against Aranya's patio doors, and the sky flashed with trees of lightning from a storm that had arrived with the coming of night. Her eyes drifted to the sheets of water slamming against the glass and then returned to the television, the reception poor due to the weather. The news was covering a fashion show in Bangkok, and Aranya leaned back on the leather couch and reached for a half-smoked joint in an ashtray by her side. The lighter in her hand was the one Kyle had given her—a gold Dunhill easily worth a week's wages.

She lit the roach and inhaled the perfumed smoke deep into her lungs, waiting for the familiar euphoric relaxation to overtake her, still on edge after the police visit. Aranya couldn't be sure that they'd bought her story, but she would stick with it—it was none of their business what Kyle was into, nor how she paid for her place and the things in it.

Aranya hadn't told them the truth about her real benefactor; she knew better than to even mention it. She couldn't imagine him having anything to do with Kyle's brutal murder, and there was no reason to drag him into her affairs. No, better to tell partial truths and wait for them to chase their tails than to come completely clean. After all, with Kyle gone, she still needed to pay the rent this month, and the police weren't about to do it for her.

She took another long hit and closed her eyes, remembering Kyle's lean waist and ridged stomach, his body a miracle of genetics and exercise. She would definitely miss him, but not because of the sex—although it had been good, after as many partners as she'd had, they were mostly interchangeable, a means to an end, the male of the species easily flattered by her enthusiasm and feigned passion, which she'd learned to exploit at an early age.

Her father had been French, a businessman with a questionable pedigree, and her mother a great beauty in Bangkok who'd fallen on hard times after three children had transformed her from an ingénue to a mother whose body hadn't recovered from Aranya, her youngest. The French father had disappeared one weekend on a trip to Laos and had never been seen again, leaving his Thai family to fend for themselves. Her mother had done what she'd had to do, but in a competitive environment that valued youth, she'd been hard-pressed to make ends meet, and the children had turned to the street for their education and sustenance.

Aranya had been the only daughter and had benefited from her mother's beauty and her father's intelligence. She only had dim memories of him, a male presence who smelled of cologne and had an occasional peck on the cheek for his girl child at bedtime.

She'd later learned that the Frenchman had returned to his country and the wife and kids he'd left there while pursuing his fortune, and had died in an automobile accident only months after landing in Paris. The news had given Aranya no pleasure —by that time she'd been far beyond blaming her parents for the world's sins or her place in it.

Prostitution had been a natural vocation for her as a teenager desperate to survive, and she'd been sucked into the life by a smooth-talking pimp who'd murmured of diamonds and yachts and trips around the world as he'd turned her out. Like all the men in her life, he'd wound up abandoning her, his life ended in an alleyway by a rival with a quicker knife hand.

Aranya's brothers had long before disappeared into Bangkok's seedy underworld, and her mother had overdosed on heroin, leaving her with nobody but herself and her wits. She'd packed her few belongings after ransacking her pimp's apartment and taken a bus to Pattaya, where she'd hoped to start a new life by the beach, where the days were sunny and the nights festive—a perfect place for a young woman with aspirations and the will to do whatever was necessary.

That had been six years before, and now, at twenty, she felt double her age, although her body and face showed no trace of the mileage on it. After over four years as a bar girl and an escort, she'd landed a patron who recognized her value. He had put her up in the apartment and furnished it for her on the condition that she be at his disposal whenever he wanted, and allowed the place to be used for meetings with his associates— one of whom had been Kyle, who'd been instantly drawn to her.

Their clandestine romance had been explosive and wild, and it hadn't hurt that he'd been as generous with her as she could have wanted. Money, jewelry, gifts—he'd been rolling in cash and hadn't minded spending it on

Aranya, who'd been more than willing to entertain him as long as it didn't interfere with her patron, who'd had no idea she was two-timing him.

Thunder roared from the patio and another flurry of rain lashed the glass. She sighed as the drug's warmth flooded her system, the opium she'd seeded the marijuana with transporting her away from her earthly cares. She was raising the joint to her lips when a rustle sounded from the entryway, and her eyelids popped open in surprise.

A figure stood dripping water no more than five feet away. His clothes were soaked, and his long hair and wild beard were matted and filthy. He was wearing some sort of tattered uniform jacket and the loose black pants of a Vietnamese peasant, a pair of worn boots without laces on his feet and a heavy survival knife gripped in his hand. Aranya's gaze met his and her blood froze in her veins at the insanity in his eyes. His face glowed gaunt and spectral, the pupils dilated and frantic, the whites yellowed from jaundice.

She tried to rise, but he crossed the distance between them in a blink, and then she was screaming in horror at his foul smell and the first blow from the knife butt, which she warded off with her arm. A flash of pain seared along her ulna as the steel hilt ripped her skin, driven by almost unbelievable strength. Her attacker barely seemed to register her as he struck again, this time slamming her across the face with the butt, the vicious blow breaking her jaw in an instant. The room spun as her consciousness receded, and her last thought as awareness faded into nothingness was that this must be the madman who'd killed Kyle.

Five minutes later, the killer wiped blood from his

mouth, the woman's throat having posed no challenge to his teeth, and tossed her front door keys that he'd found in Kyle's pocket onto her chest. The ever-present rage burning behind his eyes softened at least momentarily, his thirst for her life essence slaked. He moved soundlessly to the front door and listened for movement, and hearing nothing, twisted the knob with filth-crusted hands and slipped through the gap. He pulled it shut and ran for the stairwell that led to the roof, where he'd crossed from the building next door, a partially built commercial structure that was deserted at night other than rats and a few desperate hounds seeking shelter from the weather.

— 12 —

Sunan and Hal rolled to a stop at the gangster's restaurant, which was closed at the early hour of morning. They stepped from the truck and skirted large puddles of muddy water, remnants of the previous night's downpour.

The Thai inspector had been waiting for Hal at the gate at eight a.m., anxious to get to the restaurant after an early morning call from the gangster's assistant. The crime boss had located the doctor and wanted his payoff when he gave them the information. Hal had counted out almost all his discretionary cash, pocketed the wad of fifty dollar bills, and joined Sunan at the base entrance after a hurried breakfast in the mess, the gathered airmen checking him out with curiosity as he'd eaten by himself in a far corner.

Four guards lounged at one of the circular tables at the rear of the restaurant, and Hal recognized two of them as the pair from the day before. Sunan nodded to the men, who were clearly more relaxed today, and one of them called out in Thai and pointed at the office door.

The gangster was waiting for them and pointed to the

chairs in front of the desk. They sat and he gave them a flash of crooked teeth.

"I find doc. You bring cash?" he asked Hal in English by way of greeting.

Hal nodded. "Of course. Where is he?"

"Let's see green," the gangster fired back.

Hal exchanged a look with Sunan and slid the small wad of dollars to the gangster. The man counted it with the speed of a bank teller and grinned again.

"He in bad way. Over at Monkey Bar."

Sunan frowned. "The opium den," he said. "I thought that had been closed down."

"Right people pay, open again."

"What's his name?" Hal asked.

"Doc."

"Of course," Hal muttered.

Sunan and the gangster had a lengthy exchange in Thai while Hal studied his shoes, and then the inspector stood. "Let's get over there while he's still there. Our man here has someone outside the place with a radio, but the information you bought is where he is now, not where he went after you were told."

Hal nodded as he rose. "Sounds like that could be expensive."

"You need woman, boy, girl, whatever, you know who to call," the gangster offered to their backs. Sunan stiffened, but Hal continued to the door, hoping the inspector would let it slide. They retraced their steps to the truck, frowns in place as they navigated the mud.

"Tell me about the Monkey Bar," Hal said once they were in the vehicle.

"It's been open on and off for years. A pair of old mama-sans run it. They sell opium, not heroin, so it's not a shooting gallery. Users smoke it, and they rent cots to them in addition to selling the drug. Also liquor and some food."

"And the police don't stop it?"

Sunan shrugged. "If someone wants to smoke opium, they'll do it one way or another. Some feel it's preferable to heroin since you avoid the needles and overdoses. Either way, as with so much in our country, flexibility is prized, and allowing a few dens to operate under the radar is considered the best solution. Tolerance of them comes and goes in waves. Right now, with so many Americans, heroin is a bigger problem. Mostly it's locals and occasional curious tourists who smoke opium. The police in the area are paid to look the other way, so everyone wins."

"Except the addicts," Hal observed. "Heroin's a big problem in the U.S."

"I'm not surprised. Any night in Bangkok you can find hundreds of GIs on leave who are smoking or shooting it."

"You sound ambivalent about it."

Sunan shrugged again. "I've spent my career chasing murderers. I've seen enough dead to fill a warehouse. There are worse things than drugs. I'm not saying they're not bad, but compared with what I deal with, they're a minor problem."

The drive took them to a seedy neighborhood on the outskirts of Pattaya, the poverty palpable in the ramshackle hovels that lined the dirt streets. Sunan parked a block from their destination and they walked along the road, a few chickens racing ahead of them for company. The stench of raw sewage and wood smoke from makeshift stoves was strong in the humid air.

They reached the building that housed the Monkey Bar—what to Hal's eye looked to be an abandoned warehouse overtaken by squatters. A skeleton of a man who could have been a hundred years old was sitting on a plastic chair in front of the main entrance, and he eyed them suspiciously before challenging Sunan in Thai.

Sunan responded with a harsh tone, and the man seemed chastened. Sunan mounted the steps and Hal hurried to join him.

"What was that about?"

"He said we can't raid him. He's paid in full for the month. I told him we were looking for someone—a white man. He said there's only one inside."

"That will make our job easy."

"Maybe. Go around the back and make sure nobody ducks out. I'll call for you when I find him."

Hal did as asked and waited by the rear door. Three minutes later Sunan's head popped from it.

"He's in here. Out of it."

Hal approached, and Sunan retreated into the gloomy interior. Hal squeezed inside and blinked as his eyes adjusted to the dim light. He looked around and spotted rows of beds, half unoccupied, with prone forms lying on dirty mattresses in narcotic slumber. Sunan walked over to one of the cots and gestured at a thin man with gray hair—obviously Caucasian and just as obviously unconscious. Beside him were a bamboo pipe and a smoldering oil lamp, and next to that a small brown bar with chunks broken off the edges.

Sunan angled his head at the bar. "That's opium," Sunan said. "They use the lamp to heat it and breathe the vapor."

"Think we can rouse him?"

"Depends on when he had his last pipe and how many he's smoked."

Hal knelt beside the man and shook his shoulder. He received an uncomprehending stare through half-open eyes for his effort. Hal stood and glowered down at him, waiting to see whether he would pass out or could respond to questions.

"What?" the man growled.

"You Doc?" Hal asked.

"Who are you?"

"I'm an investigator helping the local police."

The man blinked several times and inhaled heavily. "Got to arrest the whole place, then. Hope you brought a big van."

"Not interested in arresting anyone."

"Then why are you here?"

"Are you Doc?"

The man closed his eyes again. "Tell me I'm hallucinating."

"Would it count if your hallucination told you so?"

His eyes snapped open, this time not as foggy. "This is real, isn't it?"

"I have some questions I need answers to."

Doc groaned and sat up. He stared at Sunan for a few beats and then turned back to Hal. "What are you investigating?"

"Murder."

"I didn't do it."

That drew a smile from Hal. "You're not a suspect."

"Then leave me alone."

Hal shook his head. "Not today. You want to find someplace we can talk? Sooner you cooperate, sooner you can get back to whatever this is."

"Killing the pain."

Sunan took a step closer. "There's another room in the front. Sort of a bar. Nobody's there. We can do this at one of the tables and be gone in no time. Or I can cuff you and you can go through hell at the station. Your choice."

Doc grimaced and pushed himself to his feet, his bare toes filthy in ratty flip-flops. He stumbled on the way to the bar area and Hal had to steady him, masking his disgust at touching the derelict.

They took seats opposite Doc, who began nodding off. Hal prodded him, and he snapped back to full consciousness.

"Ow."

"I'm investigating a series of murders, and your name came up."

"Me? Who's dead?"

"Sergeant Kyle Walkins, Cody Simmons Nicholas Crosby. Barry Fletcher. Tom Reed."

Doc processed the information and his eyes widened. "Shit."

Hal nodded. "Exactly."

"Why do you want to talk to me?"

"We know you were involved in drugs with some of them."

"What?"

Hal's eyes narrowed. "We know about the heroin."

Doc's expression changed. "Oh. That. It wasn't for me, if that's what you were thinking. I stick to opium. Besides, I didn't kill anyone. I've been on the pipe here for…three months, at least. Not a lot of motivation to murder."

"We're trying to figure out who killed these men. We

think it might be related to the drugs."

Doc licked his lips. "I could use a beer or something."

Sunan rose and walked over to where an old woman sat by a cooler. When he returned, he set a frosted bottle on the table in front of Doc, who took it with a shaking hand and drank half in a couple of swallows. He set it down and nodded at the Thai.

"Thanks." He paused. "How were they killed?"

Sunan glared at him. "It's been all over the news."

"Humor me. Like I said, I've been here most of the time. You see any televisions or newspapers?"

"They were all killed violently. Defensive wounds on their arms. Throats brutalized," Hal said.

"Brutalized how?"

Hal looked to Sunan for permission, and Sunan nodded. Hal sat forward. "They were ripped out."

Doc's face blanched. "Sweet Jesus…" He swallowed hard. "It's him…"

"Who?" Hal demanded.

The older man finished the beer and burped. "That's classified."

"I've got a clearance to top secret." Hal eyed him. "Besides, you aren't in the service, are you?"

"I…I was a civilian adjunct. Medical. Brought in for a special project." He glanced at Sunan. "Maybe your friend here can take a walk?"

Hal looked to the inspector with raised eyebrows. Sunan nodded and rose. "I'm going to see what else they have besides beer. You want anything?"

"Coke, if it's cold," said Hal.

"Another beer for me, Captain," Doc replied, earning a glare.

Sunan stalked away and Hal faced off with Doc. "Okay. Talk."

Doc rubbed his face with a dirty hand, his nails ragged with half-moons of grime in the beds, and when he looked Hal in the eyes, he appeared to deflate.

"I was brought in for a classified project. A prisoner. I was in charge of evaluation and stabilizing him while military intelligence figured out what to do with him."

"Why didn't they bring in a military physician?"

"My area of specialty isn't common in the army."

"What does that mean?"

"It means you don't need to know. Anyway, I was caring for a prisoner with a violent history. The heroin was to keep him sedated. We tried other agents, but that worked best to keep him calm."

Realization played across Hal's features. "VX-99..." he whispered.

Doc's eyes widened. "How could you know that?"

It was Hal's turn to stonewall. "You don't need to know."

Doc nodded with a grim smile. "Touché."

Hal frowned. "But I don't understand. The base isn't a prison. Why not fly the prisoner to the States?"

"It was decided to keep him here for the time being. I didn't make the decision. But we all thought we had him under control." Doc shook his head. "That was a mistake."

"What happened?"

"We got complacent. He must have built up a tolerance to the heroin over time and faked being out. One morning we came in, and he'd managed to kill his guard and escape."

"Wait. He killed a guard?"

"Correct."

"And then what?"

"And then my contract was terminated, and I decided to hang around and enjoy Thailand. Too much, as it turned out."

"How long ago was this?"

"Maybe…five, six months? It's a little hazy. What's the date?"

Hal told him. Doc nodded. "Five months."

"Tell me as much about him as you know."

"You know about the VX-99. What else is there to tell? He's barely more than an animal. A murderous one."

"Where was he captured and by whom?"

"I don't know. That wasn't important for my job. All I know is he's survived by killing animals, livestock and dogs, that sort of thing, and sometimes, people. I pieced that together from snatches of conversation. He'd been out in the wild for years." Doc paused. "He's a cannibal. Or more accurately, he kills anything he can, and he's not above eating human victims. But he's clever, too. He knows how to hide, obviously, if it took years to find him. The heroin calmed him to the point where he almost seemed normal—as long as the doses were right."

"You think he's doing heroin now?"

"Not if he's on a killing spree."

Hal digested that. "Why is he after Americans?"

"One of the men you mentioned was an orderly who cared for him. The other was a military policeman. The sergeant was in charge of sourcing the drugs, so he had some interactions with him as well. The others…I don't know. Don't recognize the names."

That would be Nick and Cody, Hal thought, confirming Sunan's impression that their murders hadn't been committed by the same perp.

"They were friends of Kyle's. The sergeant."

"Sorry. Still doesn't ring any bells."

"Are there any photos of the killer you know of?"

"I can't answer that for you. Sorry. I don't know, but I assume there have to be."

Hal spent five more minutes picking Doc's brain, but learned little more. Doc was fading by the time Hal decided to call it quits, and was getting visibly anxious as the drug left his system.

"Really ought to think about shaking the monkey off your back," Hal said.

"Yeah. It's occurred to me. At some point my savings will run out, but my organs will probably go first." He paused. "I was diagnosed with stage four prostate cancer about the time our man went missing. There's no cure."

Hal swallowed hard. "I…"

"Don't judge those whose shoes you haven't walked in, son. We all have our burdens. Now leave me in peace, would you? Your buddy probably drank my damned beer, too. Figures."

Hal nodded and stood. "Anything else you can tell me?"

Doc looked up at him with a hunted expression. "If you see him, kill him—or he'll rip your heart out and eat it without a second thought. He's relentless, and…he's not a man anymore." Doc paused, seeming to consider his words. "Kill him and do the world a favor. I wish I'd had the balls to give him a hot shot when I had the chance." He closed his eyes and sat back. "Now get out of here and let me be."

— 13 —

Hal filled Sunan in on what he'd learned on the way to the police station, omitting the part about the VX-99 because of security concerns, and instead painted the escaped killer as a lunatic with the strength of five men. Sunan absorbed Hal's report in silence and, when he was done, had a few pointed questions.

"I don't understand why the Americans would have this man as a prisoner and allow him to escape."

"Mistakes were made. It happened. That's all we care about," Hal deflected.

"And now he's out there, killing other Americans."

"Thais as well. We can't be sure."

"That's my line." Sunan frowned. "We need full disclosure from your military. He's one of yours. We need their help tracking him down."

"I agree, but I'm not running the show. I'll have to talk to the colonel. Worst case, I can try going over his head." Hal didn't mention the classified experimentation that would limit any cooperation from the U.S. side.

"We need everything they have on him."

"I understand. I'll do the best I can," Hal said, hating the assurances he knew could well be false, but having no viable alternative under the circumstances.

Sunan seemed to intuit Hal's reluctance to discuss the matter further, and the tension in the vehicle on the way back to Sunan's headquarters was thick as fog. Halfway to the station, the dash radio crackled and a voice called out Sunan's vehicle number in Thai.

He reached for the mic and listened, crestfallen, as the voice spoke in crisp sentences. Sunan responded and barked instructions, and then reseated the mic and looked at Hal.

"Aranya's been murdered. The housekeeper found her. Sounds like our man."

"Jesus," Hal managed, an image of the young woman's face springing to mind.

"We need to head over there."

Hal nodded. "Of course."

The trip to Aranya's apartment seemed to last forever, both men lost in thought. When they arrived, the now-familiar cordon was in place, and police vehicles on the street were blocking the curb.

The scene in the apartment was as bad as they'd feared, and Hal swallowed back sour bile that rose in his throat at the sight of the mutilated young beauty, now nearly unrecognizable in a rust-colored lake of dried blood, her face broken and her throat torn out. Sunan went about his work with determined precision as Hal stood by the small kitchen, the forensic technicians waiting with him as the inspector studied the scene.

He bagged the keys and walked to the nearest tech. "You get photos of the footprints?"

"Yes. The entire apartment, as usual."

Sunan handed her the keys. "See if you can pull prints."

"Will do."

Hal caught his eye. Sunan leaned into him. "Not much we can do here. But it's definitely him."

"Why would he come after her? She's not American…"

"Maybe we've been misinterpreting something. Or maybe the Americans are only his latest victims. Who knows how many hill people simply disappeared without a trace?"

It was a chilling thought. Sunan threw a final glance at Aranya's remains and strode to the front door. A uniformed officer stopped Sunan and whispered something in his ear, and the inspector nodded and moved out into the hall with Hal, where a woman in her seventies was standing with her hand over her heart, her face so deeply lined she more resembled a Shar-Pei than a human.

"Tell me what you told the officer," Sunan instructed, after introducing himself and flashing his badge.

The woman spoke for a minute in barely audible Thai. Sunan interrupted several times and, when she finished, jotted some notes and read them back to her. She nodded, eyes frightened, and Sunan excused her. She went back into her apartment and closed the door, and Sunan motioned to Hal to follow him out of earshot from the officers. At the end of the hall, where the emergency exit to a balcony was taped off for later attention by the techs, he stopped and turned to Hal.

"She said she thought she heard a scream last night, but couldn't be sure—thought it might have been her ears playing tricks on her or something blowing loose and screeching outside from the storm. Patio furniture."

"What time?"

"About eleven. So not that late."

"She didn't think to call the police?"

"She's old. She didn't want to call and have it turn out to be nothing. I can understand."

"So she didn't see anything?"

Sunan shook his head. "No. Not last night, anyway."

Hal studied Sunan's face. "What does that mean?"

"It means that Aranya apparently wasn't exclusive with her charms. The old lady, like many her age, is a snoop. Her pastime is watching the street outside. I asked her about visitors, and she said Aranya had a young, colored boyfriend who came fairly often, usually on weekends, sometimes with a couple of white friends."

"That would be Kyle and his buddies."

"I assume so. But this is where it gets interesting. She also said that there's another man who predates Aranya's fling with Kyle. An older man, white, who's been seeing her since she moved in. Not as regularly, but at least a couple to three times a week."

Hal blinked. "Older? How old? Could it be...Doc?"

"I don't think so."

Hal scowled at Sunan. "Spit it out. What did she say?"

"That he usually wore a uniform. An officer's uniform, she thought. And that he was maybe fifty, and fit. Looked like a professional soldier, she said."

Hal gaped at Sunan, processing the words, and then his expression clouded and he turned toward the apartment.

"Get me to the base. Now."

— 14 —

Hal brushed past the startled aide and marched to the colonel's office, ignoring the younger man's protests. He knocked on the door, containing his urge to throw it open unannounced, and only swung it wide when the colonel called out.

"Yes?"

Hal entered and stood in front of the colonel's desk, eyes blazing. The colonel regarded him as though he'd landed in a spaceship.

"Have you lost your mind, Shaw?" he snapped.

"There's been another murder. Three, actually, since we last spoke."

The colonel's face didn't change. "And when did that authorize you to barge in on a superior officer and show such contempt for protocol?"

"One of them was Aranya."

Hal watched the colonel's eyes, which momentarily seemed to lose focus as he slowly lowered the pen in his hand to the desk and sat back.

"What are you talking about?" the colonel stammered.

"Her neighbor identified an older officer who visited

221

her regularly. She described you."

"This is preposterous," Hedges growled.

Hal held his ground. "I can have her identify you out of a lineup."

Hedges' outrage collapsed. "I...tell me what happened."

"No. That's not how this is going to work. You're going to tell me the truth. Everything. No more dancing around it and hiding behind need to know." Hal paused. "I also talked to Doc."

"Then why do you need to hear it from me?"

"Humor me. Or we can do this in a more formal setting. One call to the general and we both know you'll be relieved of your command, and then this will become official."

The colonel regarded Hal with new appreciation, his breathing shallow. Beads of sweat had suddenly appeared on his forehead in spite of the frigid temperature.

"I was seeing Aranya. There's no law against that." He hesitated. "I kept it secret because I have a wife and kids back home. Surely you can understand that."

Hal nodded, unwilling to say anything that might disrupt the colonel's admission now that it had started.

"She was a doll. I can't imagine why anyone would hurt her. She was harmless."

"The same killer who butchered Kyle did it. Your man. Corporal Kendrick."

Hedges looked shocked. "How...how can you be sure?"

"The body's in the same condition as the others. There's no doubt."

"I don't understand. Why would he go after her? That makes no sense."

Hal decided to deliver a body blow. "She was seeing Kyle."

The colonel's expression melted like wax before a flame. He looked away from Hal and nodded.

"I had my suspicions. She was young. It's not entirely a surprise."

"Kyle was dealing drugs. Or smuggling them. Which you know. He was getting the heroin you used to keep Kendrick under control."

"You have it wrong. He was chartered with obtaining medical supplies—heroin—for the prisoner's containment. He wasn't smuggling. It was aboveboard."

"He was buying twenty kilos at a time, a couple of shipments a week."

The colonel's eyes widened. "You think Kendrick is killing them for heroin?"

"No, I'm informing you that there was, or still is, a major heroin ring operating on this base."

"What does that have to do with Kendrick, then?"

"Maybe nothing. But it's the common link between many of the victims so far."

"How were the first two involved in this ring you assume was operating?"

"I don't know all the details."

"Well, if there was a ring, it sounds like Kendrick did us a favor by eliminating them."

"Tell me everything about him. Don't leave anything out. Start with how you captured him."

The colonel rambled for ten minutes, his thoughts clearly scattered as he absorbed the news about Aranya. Kendrick had been living east of Pattaya in the lower hills, living off animals and occasionally butchering a farmer. Several people had sighted him, and the U.S. military had been called in when it had become clear that it was an American committing the atrocities. A search had been mounted, and he'd eventually been run to ground using local trackers and dogs, and he had been sedated with tranquilizer darts before being taken into custody at the base.

Military intelligence had stepped in and determined that its best interests lay in keeping him well away from the U.S., where he'd have constitutional protections, and decided to keep him on ice in Thailand until they figured out a longer term plan. The heroin had kept him docile, but they'd misjudged his intelligence, and he'd given them the slip early one morning and disappeared.

"He killed a guard," Hal stated flatly. "How did you cover that up?"

"Died in the line of duty. The family never suspected a thing."

Hal's lips compressed and his jaw clenched. "You've endangered lives by not telling me the truth before."

"I was under orders from higher up to contain this and limit any discussion with you to what was essential to finding Kendrick." Hedges paused. "You said you found Doc?"

Hal nodded. "He's dying."

"Could he have been involved in Kendrick's escape?"

"Not that I can tell. But you've got a bigger problem. If Kendrick is a tracker and he's become fixated on following the chain through to the people responsible for his capture and imprisonment, you could be the next link."

"What do you mean? Aranya wasn't involved in any of that."

"She was with Kyle. A key to her front door was

found by her body. Kendrick must have gotten it from Kyle. If he's crazy and fixated, he might be killing everyone he comes across with any connection. Which, given your role in this, and especially since you've been at the apartment numerous times, could put you in the crosshairs."

"That's...that's impossible," the colonel said, but his voice betrayed his doubt.

"For your sake, you better hope it is."

Hedges frowned. "That sounds like a threat."

"I don't make threats. But if you've left anything out, it could well be your ass on the line, so best think long and hard about coming clean." Hal paused. "Sir."

Five more minutes of interrogation and Hal was done. He stormed from the office, his dislike of the colonel threatening to tip him over the line into insubordination territory. It would do no good to have the man sabotaging his efforts behind his back, and he needed to maintain his focus on catching Kendrick, so Hal checked his rage at the colonel's posturing and made for his quarters to restock on money and strap on his sidearm— after trips to opium dens, meetings with gangsters, and near misses with killers, it seemed prudent to be armed.

He changed his shirt, which was soaked through, and then marched to the gate, where Sunan had again been barred entry by the petty Thai guards, the roar of jets preparing for takeoff on the tarmac a reminder that only a few hundred miles away a war was being waged by the most powerful military in the world against a collection of peasants with only rusty AKs.

— 15 —

Sunan eyed Hal from beside the truck, taking in his pistol and the angry expression on his face. "Well?"

"He admitted to it, but it doesn't really get us any further along than we were."

"What exactly did he say, and how did he react?"

Hal gave him a report. Sunan listened quietly, but interrupted him toward the end, his eyes excited.

"Say that again," he demanded.

"He was living east of Pattaya and had killed a few peasants that they know of."

"No. That's not what you said."

Hal appeared confused. "Yes, it is. He was living off livestock and killing peasants. How does that help us?"

"Livestock. That would be cows, right?"

"I assume so."

Sunan swore in Thai and opened the truck door. He reached in for the mic and slid behind the wheel to start the engine.

"What is it?" Hal asked.

"I need to talk to my subordinate."

"Why?"

"Before Kyle's murder, we received a call from a farmer in a rural community halfway between here and Pattaya. Several of his cows had gone missing."

Hal immediately understood the curse. "Did you investigate?"

Sunan keyed the mic. "That's what I intend to find out."

After several false starts, Sunan reached Panit at the station. He rattled off a string of questions and, when he was satisfied with the answers, turned to Hal with a grim expression.

"The farm is about ten kilometers from here, near Bang Sare. Panit took down the farmer's complaint, but there wasn't much there. Two missing cows. It could be nothing."

"The location's suspicious. And it fits his prior MO."

"Which is why we're going to talk to the farmer in person," Sunan agreed, and rolled away, the air conditioner laboring to cool the cab against the oppressive heat of the afternoon sun.

The farmer's plot was a lush green spread with a two-bedroom shack near what passed for a road. Several toddlers covered in mud were playing in the front yard and stared up at Sunan and Hal as though they were giants. Sunan asked the oldest looking where his father was, and the little boy pointed to the fields and said something unintelligible. Sunan thanked him and they set off along a trail that snaked through the expanse, hopeful they'd find the farmer in short order.

A crane flapped into the sky from nearby with a rush of wings, startling Hal. Sunan was unaffected and continued plodding east until the trail ended at a small stream that bisected the property. Hal looked around and saw nothing but elephant grass stretching in every direction.

"Now what?" he asked.

"He's got to be around here somewhere."

"It's a big spread."

"We can follow the creek and see where it leads."

"Wouldn't it be smarter to wait at the house?"

An hour later, no farmer in sight, they slogged back to the shack, their clothing dripping with sweat. Sunan started the truck engine and they sat drinking water, waiting for the man to put in an appearance. They were rewarded for their patience as the sun began its descent when the farmer came into view, a machete in one hand. The children went running to him and the little boy pointed at the truck. The farmer eyed it and strolled toward the vehicle as Sunan and Hal stepped out into the heat.

Sunan introduced himself and showed the farmer his badge, and then a long discussion ensued, with the farmer doing most of the talking, becoming more agitated as he spoke, motioning with the machete at the distant tree line. Sunan frowned toward the end and looked to Hal, who was pretending interest even though he wasn't following a word.

"He said he lost another one. He's been out looking for it and just got back."

"And?" Hal asked, reading Sunan's eyes.

"He found its remains at the far end of the property."

"Remains?"

"It had been killed and butchered. His words, not mine."

"Is cattle rustling a problem here?"

Sunan shook his head. "No."

"When he says butchered…"

"I asked him. Someone or something slit its throat and cut steaks from its back and flank. But left most of the meat."

"Doesn't sound like a thief, does it? They'd have led it elsewhere to slaughter or removed everything edible."

"Undoubtedly. I asked him to show us where he found it. He agreed."

"So another hike," Hal said.

"That's the only way to get there."

"Did you ask him if he's seen anyone suspicious?"

"Yes. Nothing. Although he seems spooked by the remains. Said it's never happened before, and he's lived here for forty-three years."

Hal considered the farmer, who looked more like he was in his sixties, and the man grinned, revealing a few blackened teeth. Hal returned the smile, and they set off after Sunan retrieved a flashlight from the glove compartment and locked the vehicle.

"What do you need that for?" Hal asked.

"He said it's a long way, and I don't want to step on a snake in the dark and add that to my misery."

"Good point."

The trek to the cow's carcass took well over an hour, the going treacherous once they crossed the creek, and the light was fading in the western sky when the farmer stopped short and pointed to a clearing ringed by bamboo. They moved as a group to a large brown mound near one edge of the clearing, covered with flies, the dead animal's flesh rotting in the heat.

"Jesus," Hal muttered, nose crinkling at the smell. "That's evil."

"Check out the cuts, though. Random. Like he was

just hacking away at the thing."

"So I see."

"Let's look around and see if he left a trail."

"You think that's likely?"

"You say he's crazy, and he has no reason to think anyone's looking for him, so why not? Maybe for the first time in this, we get lucky," Sunan said.

They spread out and walked the area, and after twenty minutes the farmer called to Sunan to tell him that he was heading back to his home while there was still enough light to make it. Sunan waved in acknowledgement, and they continued working the perimeter of the field until Hal called out from one of the bamboo thatches.

"There's blood over here. He went this way," he said when Sunan joined him.

Sunan peered at the brown smears on the bamboo stalks and nodded.

"Good catch."

Hal pointed at the ground, still soft from the prior evening's rain. "Are those tracks?"

Sunan moved to the faint impressions and studied them, and then stood and drew his pistol. "Looks like it."

"Don't suppose we can call for backup."

"Radio's an hour back at the road. You want to follow these or risk losing them to another rain?"

"Not much choice, is there?"

Hal eyed the tracks. "No."

They crept along a trail that led up a mild incline, and as the sky darkened with a final marbling of apricot and magenta, they arrived at an ancient wooden fence.

"This is how he gets in," Sunan said, pointing to a section where the cross posts were shattered.

"And out again." Hal drew his own weapon and

glanced at the heavens. "You think he might be nearby?"

"This is the third cow. Perfect place to lie low. I say we keep going."

Hal glanced at the flashlight in Sunan's hand. "We have big rattlers back in West Texas."

"We have vipers here, too. And cobras."

Sunan flicked on the flashlight as they continued along the track and stopped short near a grove of trees. He played the beam across another carcass, this one picked clean, bones gleaming white in the light, only a few patches of hide remaining.

"Cow number two," Hal whispered.

"He's around here somewhere. I can feel it."

"Not sure that's all that reassuring."

They made their way from the skeleton, and Hal grimaced as they neared a rise where a row of dark cave openings stretched along the base. He pointed to his right and Sunan followed with the flashlight beam, where relatively fresh stools were clumped near a tree. Sunan nodded, and Hal swallowed back the tang that automatically rose in his throat at the stink of human waste.

A sound from the nearest cave stopped them in their tracks, and Hal whispered to Sunan, "You hear that?"

The inspector nodded. "How do you want to do this?"

Hal hefted his Colt 1911 .45 pistol and his eyes narrowed. "I'll go first. Give me the flashlight."

"Why you?" Sunan asked.

"He's one of mine. I'll deal with him."

Sunan handed him the light and they crept toward the cave. As they neared the mouth, a low growl emanated from inside that chilled their blood. Both raised their weapons, their pulses hammering in their ears as they took cautious steps toward it, pistols trained on the yawning opening.

— 16 —

Hal stopped near the inky maw and his shoulders relaxed as he played the light into the opening. He twisted to where Sunan stood a few yards behind him, pistol clenched in a two-handed grip, and called out in a stage whisper, "It's just a dog. Looks terrified."

Sunan exhaled with relief and then a blur from one of the trees dropped toward him and knocked him sideways, sending his pistol flying. Hal gasped at the apparition that had materialized from the darkness and swung around with his gun at where Sunan was trying to fend off the brutal attack.

Hal tried to draw a bead on the assailant, but the man was moving at incredible speed, landing blow after blow in spite of the slim Thai's defensive blocks, a testament to the ineffectiveness of martial arts against a madman. Hal forced himself to remain calm and squeezed off a shot that hit the attacker in the upper shoulder blade, earning him an animal howl of pain and fury.

The killer spun and bolted away, and Hal fired three more times before he disappeared into the shadows. Sunan groaned from where he'd fallen and Hal moved to him, flashlight still trained on where the attacker had vanished.

"How bad?" Hal asked.

"I…not good. Arms are torn up. And I stopped your bullet with my shoulder."

"Damn. Sorry."

"Go after him. He's wounded. I'll be fine."

Hal retrieved Sunan's gun and handed it to him. "Watch out for the dog."

"Get going."

Hal didn't delay or argue. He took off after the killer at a run, following a glistening trail of crimson drops on the grass, the flashlight bobbing like a living thing on the track in front of him. He rounded a bend, and the jungle closed in around him. He slowed to take his bearings and paused, his breath a rasp from the exertion.

If his quarry was still running, he was doing so in silence—which Hal didn't see as possible given the heavy boots the man was wearing, much less while losing blood from a substantial wound. Hal resumed the chase, but moved more slowly, not wanting to underestimate the killer again. He emerged from the brush in another clearing, this one encircled with trees, and followed the blood to the far edge, where it disappeared into the gloom.

A rustle from his left stopped Hal in his tracks. He spun with his gun in the direction of the sound and barely had time to pump out two rounds before Kendrick was on him, blood coursing from his wounds and frothing from his nostrils as he tried to skewer Hal with the knife. The blade slashed through Hal's shirt and a flash of pain seared along his ribs, and then the hilt slammed against his temple, dazing him and causing him to drop the gun.

Kendrick howled in triumph, but the sound was quickly replaced by a renewed bellow of pain when Hal slapped his open palms against the man's ears, rupturing both eardrums. The knife came at Hal again, but he was ready for it, and he dodged and jammed his thumbs into the killer's eyes. The killer roared in rage and agony, and Hal threw himself to the side and scrambled for his pistol while Kendrick was blinded. His fingers felt the gun grip, and then a kick lifted him into the air, his ribs cracking from the force.

Hal landed hard and winced in pain, and then twisted as Kendrick stood over him, knife in hand, blood streaming freely down his chest. Kendrick let loose a bloodcurdling scream and brought the knife back for a killing blow. Hal's gun barked three times, the big rounds pounding into the killer at point-blank range. Kendrick jerked back as the top of his skull blew off and then tumbled to the ground. His body spasmed once, and then again, and finally lay still.

Hal sat up, his ears ringing from the shots, and probed his side, his ribs throbbing. It was bad, but he'd been hurt worse. He holstered his pistol and tried the other side, and his hand came away slick with blood from the knife wound. He hissed at the sting and wiped his fingers on his pants, shaking his head at his predicament—hurt, ribs broken, cut up, in the middle of nowhere with nothing but cobras and wild dogs to keep him company. He looked up at the gibbous moon and, after drawing several tentative breaths, stripped off his shirt, tied it in a makeshift bandage around his torso, and forced himself to his feet, shaking from the effort and the pain.

"At least you're alive," he muttered to himself. He looked around in the grass and spotted the flashlight. He scooped it up with a grimace before pulling his pistol free and walking over to the dead man to play the beam over his ruined face. The final slug had mushroomed on exit, and there wasn't much left of his head, which had split apart like a melon dropped from a second-story window. Even in death the man's features were twisted in hate, and it took every bit of self-control Hal had to keep from emptying the pistol into him.

Hal knelt unsteadily beside the dead soldier, half expecting Kendrick to lunge at him at the last minute, and felt his neck for a pulse. Feeling none, he straightened, and after a final glance at the killer's corpse and a tentative probe of his throbbing temple, he turned to find his way to Sunan so they could begin the long, hard slog back to the truck.

— 17 —

The hospital in Pattaya was primitive by American standards, the equipment largely relics from decades earlier. Sunan was in a private room on an IV drip of antibiotics. Both his arms were bandaged, but the surgery to remove the bullet from his shoulder had been successful.

Sunan looked up when Hal entered, and managed a weak smile.

"Well, we made it," he said.

"Barely."

The trek back to the truck had taken everything they'd had. Hal had fashioned a pressure bandage to stem the worst of the bleeding from Sunan's gunshot wound and had supported him on the hike back, which had taken three times as long. It had started raining halfway through, which had made the already miserable journey even more difficult, the ground slippery beneath their feet with treacherous mud.

When they'd finally made it to the vehicle, Hal had driven hard in the downpour to get Sunan to medical care, ignoring the ache in his sides from his own injuries. At the hospital, the emergency team had quickly carted

Sunan into surgery while a physician stitched up Hal's knife wound, swabbed his bruised temple, and taken X-rays of his ribs. Three fractures, fourteen stitches, and a painful shot of antibiotic later, Hal had returned to base after being told that Sunan was stable.

Thirty-two hours later, Hal's expression was dour as he approached Sunan's bed.

"What's wrong? You got your killer. You should be happy," Sunan said.

Hal took a seat and shook his head. "Yeah. Right." He paused. "I'm sorry. I've just got a bad taste in my mouth from all of this."

"Why?"

Hal frowned. "There are some things I can't tell you due to national security."

"Then leave those parts out."

"Let's just say that it's possible the killer got that way due to an experiment gone wrong. One that's been covered up by everyone involved. Now that he's dead, everyone's breathing easier, but nobody seems to be interested in taking responsibility for their role in creating a monster."

"That sounds about right for government work. It's not just yours. They're all crooks and thieves."

"Right. But we're supposed to be the good guys."

Sunan sighed. "There are no good guys in war or government work. Only different shades of bad. That's always been true. It attracts a certain type. Always will."

"Maybe. But I believed differently until now. Watching the cover-up roar into full swing, everyone trying to rewrite history...and when I pressed the colonel about the drug ring, he gave me the brush-off. Seems like he might have more to lose than I thought; or worse, that maybe the smuggling wasn't just a couple of guys."

"There have always been rumors of government involvement," Sunan said. "Common knowledge here on the ground."

"It makes me sick to be a part of it."

Sunan shrugged and then winced in pain. "Then don't be. Find a new line of work."

Hal nodded. "That's what I've been thinking. I joined the marines out of a sense of duty and honor my daddy instilled in me. Same reason I wanted to be a lawman. Now it seems that it's nothing but acting as an enforcer for a bunch of crooks. I didn't sign up for that."

"When's your tour up?"

"Six more months."

"What are you thinking about doing?"

"I don't know. Honest work of some kind. Whatever it is, not this."

Sunan nodded. "You're being hard on yourself. You stopped a killer. That's something."

"It is. But he wouldn't have been one if he hadn't been turned into one. So everyone that died goes right back to that." Hal paused. "Which you can't discuss with anyone."

"I understand. Nobody talks to me anyway, so I'm not sure there's anyone to tell."

Hal stood. "The doctors say you're going to recover fine. You'll be dancing on tables in no time."

"I'd have been better if you hadn't shot me."

"Sorry 'bout that."

"I'm kidding."

"I know." Hal regarded the bandages on his appendages. "Your arms looked like hamburger. You're lucky you didn't lose them."

"At least we know what caused the defensive wounds."

"High price to pay for knowledge."

Sunan closed his eyes. "You think the colonel's in on the drug ring?"

"Probably."

"Then you're probably better off getting out of here sooner than later. He might want to shut you up."

"That occurred to me. I'm headed to Bangkok from here."

"And then?"

"I'll run out the clock. The general will see that I get plenty of R&R. Maybe something stateside after for the duration. But I'm done."

Sunan nodded again. "Sounds that way. Good luck. And watch yourself in Bangkok."

"You take care. It was good working with you."

"Except for the part where you shot me, same here."

Hal grinned and Sunan managed a pained smile. Hal walked to the door and paused at the threshold. "You need anything before I go?"

"No. I'm fine. Thanks for getting me back in one piece."

Hal inclined his head as though ready to say something more and then reconsidered. He pushed past an unfortunate on a gurney, who was moaning like a wounded animal, a stump where his leg should have been seeping blood through a bandage, and continued down the hall, his kit bag in hand, shoulders square, radiating an authority he didn't feel. Outside, he paused on the sidewalk and looked up at the clouds, the sun warming his skin. Thousands of butterflies, their wings bright yellow, drifted across the sky like petals blown on a strong breeze, and he watched them absently as he considered his options.

After a long moment, Hal drew a deep breath and marched down the sidewalk to where a row of taxis were waiting, the drivers clumped nearby, smoking and laughing. A brief memory of Aranya's untroubled face and playfully mocking eyes flitted through his mind and he shook his head to clear it as he neared the queue, knowing in his core that his dreams would be haunted by images of Kendrick and his victims for many nights to come.

The Bone Collector

by

Jeff Olah

— 1 —

The living room was cold. Definitely too cold, but for the last several days, every room was too cold. Every hallway, every locker room, every doctor's office, and every single place that Blake Chambers had been since that day. Just too damn cold. He didn't know what he was more afraid of, the fact that this—whatever this was—had somehow changed a part of him that he couldn't control, or the possibility that he'd never again suit up as a professional football player.

His season had ended just over ninety days before. Sitting alone in the dark, attempting to control the massive headache that had returned for the second time that day, Coach Mays texted him, asking how he was doing.

He knew what was happening. What the text message was really asking. Blake had missed the previous three appointments with the team doctor and continued taking Sumatriptan—the medication he was prescribed for migraines—even though it had stopped working six days ago. Now the only time his head stopped hurting was when he was asleep, which was almost never.

Through squinted eyes, Blake looked at the backlit

screen. Three little words. *How ya doin'*? But it was more than that. The Coach knew the answer to that, so did the trainers, the team doctors, his teammates, and especially the owner, Thomas LeClair. The man worth nearly fifteen billion dollars knew exactly how he was doing. They just needed him to confirm what they all believed...that he was done with football forever.

Returning the text message, Blake Chambers lied, well mostly.

Blake typed out a quick response. *Getting better every day. See you in a few weeks.* This wasn't going to satisfy Coach and definitely wouldn't go over with the team doctors. They'd need to see him. They'd already given him more than enough opportunities to come in on his own; however, Blake already knew what awaited him once he entered that building.

Another text. This time a group message that included a few of his teammates. They were also his friends. The Coach must be desperate. Blake didn't blame him.

Blake, you know we need to see you. If you're not here at some point today, I'm sending Tucker and the boys to bring you here.

Perfect, now he really did have a problem. This was the off-season and with little besides hitting the weight room to occupy his friends, he knew they'd jump at the chance to harass him. It was what they lived for. The six-month gap between the final game of the season and the first day of training camp was usually a time to heal the bumps and bruises of the previous six months. And it was also a time when Blake's position as their leader on the field took a backseat to just being one on the boys. However, this year was going to be different and not in a way he'd enjoy.

Sliding to the edge of the oversized white leather sofa,

Blake clenched his jaw, gripped the arm, and pushed into a standing position. Most times his size was an advantage. At six foot six and two-hundred fifty-five pounds, he was the largest quarterback in the league and quite nearly the quickest as well. But today his massive frame was proving to be his Achilles heel. With each agonizing step toward the kitchen, he envied those of normal size and stature.

Stepping into his sun-drenched dining room, Blake leaned over two of the high-backed chairs and paused as another wave of nausea enveloped him. Attempting to recall the physician's exact words, he closed his eyes and cupped the sides of his head.

This is your fourth concussion in five seasons. I have no choice but to report this to the head office and Mr. LeClair. However, my personal recommendation would be for you to hang up your cleats. There's no reason to kill yourself; you've had a great career.

Hang up his cleats? Blake Chambers wasn't ready to hang up anything. He'd broken the single season rushing record for his position two years before, but had also taken more helmet to helmet contact than in any other year, which most directly added to his current condition. Gifted with the ability to run the ball as a quarterback had brought about financial wealth beyond his wildest dreams; however, it wasn't until the previous eight months that he'd wished he had a better throwing arm.

As the bile rose from the back of his throat, Blake hurried to the kitchen sink, leaned over the stainless steel bowl, and emptied the contents of his stomach. As his back arched and his stomach convulsed, he gripped the edges of the counter and hoped it would pass quickly. Without having eaten much the previous two days, the foul smelling projectile quickly passed and the final few convulsions were nothing but dry heaves.

Using his elbow to turn on the faucet, he stared down at the mess as it slowly washed down into the drain, spitting what remained in his mouth into the swirling water. Rinsing his hands, Blake cupped them together, ran them over his face, and brushed his fingers through his thick black hair.

Shaking his hands over the sink, his cell phone began to ring from the living room. Blake instantly felt a chill run up his spine and for the moment he was clear. The massive headache that had crippled him for the last several days disappeared in the blink of an eye. His stomach righted itself and a sense of calm started to wash over him.

Turning away from the sink, he stepped guardedly into the dining room, unsure when the debilitating symptoms would return. As he continued, he moved more quickly with each step, and striding into the living room, he grabbed his phone from the sofa and stared at the screen.

"Here we go."

Taking in a deep breath, Blake answered the call and hit the speaker icon.

"Coach, hey I got your—"

"Blake…where are you?"

"Home, I was just getting ready to—"

"You're not going anywhere Chambers, except straight to Miller's office."

"Coach, I'm good. Things are getting better. I'll head over there tomorrow morning, I promise."

"Yes, you will. I'm sending Tucker by to make sure you get your ass out of bed. And I don't mean at three in the afternoon. You know LeClair has been by here three times today, and I'm running out of excuses."

"Sorry Coach, just real busy."

"With what?"

Coach Mays was right. There wasn't anything that Blake needed to do. Not today and not since the season ended. He was single, had no real family to speak of, and every last one of his friends were either on the team or the coaching staff. Football was his world and had become his life. Now, he just hoped it wasn't also the thing that took it as well.

"Nothing Coach, I'll be ready to go first thing. Just have Tucker use the code to come through the front gate…same as last time."

Coach May's voice softened. "Listen kid, we all only want what's best for you. Doc says we need to get out ahead of this thing, get it taken care of before it gets any worse. You know as well as anyone that isn't something to play with. Let's get you in and get this wrapped up. I want you back in that locker room."

The man who'd coached him for the last six seasons sounded genuine, but there was no way to tell. Coach Mays spent the better part of his career getting grown men motivated to do things they weren't even aware that they were capable of doing, all for the benefit of the men in suits writing the big checks. Although at this point, Coach Mays' sincerity didn't much matter; Blake would just tell him what he wanted to hear.

"I'll be ready Coach, I'm just…"

Blake's words trailed off as another surge of nausea began to rise in his gut. He knew what was coming and what was to follow. Ending the call, he tossed his phone into the front pocket of his sweatpants and staggered out of the living room and into the hall.

Keeping himself upright, the skull-splitting headache from earlier returned with a vengeance. He gripped the side of his head with this left hand and guided himself along the wall with his right.

Moving through the sparsely furnished ten-thousand square foot home, Blake closed one eye as the searing pain intensified. He moved quickly through his bedroom, closed the shades, turned off the lights, and dropped face-first onto the white down comforter draped lazily across his custom sized mattress.

Gritting his teeth and smashing his face into the pillow, Blake prayed that sleep would take him quickly. He was no longer sure that death was something to fear. And at that particular moment, he was thinking that it may just come as a relief.

— 2 —

His bedroom was darker than he remembered, but it wasn't exactly night. The previous seventy-two hours had moved by in a blurry haze of false memories and only partially coherent daydreams. His head was also still controlled by the dull ache that radiated from the base of his spine, but didn't appear to be any worse than normal, at least for the moment.

Slowly rolling up onto his right elbow and pulling his head away from the pillow, Blake scanned the room. Squinting through the shadows, he paused as a wave of disorientation gradually began to settle in. Staring at the chest of drawers positioned along the far wall, indistinct visions of the previous two days flashed through his mind.

An overturned box of cereal had its contents spilled throughout a minefield of what looked to be four empty prescription bottles. Further on, toward the right edge of the antique stained dresser, a mound of what he figured were the clothes he'd changed in and out of over the last several days. The small pile appeared to have outgrown its current home, and dropping to the dense Persian area rug below, traveled away from the room and out of sight.

Tracing the path of the forgotten garments, Blake pushed himself up to a seated position and now rested with his shoulders against the padded headboard. Testing the pain at the back of his head, he slowly pulled back the comforter and slipped his legs over the side of the bed.

Sliding to the edge of the bed, he closed his eyes and began to stand. With the muscles in his back, neck, and shoulders tensed, he quickly opened them again and took two steps toward the master bath.

"Okay, I can live with that."

Knowing that even the slightest bit of overconfidence could be his undoing, he quickly took another two steps and reached out for the wall. He paused for a beat, took a deep breath, and keeping his left hand squarely placed against the wall, stepped cautiously from the rug to the aggressively cold Italian marble flooring.

With a few more guarded steps, Blake now stood in the archway at the entrance to the master bath. Continuing to put together the events of the last few days, he presumed he hadn't made his way to the opposite end of the sprawling single level home more than once or twice over the last two days. And although the air around him continued to chill the skin along his bare back and chest, something was different.

A small pile of towels sat just below the sink. They appeared—from where he stood—to be wet. Not like they had been used to absorb what remained after a shower and then tossed to the ground. This was something altogether different, and as he proceeded out onto the cold tile, a hint of color fading in from the right caught his eye.

There was no mistaking what it was, however the discovery stopped him dead in his tracks. Blake initially figured what he was seeing was the result of his inability to fully function as a human being over the last several days, coupled with his failing memory, but this definitely wasn't that.

Although he was unable to recall exactly what had taken place eight feet from where he stood, the thin trail of blood traveling away from the shower forced him to slowly take a step in the opposite direction.

He quickly looked himself over, and although his head still pounded and his mouth tasted like he'd gargled expired milk, he could see the blood wasn't his. Another step back and once again standing in the archway, he squinted through his bedroom, into the failing daylight.

Nothing was out of place; however, running his eyes back over the tan Berber carpeting to the French doors at the opposite end of the bedroom, he swallowed hard. Caked on the handle and running down over the threshold, another ominous red trail could be seen glowing black from his vantage.

Backing toward the walk-in closet, Blake tried to remember when he'd last fired the Ruger SP101 he'd purchased five years ago. He always told himself he'd find a local firing range and become comfortable with the revolver, even though he'd never fired one. Days turned to weeks and weeks to months and years, and now he couldn't even remember which pair of sneakers he'd buried it behind.

Turning on the light, he moved into the fifteen by twelve foot closet and quickly scanned the floor. He was now having trouble even remembering which side of the closet he'd hidden the weapon. He looked right and then left, studying the double row of expensive footwear for a sign, anything to trip his memory. But nothing did.

As his heart continued to pound against the inside of his chest, he turned from the floor, pulled down a hooded sweatshirt, and slipped it down over his head. Contrary to the moment, he let out a short laugh and shook his head at the fact that he was possibly living the last few moments of his life, and his only response was an attempt at fending off the cool interior temperatures.

"Ridiculous, but what—"

His attention pulled back to the master bath, a weakened voice broke the silence.

"Blake."

It was familiar. Somewhat slower and a bit off tone, but familiar. Attempting to place the voice, he walked out of the closet and moved to the left side of the archway. Leaning into the wall, Blake craned his neck forward and attempted to get a better view of what he'd heard.

Squinting with one eye and preparing to run, he said, "Hello?"

Again—exactly as it had twenty seconds earlier—the voice came through weak and broken, and sounded as if the person was weeping. "Blake?"

He knew. It couldn't have been any clearer. Entering the oversized bathroom and sidestepping the pile of soaked towels, Blake stood at the entrance to the massive eight-foot shower. Gripping the leading edge, he moved to a squatting position and stared back at his friend.

The intermittent slivers of light filtering in from the adjoining room swept across the large man's face. They colored his tears with an ominous glow and reflected against the shallow crevices in his ebony skin. He stared up at Blake and as fat drops of thick blood dripped from his hands, he began to shake.

Blake looked into his friend's eyes. "Dwight…what

the hell is going on?"

The giant of a man backed into the corner. "Blake, I can't… I just…"

"Dwight, look at me." He waited as his friend attempted to focus. "What happened…are you in trouble?"

The large man wiped at his face and began to nod. "Yeah…it's not—." He paused, searching for the words. "It's not me, I didn't do this. It was them, the others, they're monsters."

Blake forced a weak smile, but couldn't hide his confusion. "I don't understand, what are you—"

Interrupting, Dwight slouched back against the wet tile and let out of heavy breath. "They're gone. All of them…they're all dead."

— 3 —

Late afternoon had slipped into night as the two men moved from the rear of the home and now sat across from one another in the living room. Blake had helped his friend get cleaned up and was even able to find the larger man some clothes that actually fit. They sank into the oversized white leather sofa and stared back at the television as it began to power up.

Blake motioned toward the window at the front of the home as Dwight had finally began to regain his composure. This was a man he'd spent the better part of the last seven years with and not once had he seen him like this. There wasn't a single question he could think of that would rightfully explain why his three-hundred-pound friend appeared in his home, covered in blood and babbling about monsters.

As the sixty-inch flat-panel LCD television blazed to life, Blake turned to Dwight. Still confused, he repeated his friend's last few statements. "Uh…so, you're saying that coach and the others are all gone?"

Dwight continued to stare straight ahead and only nodded.

"And you came here from Tucker's house?"

Again the large man simply nodded.

This had to be a practical joke. He and his teammates would go after one another relentlessly once the season started, but were typically less aggressive during the few months they had off each year. It was a time they used to decompress from the never-ending abuse their bodies took the previous six months. But the look plastered across his friend's face and the very realistic scene that had played out in his master bath told him otherwise.

Massaging his temples, Blake slid to the edge of the couch, and leaned in toward his friend. "Okay, I need you to run it back for me. What the hell has been happening the last few days?"

Turning from the television, Dwight spoke quietly—almost in a whisper. "We've all been trying to call you for the last three days."

"Yeah, I guess my phone died."

Dwight shook his head. "That's why I came here. No one could find you...no one had heard from you."

"And?"

"And what, Blake? Haven't you been watching the news? Seen what's happening out there?"

Blake could see that his friend truly had little understanding of his condition, and not wanting to go into detail, gave an answer that he'd hoped would suffice. "I've been sick, haven't left the house in like four or five days."

"What about the news, the internet? You really have no idea what's going on out there? It's like World War Three; those things are everywhere, destroying everything. It doesn't even seem real. I just can't believe—"

As if adding an exclamation to his statement, a

thunderous pair of explosions echoed somewhere in the distance. The first rattled the windows as Blake leapt from the sofa and the second, much closer, sounded as if it lifted the home from its foundation.

Back to his friend, Blake's eyes were wide. And momentarily forgetting about the pain radiating from the back of his head, he reached for the television remote. "What the hell was that?"

"That's it," Dwight said. "We need to go."

Flipping from one channel to the next, Blake quickly landed on one of the many stations attempting to answer the same questions he was now asking his friend. The pair of CNN reporters appeared to be just as confused—one even alluding to the mass hysteria as a *Zombie Apocalypse.*

"They're kidding, right? The Zombie Apocalypse?" Turning from the television back to the front window, Blake watched as miles away the sky lit up in a bright fireball. "Dwight, what is this? What's really going on out there?"

"Blake, I don't know. I just don't know. There are these things—I don't even know how to describe them. They're…they're something I've never seen. Something that's not real, couldn't be."

"I'm not sure I understand, how have you—"

The reporter's even tone coming from the television suddenly changed and both Blake and Dwight turned to look. She stared blankly into the camera and said, "We have footage from upstate New York of what appears to be a bewildered man who is attacking another…oh my God."

She stopped speaking and held her hand over her mouth as the video clip rolled. Black bars filled the right and left corners of the screen as the grainy cell phone footage began to play. The picture bounced up and down, moving in and out of focus as the man behind the camera kept shouting the same three words the reporter had last spoken.

"OH MY GOD, OH MY GOD, OH MY GOD, OH MY GOD..."

The sound of a door slamming preceded the video finally coming clear and being held up to a window. Beyond that, a street could be seen with multiple people darting from the left side of the screen to the right. A few looked over their shoulder, but most simply ran as though their lives depended on it.

As the clip continued, a man entered the frame. Tall and thin—he was probably right at six feet, but couldn't have been more than one-hundred-fifty pounds. He was moving considerably slower than the others, and as he came into full view, it was apparent why. His left leg seemed to be broken and was severely mangled just below the knee. He was now dragging what remained of his left leg and doing his best to move in the same direction as the others.

As a large shadow entered the lower left of the screen, a loud snapping sound began drowning out the muffled screams of the runners. It sounded vaguely like the breaking of bones, but the irritating cracks came in rapid succession, almost like rounds fired from a semi-automatic weapon.

Turning from the television and suddenly feeling much warmer than he had in days, Blake said, "What is that? Sounds like—"

The rest of his sentence trailed off as the look on his friend's face pulled him back to the screen. "That's it...that's what's out there."

The friends again stared at the flickering screen, only now neither was able to form a rational thought, let alone put words to what they were seeing.

A grotesquely disfigured man—or at least that's what this thing looked like it had once been—leaned into the shot. The first thing Blake noticed was the odd coloring of its skin. It was something reminiscent of cloudy water, not quite white or tan, but more of a translucent pearl, with blue veins weaving odd patterns across the majority of its hairless body.

The unthinkable beast stepped forward and eyed its target. Extending its densely muscled right arm, it reached out for the injured left leg of the man on all fours, now heading toward the right corner of the screen.

Through the grainy cellphone video, it looked as though the creature's hands had somehow morphed into thick meaty claws, and its nails into dangerously jagged talons. They clicked and scratched as the fast moving beast scurried across the asphalt toward its victim. And with a single swipe of its right arm, it clutched the screaming man by the ankle and began pulling him backward.

Shouts of horror could also be heard coming from the individual holding the phone as they took a step back from the window and the camera refocused. The frame a bit wider now, and the scene coming clear, the totality of the creature came into full view. And as it turned to face the window, the camera momentarily shook and then the video went to black, but not before Blake and Dwight looked into the eyes of what was about to change civilization forever.

— 4 —

With the image burned into the deepest part of his mind's eye, Blake tried making sense of what he'd just witnessed. And as the reporters continued their discussion of what they thought was happening, he only stared at the screen, attempting to forget the pain that had returned at the top and sides of his head.

Clutching the remote—his hand shaking as he muted the volume—Blake fought to keep his composure. That thing that was once human had somehow transformed into something nearly indescribable. What he couldn't piece together was how. It just didn't seem possible, not now, not ever. Although, in his current condition, he couldn't say for certain that he wasn't hallucinating, or even dreaming.

Back to his friend, Blake pointed to the front window. "Is that what caused whatever is going on out there?"

Dwight nodded. "I think so."

"That's not possible, how on earth could that thing—"

"Blake, there are hundreds of those things, maybe thousands...maybe more."

"Come on, how did no one know these things existed before two days ago? There was nothing on the news, nothing on the internet. There's no way all of this just popped up out of the blue—someone must have known something."

"I don't think so man. They really don't know what this is. They keep calling it a virus or something. Yesterday one of the news stations even said it was Ebola. People started losing their minds, calling it the apocalypse, saying that we're all gonna die."

Blake didn't initially respond; he instead moved around the sofa and stopped at the edge of the large front window. He leaned to the left and looked out over his property, scanning the massive front lawn.

"Okay, you show up in my home covered in someone else's blood and tell me the world is going to hell because of some super virus. So, if everything you say is correct, and I'm not going completely insane, we need a plan to…"

As his words trailed off, Blake noticed that Dwight had looked from the television to the window for the third time in the last ten seconds.

"What?"

Dwight nervously rubbed his hands together. "We need to get the blinds shut, all of them."

"Why?"

"Those things are more active at night and I think they may even see better when it's dark."

Shaking his head and letting out a heavy sigh, Blake was skeptical, but figured it couldn't hurt to humor his friend. He moved deliberately from one window to the next, closing off view from the outside world, and allowing himself a brief moment to digest all that had taken place over the last few hours. He still wasn't exactly sure what was happening, but he had a feeling he was about to find out.

As he made his way from the south side of the home and back into the front room, he grabbed the remote, switched off the television, and dropped back onto the sofa. "Okay, we're good."

"Wait," Dwight said, "shouldn't we keep that on, maybe get some updates?"

"I just need to wrap my head around this first, get some perspective."

Dwight furrowed his brow, but didn't respond.

"Okay," Blake said, "tell me everything."

"What?"

"I want to know exactly how you ended up here and what you've seen out there. I've been dead to the world for the last three or four days, so for me this isn't real."

"Trust me, Blake; this is real."

"So then, tell me what happened."

Dwight slid back against the cushion and allowed the oversized sofa to envelop him. He took in a deep breath and looked away from Blake. "I'm scared."

This was new, and almost as disturbing as what he'd seen on the short video clip from upstate. The man he'd known better than anyone else wasn't scared of anything or anyone. Pushing three-hundred pounds and with arms the size of telephone poles, his good friend had never even spoken those two words before today, at least not in Blake's presence.

"Of what?"

Rubbing his meaty hand over his face, Dwight fought back tears as he began. "Blake, I had to watch two of those things fight each other to get to Tucker. They did things to him that I've never seen before. I don't want to remember, but I also can't stop seeing it."

"I'm sorry."

"There was a big one, probably bigger than me." Dwight shook his head. "He jumped from Tucker to Coach and dragged him out onto the balcony. That thing, it ripped Coach's arm off without even trying."

"Dwight, you don't have to—"

"It was fast and strong. Stronger than anything I've ever seen. It howled like an animal and then started biting him…over and over again. Pulling Coach apart and eating him, I can't even tell you how bad it was."

Blake sat in disbelief searching for the words, something that would help his friend, something to offer a bit of relief from what he'd been through. But nothing came.

Dwight finally sat forward, wiped away the tears running down his face and forced a half smile. "They saved me."

"Who saved you?"

"Morales, Finn, and Coach. We'd heard they were setting up shelters in the city and drove to Tucker's house to pick him up. But it was a mess before we even got there, I almost didn't make it out."

"How *did* you get out?"

"I rushed the one that pulled Coach out onto the balcony, but it was too late. I hit that thing hard from a full sprint. I went over the railing and I landed on top of it. That thing hit the ground so hard that its head exploded against the concrete. I got up and ran—didn't really know what else to do, so I kept running. I made it to the dock and then just kept going."

"You took Tucker's boat—came all the way up here through the Long Island Sound?"

"Yeah, I don't think those things can swim."

"But why…why come here?"

The first real sign that his friend was still here. Dwight actually formed a full smile. "You really think I was going to let you miss all this fun?"

Blake returned a half-hearted smile and nodded. "I think you could have made an exception this—"

Another explosion shook the home. This one was even closer than the previous two and lit the entire living room through the closed wood blinds.

Before the shock wave ended, Dwight stood and started for the rear of the home. "Blake, we have to go…right now."

— 5 —

Blake filled a single backpack and made his way from the bedroom into the kitchen. He opened and closed every cabinet and drawer on his way to the rear of the home, before stopping in the dining room and looking back across the interior. He shoved his hand through each pocket of the black bag, and with each second that passed, his heart rate climbed.

"What is it?" Dwight said. "Your meds?"

"Yeah man, I'm completely out."

"Gonna be bad?"

"I really don't know. I've been on them for so long, I don't remember what it feels like to be normal, or how bad the pain is going to get."

Dwight didn't respond. He looked away and focused on the back door.

"Yeah," Blake said, "I know man, but having that gun would have probably made things a bit more—"

"You left it at the apartment?"

His second residence, a twelve-hundred square-foot apartment he'd rented for the last several seasons, sat less than a mile from the stadium and offered a much shorter commute for those nights he preferred to stay in the city and avoid the trip back to Westchester County.

"Yeah, dumb move I know. But I was getting a weird vibe the last few times I stayed in the city. Just forgot it was even there."

Dwight looked back at Blake, but didn't say anything. His eyes were wide and he appeared to be breathing more rapidly than before. He turned nervously toward the rear of the home and then quickly back to his friend, looking more like a child who'd lost his parents than a three-hundred-pound professional athlete.

"Big D…you okay man?"

"We have to go; we need to get to the city."

"Your nephew?"

"Yeah, he said the National Guard set up a shelter at the library. They were going to take a stand at the Queensboro Bridge. They aren't letting those things into the city. We need to get down there by morning."

Blake turned toward the rear of the home, back toward the front door, and then to his friend. "There's not a chance we could just drive there?"

"Impossible, roads are so blocked we wouldn't even make it to the 95."

"So, Tucker's boat?"

"It's our only shot; we're not getting into the city any other way. At least not tonight."

Blake stared at his friend, not quite sure what he should say. What could he say? He still wasn't even sure he believed any of this and now he was leaving his home to get on a boat in the middle of the Long Island Sound and run from something he wasn't sure was even a threat. He trusted his friend and would keep an open mind, but was more than confident the pair would be right back in his living room by morning.

"Okay, let's go."

"It's off to the left, at the far end of the dock. We need to stay quiet and out of sight. Those things—"

Motioning to the rear slider, Blake pointed toward the rear of his property. "I'll follow you out."

Blake pulled open the door and paused as Dwight craned his neck through the opening. His massive friend looked left, right, and then back to the left again. "Okay."

As Blake slid the door closed and engaged the lock, Dwight had run the short distance to the head-high shrub at the edge of the yard and stopped. The large man turned to face Blake and was now frantically waving him over.

With wide eyes and quivering hands cupped around his mouth, Dwight whispered under his breath. "Let's go."

Blake jogged across the lawn, slipping his arms into the straps of the backpack as he ran. He moved to his friend, and as he reached the head-high shrub dividing his yard from his neighbor's, he looked past Dwight and stared down the length of the one-hundred-foot dock.

"You good with navigating that thing in the dark? We may just want to—"

A loud crashing sound pulled Blake's attention back over his right shoulder. It was loud—not unlike a window being smashed—but it was also muffled. And it was close, much closer than he was comfortable with.

He turned and stood on his toes, reaching for Dwight's left arm as he peered over the shrub and into his neighbor's home. It was dark, much darker than his own; however, as he scanned the world beyond, not much more than a few out of control fires in the distance lit the night sky.

Once his eyes adjusted for depth, Blake squinted and looked to where he calculated the noise had originated. His neighbor's rear slider remained intact, and although getting a clear image of anything beyond the first few feet from the door would be impossible, he had a bad feeling.

Dwight was now also on his toes, attempting to follow Blake's eyes as they moved from one window to the next. He held his right hand over his eyes, trying to shield them from the glare cast by the heavy moonlight, nudging Blake as he shook his head.

"I don't think it was coming from—"

A ghostlike shadow moved from one side of the rear slider to the other. It jerked oddly as it rushed by, disappearing into the living room before either man could get a good look at it. However, they didn't need to. Dwight knew what it was and had already dipped below the shrub, again beginning to breathe rapidly as he turned toward the dock.

Blake had also seen what had driven his friend away, but he continued to stare into his neighbor's home even as Dwight tugged at the backpack hanging from his shoulders. He was more curious than frightened and wasn't exactly certain of what it was that he'd seen. Was it one of those things from the news or was it simply the reflection of the sparse cloud cover running through the light afforded by the full moon?

Dwight grabbed a handful of Blake's shirt and tugged him backward, their faces only inches apart. "We have to get the hell out of here, I mean right now before that thing sees us. Trust me, whatever it is, it's way faster than either of us."

Blake pulled away. Out of the corner of his eye, he was able to see the translucent white figure yet again. This time, it was moving much slower and back toward the kitchen. As it came into full view, a woman's screeching voice could be heard from inside the home.

Although she was more than thirty feet away and behind the heavy glass slider, her tortured plea echoed through the night as though she sat only feet away.

"JOHN NO... PLEASE NO. PLEEEEEEEASE NOOOOOOOOO."

The white shadowy figure emerged from the cover of darkness and stepped back toward the massive glass door. It held the woman by the neck and appeared to be examining her nearly naked body. Blood ran down its thickly muscled back and disappeared into what remained of the tattered green scrubs the beast was wearing.

Blake instantly recognized the aggressor as his neighbor John Santori. A man who up until now had saved the lives of others as a career. The gentle, soft-spoken man was rarely seen around the upscale neighborhood without a smile and a few kind-hearted words for anyone he happened by. But whatever that thing was, it was no longer the highly paid trauma surgeon from Long Island.

Unable to turn away, Blake's eyes finally fell upon the woman. Her name was Tamara, and although she'd lived next door for more years than he could remember, he'd only ever spoken to her twice. He knew that she was a writer of some sort—maybe fiction, maybe self-help—he wasn't sure. Either way, she was a bit of a mystery.

The beast who was once her beloved husband lowered his right arm. He brought her face down in front of his and let out a shriek that sounded more like a wounded animal than anything produced by a human. She turned away and her terrified eyes briefly drifted toward Blake.

A look of confusion and shock crossed her face, but before she could turn away, her aggressor had taken notice. The beast quickly tossed her to the ground and followed the path of her eyes. It now saw what she saw.

Not more than thirty feet away and only separated by a thin pane of glass, the former surgeon looked down from the raised living room and into Blake's eyes. Leaning forward, its grotesque features were illuminated by the intensified moonlight.

"Holy shhhh—"

It wasn't real, it couldn't be. The thing that was his neighbor had transformed into something completely unrecognizable as human. Its pupils had morphed into yellow slits that ran down the center of each eye, and what was once its mouth was now a bulging sucker that framed two rows of broken and jagged teeth. Thick trails of blood ran from its swollen lips down onto the translucent skin that wrapped tightly around its hairless torso.

The beast lowered its head and cocked it to the right. He glared at Blake as if he was sizing him up, scrutinizing him for any outward signs of weakness. And when Blake failed to look away, it pounded its arms against the metal door frame, tilted his chin back, and shrieked with such force that the windows along the first floor rattled in their frames.

As the wave of sound echoed into the night and then died away, the beast again pounded its meaty arms against the frame of the massive glass slider. With the upper right corner now bent outward, the former surgeon took notice and began slamming it harder with each progressive strike. Another six blows and the door exploded from its track, crashing to the concrete patio below.

The world instantly went quiet.

Blake felt his pulse racing as he calculated the odds of making it to the boat. He slowly brought his hands down and tightened the straps of his pack, attempting to calm his labored breathing.

Out of the corner of his mouth he whispered. "Dwight, you ready to—"

Breaking through the aggressive silence, Tamara's voice roared from somewhere behind the beast that had stepped out over the demolished threshold.

"RUUUUUUNNNN!"

— 6 —

Blake was confident that even in his current condition, he could outrun his much larger friend. Given the relatively short distance and the intensity of the situation, he figured he'd reach the end of the dock a few paces ahead of Dwight. The only variable that remained in the out of control situation was that thing that used to be his neighbor, now running on all fours in a direct line toward them. Would they reach the boat before their pursuer or would they end up like the man from the grainy cell phone video? Either way, Blake would have his answer within the next few seconds.

Dwight was already in a dead sprint by the time Blake reacted. The massive offensive lineman moved with a speed Blake wasn't quite sure he'd ever seen. His good friend was one of the faster big men on the team, but this was something altogether different. It was fear pushing his friend forward as they transitioned from the lush green lawn, out onto the eight-foot-wide raised dock.

Fear and adrenaline.

Blake leaned forward and pumped his arms, attempting to squeeze every last bit of speed out of his tired body. The pain at the back of his head returned yet again, and this time it was begging him to stop. However, the pounding against the inside of his skull was also serving a purpose. It was drowning out the riotous footfalls from the opposite side of the head-high shrub that grew closer with each second that ticked away.

As they reached the midway point, Blake was closing in on his friend and would assuredly reach the boat first. He wasn't exactly confident in his abilities out on the water, but knew he'd have to be the one to at least get the boat away from the dock. He'd have Dwight take control once this nightmare was behind them, but for now he only focused on ignoring the excruciating pain in his head, and living long enough to see how bad it was going to get.

He shouted to his friend as they now ran shoulder to shoulder. "Dwight, that thing ready to go?"

His friend nodded. "Just get in and untie us, I'll do the rest."

From behind, another ear-splitting screech rang out. It was close. Too close. The shrub between the two homes gave little resistance as the beast giving chase plowed through, sending splintered fragments of wood and leaves skyward.

As it skidded to a stop along the left side of the dock, the beast dug its razor like talons into the red cedar. It locked eyes on the two men nearly fifty feet ahead and lunged forward. Again on all fours, it breathed heavily through its flared nostrils, spitting blood and mucus as it picked up speed. Its joints snapped and clicked, and as it began closing the gap, Blake did what he'd told himself never to do.

Now a full stride ahead of his friend, Blake turned and looked over his shoulder. Even though he'd been taught since the third grade that doing so meant a reduction in speed, and that giving up even a quarter second to a defender could be the difference between winning and losing a game, tonight the fear of the unknown briefly took control. This wasn't a game, and losing a fraction of a second to the raging animal at his back could mean a hell of a lot more than any game he'd ever played in—it could mean his life.

Ten strides, a quick left turn, and a short jump into the twenty-nine-foot boat. That was all that was left. Well, that and the problem of pushing away from the dock before that thing joined them. Lowering his throbbing head, and attempting to increase his speed, Blake aimed for the edge of the wooden platform. He needed to take a chance, it was the only way.

Over the antagonistic galloping sound at his back, he shouted. "Follow me, and stay close."

And with less than ten feet before the turn at the end of the dock, Blake drifted left. He took the final two strides, planted his left foot and leapt over the short gap between the two platforms. Landing lightly, it took him another few steps to recover before he was on the move again.

Dwight had also cut the corner and made the jump, but the big man had lost another step or two. He was a full three seconds behind Blake when the beast slowed into the turn, digging its talons into the fine-grained wood. It growled in frustration as it continued sideways and nearly slid into the Long Island Sound.

Blake was first. He took one final step and hurdled the side of the Century 2901. Without turning, he moved quickly to the stern and released the line from the dock. As he twisted right and started for the bow, Dwight cried out through heavy breaths.

"Blake…just…go…"

His attention pulled back to the dock, Dwight was slowing under the weight of his own body, just as the beast dug in yet again and used its rear legs to propel itself into the air.

The nausea growing in the pit of his stomach forced Blake forward as he shouted, "JUMP!"

The beast came in fast behind Dwight, and the big man used what little strength remained in his fatigued body to dive head first toward the boat. They were both momentarily airborne, with the massive translucent body of the former surgeon blocking out the light of the moon. As the pair collided mid-air and came crashing into the starboard side of the boat, Dwight was pushed inside, while the beast fought to get a grip on the outer edge.

Blake had untied the bow and was moving back to his friend as the twenty-nine-foot vessel began drifting away from the dock. He helped Dwight to his feet and then stepped carefully past him as the beast dug the talons of its right hand into the stern seating and began pulling itself into the boat.

Blake rapidly scanned the darkened interior and floor as the thing that used to be his neighbor reached for the railing with its left arm and howled. It sniffed at the air and popped its sucker mouth in anticipation of the flesh it was coming for.

Blake called out to Dwight as he dug through the storage panels along the port side, pushing aside three boxes filled with can goods and dried fruit.

"Now buddy, get this thing moving!"

As his voice slowly faded into the night air, Blake kept one eye on the advancing beast—who continued to claw its way along the slick exterior—while digging through the shallow storage panel. And pushing aside a second brightly colored life vest, he found exactly what he'd been searching for, a ten-inch fixed-blade stainless steel hunting knife. He'd have to get in close, but at this point, he had no other choice.

The engines roared to life and as the Century 2901 lurched forward, Blake gripped the railing and took a deep breath. The beast had slipped back and was now being dragged through the frigid East Coast waters, only clutching the railing with one arm.

As Blake stepped forward, the beast growled and swung its free hand wildly in his direction. He took another step forward and held the ten-inch knife out in front, hoping above all else the forward motion of the speeding vessel would be too much for the enraged former surgeon.

To his dismay, the beast who'd tracked them from land to sea appeared to be again pulling itself up toward the stern. It was now or never. In another ten seconds, there wouldn't be a thing he or his friend could do to combat their much larger opponent. They would die right here, tonight.

Before the beast could pull itself another inch toward him, Blake moved to offense. He shook his head and then darted quickly to the stern, bracing his leading foot against the bench seating. And in one motion he swung the heavy stainless steel blade in a downward arch, hoping to extricate the thick claw of his attacker from the railing.

At the same moment the beast swung its free arm back toward Blake. Its hook-like talon caught his left arm and began to tighten around his wrist. Blake did the only thing he could. He swallowed hard and allowed the translucent animal to pull itself toward him.

As the pair were nearly face to face, and Blake's heart-rate skyrocketing, he leaned in and with his free right arm, drove the ten-inch stainless-steel blade deep into the beast's head. It blinked twice and loosened its grip around Blake's arm. Its sucker lips came together and popped involuntarily as it went limp and slipped slowly into the dark water.

Blake waited as the grotesquely disfigured face of his former neighbor disappeared from sight. He dropped the knife, took another deep breath and moved to his friend.

"He's gone."

Dwight quickly cut back the throttle and brought the boat to a slow idle. He turned to Blake and threw his thick arms around him. "Man, I don't know…"

Blake could hear the big man's voice fading as the all-too-familiar pounding in his head began moving from the base of his neck and into his temple. He pulled back from his friend as the ensuing nausea forced him to his knees.

His friend was now shouting. "Blake my man, what's wrong? You're freezing, what can I do…"

Again he was gone. And now Blake dropped to all fours and began dry-heaving. His back spasmed with each wave, and as he reached for the railing on the port side, his vision began to narrow.

Nothing was left. Only the darkness that filled his eyes and the sense that he was being pulled backward into the void from which there was no escape.

— 7 —

Awakening to the warmth of the sun on his face was different. So was the man staring down at him. Blake rolled onto his side and tried to place his surroundings. There were voices, at least two, and one of them was a child. His memory had been spotty at best, even before his most recent injury, but this was different. As he pushed himself into a seated position and looked around, none of this, not a single thing, was even vaguely familiar.

Well…almost nothing.

The man seated to his left smiled excitedly through a thick beard. He was clean, appeared relaxed, and was nothing at all like the man he remembered. This version had to be an illusion. The man in the loose-fitting hooded sweatshirt, blue jeans, and black ball cap that read BXF Technologies was someone else, it had to be.

"Dwight?"

The name felt odd as it left his mouth. His tongue was dry and his throat sore as he tried putting the pieces together. He remembered the grainy cell phone video on the news, the terrified look on his neighbor's face, and even more clearly, he remembered her husband or whatever that was chasing him to the end of the dock and into the boat.

"Where are we?"

Dwight sat forward and ran his hand over the dense beard that had taken over his face. He continued to smile, almost involuntarily. as he decided the best way to explain their current situation. Pushing away from the seat and standing, he scanned the interior.

"Things are different, much different."

Blake matched his friend's smile, leaned back, and nodded. "Yeah, I can see that. Where the hell are we? And…and, I thought I heard someone else, maybe a kid?"

"Look around," Dwight said. "What do you see?"

"I don't know man. I wake up and you're in someone else's clothes, you've grown beard, you look like you've lost thirty, maybe forty pounds."

"Good guess, it's actually twenty-eight."

"Okay," Blake said. "What is this, where are we?"

Dwight stretched his arms out over his head, looking like he was getting ready to make some grand announcement and then quickly said, "We're on another boat…well, actually more like a yacht. We're safe here for now and with what's going on in the city, we really don't have a choice anyway."

He didn't know what to ask first. This wasn't real, it couldn't be, none of it. Not the nightmarish creature he saw on the news, not his neighbor, and not him shoving a ten-inch hunting knife into the head of another human being.

"How long have I been out?"

"Don't know…a few weeks, maybe a month."

"What?"

"You haven't been out the whole time, but you've

been real sick. Throwing up, seeing things, and talking to people who weren't there. Brian thinks it's your injury and also coming off your meds."

"Brian?"

"Yeah, this is his yacht. I mean it's his now."

Blake wasn't completely sure he understood half of what his friend was explaining. There was too much of a jump this time. He'd lost a few days here and there, even an entire four-day weekend once, but this didn't seem possible.

"Brian, is that the kid's voice I heard?"

"No," Dwight said as his smile returned. "That kid is Jordan, Brian's son. They'll be back in a while."

Blake again shook his head and ran his hands over his face, almost surprised by the facial hair he'd grown. He imagined that it matched his friend's, but in a much lighter shade. He hadn't gone a single day in the last ten years without shaving, and knew that he'd hate what he found in the mirror.

"So...what the hell happened, why are we here?"

"You went down pretty hard that night. I tried to wake you up, but nothing was working. You were still breathing, so I went looking for help. Took us down the East River, tried to find a spot to get us into the city, but that's when all hell broke loose."

"Whatta ya mean?"

"Couldn't even get close, it was like everyone with a boat had the same idea. I couldn't even get within a mile of RFK; people were losing their minds. People fighting, jumping onto other boats, throwing each other into the East River, gunshots—it was out of control."

"So?"

"So, I turned us around and just looked for

somewhere quiet to ride it out. By morning you seemed okay and even woke up to eat. You were talking nonsense and didn't know who I was, but you ate and then just went out again. It was like that for a few days."

Blake looked around. "How'd we get here?"

"After four or five days, I tried to get us back into the city, but it was the same as before. And now there were more people, a lot more. Some were in really bad shape; the attacks were happening all over the place. So I turned back again, was gonna try to dock somewhere over by Kings Point. Maybe get into the city from the other side. I didn't know what else to do and we were running out of food."

"Is that where you found these guys?"

"Yeah, it was late in the afternoon and we'd just run out of fuel, hadn't found anywhere yet, so I dropped anchor. Brian saw what happened and came out to see if he could help. The boat belonged to someone in his family, but he and his son had been out here since the third day, said they were just going to wait it out on the water."

Blake's stomach growled. "And how long have I been a burden to these people?"

"Like I said man, I lost all track of time and haven't cared much to find out. It really doesn't matter anyway, we're just a number now."

"Just a number, what are you—"

Through the cabin door, a whoosh of stagnant air preceded the two men. The first, a thirty-something man, with thick black hair and a large smile, wore tan cargo pants and a navy blue sweatshirt. He moved quickly to Blake with his right hand extended and a boy of maybe ten or eleven at his left side.

"Blake, I'm glad to see you up and around. My name is Brian Chow and this is my son Jordan."

The small-framed man waited for Blake to return the gesture and turned to Dwight. "Is he okay?"

"Yeah, just gave him the rundown. I think he's still trying to put all the pieces together. Doesn't remember much, but he's good."

Blake regarded Brian with a smile of his own and pushed away from the sofa. Extending his right arm, he leaned forward and shook the smaller man's hand.

"My name is Blake Chambers, it's nice to meet you Brian Chow." He looked from Brian to Dwight and finally back to Jordan. "Thank you all for saving my life...or at least what's left of it."

— 8 —

The three men sat around the oval-shaped mahogany table out on the open-air sundeck. They watched as the sun drifted from the low cloud cover into the western skyline. Over Blake's right shoulder, the thick black smoke from days before began to settle above the city, and from their vantage, Lower Manhattan looked like an absolute war zone.

Buildings with large portions of their external skeleton either burned away or completely eviscerated stood against the darkening backdrop. Fires dotted the desolate wasteland, slowly losing their ferocity as the city settled in for what came next. And for the third time in as many minutes, the calm of late afternoon was broken by the distant screeching that appeared to originate somewhere many miles away.

"The military," Blake asked, "they getting this thing under control?"

Dwight looked to Brian, who in turn leaned back in his chair and called for his son. "Jordan, where you at bud?"

"Back here, Dad." The boy's youthful voice, full of

enthusiasm and expectation, came through the open door of the main salon. Seconds later, he ran out onto the sundeck, sweat running from his hairline down into the collar of his heather grey t-shirt. As his eyes fell upon Blake, he smiled shyly and then quickly turned to his father.

"Yeah Dad?"

Brian also smiled as he turned from his son to Blake, and then back to his son.

"Can you go down to the lower deck and get us a few waters? And maybe if there are any chips left, you can bring those too?"

"Okay." The boy smiled…bigger this time, and then darted by his father to the steps leading to the lower decks.

Brian waited until his son disappeared before turning back to the other men. He looked to Dwight, leaned into the table, and then turned to Blake. "He knows what's going on out there, he's even seen it happen. I'd just like him to have a few days without having to think about it."

Blake nodded. "Makes sense."

Brian continued, "This thing is a mess; it doesn't look like there's a way to control it. Not law enforcement, not the military, not anyone."

"What is it—have they figured it out?"

"There wasn't really a whole lot of information that got out to the public; however, I had a friend in the CDC. She told me this thing was somehow related to the Ebola virus. It mutated into whatever the hell this has become."

Blake furrowed his brow. "You *had* a friend at the CDC?"

"Yeah, but since the grid went down, communication has been all but impossible. The last I heard from her, there was a team of virologists attempting to find a way to reverse engineer this thing, find its weakness."

"And?"

"I don't know, we never heard back. She and some of the others were going to be evacuated early on, but she said she didn't know where they were going. I never did hear from her after that."

Blake studied his new friend. He was young and professional looking, but nothing out of the ordinary. Nothing that gave him the impression that this man knew a thing about what had changed his neighbor, but also nothing that told him that this man was telling him anything other than the absolute truth.

"I'm sorry, but how is it that you had a direct line to someone at the CDC? You work for the government, maybe the military?"

Brian fought back the urge to laugh. He turned to Dwight and smiled. "No, I'm just a high school teacher. Honors Biology, ten years. Barbara, my contact at the CDC, was just an old college friend. We spoke a few times a year, but she called me the morning this thing hit the news to tell me that it looked like we may be in for something big, something we've never seen before."

"We?"

"Us, all of us. All of humanity. Well, those of us still upright."

Blake looked out toward the city as the sun finally dipped below the horizon. "Those things, what are—"

Interrupting, Brian quickly said, "Variants, they're calling those things Variants."

"Catchy."

"Yeah, it fits."

"Okay, so what's the plan? There's obviously a reason

we're out here on the water and not being protected by large men with automatic rifles."

"I'm not exactly sure *what* the hell is happening out there, but they pretty much torched the entire city. I would guess that those things were getting the upper hand and they had no other choice."

"So," Blake said, "they evacuated the city?"

"Don't know, but those things are everywhere, more of them every single day; it's spreading like wildfire."

"How?"

Again Brian turned to Dwight.

Dwight motioned toward his friend and then turning back to Brian said, "I told you, he doesn't know about any of it. I mean, if you hadn't come along, I wouldn't know much more than him."

"Blood," Brian said, turning back to Blake. "It looks like those infected end up bleeding out because of the Ebola and are highly contagious once they do."

"Okay, have they figured out how to avoid this thing?"

"Just stay away from anyone who looks like your old neighbor. Other than that, it's anyone's guess. And we've been kind of cut off out here, so any new information is going to be slow coming, but I'm okay with that. We've got enough food and water to last us at least another thirty days."

"And after that?"

Brian's face had changed over the last several minutes. He now appeared irritated as he again turned to Dwight. "Your friend ever look at the bright side?"

"Bright side?" Blake slid forward in his seat and sat up tall. "Hey, I do appreciate what you've done for me and my friend, but from what you've described here today, there is no bright side, and it doesn't sound like there's ever gonna be one, so excuse me if I don't share in your—"

"DAD!"

The boy's enthusiastic voice carried into the sundeck, interrupting Blake's rant.

Brian shouted back. "Yeah buddy?"

"Dad, there's someone coming…another boat."

— 9 —

A dirty orange and yellow skyline framed the Long Island Sound in a menacing glow as the men hurried to the rear stairs and down to the lower deck. The unidentified thirty-foot fishing boat that Brian's son had warned of now drifted slowly over the calm waters and appeared to have cut its motor as it drew to within twenty-five feet.

Quickly kneeling alongside Jordan, Blake placed his hand on the boy's shoulder. He looked back at Dwight and then quickly over to Brian. His new friend now stood at the edge of the lower deck with a shotgun slung over his right shoulder and was motioning for his son to join him.

Blake hadn't seen the ominous looking weapon before this moment, and also hadn't noticed Brian retrieving it on the way down the stairs. However, the way the former biology teacher held it told him that this may not have been the first time.

Before the boy moved away, he turned to Blake, his smile even bigger than before—if that was even possible. He leaned in and whispered as if what he was about to tell Blake was something only for him.

"Mr. Chambers?"

"Yeah?"

"You're my favorite quarterback, like ever. My dad knows, but he told me not to bug you."

Blake had already begun to forget about his former life, even more so now that the world was falling down around him. The only thing on his mind was surviving to see another day, hell even just another hour. His time as a professional athlete was over long before the world went to hell. But now it only seemed like a distant memory, almost as if it were someone else.

He looked out toward the burning city and then returned the boy's smile. "Tell you what, when all this is over, I'll take you and your dad to the stadium and we'll throw the ball around, sound good?"

Unable to respond, the exuberant young boy turned away from Blake and ran the short distance to his father. He pulled at his father's shirt and pointed to Blake. "Dad, Mr. Chambers said—"

"Gimme a minute Jordan, let me see what these people want."

Furrowing his brow, Blake looked to Brian and said, "I'm guessing these aren't friends of yours?"

"Nope," Brian said, drawing out the word. "We haven't had to deal with this just yet."

"Deal with what?"

Brian didn't respond. He instead continued watching the approaching boat, stepped forward to the edge of the deck, and pulled the shotgun off his shoulder. He now held it in both hands across his chest, and attempting to get a look at the individuals behind the shaded canopy, scooted his son in behind him.

The smaller vessel continued traveling slowly forward, and as it came to within a few feet of the lower deck, two men moved out from behind the canopy with their hands in the air. Their eyes darted between the three men and the boy, and the smaller of the two began to move toward the side of his boat as Brian stepped forward.

"Put your hands down."

The much smaller fishing boat came to rest with its starboard edge against the center of the lower deck. Brian waited as the two men dropped their arms to their sides and pointed the barrel of the shotgun out over the water.

"Gentlemen we aren't taking any passengers, so wherever it was that you were headed, you'll just want to keep going."

The men looked at one another. The larger of the two, a thirty-something, dark-haired, sinewy man, tugged at his greying beard. He turned back to face Brian, a thin smile forming at the corners of his mouth as the cracks in his weathered brown skin began to deepen. Turning his eyes down, he looked over his tattered white button down and his bloodstained charcoal trousers and said, "We can't."

The man's voice came out dry and weak. He looked back at his friend and then quickly to Brian. "Sir, we have nowhere else to go. Our boat is almost out of fuel and we haven't eaten in days." From his dried out, overly hollowed facial features, he appeared to be telling the truth, but something about the way he spoke the words seemed disingenuous.

Brian shook his head. He looked around the lower deck, let out a long sigh, and turned back to the two men. "Listen guys, we've got our own set of problems out here and unfortunately we can't help…I'm sorry."

Had Brian noticed the same thing that Blake did? Was he also skeptical of the two strangely desperate men? Did he know something that he wasn't sharing, or was he simply trying to keep the situation from escalating? Even though Blake had been in their care for what he was told was likely close to a month, he'd only come to know the younger man and his son a few hours before. He had no way of knowing how this was going to play out.

"We can't go back there," the disheveled man said. "We only just barely got out—"

Blake leaned forward and grabbed the side of the boat. He regarded the men with a quick nod and then motioned back in the direction they'd come.

"Where you boys comin' from?"

They turned their attention from Brian over to Blake. The smaller man quickly smiled. He couldn't hide what he'd just discovered and began elbowing his larger friend as he began to laugh. The larger of the two men squinted through the waning sunlight and matched his friend's grin.

"Are you kidding me?" The man's voice was different now. Gone was the weak tone and the downcast manner in which he initially spoke. It was only four words, but they came out fast and excited, as if the man had just found something he'd lost.

As he continued, he pointed at Blake. "I've lived in this hell hole my entire life, been to more games than I can remember and it's here, out on this water, after the end of the world, that I run into this guy."

Blake began to laugh. "Hey, I'll bet you never—"

The man cut him off, still not quite finished with his thought. "Blake Chambers... Blake freakin' Chambers. How awkward is this?"

"Awkward?" Blake said.

"Well," the man said, "not yet, but in the next few minutes, I'm sure it's gonna be."

Blake looked the men over, attempting to get a read on just what they had in mind. The smaller of the two began shifting his weight from one leg to the other, while staring at the weapon in Brian's hands. Whatever this was, it wasn't good.

Silence hung in the air, exaggerating the overtly uncomfortable situation. Finally stepping forward, Blake held out his right hand. "Hey guys, I'm sure we can work something out, isn't that right Brian?"

Before Brian had a chance to respond, the larger man stepped forward, pulled a pistol from his lower back and pointed it at him. The man's eyes narrowed as he began to speak.

"It's really simple. We don't want a damn thing you have. We don't want your food, we don't want your water. Hell, we don't even want to hurt you...but we will."

Brian held the shotgun steady while looking from Blake to Dwight to his son and finally back to the men eight feet away. "What *do* you want?"

The larger man nodded. "Okay, now we're getting somewhere." He took another step forward and craned his neck to the right, attempting to make eye contact with Jordan. "My name is Victor and my friend here is Jesse. He's quiet, but also has a bit of a temper and he's already had a rough day, so let's just get right to it."

Brian continued to grip the shotgun and had yet to move. "I'll ask you again, what do you want?"

"Calm down," Victor said. "There's no need for this to go somewhere it shouldn't. All we want is a ride. This piece of crap really *is* just about out of gas and we need to get into the city."

Brian shook his head. "Not gonna happen."

"Well then," Victor said, "I guess this does need to get ugly, and here I thought we'd have a nice—"

"No, that's not…it's not…the city, there isn't anything to go back to. You had to have known, I mean the sky has been lit up for days."

"Yes, I know. But I'm still gonna need you to get us there."

"And if we don't?"

"Brian is it?"

Brian nodded.

"Okay Brian, right now I'm asking nicely, which I don't normally do. But given the fact that if I shoot you and your friends here, there is a pretty damn good chance that you'll shoot me back. And I really don't feel like getting shot. I'm hungry, I'm tired, and it's been a long day. I'm also pretty sure your friends here don't want to die today either, so let's just do away with the chit-chat and get this beast moving toward the city. Whatta ya say?"

— 10 —

Growing closer to the city, the air out on the open sundeck was much warmer than in the secluded cove out past Manhasset Bay. The air reeked of burning embers, rotting flesh, and something only comparable to spoiled milk. The noxious combination now appeared to have taken up residence in their nasal cavities, and breathing through their mouths had long since become a monotonous chore. The night was already long, but under the current conditions, it seemed like an eternity.

Blake sat with Dwight, Jordan, and the man they'd come to know as Jesse. The small man had only spoken twice in the four hours since leaving the bay, and as the group of four watched the smoldering city grow closer, Blake continued to try to draw him out.

"I think we may want to head inside, get the doors and windows sealed off. Jesse, what do you think?"

The small man with thin lips, coarse wiry hair, and a set of eyes dark enough to blend into the night shook his head. He stood from his chair, walked to the end of the deck, and turned toward the city.

"We need to keep our eyes open. After we pass the 59th Street Bridge, it'll be on our right."

Dwight pushed away from the table, stood, and started toward the interior cabin. "What will?"

"Don't worry about it, we have friends waiting for us."

Dwight stopped at the door. "No, you don't. There isn't anyone left in the city. They're all either dead or turned into one of those things. And you'd know that if you'd seen what happened out there."

The little man pulled a pistol from his waistband and pointed it in Dwight's direction. "We know what we're doing, and if you had any brains in that big ass head of yours, you'd be begging me to take you with us."

Blake had very little knowledge of handguns; however, the one Jesse was now pointing at his friend looked an awful lot like the one Victor had used to convince Brian to allow him and his friend aboard. They could have been a matching pair.

From his seat at the weathered teak table, he'd be guessing at the gun's make. Although Blake figured it to be a nine millimeter and as the small man waved it in his direction, the cloudless night reflected the moon off its stainless steel finish.

"Where?" Blake asked. "Where on earth could you and Victor be going that is any safer than out here on the water? I can't imagine that anything in the city is worth risking your life for. Seems like a suicide mission, if you ask me."

Jesse smiled for the first time all night. "I've always hated football."

Blake motioned for Jordan and pushed away from his seat. "What does that have to do—"

"You probably think that your opinion matters. That I should listen to you because of who you are... I'm sorry, because of who you used to be. But you're wrong. No one cares about who you were, who he was, who I was, not anymore. Now is just about now, what you can do and what you can take. There is no one coming to save you, or me, or anyone else. You just have to figure it out for yourself."

Blake motioned toward the interior and leaned down, whispered to Jordan. "Go inside with Dwight, the smell out here is getting worse." Then to Dwight he said, "Find out from Brian how much longer, I'd like to help Victor and Jesse here get on their way."

Dwight chuckled as he gave a thumbs-up and followed Jordan through the door. "Same old Blake."

They disappeared behind the stained glass doors and Blake paused a beat before quickly moving away from the table and flipping his chair over backward in the process. He quickened his pace as he crossed the deck and moved to Jesse. The smaller man in turn raised his pistol and placed it against Blake's chest.

"You don't like football?"

Jesse grinned. "No, I think it's a joke. I think you're a joke. How many games did you miss last year because of that *injury*?"

"Listen little man, if you didn't have that gun—"

"But I do, so why don't you back up?"

Blake looked down at the nine millimeter resting against his sternum and then back at Jesse. He wasn't sure whether the nausea rising in his stomach was from the thinly-veiled threat or if his body was once again choosing the most inopportune time to self-destruct. And as the distant white noise began to fill his ears, he knew what was about to happen.

"BACK UP MAN!" The smaller man was now shouting, but Blake couldn't make sense of exactly what he wanted. The words came to him in an order he was unable to decode and as he felt his knees beginning to weaken, he leaned into the smaller man and attempted a plea for help.

"I have…you need…get Dwight."

Jesse lowered the pistol and backed away, allowing Blake to crash to the deck. The smaller man stared at him with a puzzled look before turning and setting the weapon on the lounge chair to his right. Kneeling alongside the six-foot six-inch former professional athlete, the awkwardness of the situation came flooding in.

"My man, get your ass up. This isn't funny, what the hell is the matter with you?"

As the smaller man stood over him, Blake's eyes began to cloud over. He swallowed hard and fought to stay coherent. The ringing in his ears was now loud enough that all outside sound was nearly muted.

As he continued to drift toward unconsciousness, Blake slowly rolled onto his back and placed his hands at his side. He figured that any movement was progress and would keep his mind in the moment. And again he attempted communication as the man standing above him looked away.

"Dwight…please… I can't."

The smaller man looked past Blake and was again shouting, although his words came through as a whisper. "I don't know; he just dropped."

There were other voices too. They were coming from somewhere else. Blake recognized the tone, but the words wouldn't come.

And now Jesse stepped around Blake, his hands in the air and his mouth moving more quickly than before. "No

I didn't do anything to him. He just dropped to the ground and started talking nonsense. I don't know what the hell's the matter with this guy, maybe he's sick?"

Again Blake pushed his hands into the cool wood flooring and attempted to sit. He was caught from behind as a pair of extra-large hands reached under his arms and began dragging him toward the interior cabin.

"You're not leaving us again."

Dwight's voice was a welcome distraction as Blake attempted to extricate himself from the grips of his downward spiral. He was pulled backward and placed in a chair as Dwight patted him on the back and moved in around him. Having his friend there gave him a familiar base from which to try to focus on the world around him. And as he stared back at the five men now gathered in front of him, his head began to steady.

The large man he remembered as Victor walked to within a few feet, bent at the waist, and stared into his eyes. He shook his head and then looked back at the other men.

"Can you get him up?"

Brian was standing with his son, alongside Dwight. "You can't do this, we helped you."

The smaller man stood a few feet away, again at the edge of the deck, now holding tight to Brian's shotgun. "Yes we can."

Dwight finally stepped forward. "We can work this out, there's plenty of room here for all of us."

"No there's not," Victor said. "Get you friend up, and get the hell off my boat."

— 11 —

The sky opened up and light rain began to push the blackened ash back to earth as Blake and his friends were led to the lower deck with guns at their backs. Twenty feet from where East 42nd Street dead-ended into FDR Drive, the luxury yacht sat on the eerily quiet water not quite three miles from the Manhattan Bridge.

Brian was the first to reach the lower deck and holding Jordan's hand, he attempted to restart the conversation. "We can work this out; there's no reason why we can't."

Victor placed his weapon against Blake's back and forced him out into the center of the deck. He motioned for Dwight to follow him and then pointed out over the darkened night. "Listen, you had the chance to offer help when we first came to you, but instead you told us there wasn't anything you could do. And now that the shoe's on the other foot, you really have the nerve to ask for the same thing you denied my friend and I?"

Brian looked around at the others and then back over his shoulder at the devastated city. "You know there's nothing out there for us. You'd be essentially sending us out there to die. You don't want that, I guarantee—"

"Yeah, I get it. It's gonna be rough out there. Those

things are definitely not something I'd want to run into, and that's why I'm going to give you a thirty second head start. Hell, you don't even have to go into the city. You can follow us or you can head back in the other direction, but either way, you'll be getting off here."

Victor looked over his left shoulder and pointed at a grouping of three forgotten boats that had gathered at the center of the East River, not more than fifty yards away. "You can take one of those, well that is if you guys are good swimmers." He pointed to Blake. "And if Mr. Concussion here can keep it together."

The smaller man moved to the edge of the aft deck and waited. He looked toward Brian and his son, then over to Blake and Dwight, motioning toward the water below. "Let's go guys, it's gonna be really cold, but at least he didn't shoot you and then throw you in. You should be thanking—"

Jesse's words fell off as he noticed what the others had only seconds before. It sounded as though every truck in the New York City Department of Sanitation was headed for their exact location. The thunderous roar shook the railing at the outer edge of FDR Drive and rippled the water near the edge of the river.

Blake furrowed his brow and as the pain in the back of his head surged, he looked toward 42nd Street. Placing his right hand over his eyes, he tried to focus on where the sound was coming from. He landed on a spot between the UN Headquarters and the park directly across the street.

His vision was still only seventy percent at best, and through the soft rain and the falling ash, nothing in the distance was clear enough to offer a clue. The moonlight danced off the windows of the UN Building in intermittent bursts that offered a strobe effect, as whatever it was moved closer.

"Oh my God!"

Jesse leaned over the edge of the deck and was the first to realize what the others were about to find out. His hands shook and as he stepped back he turned to Victor. The men stared at one another, unable to put to words the unimaginable scene playing out less than a hundred yards away.

Their translucent skin—peppered with damp flakes of black ash—glinted the silvery moon as they galloped along 42nd Street toward the turn at FDR. Those leading the pack—that numbered in the hundreds—made quick work of the short retaining wall and charged across a short greenbelt.

Victor raised his pistol, pointed at the former biology teacher, and motioned toward the water. "Go." He stepped backward quickly, moving to the stairs, and fired off a single round that nearly clipped Brian's right ear. "I won't ask you again."

He wouldn't have to. It was already too late. The first few Variants had leapt the railing at the end of 42nd and were moving at a speed which seemed improbable, given the awkward jerking gait with which they moved from one stalled vehicle to the next.

Blake took a deep breath and shifting his weight onto his right leg, pushed Dwight toward Brian and his son. In the same motion he moved left and reached out for the collar of Jesse's jacket as the smaller man tried to follow his friend up the rear stairs.

He missed Jesse's collar, but as he followed through he was able to swipe at the smaller man's feet and upend him halfway up the staircase. To Dwight, Blake said, "Get them to the wheelhouse."

As Victor reached the second level and Dwight, Brian and Jordan climbed the stairs on the port side, and Blake pulled Jesse back to the lower deck. The much smaller man got free, kicked Blake in the right side of his head, and both men tumbled to the hard wood decking.

The younger man was thin, but quick. He got to his feet first and scrambled back to the edge of the stairs, retrieving his nine millimeter. He smiled at Blake and shook his head. "I told Victor one of you would end up doing something stupid. He figured it would be that idiot with the kid, but I told him it would be you. And by the way, I still hate football."

Jesse raised his weapon, but paused as Blake gripped the side of his head and waited for the inevitable. The smaller man looked to the deck above just as the luxury yacht listed right. He began to speak, but stopped as the clicking and popping filled the air around them.

Craning his neck back and to the right, Blake watched as dozens of Variants leapt the four-foot barrier and splashed down into the frigid water of the East River. Most tumbled over one another, their dirty translucent skin glowing as they struggled to maintain buoyancy.

One by one, they slowly dipped beneath the surface of the blacked out water and faded into obscurity as others piled in from above. These monsters were of little concern to Blake or any of the others as it didn't appear they could swim. Not one had surfaced since careening into the water less than ten feet from where they stood.

Their concern, and specifically the small man standing five feet from Blake, were the few more agile Variants that were able to make the jump from the roadway to the one-hundred-fifty-foot super yacht. There weren't many;

however, the first one that did now sat perched ten feet above the lower deck, its yellow slits focused on Jesse as it slurped a thin line of blood from its sucker lips.

Jesse momentarily forgot about Blake and quickly moved the pistol to the deck above. The beast hunched on its rear legs, growled at its much smaller adversary. It beat its chest and raised its right arm, extending a hooked claw in the smaller man's direction.

As Blake pushed back into the shadows afforded by the starboard side stairs, Jesse squeezed off three quick shots.

— 12 —

The beast seemed to float in the air and time stood still as it moved toward the three rounds fired from Jesse's nine millimeter. The first two went wide to the left. And the third tore away a two-inch chunk of the Variant's right shoulder, exposing a dense layer of pearlescent muscle fiber, interlaced with a network of deep blue veins.

As it crashed down on top of the small man, it rose onto its hind legs, pinning him to the deck, and cut its angular chin toward the moon. It howled with the unrestrained anticipation of an animal about to feed for the first time in days. And as it dripped blood from its round swollen lips, Jesse begged for mercy.

"PLEEEEEASE!"

The Variant peered back at its much smaller adversary, as if attempting to understand, or maybe it was simply savoring the moment. Either way, as it began to lower itself, the hook-like claws extending from its back feet dug into Jesse's upper arms, spilling blood out onto the light colored wood flooring.

"KILL ME... JUST KILL ME ALREADY!"

The Variant snorted and locked eyes with Jesse. It

watched as a thin trail of blood escaped its victim's body, sniffing at the air in short bursts. And again leaning forward, it quickly looked from right to left and then drove its meaty right hand into the smaller man's chest, its hooked claw eviscerating skin and bone alike.

Blake could only watch as Jesse slipped from this world into the next. The monster perched over him quickly began tearing away pieces of wet sticky flesh, consuming the scraps one handful at a time. It lowered its head and forced its popping sucker lips onto the dead man's subclavian artery, slurping the warm blood that appeared black under the night's sky.

Blake gripped the back of his head, and from the shadows, prayed that his body would cooperate at least for the next few minutes. He slid slowly up the wall at his back as another terrified voice rang out from somewhere above. It wasn't Dwight and it was too throaty to be the boy, but he couldn't be sure it was Brian.

As the beast ten feet away continued to feed, Blake got to his feet and started for the stairs. Turning, and taking the first three steps, the Variant hunched over Jesse cocked its head. It didn't look in his direction. Instead it turned its wet nose toward the sky, closed its yellowed eyes and just listened.

Blake stared at the creature, his heart pummeling the inside of his chest and the pressure building rapidly at the base of his skull. He raised his right foot to take another step as an anguished cry for mercy came from above, quickly followed by a thunderous explosion.

Another two steps and the deck above came into focus. His best friend stood six feet from the door to the interior cabin, shoulder to shoulder with Brian. The young boy—tears flooding down both cheek—stood behind them trembling as he cut his eyes from one side to the other.

One the opposite side of the deck, two large Variants fought one another for the rights to the man with the jet black hair. Victor was still gripping his pistol as he was being lunged at from both sides. However, he was unable to get his arm up in time and fired two quick shots from his hip. Both went wide right, and without finding a target, raced off into the night sky.

Blake quickly turned and looked over his right shoulder toward the city. He could see that they had drifted far enough away from the river's edge that they no longer had to be concerned with taking on any new passengers. Those piling in from behind the railing at the end of 42nd Street came to an abrupt stop, although a few continued to follow their fellow Variants into the East River.

With the beast on the lower deck continuing to focus on Jesse's lifeless corpse, and the two much larger Variants having cornered Victor near the overturned table on the port side, Blake's mouth went dry. His hands shook and the pain at the base of his neck returned with a vengeance. He had maybe another thirty seconds, maybe less, probably less.

The nausea also came flooding back. He dropped to his knees and braced himself against the stair above as he began to dry heave. Looking up between the excruciating waves of pain torching his midsection, Blake locked eyes with Dwight.

His friend quietly began guiding Brian and Jordan toward the darkened doors of the interior as the two massive Variants finally descended on a cowering Victor. The pair pushed the screaming man's body into the corner and began the process of pulling him apart.

Victor's incessant wailing lasted less than ten seconds as the Variant on his left ripped into his neck and pulled away his throat, from chin to clavicle. Blood splatter rained down over the deck, as well as large chunks of tattered flesh and splintered bone.

Dwight used the diversion to rush Brian and Jordan inside, but waited at the door and turned back. He waved frantically, calling for Blake to follow them inside, but Blake knew that even if he made it inside and to the halfway secure wheelhouse, those things would eventually get in. There would be no denying them; they would never stop.

He could make a run for the upper deck and hope that somehow those things would follow, and at some point throw them off balance and in turn off the yacht. But that was pie in the sky, and Blake never operated on pie in the sky—he was more into certainties. That plan wouldn't have worked under the best of conditions and tonight wasn't that night.

Blake was also a guy that wasted little time coming to a decision. Years of being chased down by three-hundred-plus pound men looking to tear your head off will do that to a person. And tonight he felt that same pressure. Only now those three-hundred pound men were all well over six-feet tall, wore a thin translucent skin, had rounded sucker lips, and teeth that looked like they were shaped with a buzz saw.

Blake wasn't going to be able to outrun these opponents. Not here on this boat and not on the decimated streets of New York City. He was sick and there was no going back. This was a condition brought about by the game he loved and the way he played it.

Those four concussions over the last several seasons brought him to a place he'd have a hard time escaping, even in a perfect world.

This was it. He actually looked forward to not feeling this pain another second, not having to fear its return and not having to rely on the sympathy of others just to make it through the day. It was time to turn the tables. Time to do the only thing left to do.

Blake stared back at his friend, wiped away a tear, and nodded.

"GO!" Blake shouted. "GET THEM OUT OF HERE!"

As the Variants hovering above what remained of Victor turned toward him, Blake took a deep breath, prayed his legs would hold up and started back toward the lower deck. As he reached the bottom step, he could feel the one-hundred-fifty-foot super yacht beginning to move forward. Brian must have reached the wheelhouse ahead of Dwight and had a similar plan in mind.

Out onto the deck, Blake sidestepped the thick pool of blood surrounding the Variant that fed on Jesse. He turned to look back over his shoulder, and as expected, the other two had taken the bait. They had decided that the opportunity for another kill was more enticing than simply continuing to ravage their motionless victim.

Blake planted his right foot as a wave of pain shot from the back of his head and into his eyes, nearly taking his vision in the process. He spotted his target pulling away from Jesse as the hulking Variants that leapt from the railing above crashed down six feet behind.

He dug in, shifted his weight forward, and lowered his shoulder as the pair coming from behind shrieked in anger. Their heavy footfalls were running a close second to the popping and clicking of their joints as they nipped at Blake's heels.

The yacht again lurched forward as Blake made eye contact with the Variant now standing over Jesse's limp body. Its yellow slits blinked twice—not unlike the shutter of a camera—as if it was attempting to make sense of this massive human doing the unthinkable.

Blake took one final step, placing his left foot in the only spot on the wood decking not flooded with Jesse's blood. He dove forward, but was caught from behind by one of the two at his back. His forward momentum carried him and the beast on his back into the surprised Variant that had dismembered the small man only minutes before.

As the three bodies tumbled one over the other toward the edge, the trailing Variant, the last to join the chase, slammed into the pile at full speed. The bone-jarring collision forced the three Variants, along with Blake, off the end of the deck and into the East River.

Blake fought to get to the surface, although the three Variants pulled and scratched at him, also fighting to stay afloat. As he kicked and pushed at hooked claws thrashing nearby, he felt a warm but painful sensation radiating from his right calf. Twisting away, he attempted to focus through the murky, bloodstained waters.

A parade of tiny bubbles passed over his face and then cleared the area around his body. The smaller Variant, the one that had attacked and disemboweled Jesse, was attached to Blake's right leg. It stared up at him from the depths, again blinking its yellow shaded eyes, and sank its jagged teeth into exposed flesh just below his knee. It wrapped its swollen lips around the meaty muscle of Blake's lower leg and began to feed.

Blake kicked harder now and drove his left foot down into the top of the Variant's head. Two blows, and then three, and then with a fourth and final strike, the Variant pulled back its sucker lips. Unable to get a breath and falling further into the darkness, the beast released its grip and dropped from sight.

Searching for the two others, Blake felt himself slipping. Although he had pulled himself to the surface, the yacht was too far away and the pounding in his head told him that this was where he'd take his final breath. He would lose consciousness and within seconds he'd end his time here on this earth, buried amongst the monsters that had also found the bottom of the East River.

— 13 —

The fading sun was high in the sky. It was warming his back and much hotter than he could ever remember. His skin felt as though someone was running a heat lamp quickly across the exposed areas between his shoulder blades. He didn't particularly like it, but he also didn't want to move. He was at odds with the weird sensation—it wasn't entirely pain, but also not a source of pleasure.

And the smell. Rotting meat was the only way he could describe the rancid odor assaulting his abnormally sensitive nasal cavity. It bled into his mouth and down the back of his throat. He waited for the nausea to return; he was sure it would come, but it never did.

He slowly lifted his head, trying to get an idea of exactly where he was, what this was. He didn't recognize his surroundings and more than that, he couldn't recall much more than the preceding three or four minutes.

Massive rocks and water. A whole lot of water, as far as the eye could see. But that was behind him and he wasn't going back. In front, there was also a concrete retaining wall and something of considerable substance beyond that. He couldn't see it from where he was, but he could sense it. Something he needed and something else that needed him.

Pushing up to his feet, he scanned the uneven surface as his vision crystalized. He could see everything in vivid detail and without the searing pain from before. In fact, he felt no pain at all—anywhere in his body.

Quickly scaling the short concrete retaining wall and the guardrail above that, he leapt out onto 42nd. Hundreds of forgotten vehicles—some still in perfectly formed lines—crowded the long onramp to FDR.

He stopped alongside a burned-out late model sedan as the street beyond the UN Building began to quake. Variants, more by the second with their clicking joints and their popping mouths, skittered out from behind the sparsely placed shadows and into the street; however, none moved to within ten feet of where he now stood.

His first instinct wasn't to run, and although he was outnumbered more than a hundred to one, he wasn't afraid...but he *was* angry. He didn't completely understand why, and at the moment he was also starving, as if he hadn't eaten in weeks. And staring at the beasts—too many to count—he wanted to feed.

Blinking through the confusion, something to his left glinted off the chrome trim of the sedan. With a rush of adrenaline, he turned toward the vehicle and caught his own reflection in the passenger window.

What the hell was this?

This wasn't him. Although he was able to connect the events that led to him being here on this street, to him being amongst the massive horde, he didn't want to believe it. He didn't want to admit that this was what he'd become, but there was absolutely no denying it. He was now one of them; he was the same, but also different.

He was big. Much bigger than before. Much bigger

than any of the others, probably twice their size. His arms held more muscle, his shoulders were more round and striated, and although his legs hadn't grown by the same proportions, the joints appeared to have shifted in a way that would make running on all fours considerably more efficient.

His thick black hair was also now gone. Only a thin layer of translucent skin covered his skull and as he leaned closer, he noticed that his mouth and chin were covered in dried blood that was a muted shade of black. It had also run from his ears and nose, clotting near the upper part of his chest and neck. He slowly wiped at it, but as it flaked away, the stench sent a surge of aggression coursing through every ounce of his body.

As the crowd began to part, he reached forward, gripped the passenger door, and almost pulled it from its hinge. In unison, the horde began to shriek, pounding their hooked claws into the long line of vehicles at their backs. The ground shook and the sound of over a hundred enraged beasts echoed through the small space between the UN Building and the open air playground, finally dissipating out into the city beyond.

He turned to face the massive gathering of Variants and dropped to all fours. The sky grew dark as he placed his swollen claw-like hands down and began to walk forward. The break in the crowd continued to grow as he drew to within twenty feet and then their incoherent wailing ended all at once.

He wasn't afraid of them. They weren't here to do him any harm. In fact, they appeared to be watching his every move, as if they'd come here expecting something from him. Something they needed from him. He wasn't sure what it was, but he assumed that since one of these things had dragged him from the edge of the East River, he would soon find out.

Thunder clapped somewhere overhead as five small shadows emerged from between the two rows of Variants. As he waited, five men, all extremely malnourished, wearing thick dusty beards walked hesitantly out into the open space. Looking back at the horde with confusion in his eyes, the first man turned to the crowd.

"Why are you doing this? We've given you everything you asked for and there's no way we can go back there now; he'll kill us...or worse."

A tall rather stocky looking Variant moved quickly away from the others and stood within inches of the man who appeared to be questioning the directive he'd been given. The beast raised its meaty arm and slammed it down hard onto the head of the already broken man, knocking him to the ground. The Variant then came back around and gripped the thin man by the neck, pulling him to his feet.

The beast brought its face even with the man's and motioned for him to keep moving. The man fought to free himself before getting back to his feet and joining the others. The five men now stood shoulder to shoulder and stared at the ground, avoiding any form of eye contact.

Watching as the men shuffled nervously, a few now shivering under the brand new rain, he was unable to control himself a second longer. It had to happen now. He was changed and although he was only able to remember bits and pieces of his former life, he couldn't imagine anything so powerful. This wasn't about hate or jealousy, or even fear, anger, or love. This was about something different. This was about survival.

Breathing out heavily through his upturned nose, he marched to the five men and stood over them. The man in the middle began urinating on himself and the man directly to his left shook his head, and under his breath said, "Keep it together man."

The two men at the far right began to chuckle and then quickly quieted themselves. They turned to one another and through the thick layer of dirt and dried blood, their faces turned a deep shade of red.

Moving away from the now embarrassed man at the center of the group, he lumbered to the two who'd attempted to quiet their laughter. Catching another glimpse of himself in the first floor windows of the UN Building, he nearly flinched. He was again caught off guard by the complete change in his appearance.

The monster staring back at him was no longer Blake Chambers. And although he still remembered his name, not much else from his former self remained. The translucent skin, the swollen sucker lips, the blacked out crevasses that encircled his yellow eyes, everything about who he used to be was gone.

This wasn't him. He couldn't understand it, how it happened. But it did, and somewhere deep down inside, he liked it. He now wanted it, he needed it. The mysterious desire to destroy, to assert his physical dominance, had to be released and it needed to happen now.

Twisting back to the two men, Blake grabbed the first by the waist and held him three feet off the ground. He raised his left arm and used the six-inch talon protruding from the end of his meaty claw-like hand to separate the man's head from his body.

Looking over the incensed horde, he brought the

man's limp body to his popping sucker lips and began to feed. He tore at the opening above the man's shoulders and slurped at the mess that he held at the end of his right arm. He was intoxicated with not only the taste, but also the visceral response from his followers.

The crowd that numbered almost one hundred again pounded the abandoned vehicles. They howled under the growing cloud cover and the rain continued to fall as they praised the merciless display of aggression.

As Blake pulled away and slurped one last mouthful, he dropped the decapitated body to the asphalt. The remaining four men now huddled together under his shadow, as the one who'd urinated on himself begged for his life.

"Please, we'll help you find more. We'll do anything…please!"

As the man's voice trailed off and the area fell into silence, Blake looked back toward the north end of 1st Avenue. Through the falling rain, he saw a brief flash of light followed by a short crack. And a fraction of a second later, his right leg began to warm as the translucent skin just below his right knee was peeled back, and the projectile buried itself into the street below. He'd been shot; however, it was only a flesh wound.

— 14 —

The pack traveled as one. They moved quickly up 42nd as two of the more agile Variants led them toward the Bryant Metro Station. Blake was out in front with the headless body of his male victim slung over his right shoulder. And as they approached 6th Avenue, the horde began to slow, looking between the three buildings that framed the massive intersection.

Unaware of why the majority of his group had pulled back before crossing over 6th, he continued toward the entrance to the station. Still carrying the shredded corpse, he stepped up onto the sidewalk and was annoyed to see the man who'd urinated on himself less than an hour before. The man ran out ahead, looked into the stairwell, and then turned back toward Blake.

The man avoided direct eye contact and pointing into the darkness said, "No...not yet, they're still in there. They're just waiting for you."

Blake stared at the man for a moment. He understood the words he was saying, but was having trouble controlling his growing impulse to continue feeding. He dropped the headless body, turned to the three closest Variants, and nodded toward the stairs.

As the trio dropped down onto all fours and rushed by, he grabbed the closest and pointed at the body he'd laid on the sidewalk. The Variant snatched up the body and dragged it to the darkened opening. And as he watched the Variant pick up the awkward bloodied mess and toss it down into the stairwell, another voice—this one much louder and more pronounced—echoed inside his head.

"GO… GO NOW. THAT IS WHERE YOU NEED TO BE. THAT IS YOUR HOME."

He shook his head and spun quickly to his left and then back to his right. No one was there. No one was speaking. The voice was coming from within his own head, and it wasn't done.

"GO INTO THAT STATION AND TAKE WHAT IS YOURS. KILL ANYONE WHO STANDS IN YOUR WAY. DO IT NOW."

The three Variants started slowly into the stairwell. They looked spooked, as if whatever was waiting below was daring them to come forward. They stepped slowly, moving cautiously as they descended out of sight.

Another ten seconds and a tortured shriek boomed from the depths, echoing out into the street. The horde that had moved closer to the stairs slowed. And as the body of one of the Variants rocketed out of the darkness, end over end, like a rag doll being tossed into the air, those closest to the entrance skittered away.

"NOW," the voice in his head said. *"GO NOW AND DESTROY IT!"*

As another disturbing howl came from the blacked-out entrance to the Bryant Metro Station, he dropped to all fours and bolted toward the darkness. His hooked talons digging into the concrete, he spat and snorted as he picked up speed. Reaching the steel framed entrance, he galloped through the busted out glass and leapt from the top step.

Blake glided over the long set of stairs, his eyes adjusting quickly to the change in illumination, and as the platform below came into view, he located the source of the Variants' distressed cries.

Reaching up, he dug his claw into the concrete overhead and slowed himself just enough to drop to the platform and avoid slamming into a sea of unfamiliar Variants. There were more here than on the street above and as he scanned the crowd, he quickly realized that these were not part of his following.

There were four of the barely recognizable beasts holding tight to one of his own. They had the much smaller Variant spread out, each gripping a limb. They were attempting to pull the wailing beast apart. Arms flexed and legs stretched beyond natural limits, the scout he'd sent into the station shrieked in agony.

He stared into the eyes of the four henchmen, staying with each long enough to let them know that this would be their final act. The defiant beasts only howled back, looking to one another and then over their right shoulders. Something or someone lurked near the second set of stairs leading to the tracks below.

As he looked over the horde beyond the four holding his scout, he spotted his third follower—the last to enter the stairwell. It had already met its fate and now lay face-down in a growing pool of its own blood.

Blake pulled back his swollen lips, exposing a jagged set of broken and bloodied teeth and roared at the crowd. As they began to fill in behind one another—now four rows deep—they howled for their four friends to end the standoff. Beating their thick clawed hands into the tiled walls and concrete flooring, they dared Blake to step forward.

He wasn't afraid, he wanted this. It would be over quickly, either for him or for them, but either way he'd find out in the next few minutes who owned this station, and he sure as hell wasn't going to let the beast hiding near the second set of stairs forget who he was.

Breathing out hard through his nose, Blake exploded away from the bottom step, his right arm extended toward the four holding his scout. As he drew closer to the opposing beasts, he noticed that they were bigger than those who followed him away from the UN Building, most at least a head taller. However, they were also a step slower than his, and as he swung his arm back to center, he ripped through the midsection of two of the henchmen, tearing out their lower intestines and evening the score with one strike.

As the two rival Variants dropped to the ground and Blake continued forward, the crowd quickly parted, revealing the beast lurking by the second set of stairs. Their leader, and the current landlord of this lair, was the biggest thing he'd ever seen. If he had to guess, the behemoth had to have outweighed him by at least sixty to eighty pounds, but again Blake assumed its weight advantage could end up being its downfall.

As the larger Variant stepped away from the railing and lumbered toward him, from somewhere in the deep reaches of his psyche, he was reminded of the story of David and Goliath. And although Blake had become a monster in his own right, this thing now standing twenty feet away was his Goliath.

As the horde opposite him began to back away, he

quickly moved left, cornering one of the others. He wrapped his meaty hand around its throat, and with only his right arm, snapped the smaller Variant's neck. He raised it into the air for the others to see and tossed it at the feet of Goliath.

His larger foe looked down and snarled. It kicked the body aside and turned its shadowed gaze back to Blake. Lowering his shoulder, Goliath moved quickly toward him. As the massive beast dropped to all fours and began to gallop, the tunnel exploded with shrieks of excitement.

As their enthusiasm quickly turned to rage, the horde again turned their attention to Blake. They'd fight their own for the opportunity to take him apart. Each with their yellow slitted eyes focused on the invisible target he wore across his chest. He had come into their home and threatened their leader. Now they wanted to show him why that was a bad idea.

Grossly outnumbered, but still determined, he would stand his ground. He would take this place from them. It was already his before he entered the stairwell and he was here to evict a few hundred former tenants. He didn't care how many of those he had to kill in the process; this station would be his.

As the crowd ahead continued toward him, his attention was pulled to the stairwell at his back. The clicking and popping of joints from those on the street above overpowered the raucous howling from those coming for him.

The comparatively smaller Variants that had chosen to stand with him were now racing down the steps in twos, threes, and fours. They scampered across the walls, moving like awkward spiders rushing around, over, and past him. They hurtled themselves at their larger counterparts without any concern for themselves.

Blake watched as the two groups slammed into one another, bodies on top of bodies, pulling, biting, and slashing. They came at one another with their jagged teeth, hooked claws, and every ounce of aggression they could muster. Thick dark blood was quickly spilled as his smaller, but more agile group of assailants instantly tore through the first line of defense, severing arms, slashing throats, and disemboweling those unfortunate enough to be positioned with their backs to the station wall.

His group appeared more organized, attacking in pairs instead of one on one. It was obvious that this wasn't their first time battling another group; however, it was the first time they'd battled for him. This looked personal and also like the group had come back here to reclaim their home.

He now knew why he'd been chosen. Why they'd led him here and what this all meant. He was the one that they trusted to take on Goliath. The only one. The massive Variant had run them from their lair and eliminated whoever came before him. Now it was time to show the much larger beast why that was a mistake.

Slamming his thick hands into the ground, Blake roared in the direction of his adversary. Goliath stared back and shook his shoulders. The massive monster opened his mouth and released a deep growl that quieted both groups. He lumbered forward on all fours and as the crowds parted, he used his well-muscled rear legs to propel himself into the air.

At the same time, Blake also went airborne and the two Alphas collided, sending them into the wall. He quickly scrambled to his feet and before Goliath had a chance to steady himself, Blake swung with a right and a left, opening up the beast from shoulder to hip.

Stepping back, Goliath howled in pain and looked over his injuries. Although superficial, just the sight of his own blood enraged the Alpha even further. He slammed his left arm into the wall, dislodging a hail of broken tile as he moved on Blake yet again.

Blake stepped back, planted his right foot, and leaned away, using Goliath's momentum against him. As his larger opponent stumbled forward, he swung down and away, slicing through a large section of Goliath's back.

The larger Alpha rolled to his feet and quickly turned back to Blake. He growled, slamming his fists into the concrete floor, but didn't move from where he stood. Turning and looking out over the station as the two groups fell back, Goliath dipped his chin and motioned with his left arm toward the tunnel that led away from the platform.

The Variants that had brought him here and fought for him slowly filtered in around, some leaving small pieces of their victims at his feet. They watched as the others hung their misshapen heads and marched further into the Bryant Metro Station and then finally out of sight. For now, they'd taken back their home. However, they also knew that this wasn't the last they'd see of the group led by the biggest Variant anyone had ever laid eyes on. This was only the beginning.

Stepping to the center and reaching to the blood splattered floor, Blake scooped up a handful of discarded body parts—ears, noses, lips—and then stringing them together, made himself a trophy necklace. He held it above his head and let out a victorious roar before sliding it over his head and around his neck.

Looking out over the crowd and across the empty

platform, he was able to force through one word.

"Ours."

— 15 —

They'd fought for rights to the station for what seemed like weeks. With every day that passed, he lost more of his warriors to the nonstop battle with Goliath's group and the intermittent explosions that leveled every part of the city above. He now sought reinforcements, not only for himself, but also for the survival of his following.

If they were to continue, they'd need to explore beyond the walls of the cramped station. They'd need to find more food. With the city nearly extinct of humans, they'd have to head back into the smaller cities and somehow draw out those who had survived...and add them to the wall.

He'd finished his body of armor with the help of two of his most trustworthy warriors less than three days before. Covered from the neck down in a patchwork of human bones, he'd left nothing to chance. If Goliath came for him again, he would definitively have the upper hand.

The final piece, a cloak made from the dehydrated flesh of his most recent kills, hung over his back as he waited for his human collaborators to move through the agitated crowd of Variants. The two men stared at the ground as they walked to the edge of the platform and stood at the foot of his throne made from the bones of those who'd gone before them.

"We have good news," said the desperately thin man on the left. "We know where they are."

He nodded and held out his hand.

"Plum Island…there are more of them at Plum Island. Probably more than fifty. We can be there in a few hours, but it won't be easy to get in and out."

Again he nodded, this time, however, he turned to the second man, looking for confirmation.

The continued silence pulled the second man's eyes from the floor. He paused for a moment and then spoke quietly, as if he was unsure if he was allowed. "Yes…there are people there, but they also know about this place, that we are here."

The first man turned and shook his head. Furrowing his brow, he began to speak, but was cut short as the quiet man continued.

"They also know about you, they've started calling you The Bone Collector. They're afraid of you, but are still coming. They're already in the city."

The Bone Collector. He'd forgotten most everything from before three weeks ago and at times even his name sounded unfamiliar rolling around in his head. But *The Bone Collector* was a name he found to be fitting. He even liked it, and if he ever had the chance to meet those who'd given him the name, he'd be sure to show them just how insightful they really were.

He attempted to vocalize his new moniker. "The…Bo—"

In the distance, the sound of multiple Blackhawk helicopters interrupted. He turned back toward the men at his feet and motioned toward the stairs leading to the street.

"How...long?"

The first man stepped forward and without looking him directly in the eye said, "Maybe ten minutes, maybe less."

He motioned toward the back of the station, away from the platform and toward the gruesome web of humans bodies set along the rear wall. Most were either already dead or incapacitated. Their dwindling supply of food, as well as what was left of his army of warriors, needed to be moved into the tunnels.

The Bone Collector stood from his throne and roared. "GO!"

The horde skittered away, joints clicking and popping as they moved off the platform and back into the tunnels. The men standing in front of the throne also ran off searching for a place to hide.

As the whop-whop-whop of the Blackhawks' blades faded, he stepped down and followed the others into the darkness. But before disappearing into the larger tunnel, he noticed one of Goliath's scouts standing at the stairs leading to the street. When the Variant noticed he was being watched, he scampered back up the stairs, shrieking as his reached the street.

Working his way through the cramped passageway, the Bone Collector reached the opening that led into three additional tunnels. Stepping from the larger opening into a small stream of blood and trash, his rear legs were taken out from under him.

The unmistakable thundering of the F-18 Super Hornet only narrowly preceded the earth shaking detonation that had him clinging to the walls of the underground corridor. Chunks of concrete were dislodged, the ground under his clawed feet shifted, and as he dropped down onto all fours, a dense wave of radiating heat tore through the network of tunnels.

As the dust settled, the world was calm. He dropped into the alcove between the two sets of tunnels and just listened. The soft wailing of injured Variants could be heard from the streets above and the hissing of a pressurized pipe that had severed now blocked one of his exits. He'd have to go back the way he came, if that were even possible.

He waited, and as the seconds turned to minutes, another explosion sounded in the distance, and then another. And after the area had gone silent once again, a fourth detonation rocked the city, although the last three appeared to be moving away from the station.

It was time to move, time to follow his humans out to the island they'd described. He leaned into the tunnel that he had come through only minutes before, and as the tiny hair-like spikes rose from his hands and feet, he hung upside down waiting for movement from the other end.

From somewhere deep in the station, probably not far from his lair, the high pitched wail of a Variant rang out. He dropped from his position and galloped quietly toward the platform at the end of the tunnel. Before he'd covered half the distance, four quick gunshots broke the tension-filled silence.

Again he advanced, although slowing twenty feet before the drop, another round of bombs fell over the city. Again much closer to the station than he was comfortable with, the ensuing fireball lit the tunnels at his back. Glancing over his shoulder, the shockwave tossed him into the air.

Thrown to wet concrete, he rolled onto his side and quickly dug his right hand into the wall. Waiting for what was to come, he lowered his shoulder and crawled forward on all fours, breathing in the ash-filled air as he moved.

Nearing the end of the tunnel, he heard a howl from somewhere deep inside the station; however, it wasn't one of his. It also wasn't one of Goliath's. The sound wasn't a Variant at all. It was something familiar, but also something he couldn't quite place, it was something from his former life, one he didn't care to remember. Whatever it was, he was going to kill it.

He moved to the edge of the tunnel and scanned the area below. Scorched bodies of multiple Variants lay in awkward positions for as far back as he could see. Spot fires peppered the landscape, still burning a path from where the fireball must have torn through the station.

Another round of gunfire broke out, closely followed by three deep thuds and the wailing of humans. They were shouting, crying, and calling for help. No one answered, but the sound of Variants skittering through the tunnels battled with the voices in his head, demanding he eliminate the human threat.

Off the edge and onto the platform below, he turned to see six of the juveniles packed tightly together in the tunnel. These child Variants watched him for a sign of what they were supposed to do. With the street above an all-out war zone and the station erupting in gunfire, there was only one way forward. He was going to kill anyone who stood in his way.

To his right, four men stood with weapons trained in his direction, at least three of which were Marines. Within the fraction of a second it took them to squeeze off eight consecutive rounds, he was on them. One in each hand, he pulled the first two off their feet and tossed the small man in his right hand out toward the station platform. The man's body summersaulted through the air and slammed into the ground with an audible thud.

The second was tossed before the first hit the ground and crashed into the side of an abandoned train car, breaking out the only remaining window. The body dropped to the tracks and slumped forward.

More shots tore through the smoke-filled station as he twisted left and clutched the other two. One by the neck and the other around the waist. He launched them simultaneously toward the rapid crack-crack-crack of the automatic weapons.

The flailing bodies ripped a path through the smoke and ash, giving him a glimpse of what lay directly ahead. Three more humans, maybe four, weapons ready and turning his way. Their hushed voices spoke quickly as they attempted to move one of the injured men he had thrown.

One of the remaining men moved away from the others and was running toward him. He couldn't understand why. He'd given these Marines every reason to go the other way; however, this soldier continued to test fate.

Waving his clawed hand through the smoke, he saw that the man moving toward him was running on prosthetics. Jutting from his lower legs were thin metal blades that propelled him forward much more swiftly than the others before him. He was going to make sure that young Marine would never forget this day.

"Help! You have to help!" Another human voice boomed from somewhere further in the station.

The man on the blades moved to the platform deck just below him and began to climb. While the bladed soldier was occupied, he scaled the wall at his back. He'd come at the Marine from the opposite side of the platform, give the small human a few seconds to see his face before ending his life.

Down onto the open floor, he scanned the bottoms of the stairwells leading to the north and east. Nothing moved. The remains of dozens of bodies—both human and Variant—lay in a perfectly formed ring at the bottom of the stairs, beyond that two more Marines leveled their weapons at a group of armored juveniles and began to fire.

Over his left shoulder, another four Variants clung to the ceiling watching over the Marines they'd captured, as well as their human collaborators. The two aggressively thin men, with a thick layer of ash hanging from their beards, avoided eye contact with the Marines and only stared at the platform floor.

Taking the pair of Marines, he dragged them toward the man with the blades. He dropped them within feet of his new target, raised his thickly muscled arms and roared through the fading smoke. As his thunderous shriek echoed through the rest of the station, he stood over the Marines, pointed down at them with a long hooked talon, and turned his eyes toward the solider with the metal blades.

Humanity was lost to him long before this moment. Over the last several weeks, he'd come to view the much smaller and weaker entities as little more than a source of fuel. And although very few had managed to survive in his presence, this insignificant human with metal sticks for legs was different. He didn't appear to be frightened, and was also the first he'd come across who not only didn't retreat, but actually had the audacity to run toward him.

To his surprise, the Marine leveled his weapon and fired off a shot that narrowly missed the right side of his head. Two more shots quickly followed, both shattering the femur and sternum bones that made up the heavy armor covering his chest and ribcage.

Wailing in pain, he twisted to the side as the Marine fired a fourth shot that slipped in between a small gap in the armor near his right shoulder. The projectile tore through his shoulder, sending fragments from the hipbone he wore as a shoulder pad into the thick column at his back.

He raced across the scorched concrete, dropped his head, and plowed into the bladed man. His shoulder caught the Marine in the chest and drove them both into the platform. The smaller man flipped backward and then skidded to a stop as his helmet ripped free and rolled out of sight.

The Marine was fighting to breathe as he rolled onto his back and reached for another weapon. The soldier took aim and fired three quick shots, the first penetrated one of the trophy ears on his necklace and the next two dug into the thick muscular flesh just above his collarbone. A wave of warm discomfort quickly ran through his neck and down into his chest.

He quickly realized what this was and knew he didn't have long. His vision began to blur and his legs felt unstable. He stepped forward, grabbed the Marine by the right blade and launched him into the air. He watched as the man's body came to rest alongside one of the other soldiers who had attempted to drive him from his home.

The Bone Collector lowered his eyes, and attempting to focus, pulled out the three bloody darts and threw them aside. The small man who he was about to kill had tried to sedate him, attempting to use a few tranquilizer darts to bring the confrontation to a quick end. Little did the bladed man know that this was far from over.

Stumbling forward, he turned to check on the juveniles. His eyes now betraying him, he was only able to make out their translucent silhouettes as he moved toward the bladed Marine. Parting his engorged lips, he only managed a single word.

"K-ill."

He extended his right arm and pointed at the Marine. The drugs now racing through his body had begun to eclipse his will to fight. He was no longer able to control his lower half and dropped to his knees. He blinked twice, and still struggling to fight the inevitable, fell face first to the concrete platform.

As the sounds of battle faded and the Marine with metal blades moved away, he was finally overcome by the powerful sedative.

— 16 —

Awakening on the asphalt, his mouth was dry and his arms and legs heavy. He moved to his knees and then pulled himself up using the open door of a torched police cruiser. The metal frame was still warm to the touch, and as he moved out into the street, the Bone Collector surveyed his devastated city.

The landscape along 42nd was much different than the last time he'd come to the surface. Too many to count, the broken bodies of Variants littered the sidewalks and streets as far as he could see. Abandoned vehicles sat dying underneath large chunks of concrete, while their interiors still glowed with the illumination of waning spot fires.

The area beyond the station crawled with activity as Variants skittered out from behind the decimated buildings along 6th Avenue. Others crept slowly away from Bryant Park, their badly fractured bodies clicking and popping out of sync in awkward fits and starts. They appeared dazed, and under the darkened sky, to have lost their natural sense of direction.

He looked out over the confused and somewhat frantic crowds, finally noticing what he was searching for.

His only remaining human collaborator was closely following two large Variants who dragged a screaming Marine by the arm through the middle of the burned out street.

He moved to them, took the Marine by the ankle and ignoring the absolute chaos, started down 42nd toward the water. Blood had run from the shoulder wound he'd suffered at the hands of the bladed Marine, although it had already begun to seal itself off behind a thick layer of scar tissue.

On the move, his cape of dehydrated human flesh flapped in the driving wind, and crossing alongside the New York Public Library, the panicked Marine he was dragging began to scream.

"I'll show you, I'll take you there!"

The Bone Collector pulled back and quickly dropped to all fours. He leaned over the Marine and attempted to speak; however, he was only able to utter a few incoherent syllables. He slowly breathed out through his nose and started once again.

"W-here...where are the others?"

The Marine's voice shook. "Plum Island. They're at Plum Island.

From further back in the crowd of trailing Variants, the remaining human collaborator moved in close. "I know where that is. I've seen it—"

The Marine interrupted as he stared up at his captor. "There are doctors there who're creating a weapon to kill you."

The Bone Collector moved up onto his rear legs and howled as he clutched the Marine with one hooked claw and motioned toward the end of 42nd with the other. He waited as the human collaborator slipped in behind and then the riotous crowd of more than sixty started toward the East River.

***

Within an hour, they'd made their way through the burned out city and down to the water. Awaiting them were just over forty human collaborators. Most were wearing tattered military uniforms and being watched over as they loaded a small fleet of eight boats. There were a handful of Coast Guard vessels as well as a few that were built for pure speed. And as the Variants that had come with him from Bryant Station leapt out onto the dock, the men backed away and moved toward the boats.

He lumbered slowly toward the end of the dock, eyeing the men who'd been chosen to accompany his group to the island. Most carried rifles or handguns. There was even one who had an AT-4 single-shot launcher slung over his shoulder. They avoided eye contact, and as he drew closer, they quickly jumped into the idling boats.

Still dragging the tortured Marine, the Bone Collector turned back to the trailing Variants and roared. As they dropped to all fours and began galloping wildly toward him, he grabbed the soldier by the neck, tossed his wrecked body into the closest boat, and quickly leapt in behind a half dozen human collaborators.

The horde appeared confused, and a bit hesitant to board the unstable crafts. Variants lined the edge of the dock and waited as the collaborators moved back. Then slowly piling in, one behind another, they steadied themselves along the sides as the boats pulled away from the dock and started for Plum Island.

Rain continued to fall out of the darkened sky. It came down much harder now, and as the eight boats raced away from the city, the downed Queensboro Bridge sat in the distance. Near the center, where it sagged into the water, there appeared a familiar sight.

The Bone Collector stood hunched over the nearly unconscious Marine and stared off the starboard side at the hull of the capsized yacht. The exposed white hull sat just above the surface like a beacon that represented the complete destruction of civilization. The symbol stirred something deep inside that he couldn't readily explain. Something about it that just felt close, almost kindred.

The long line of waterborne vessels moved through the glassy water without incident and within a mile of the island, he noticed that one of the boats they'd left behind had been boarded and was now in pursuit. From this distance, it would be impossible to see the person who thought it would be a good idea to give chase; however, he figured he knew exactly who it was.

He wanted nothing more than the opportunity to end that man's life.

Now less than sixty seconds from shore, a pair of flares lit up the sky and two of the boats fell back. They'd spotted the same speedboat he had and decided to deal with it before approaching land. He didn't like the slight delay, but it was something that had to be done. That boat was gaining on them, and as they grew closer, the possibility of the man aboard shooting off another flare and signaling the unsuspecting inhabitants of Plum Island was too much of a liability.

The first boat reached the shore just slightly ahead of his, plowing through the two sets of electric fences. And as the aggressively impatient Variants began running out onto the soft sand, the Bone Collector looked toward the horizon and the white domed buildings he was about to overthrow. He would take the island and everything on it.

This place was his now and every remaining soul left on this rock was going to remember his name.

— 17 —

Collaborators followed Variants away from the beach as gunfire erupted from the towers that protected the white domed buildings. Lighting up the sky, the rounds buried in the sand and tore into the first few boats lining the shore. As he watched the chaotic mess just beginning to unfold, the Bone Collector grabbed the man to his left—the one who'd followed him from the city—and pointed toward the trees.

"Doctor...where?"

The man hesitated. He was shaking and looked quickly from the boats to the treeline and back.

"Uh... I'm not...uh—"

The Bone Collector wrapped his thick claw around the man's neck and roared.

"WHERE?"

The man flinched as he was dropped back into the boat. From just beyond the trees, a Blackhawk lifted above the tarmac, firing on the beach as it ascended. Variants skittered away, their joints clicking and popping as they rushed from the area looking for cover.

"There," the man said, "the buildings are over there. Look for number three."

From over his left shoulder, a flash streaked away from the beach. Illuminating the sand, a rocket shot across the sky and slammed into the side of the helicopter. A massive plume of orange and yellow backlit the entire island as the fiery wreckage dropped quickly back to the tarmac.

"GO!"

Tossing the man out onto the beach, the Bone Collector watched where his Variant warriors were entering the interior of the island. He gripped the back of the man's jacket and pulled him forward. They quickly moved through the trees and then along a concrete path between two buildings.

From the rear, another boat appeared out on the water. It had come from the right side of the island and moved with considerable speed as it approached the shore. A soldier stood positioned behind the Gatling gun firing at those still on shore. But as it drew to within fifty feet, the human collaborators hiding at the treeline began firing back. Within seconds, the blacked out military vessel glided to a stop.

Out into the center of the facility, he followed a group of Variants as the air raid sirens blasted from somewhere further in the facility. Off to the left, the wrecked Blackhawk lit the tarmac, casting shadows over Variants attacking a pair of Marines near the entrance to one of the domed structures.

Automatic gunfire and tracer rounds shot across the common areas and targeted a large grouping of Variants galloping away from the scorched airfield. They dropped faster than he could count, heads exploding and limbs being ripped from bodies. Unfazed, his translucent soldiers continued to charge toward the five Marines positioned along the center of the lawn.

In the opposite direction, a man and a woman carried a Marine down a set of steps and once they reached the bottom, they sat the soldier in a wheelchair. Behind them, two more women and two little girls followed. They were moving quickly down a concrete walkway toward the one of the other buildings, and as the young blond Marine quickly scanned the lawn, the others ran on ahead.

His instinct was to chase down the man in the chair and the one pushing him, although a voice from over his shoulder pulled him back.

"Hey...that's her." The collaborator he'd pulled from the boat squatted beside him, pointing toward the women moving away from the man in the chair.

"That's the doctor."

The Bone Collector brushed the man aside and watched as another wave of Variants moved on the five Marines fanned out across the lawn. He found an opening and lumbered quickly to the middle of the group. Support also came from behind as his human collaborators laid down cover fire with their shotguns and M-16s.

The man in the wheelchair stopped and shouldered a rifle as the others continued on toward the building in the distance. He took aim and fired a shot that hit one of the human collaborators dead center in the face, a river of blood bursting from the man's obliterated skull.

As the blond wheelchair-bound Marine shouted at the women, they were escorted away by an older man with a shotgun. And as they started up the steps into the building, two additional Marines moved away, sprinting for the center of the lawn.

He wanted the blond Marine in the chair. He wanted

him for himself. The only thing he wanted more was the woman doctor who he was told was creating a weapon that would destroy him. He didn't understand why, but he was curious about this human and how easily he'd gotten to her. It would be over in less than a few minutes, and those who moved into his path would pay the price.

Another woman, short haired and muscular, returned and crouched next to the man in the wheelchair. She also carried a weapon and after exchanging glances, she turned and began firing at his Variants, leveling at least six before taking a breath. However, he didn't care. He only wanted to get to the man in the chair and then to the woman doctor. He would give every last one of his followers to get what he came for.

The man in the chair again shouldered his rifle and began taking aim at the human collaborators. The Bone Collector moved in a straight line to the machine gun nest and in full view of the man in the chair, gripped one of the Marines, held him in the air and with one twist, snapped the soldier's neck.

Tossing the limp body aside, he turned and started for the Marine in the chair. The young blond man leveled his weapon and began to fire. Rounds exploded into his armor, slowing him down, but not stopping him. He was angered and as the small man in the chair fired again, he drifted back into the cover of his army of Variants.

As the short-haired woman changed her magazine and continued to fire, another joined the fight. It was the man with the shotgun, who'd guided the woman doctor and the others into the building at the far edge of the greenbelt. He came in next to the man in the chair and immediately shouldered the weapon and fired on the Variants attacking the Marines at the center of the lawn.

The man in the chair shifted focus and also began firing at those near the machine gun nest. They picked off the Variants one by one, but were only able to save two of the men before they were overrun. The pair of Marines quickly fell back, firing as they moved away from the nest.

With only seven of his Variant warriors remaining on the lawn, The Bone Collector moved to the front of the pack. The only thing between him and the woman doctor was the blond Marine in the chair and his two very foolish friends. He would kill the men and take the woman back with the others. He would make her watch as he took their lives.

As the Bone Collector hunched forward and started toward the trio, the man with the shotgun stepped away from the others and fired one devastatingly accurate shot that exploded through his armor and blew off his left arm just below the elbow. Fragmented pieces of flesh and bone shot into the army of Variants already darting forward.

The Bone Collector howled in pain as he looked from left to right searching for a place to retreat. The blond Marine in the wheelchair was already tracking him and fired off three quick shots into his armored chest plates. One of the rounds tore into his flesh, forcing him to the right. And before the next barrage began, he quickly dipped his head and vomited a thick white substance out over his amputated left arm.

The man with the shotgun, as well as the two remaining Marines, continued to fire on another pack of Variants as they dropped to all fours and galloped across the greenbelt. The three men were able to eliminate two of the skittering creatures, although the others were able to make it through unharmed.

Turning away from the trio, the Bone Collector looked back toward the building that the woman doctor had disappeared into, and roared as the Marine in the wheelchair again fired into the bony armor on his back and right side. His thickly pained howl echoed across the lawn as four of his Variants plowed into the two remaining Marines, knocking them back into the grass. The soldiers were able to cut down two of the beasts, but in the end were overcome by the unfair odds.

The man with the shotgun moved in as the two Variants lost interest in the dead Marines and again opened fire on them. He was able to eliminate the pair with three quick blasts and then twisting back to his left, leveled the barrel at the Bone Collector.

He lumbered forward, moving toward the man with the shotgun and took a blast to the side of his already splintered chest plating, sending fragments of bone and flesh rocketing past his face and neck.

As the man with the shotgun pumped the weapon, the Bone Collector grabbed it with his uninjured hand and tossed it away. Quickly turning back before his much smaller adversary had a chance to react, he gripped him around the throat and lifted him off the ground, blood running down his densely muscled arm. And with one flex of his meaty claw, he snapped the man's neck and tossed him aside.

Turning his attention back to the Marine in the wheelchair, the soldier fired off two quick rounds and shouted.

"NO!"

The Bone Collector dropped to all fours and launched himself into the young Marine's wheelchair. The ensuing collision sent the smaller man flailing backward and onto the paved walkway. The Marine scrambled back to his rifle and rolled over onto his back, as the woman who remained at his side lunged forward and drove the blade of her knife into the Bone Collector's back.

Twisting left, he swatted at the woman and knocked her back into the steps of the building. He then turned back as the Marine cursed at him and fired a round that tore off a large piece of his right ear. Reaching down, he grabbed the man with the messy blond hair by one of his broken legs and tossed him down the concrete path.

As the injured Marine clawed to get away, the Bone Collector moved in over him and hoisted him into the air. Spinning back toward the building, the woman he'd tossed away had returned. She leapt onto his back and again drove the knife into his thick muscles. Using the jagged edge of his severed left arm, the Bone collector slashed at her, knocking her back to the ground.

The Marine he held at arm's length again cursed as he struggled to breathe. The small man gripped his thick forearm with one hand and began striking him in the eye with the other. The Bone Collector howled as the man's knuckles tore into the soft fleshy tissue just below his eye. He'd given the young Marine enough time. He needed to end this and get back to the reason he came here.

As the Marine fought to take another breath, blinking and squirming as he was raised higher into the air, the Bone Collector tightened his grip and twisted his vice-like clawed hand to the left, snapping the young man's neck. It was over. He tossed the young Marine's body aside and looked toward the building at the end of the concrete path.

The woman with the knife started to crawl toward the Marine's motionless body. She was shouting something incoherent, and as he reached for her, a single shot from somewhere in the distance plowed through his back armor. He rounded his shoulders and grabbing the woman by the hair, started for the building straight ahead.

She struggled under his grip and called out to the fallen soldier as he pulled her toward the steps at the front of the building. Twisting and peering over his left shoulder, the Bone Collector saw the Marine who'd shot him in the back now firing on another pack of Variants. As he reached the steps he handed the woman off, quickly climbed to the door, and nearly ripped it from its hinges.

He looked to the dozen Variants that had rushed from other areas of the facility and pointed into the building.

"I...want...all...of them."

Out onto to the concrete path, he led the way back to the waiting boats. The woman doctor cried as he carried her over his shoulder. She pounded her small fists into what remained of his bony armor and spoke softly into the night. She was attempting to convince herself that everything was going to be alright, that she was going to find a way out of this.

Reaching the beach, the Bone Collector waited as his Variants placed the other women and the two little girls into the first boat. He waved them on and watched as they skittered into the adjoining vessels. And finally climbing in behind them, he nodded to his human collaborators and pointed his hooked claw out over the water.

"Go."

A minute later, they were racing back down the East River toward New York City. Toward his home.

— 18 —

He had forgotten just about every detail of his former life. The only thing that remained was the vague memory of his former injury. The headaches, the nausea, the excessively debilitating and frequent blackouts, those things were gone. The side effects of his many concussions were part of who he used to be. But he didn't miss that person, and only rarely had flashes of what it meant to be human. What it meant to be less than what he'd become. The Blake Chambers from three months ago was gone, and as he led his army of Variant warriors back to his lair, he was okay with that.

In less than two hours, they'd reached the docks and unloaded their civilian prisoners. Thick rain now washed away the layer of ash that covered every inch of the city. It pelted his head and neck as he scanned the far end of 42nd for the only thing that would stand between him and the Bryant Metro Station. The Bone Collector hadn't seen Goliath in days, but returning home, he had a feeling that tonight would be different.

The half dozen Variants who carried the women and two small girls began to move at an increased pace. They had made their way to the front of the advancing horde, climbing over torched vehicles and skittering along the destroyed sidewalks. However, he wanted them closer, he felt the need to keep his human prisoners alive for the time being. He wasn't going to allow one of the rival groups to destroy the woman doctor or the children.

He dropped to all fours, pounded his fists into the asphalt and shrieked at the offending Variants. Their heads shot back, a few returning his animalist howl, and although they continued on, the group slowed their pace.

Shifting his gaze, he watched as the woman doctor pounded the back of the large Variant he had allowed to carry her. She squirmed, frantically attempting to free herself and screeched as her captor tightened his talon down around her ankle, cutting into her flesh.

The woman doctor fought harder. She continued to slam her fists into the back of the Variant, and when he didn't respond, she pulled back her left leg, and kneed her unsuspecting captor squarely in the throat. As the Variant's head shot back, she could feel the fleshy part of his neck give way under her kneecap.

The massive beast screeched in agony and tossed her to the cold wet concrete. Her body slammed into the ground, and as she rolled onto her back, she was already kicking and screaming.

"No!" she shouted. "Leave us alone."

The Variant was over her before the last word left her lips. He ran his thick claw over his injury and then tilted his head from side to side. The woman doctor scooted backward as the Variant slashed at her, finally grabbing ahold of her left boot and dragging her toward his awaiting mouth.

She screamed and tried to pull away, but he was simply too strong. He allowed her to dig her fingers into the concrete and scoot backward a few inches and then appeared to smile as he dragged her back. The Variant looked like he was toying with her, like he enjoyed the escalation of fear that she was experiencing.

She pulled away once more and as the muscular Variant began to drag her back, the Bone Collector stood up on his rear legs and lumbered up onto the sidewalk. He moved in behind the Variant, and with the woman doctor still shouting into the night, he raised his severed left arm and jammed the exposed bone into the back of the beast's head.

The woman doctor pulled away and fell onto her back. She stopped fighting and only lay on the concrete with her head atop a damp black ball cap. She stared up at the sky as the Bone Collector gently pulled her off the sidewalk with his right arm. She appeared to be mumbling to herself.

Tossing her over his shoulder, he continued to stare at the ground, and in particular at the soaking wet black ball cap that her head had fallen on. He knew it was familiar, but he wasn't exactly sure why. The letters meant nothing to him now; however, he had a feeling that they must have at one point. *BXF Technologies*. He wanted to remember, but for now it would remain a mystery.

Back out into the street, the skies rumbled. He'd heard the familiar sound all too often over the last several weeks. They were coming yet again. They were coming to destroy the city. They were coming to destroy his home.

A pair of jets streaked across the skyline. They disappeared behind the torched buildings of downtown before he was able to see where they had come from. Calling out to his small army of Variants, the Bone Collector pointed his hooked claw toward the Bryant

Metro Station.

"GO!"

Before he could get a secured grip on the woman doctor, they were on the move. They'd reach the stairs to the station in just under sixty seconds; however, as the sounds of the jets bled into the silence of night, it was replaced with another familiar sound. The whop-whop-whop of a Blackhawk helicopter boomed from somewhere near the East River.

Fighting to run, he could see ahead as the woman with short hair—the one who fought beside the young Marine in the wheelchair—had gotten free. She had fought with one of the female Variants and was now chasing after another who was carrying the two little girls.

Pointing at her with a long hooked talon, the Bone Collector ordered two of his Variants after her. They moved in quickly and took her to the ground. The woman struggled to get free, but the female Variant she'd been fighting with came out of nowhere and leapt in on top of the others.

Moving toward the commotion, the Bone Collector drew back his injured left arm. Holding tight to the woman doctor over his right shoulder, he was stopped in his tracks as the three Variants released the short-haired woman and skittered over to his side. The other Variants released their human prisoners, moved in around him, and stared up at the building directly ahead. He also released the woman doctor and watched as she walked slowly to the opposite sidewalk.

He knew he'd run into them again; he was just hoping he'd get to his lair first. Out here on the devastated streets of New York City, he and his small army of Variants would suffer from the sheer number of those who stood with Goliath. But he wasn't intimidated, he'd been waiting for this moment.

As his human prisoners scrambled together and moved away, the first shot was fired. One of his collaborators shot at the opposing Variants, who'd crawled down the face of the building and now stared back at the Bone Collector and his small group of warriors.

A second shot was fired by one of the collaborators as both groups charged forward. Their translucent bodies crashed into one another, a few of the smaller Variants slamming backward into the street and then attempting to rejoin the fight.

The mess of disjointed arm and legs and mouths and snapping jaws became a blur as the Bone Collector lowered his head and drove his hulking body through the middle of the crowd. As he turned to survey the damage, one of his own leapt onto his back.

The female Variant who'd attacked the short-haired woman dug her claws into his armor, only to be pulled off and speared with the bone of his exposed left elbow. He raised her into the air, allowing the others to see, before gripping her right arm and pulling it off. The giant Alpha tossed her body into the street, and as his human prisoners moved out of sight, he spotted his next victim.

Behind the chaos of the two Variant gangs stood the only other creature that matched his size. Actually, Goliath was a head taller and must have outweighed him by at least sixty pounds. The Alpha was bigger, but again slower, and tonight he'd use that disparity to rid the world of his only competition. Once and for all.

From across the street, Goliath locked eyes with the Bone Collector and snarled. He raised his massive arms in the air and then brought them down on the burnt-out minivan to his left, virtually smashing it into the ground.

The Bone Collector let out a howl that shook the street as he started toward his target. Moving through the densely packed crowd, he could hear the Blackhawk now overhead, beginning to descend. And coming out on the other end, he was caught off guard as the larger Alpha dropped his shoulder and rammed into him like a ten-ton wrecking ball.

The two behemoths slammed into the asphalt and rolled onto the sidewalk, crashing into the torched building. Coming to an abrupt stop against the brick façade, the Bone Collector found himself in new territory. He now lay under the bigger Alpha with only his right arm as leverage.

Goliath had him by the throat. He lay on his back with his head propped at an awkward angle against the four-story building. He slipped his blown apart left arm out and punched up toward the massive Alpha. He came away with nothing; the much larger Variant was positioned too far from his torso.

He rolled slightly onto his left side and forced his good arm up through the middle of Goliath's, attempting to push the mammoth beast away. Again no luck, his one arm was no match for the strength of the more massive creature.

As Goliath continued to clamp down, he could feel his throat closing under the immense pressure. And looking over his aggressor's right shoulder, he was able to see one of his collaborators firing on the chopper now directly overhead. The scared human was able to strike the hovering Blackhawk with at least six rounds.

Men in military uniforms hung from the opening, and

even from this distance, the surprised look they all wore was clearly evident. One of the Marines—the man with metal blades for legs—fired from the open door. And as the Blackhawk began to drop more rapidly, he eliminated the collaborator with one shot to the head.

The Blackhawk was less than three seconds from crashing back to earth as the soldiers aboard began to bail out. One by one, they moved to the door and jumped. The last to make the leap carried a dog in his arms and quickly disappeared in the hail of ash and rain.

His vision was fading quickly under the tightening grip of the larger Alpha. A surge of white hot pain shot through his neck and into the base of his skull. The Bone Collector bucked under the massive Variant and his mind momentarily cleared.

The wet dusty ball cap from 42nd Street belonged to his friend. He couldn't remember his name, although the man's big bright smile was tattooed somewhere in the deep reaches of his mind. His friend must have made it off the yacht, although being in the city, he'd surely perished, and it may have even been at the hands of one of his own.

As the vision started to fade, the chopper slammed into the side of the building in an explosion that shook the entire city block. It blew into a thousand different pieces, forcing Goliath into the air and onto his back at the center of 42nd Street.

As the shredded pieces of the Blackhawk's blades tore into the asphalt all around him, the Bone Collector quickly got to his feet and used his right arm to pull one of the still flaming pieces from the asphalt. He moved in over a dazed Goliath and shoved it through the massive Alpha's chest, extinguishing the bright orange flames.

The beast was gone as fast as he'd come. The Bone Collector leaned over his former adversary and vomited a mouthful of black blood out over the limp body. He'd taken back the city and his home. And as he watched his human prisoners run off toward the destroyed public library with the remaining Marines from the Blackhawk, he looked around and roared into the night.

In unison, more than a hundred Variants began to wail. They watched as their leader was defeated, and although their guttural moans held a twinge of anguish, they absolutely were not grieving. These creatures still outnumbered his own by more than two to one. What they were doing was calling for his head.

The Bone Collector roared back in defiance, and as his small group of human collaborators and Variant warriors gathered around, he started in the direction his prisoners had run.

Lumbering forward, he scanned the streets as the familiar roar of jets once again filled the air. He pushed on and as he reached the front of the crowd, the other gang of Variants rushed in off the sidewalks.

They skittered along the tops of burned out vehicles, in between abandoned delivery trucks, and over shattered newsstands. They were chasing him and his Variants as the Marines from somewhere in the opposite direction fired automatic weapons and launched grenades. 42nd Street was now an outright war zone.

Within fifty yards of the upcoming building and along the left side of the street, he looked toward a set of windows on the fourth floor. Through the intermittent gunfire and the random explosions, his vision crystallized. From his vantage, he could make out two separate faces.

A large man and a boy sat facing the street and

watching the mayhem. The defeated eyes of the man glowed in the night behind a dirty ash-covered window. He was hunched over the small boy who had tears running down his face. The man hugged the boy and appeared to be talking to him.

In a brief moment of clarity, he realized what he was looking upon. Dwight had indeed made it off the yacht. He had also somehow managed to save the small boy they'd been traveling with. And for reasons unknown to him, he turned away from the window and pointed his Variants in the opposite direction.

He dipped his scarred head, twisted his massive shoulders, and lumbered toward the New York Public Library. Movement ahead gave him hope that his human prisoners were somewhere in the building. But as he turned to face the set of doors directly ahead, he eyed the bladed Marine behind the barrel of his weapon.

There was an explosion in his mind as he felt the realization crashing in around him. He knew what this was—what was about to happen. He remembered. And even though it was only a flash, it was everything. Who he had been, his friends, his family, every single detail of his former life…all at once. He also had the memory of what brought him to this place. Tumbling off the yacht and waking along the edge of the East River. He saw their faces, each and every one of them. His victims, be they human or Variant, in their final moments.

While neither elated nor angered, he was accepting. There was no emotion, and he had no choice.

Less than a fraction of a second later, a crack echoed through the streets and the bullet racing away from the doorway entered his head. He dropped to his knees, his shoulders slumped forward, his face now caved in, and the back of his skull blown out onto 42nd Street.

Blake Chambers died in the frigid waters of the East River more than a month before. And now, out on the destroyed streets of New York City, the Bone Collector was also gone.

Extinction: Trippin'

by

Mark Tufo

An Extinction Cycle Novella

Prologue

"*Gawd when is this lecture going to be over?* Bitch can drone for hours!" Rebecca Kranston flung her head back, her long blond hair draping over the back of her chair. She was seated near the back of the large amphitheater lecture hall in the newly constructed Sanford S. Atwood Chemistry Center.

"Shhh…Becky," her sorority sister Claren laughed nervously.

"Are you kidding me? I could get out into the aisle and start fapping and Professor Flappy Mouth McFlapperson Springsteen wouldn't notice. She'd just keeping talking in that boring-ass monotone way that she does. I bet she doesn't even breathe."

"Will you be quiet? I'm trying to take notes." Devon McCourty had turned around to berate the young woman.

"Then maybe you should have sat closer," Becky shot back, then she sneered at him. "Or are you just looking to see if I'm fapping?" She spread her legs apart and brought her pointer finger to her lips in a seductive manner.

Devon immediately blushed a deep shade of crimson before turning back around.

"I thought you looked a little light in your loafers," Becky laughed.

Claren was embarrassed and wanted to move as many rows away from the caustic girl as she could. But it was common knowledge on campus that Becky Cranston's parents had money and she had the looks of a top tier model, two things that made her a powerful ally or a terrible enemy and she preferred the former much more than the latter.

"Come on Claren, let's just go. I can barely stay awake."

"We can't, Becky. You're close to failing this class and attendance is almost twenty percent of the grade."

"Fine, wake me when it's over." She'd no sooner closed her eyes when the campus alarm rang out. This had just been installed due to the recent glut of campus shootings. "Great," she stated as she opened one eye. "Another murdering, suicidal asshole with a gun. Why doesn't he just shove the muzzle up his ass and blow holes in his brain?"

"Let's go, let's go!" Professor Springsteen shouted. At thirty-two, she'd been one of the youngest to ever reach tenure at the university. At seventy-two, she was one of the oldest still teaching. She'd lost her love for it nearly two decades ago but truly feared what she would do with the rest of her life if she didn't keep doing it. Each building had "safe-zones" designated for just such emergencies. The Professor had moved to the far left and was holding open a door to the stairwell that led down into the underground labs. These were initially put in for faculty to work on level-2 pathogens, but parents' and students' rights activists had taken a great affront to having potentially lethal viruses being studied right under a lecture hall and until a virtually unattainable degree of safety could be reached, the state of the art facility was collecting dust.

"Screw this. It's just a drill. Let's go back to the house and do some shots." Becky had grabbed Claren's arm and was pulling her away from the steady flow of students swimming downstream.

"We can't know that, Becky, and if it is a drill, the Professor will be taking attendance down there."

"When did you become such a slug, Claren? Don't worry about it. My parents will buy a wing or something and I'll graduate just fine."

"Yeah, but what about me?" Claren asked as Becky pulled her out of the classroom.

They ran out of the hall, through the open atrium, and were standing on the top step of the large stone staircase. Students were running recklessly in every direction.

"Doesn't look like a drill, Becky," Claren said nervously.

"Makes it that much more exciting!" Becky was taking the stairs down, two at a time, a reluctant Claren in tow. "I want to see the shooter before the police kill him, but I don't hear...oh there it is." The staccato burst of a weapon broke through the screams of frightened students and faculty running for cover. Becky was pulling Claren forward while also looking for the camera app on her phone so she could take video of the man during his last few breaths before the authorities got to him.

"Maybe it will be a head shot! We can watch his brains get splattered all over the pavement and I could have that on my phone forever! Wonder how many likes I could get on Facebook for that! I'll be an Instagram smash!"

Claren had finally dug her heels in when there was

constant gunfire to the side of them and she realized there was more than one active shooter. Even Becky had stopped to take notice. "Mr. 'super geeky lonely with a gun' has a friend?" Becky asked.

They'd been still for a few seconds when they heard and saw four students off to their left come screaming and running from around the corner of the residential hall not more than fifty yards away. Claren realized just how exposed and vulnerable they were in the middle of the open quad, which led to all points within the six-hundred acre campus.

"This...this isn't a drill and we're in danger." Claren had decided to change who was leading and grabbed Becky's arm. She was pulling her back to the building they'd moments before evacuated; the sight in front of them stopped the girls short. Five impossibly deformed creatures covered from head to toe in blood had pulled down the slowest of the quad runners. Blood arced high into the air as they tore into him with their claws and teeth. They'd ripped at him so vigorously, body parts were flung into the air. Becky had nearly thrown up when she'd seen what looked suspiciously like a liver fall wetly to the ground. Four had stayed to enjoy their meal, the fifth was looking for desert.

"Come on!" Claren urged Becky who was shutting down from the shock of the sight.

"What are they?" Becky asked as she kept her head turned to the action. Two of the creatures left their mutilated kill and were moving incredibly fast toward a remaining trio of students, one who'd had the misfortune to be barefoot and had stepped on something sharp, slowing him down considerably due to his limping gait.

"Oh, gawd." Becky reached up to her mouth in a

desperate and failed attempt to hold back the bile that poured forth from her stomach. Warm chunks of her half-digested bran muffin flowed through and around her fingers. One of the creatures caught the scent of her vomit and immediately looked over to the two girls.

Claren turned in time to see that the thing had spotted them. Becky had long strings of stomach juice hanging from her mouth and dripping from her hand.

"Becky come on!" Claren urged again. The beast's mouth puckered as it zeroed in on its next meal. A ravenously long tongue poked out from that round orifice, sampling the air. It had halved the distance in under three seconds. Claren's left foot had just come down on the first step of the Aston building when she heard shots. A security guard standing atop the stairs had completely unloaded his service revolver into the diseased being just as it leapt for the girls. He waved them on...as if they needed the added impetus. He was fumbling in his pocket for extra rounds when Claren came abreast of him.

"Thank you," she managed to say as she pushed into the door at full speed. He briefly acknowledged the girl with a head nod, but before he could reload he was struck hard from the side and his shoulder blade bitten through. A searing pain rocketed up his spine and radiated out across his brain plate. He flailed out and struck the creature on the top of the head with the butt of his weapon. Though he repeatedly brought the weapon down, he did not revel in the crunch as he crushed its skull in. The pain from the bite wound was akin to pouring scalding bacon grease onto an eyeball—or so he imagined. He collapsed next to the two fallen creatures, taking in heavy breaths as he attempted to staunch the flow of blood from his side.

Byron Martinez had wanted to be a policeman for as long as he could remember, he'd even taken the entrance exam and was prepared to enter into the next cadet training cycle. That was until his long time girlfriend, Penelope Whiteside, had gotten pregnant. He'd married her within the month and she'd convinced him that being a cop was too dangerous for a man with a new bride and baby. He'd agreed. They'd settled on campus security thinking the worst he would have to deal with was vandalism and excessive drinking.

"I did pretty good, Pen," he said as he tore a strip from his undershirt and stuffed it into a hole that would not coagulate. "Tell the baby I love her." He tried to stand, but felt incredibly light-headed and burning with fever. He yanked off his blue security uniform shirt, he hardly noticed the blood-red blotches forming up and down the length of his arms. He screamed out in pain as the joints in his elbows and knees began to click and pop loudly. He was angry, angry that he was going to die young and alone, with his wife and beautiful baby at home; angry that he would never see her grow up and start a life of her own. Then he became violently irate because he was so hungry. Suddenly he was starving. He turned to get on all fours, and noticed his reflection, clearly visible in a window. He was unsure of what was staring back at him...but at that moment he didn't care. All he wanted, no—all he needed, was to eat, and his food had just run through that very doorway. He bit off a large fibrous chunk of meat from his own arm before he bounded off.

He smashed his head full force into the door; a starburst formed in the heavy glass. He reared back and struck again, this time making it halfway through. His savagery intensified as a large, long, jagged piece of the window scraped down his forehead, tore through his eye, and traveled halfway down his chest, leaving a deep laceration that bled voraciously. He screeched out in pain, yet he backed up again and blew through what remained of the barrier. He could smell the girls; their perfume and soap and the blessed scent of their meat enticed him like no other dish had ever done before.

He loped into the massive foyer, his head swiveling about as he looked for them. He hit the arm bar for the classroom door and just caught a glimpse of them at the far side of the room as they went through another passageway. The one in front had spotted him, the one leaking viscous viscera from her mouth had not.

"Shit!" Claren had looked up when she heard the door slam into the wall. Becky had been slowing her up since they'd started their retreat and she had a moment of weakness and self-preservation where she just wanted to let go of the other girl's arm and get to safety. If she'd stopped to think about all the mean things Becky had done to her during her sorority rush week she would have tied a bow around the girl and pushed her back toward the raging beast coming their way. Instead, she pulled her even harder. Becky was stumbling down the stairs; she'd broken the heel on one of her shoes and the other had twisted off when she stepped down awkwardly. She screamed out and nearly tumbled down from the severe sprain.

"Open the door!" Claren begged. She was two flights down when the monster peered over the railing above them. He screeched wildly when he saw the women.

"I can't move, Claren! My ankle is broken!"

"Get the fuck up, you mean bitch, or I'm going to drag you by your hair!"

The thing above them was leaping down entire half flights of stairs crashing into the walls on each landing. It would shake away the cobwebs and leap again.

"Open the door, please dear God open the door!" Claren was three steps from the bio-hazard marked door. A panicked Devon McCourty's face appeared in the small wire meshed safety window. Claren reached out and tried to twist the locked handle; it did not move. She banged her hand against the glass, Devon flinched and backed away as she did so.

Something in Becky reawakened when she saw Devon's face. She was leaning against the door, propped up against Claren. "Listen you sniveling little momma's boy, open this motherfucking door or I'm going to kick you in that pasty little worm you call a dick!"

Devon stepped forward half a step and placed the extended middle finger from his right hand against the glass, just as a huge spray of blood coated the entire viewing pane. Claren could not even cry out as her carotid artery was severed from the vicious bite. Her head lolled to the side as the monster began to severe through muscle and finally bone. Becky had backed away, hopping on her remaining good leg. She hid in the small concave of concrete that the stairwell had afforded, attempting to cover her ears to the wet, syrupy sounds of her friend being eaten, but the lip smacking and mouth puckering noises were too loud. She barely felt the piercing claw penetrate her calf as it dragged her out from beneath the stairwell, and she certainly didn't hear her own screams as it stripped her thigh muscle completely off before settling into her midsection and the soft internal organs housed there.

— 1 —

Lawrence Tynes, or BT, Big Tiny, as he was known to his friends, was sitting on a chair, resting his elbows on the deck railing as he looked over the expansive clearing down below. He was a large man, hence the nickname. At 6'5" and two hundred and fifty pounds, he was taller than most, even in the seated position. He was on watch this cool October morning, though not a zombie had been spotted in nearly two weeks. When the world had made sense, he would never have visited the remote Maine woods—much less lived in them. Now he could not imagine leaving. Though he had lost his fiancée in those first chaotic days of the zombie invasion, he'd been given a much cherished second chance when he'd hooked up with the wise-cracking, germ-a-phobic, OCD-addled and ADD-infused walking neurosis named Michael Talbot, a man who he counted among his best friends. In fact, he was like a brother to BT. A lot of good came with throwing his lot in with a man whose credo was act first, worry later, but there was also a lot of bad. And part of that was coming out the sliding door right now.

"Whoa, I didn't know I was going to be out here," Trip said as he gazed about, finally settling on BT.

BT could only shake his head. The other man, John the Tripper, or more commonly called "Trip," gave burnt-out freaks a bad name. Trip was hippie, health-food, kale-eating thin, though he ate more junk food than the participants of a World of Warcraft convention. He had graying hair pulled back in a ponytail and a thin beard that fell midway down his chest. And if he wasn't smoking a joint, he was thinking about it. Of all the people that called that house a sanctuary, it was Trip that BT avoided being around the most. He hardly ever made sense, but when he did it was terrifying.

BT let his head rest against the railing. "What are you doing out here, Trip?" Sometimes he didn't know why he bothered asking the other man questions.

"I'm on yeti detail," he said matter of factly before pulling a perfectly spun joint from his breast pocket.

He could not be trusted to stand regular watch, so Mike had come up with Yeti Watch for Trip. It had been a success in the sense that Trip no longer complained about not having zombie spotting duty, but a failure to everyone else because he'd pulled the house alarm four times having "spotted" the other, more elusive monster.

"You think if I act crazy I can get out of guard duty?" BT asked.

"I find it strange they think you're normal." Trip exhaled along with a heavy plume of smoke.

"Hey, go smoke that shit somewhere else."

"Shit? How dare you!" Trip looked genuinely insulted. I'll have you note this comes from the finest back alley gardens of Detroit!"

Mike came through the doors waving his hands to push some of the thick cloud aside. Heavy bags hung down from his red-rimmed eyes.

"How's she doing?" BT asked.

"The pneumonia is kicking her ass, her breathing is labored…I'm not sure." He was talking about Carol, his mother-in-law. "Her chest sounds like she's blowing bubbles in chocolate milk."

"That's a good thing, isn't it?" Trip asked.

"Not this time," Mike said as he clapped Trip lightly on the shoulder, giving him a small smile. "I don't know if the antibiotics are going to kick in before her breathing gives out. I need to get a hold of a nebulizer for her; breathing treatments might be her only shot."

"When's the last time you slept?" BT asked.

"What day is it?" Mike half-joked.

"Twelve days before Halloween—I can't wait to go trick or treating. You think the neighbors will have some Mars Bars?" Trip asked.

"You're pushing sixty. You can't go trick or treating, crazy bastard," BT said.

"Sure I can, if I wear a headband my wife says I look like Tommy Chong, though I can't see the resemblance."

"Just stop talking." BT put his hand up. "Listen, Mike, I'll make a run to the hospital, pick up the machine, be right back."

"I'll go with you," Mike said.

"No way. Go get some sleep. You look more like a zombie than anything I've seen recently. I'll get it done, don't worry. There doesn't seem to be anything out here anyway."

"If it's all the same, I think I'd rather go. I need to get out of here. Tracy is pretty worried about her mother and with my penchant for getting into trouble, well let's just say I don't want to be anywhere near her when I screw something up. Plus, hospital runs never seem to go well.

I'd feel better if I was there to help."

"I'd like to go, too. Make sure you both are alright," Trip said.

"You sure this doesn't have something to do with pharmaceuticals?" Mike asked.

"Tell me the thought of grabbing whatever you want from a pharmacy doesn't hold intrigue?" Trip asked.

Mike could only shrug and smirk.

"Hell no, Mike, he's not going. I'd rather go without a rifle." BT protested.

"Fine…whatever. I feel like this is prime Yeti spotting time anyway." Trip said. BT watched as Mike's head sagged. If he falsely pulled the alarm, Carol and Tracy could potentially lose out on some much-needed rest.

"Jackass," BT said begrudgingly. "Okay, we'll take your smoked-out ass, but you start doing or saying any crazy shit and I'm going to lock you up in the psych ward."

Trip thought on it for a moment. "I'm cool with that. You have no idea the plethora of incredible drugs and crayon colors you can get there."

"Alright let me tell the missus, grab some gear, and we'll head out. Hopefully, we'll have a little bit of luck and this will go smoothly," Mike said as he went in.

"We don't need luck, there's me!" Trip was beaming.

BT tapped his head against the railing. "Let's gear up, Trip. The quicker we go out and do this, the quicker I can be rid of you."

"That's the spirit," Trip said. "I'll be right in…I want to finish this," he said as he held up the half burned blunt.

BT was down in the basement getting his gear together. He had an AR-15, five magazines of thirty rounds each and a Desert Eagle Colt with an additional fifty rounds. He tied up his boots, put on a very large bulletproof vest, and finally adorned himself with a tactical belt to carry all the additional ammunition.

"Going to get some milk?" It was Mrs. Deneaux, she'd been in the family room across from the makeshift armory. The older woman was the definition of a frenemy. If she was on your side and not trying to seek an advantage from your death, she was an incredible ally—smart as a whip and a dead eye shot. She'd been responsible for their safe extraction from a number of volatile situations. Unfortunately, she'd also been linked to at least two of the members in the household's deaths. Yet she'd still found a way to fall under the Talbot protective umbrella. BT was convinced a spider wearing a clown outfit would be more appealing than that woman.

"Nebulizer," BT grunted as he cinched his belt tight.

"Hospital run! Fantastic. I've been wanting to do something."

"Fuck no, I'm already taking the stoner. I'll leave the black widow behind this time."

"Are you really going to trust that simpleton with watching your back?"

"I haven't seen a zombie in two weeks, I think I'll be fine. Plus Mike is coming."

"And yet you are wearing protective gear and you've brought enough ammunition for a sustained firefight. And we all know, that wherever Mike goes, fun is sure to follow. No, I think I'm coming…if for no other reason than I am bored senseless in here."

"Just great. This is shaping up to be a killer day and there's nothing wrong with being prepared."

"Dear boy that's all I'm saying. You're better off

throwing wet Twinkies at the zombies than having Trip by your side. Mike can be wonderful as well, but wholly unpredictable. I can be of great help."

"Or detriment," BT added. Deneaux smiled wryly.

"Let's pretend that there is nothing for me to gain on this trip other than getting out of this infernally stuffy house. Stretch my legs, shoot a few bullets at zombies, normal all-American things."

"Yeah I'm sure you were the queen of beer, hot dogs, and barbecue."

"It's settled then. I'm glad I already packed." Deneaux stood, BT noticed the small hand cannon she had strapped to her hip. She adjusted her fanny pack full of rounds.

"I should have just stayed in bed." BT went upstairs. When he entered the kitchen, Trip was at the sink filling canteens with bottled water.

"Why wouldn't you just leave the water in the bottle it came in, Trip?" BT asked.

"That would have been a pretty good idea, too," Trip said as he handed a full and closed canteen to BT.

"No, give me the one you're about to fill now. That way I can make sure you don't put anything in it."

"Then how will I get the water in it?"

"I meant anything *extra,* I've heard how you work."

Trip topped the canteen off, spun the top on and handed it over. BT watched as Trip filled a third and a fourth.

"How did you know Deneaux was coming? I haven't said anything."

"How would I not?" Trip asked over his shoulder.

"I don't know. I just want to get this over with." BT absently took a heavy swig from his canteen.

"Oh…okay," Trip said as he also took a heavy drink. "We should properly hydrate," he said to Deneaux as she came up the stairs.

"You're letting him fill the canteens?" She arched an eyebrow at BT. "I wouldn't let him mow my lawn," she said as she also took a large swig.

"You cut grass? What kind of monster are you?" Trip asked. "You know the smell of fresh cut grass that you smell after a mowing? Well, that's a distress signal, that's basically grass screaming!"

"This is who you want to go out with?" Deneaux asked of BT.

BT grabbed the keys to a Ford F150 pickup truck, one of three that Mike's brother, Ron, still owned.

"Bring her back in one piece please," Ron asked.

"Relax. I'm not your brother," BT replied referring to Mike's penchant for dismantling Ron's vehicles at record-setting paces.

"Not cool," Mike said as he came down the stairs. "Let me just tell my kids goodbye and I'll meet you outside."

"You're not driving, right?" Ron asked his brother.

"Everyone is a comedian," Mike replied before going downstairs.

"I'm serious!" Ron called after him.

Mike hopped into the back of the cab with Trip, who handed him a near to overflowing canteen. "You should take a sip, so I can close this."

"You know you could have just dumped out a bit," Mike said absently as he took a heavy drink then spun the top on.

"I could have, but that would have been wasteful," Trip responded, Mike didn't think on it again—at least not then.

They rolled out of Ron's narrow, tree-lined driveway and onto a roadway that wasn't much wider. There were times BT didn't like the cluster fuck of trees. It was too thick; too many things could hide in there. He'd often complained that an army could be in the brush. It was a cool day, even by Maine's autumn standards, so by the time they hit Route 1, BT had rolled up the window. Leaves, branches, and the occasional burned out husks of cars were all that were on the roadway. Of course, there were more survivors out there, but there were also still plenty of zombies, and the best defense against the brain-eating hordes was stealth. If they didn't know you existed, they could not eat you. Add to that, the fragile peace that had once existed amongst strangers was destroyed the moment civilization had been flushed down the drain. Just as likely to get your brains blown out as get your kidney eaten in this brand new world.

"Is that fog?" Deneaux asked pointing up ahead on the roadway.

"I hope so. If it's smoke, that would mean half of Belfast has gone up in fire...including the hospital," BT responded. The nose of the truck had no sooner hit the strange apparition when BT felt a lightness to his head and a heaviness to his eyes. "I...ah...feel frunny." The words taking on an elongated slant as if he were racing away from them.

"What the fuck Trip!" Mike shouted out in remembrance of past events.

"I'm sorry; I had to." Was all any of them could remember Trip saying as the truck veered off the side of the road.

— 2 —

"What the hell?" BT lifted his head off of the steering wheel, a line of drool connecting him to it. Deneaux had her head back against the seat rest, she was snoring. As BT regained his wits, he saw Trip by the front of the truck talking to Mike, his back to the cab, a ring of smoke encircling his head. They both turned when they heard the door open.

"I had to man!" Trip pleaded.

"Had to what? Drug us? Not all of us want to be as fucked up as you, little man. Now it's time for you to pay! Simple little run to get a damn breathing machine but you had to make us join your little drug-fueled party. You've exposed us all to unimaginable dangers. What if zombies had come, you idiot!" BT was as angry as Mike had ever seen him.

"Oh, it's worse than that. Before you see if it's really possible to shit down someone's neck, BT I think you should look around." Mike said.

BT paused, not sure how Mike knew what he wanted to do to Trip. After a moment he let it go, partly because he figured Mike had reasoned it out knowing he generally wanted to rip other people's heads off when they gave him a hard time, but mainly because he could not for the life of him figure out exactly where he was. It was a street lined with trees, but not the pines, oaks, and maples of Maine that he was used to. He was seeing magnolias, dogwoods, and southern pines. That last tree broke something loose in his mind; he noticed that the weather had changed dramatically as well. It was warm—extremely warm—and the humidity level was uncomfortably high.

"You're going to want to hear him out," Mike said, doing his best to shield Trip from the raging bull that was BT.

"Atlanta?" Mrs. Deneaux asked as she exited the truck. She had one hand to her head. "What are we doing here?"

"Numb nuts over there drugged us and flew us down here or some shit."

"Flew? Not unless he had access to a rocket; it's been less than fifteen minutes." Deneaux had turned her slender, watch-clad wrist to look at the time.

"I don't feel messed up. There's no way we could have been drugged, passed out, and then feel fine in that amount of time." BT was shaking his head.

"It's just a little something to help with the transition," Trip said as he eyed the big man warily.

"What are you talking about? Mike, you seem mighty alright with whatever is going on." BT was trying to get his bearings.

"Not my first rodeo, brother." Mike was establishing a perimeter while Trip caught them up to speed.

"Most that stay awake for the crossover suffer some ill effects," Trip said.

Deneaux, ever the astute one asked, "So how many

crossovers must you have stayed alert for?"

Trip did not dignify her question. "There are people here that need help. And I can't be everywhere," he pleaded.

"Trip, man." BT was perhaps not scared, but definitely concerned. He had no idea how he had got to where he was, and the only one with any answers hadn't had a cohesive thought since the Nixon era. "The beginning, Trip. You need to start from the beginning—and not the beginning where you were born, but from the moment we hit that mist."

"It's not really mist."

"I don't care!" BT roared.

Trip's hand was shaking as he took another drag. "Yo, Ponch you sure you don't want to be over here?" Mike ignored the nickname Trip had given him and continued walking around, keeping an eye out.

"Let me just check this place out, Trip. You tend to drop us in some pretty tight spots." Mike replied.

"I'd wait for him to come back, but this is too urgent." Trip said.

"What's so urgent?" Deneaux turned when she heard a loud screech, unlike anything she'd ever heard before, off in the distance. She wished it was "far off" but she didn't get that impression.

"Is this the night runner world?" BT asked. Mike had told him all about that particular adventure where they'd met a man named Jack Walker and there were zombies, night runners, and another monster. "What was that other thing? Yeah the whistlers. Are they here? Is that what's screaming?"

There was a barely audible "no" from Mike, who was attempting to locate where the sound had come from.

Trip thought about it for a second. "Similar, but not whistlers. It's something new and terrible. They were human once; whistlers weren't."

Another screech—more than one, and definitely closer. "That doesn't sound friendly." Deneaux snubbed out a cigarette. "We should find cover."

"Fuck that. Let's get back in the truck and get to Maine. We're in the South somewhere, we could get back there by tomorrow morning at the latest." BT was heading for the vehicle.

Trip's expression was sad. "What you seek is not there in this world." He did not elaborate any further, though his countenance gave it away.

"Bullshit. Those crazy bastard Talbots could stand at ground zero during a nuclear explosion and walk away talking about what a great rush that was."

"I could see that," Deneaux cackled.

There was the crack of multiple gunfire somewhere to the east, followed immediately by a large explosion that rumbled the earth beneath their feet. They all looked up as they heard the air tearing sound of jets flying overhead.

"It's not safe here." Trip was urging them over to a house on the far side of the road.

"I'm with him," Mike said pulling in to the relative safety their numbers afforded.

Deneaux was in self-preservation mode and began to leave immediately. "Come on big man," she called. "If whatever is coming enjoys eating human flesh you are going to look like a banquet."

"Fuck off," he muttered. "When we get in there, Trip, you're going to tell me everything. You understand?"

Trip said nothing but kept shuffling along.

"If you don't, I'm staying right here. And with my

dying gesture I'm going to point out exactly where you are."

"Now who's the asshole?" Deneaux was up two of the steps that led to a wraparound porch.

"BT, come on man, we're already here. That's not going to change," Mike said as he halted his escape.

BT merely folded his arms across his chest while he looked intently at Trip.

"Everything…I know," Trip promised.

"That could be absolutely nothing." BT harrumphed but still made his way to them, a little extra pop to his step when a screech much louder than the first echoed down the street.

Trip opened the door and urged the others in. The house was immaculate. It did not appear to any of them that anything was out of place or that the occupants had left hastily, taking only what they could. To their right was a living room, the left the kitchen. Directly ahead of them, away from the foyer, was a large staircase with a landing halfway up. That was what Trip was heading for. BT closed the door and threw the deadbolt before following.

Trip went to the right once he got to the top, straight through the master bedroom and into the master bath.

"Nice to see that someone still makes a bed in this day and age," Deneaux said as she sat down upon the king-size mattress. "I personally wouldn't have gone for the purple and gold motif." She'd picked up a corner of the comforter. "But to each his own."

BT had gone to the side of the window, moving the curtain slightly to get a look and see if anything was happening. Trip came out carrying two bottles of hair spray and an assortment of perfumes, he dumped them onto the bed and began spraying copious amounts of product into the air.

"What are you doing, you insipid fool?" Deneaux had arisen quickly from the bed and was getting away from the aerosol assault.

"They have incredible senses of smell! We need to be masked," he answered.

BT waited until the first of the cans petered out and watched as the thick wet vapor settled. He could barely catch a full breath; his lungs choked from the chemicals. "No more." BT held up a hand." Trip did three quick squirts before BT could cross the room and take the bottle away.

"The fuck is wrong with you, man?" BT was angry.

"House is clear," Mike said as he was about to enter the room. "Holy crap, what is that smell? BT, you trying to freshen up?"

"Shhh." Trip looked visibly nervous and pointed to the window.

"My god." It was Deneaux, peeking around the edge. BT and Mike ran across the room and were careful to not reveal themselves as they got into position to look out as well. Mike couldn't be sure about BT, but he felt as if he swallowed a handful of live worms and they were wriggling frantically in his stomach as the acids there slowly ate away at them.

Trip had said the things that were down there were once human, though none of them could fathom how that was possible. The two they were looking at were staring at something in the roadway; BT thought it could be Deneaux's damned stubbed-out cigarette. The aberrations were on all fours, their joints bent in completely unnatural angles—but that was far from the worst of it. Any skin not covered was blotched completely in bursting red pustules, in place of their hands and feet were these strange hooked claws that clicked on the ground as they walked and surveyed the area. And still, that was not the most terrifying aspect. When the larger male looked up and began sniffing at the air, BT thought he was going to have to bring Mike over to the bathroom before the other man lost the contents of his meager breakfast.

"Think I'm going to catch my breath," Mike said as he withdrew and sat on the floor.

A bleached-out, round mouth full of razor sharp teeth was puckering and suckering. BT could not help but think he was looking at some sort of parasitic worm when he saw that orifice. The eyes were cat-like with vertical pupils and surrounded by the red of broken blood vessels and hemorrhaging cells. What hair remained on its head was in wilted, sporadic clumps. The smaller female made a pitiful retching sound and a black, tarry substance consisting of blood and some other unknown compound fissured from her mouth, completely coating the cigarette butt. The male loped a few steps, clicking as he went, attempting to pick up the group's scent. His gaze more than once fixated on their window.

"Don't move," Deneaux hissed. Every instinct in BT had been to flinch, pull back and hide under the bed. He remained steadfast, impressed with how calmly Deneaux held her spot. Then he realized it's easy to not get alarmed when you don't have a beating heart, conscience, or soul. Dwelling on that thought was the only thing that got him through those next few horrific moments. There was gunfire a street over; the male's head swung and the two bounded off. The speed with which they did so gave

BT pause. He'd thought the speeder zombies were fast. The things down there on the street had a gait closer to that of a gazelle. It was inhuman, to say the least.

"Start talking, Trip, or I'm going to toss you out the window and give it my best go getting back to Maine, no matter what you said may or may not be there." BT moved away from the window, feeling better for it. Deneaux stayed where she was, keeping a look out to make sure their visitors didn't come back.

"We have to help here," Trip beseeched.

"Let's start with what those things are." Mike flipped a thumb over his shoulder.

"Yeah what are those things, man?" BT echoed.

"They're an experiment. The U.S. Government, under the guise of creating a cure for Ebola, was actually working on weaponizing it."

"Weaponize Ebola? Have they lost their minds?" BT asked.

"You can see it didn't work," Trip continued.

"No shit, tweak," Deneaux said, not pulling her stare away from the street.

"There was a scientist that mixed it with a Vietnam era compound called VX99…it was supposed to make super soldiers. That didn't quite work out the way they planned."

"So they took a failed chemical from forty years ago and mixed it with one of the world's most deadly viruses?" BT asked as Trip nodded. "Good to see the government is just as fucked up across multiple worlds. I mean that's what we're dealing with right? This isn't our reality?"

That got Deneaux's full attention. She finally moved to watch the conversation.

"There are more realities than you can imagine." Trip seemed nervous, not knowing how much he could actually say.

"So who the fuck are you to go skipping through the universe?" Deneaux asked.

"It wasn't always like this; I wasn't always like this. I was a Mensa member…I was studying astrophysics."

BT snorted, not really believing that the ultimate pot smoker could be capable of grasping anything more difficult than the mechanics to spin a bone. Then again, the proof was somewhat in the pudding, it was obvious they weren't in Kansas anymore, or Maine in this case. Mike wisely said nothing.

"That part is a story for another day. We're under too much of a time constraint for that explanation."

"Time crunch? We've got all day as far as I'm concerned. I'm not going out there until whatever fog you placed on my head is lifted and I'm back at Ron's house. Shit, I might be there already, sleeping peacefully after having just done a non-eventful guard duty. I'm figuring that's what is going on anyway—it got so boring that I had to go and invent this nightmare so I could keep my brain stimulated. Fucking oww!" BT blurted out.

Deneaux had gripped his ear and twisted it hard. "Nope, not a dream," she said.

"Maybe you should have tried that on yourself, you old bat." BT was rubbing the side of his head furiously.

"I'm not the one doubting where I'm physically standing." She went to light a cigarette but thought better of it and put the pack away.

"This world is in trouble and there're a few very key people whose survival is paramount to its continuation."

"Not him?" BT asked pointing to Mike.

"Not in this realm. There's a Master Sergeant Beckham; he is the leader of a Delta team. He's on his way here."

"Here, here?" BT was pointing to the floor.

"Army guys? Would have figured it would be Marines," Mike said, reverting to his inter-service rivalry.

"And they say I'm ego-centric," Deneaux quipped.

"No, he's headed for the CDC where he needs to rescue a scientist there. Her name is Kate Lovato; she's going to be the key to finding a way back from what has been unleashed here."

"What is our role in all of this?" Deneaux asked. BT looked lost, deep in the significance of what was being explained to him. It was not a concept he was transitioning into well.

"Their odds of success are dismally small. We're here to help better them."

"How?" BT had not looked up.

"I don't know," was Trip's reply.

Anger immediately flared up in the big man. "Oh. So *now* you don't know. You suck us into this cesspool of a world, explain to us where we are, what's happening, and what needs to be done, but you stop just short of telling us *how?!* Well isn't that just fucking special!" BT was pacing back and forth across the room, his anger mounting with each step. "Why? Why should I...why should we care what happens to this fucked up place? They made their monster infested bed, let them lie in it. It's not like we have spare resources...how can we possibly make much of a difference here?"

"It's not that simple. This world is the same, but different. All realities are tied together in some ways; some ties you can see, others you will never understand.

Your world, Jack's world, the whistler world, Master Sergeant Beckham's world…well, countless others. Each plane of existence subtly intersects and influences the others. If this world falls, the effects ripple out and can turn favorable outcomes to unfavorable ones…and vice-versa, but that's nothing we can predict. In this case, all I can tell you is that it's imperative that we at least give this place a chance to succeed."

It made sense—and that infuriated BT even more.

"I think what we should be asking here is this: we've all known Trip's crazy ass for months, and, just being honest here buddy, but you haven't made much sense for the vast majority of it. Yet here you are, talking not only like a normal person, but an educated one. I'm almost having a harder time believing *that* than anything else," Mike said rubbing his hand over his goatee.

"Side effect of the shift. Keeps everything in focus for a while," Trip responded.

"That's a side effect?" Deneaux could not help but ask.

"It's limited, and I can't stay this way long. It's my understanding that my mind would snap like an overstretched rubber band if I were exposed to the infinite number of realities I've been through for too long; the Trip you know protects me from that overload."

"Pretty sure that already happened," BT mumbled.

"So, say we help this Beckham and Lovato. What happens to us then?" Deneaux asked, looking out for her end game.

"Most times we just go back to where we came from," Trip answered.

"Most times?" Mike asked.

"There's been…difficulties before."

"I'm not going to go skipping through history like Scott Bakula in *Quantum Leap!*" BT shouted.

"It would be funny to see you as a small white girl," Mike said referring to the show's lead character being portrayed as the person he inhabited for his brief stay in one period.

"Mike, how do you come back from something like this?" BT asked.

"Shit, bud. I hate to sound like a commercial, but you just do it and get it done with. You knew what you were signing up for when you met me."

"Ain't nobody knew what they were getting into when they signed up with you, least of all that poor woman you call your wife. What kind of leverage do you have on her that she hasn't just left your sorry ass?" BT asked.

Mike looked down to his crotch.

"Please," BT sneered. "If anything, that's another in the minus column for you."

"So, now what?" Deneaux interceded before the two men could degrade the conversation down to name calling and schoolyard insults.

"I thought you'd never ask," Trip said.

— 3 —

Gunfire was happening all around them. Unlike the world they'd just left, this one was clearly in the early throes of human extinction, poised on the edge of that black horizon. Trip led them out the back door of the house. From there they went through a gated fence and into some dense woods. Mike was happy to note that unlike Maine, there was no heavy brush to impede their way.

"I'm not going to be here soon." Trip had stopped navigating to look back at them.

"Fuck. Move quicker then! At least get us into the position you think we're supposed to be in," Mike urged.

"Shocker. You're going to check out just as it gets intense," BT said.

"When I said I wanted to stretch my legs, this isn't what I meant," Deneaux said as they were at a slight jog.

"Emory University." BT read the first sign when they emerged from the woods. There was a large white building with multiple windows. They figured it to be dorm rooms, if the random and various decorations adorning the windows were any indication. There were no students milling about, heading to or away from their classes. In fact, it was preternaturally quiet on the campus as they went farther in. Trip had told them that the CDC complex was on the other side of the university. And though they didn't know the mission, it made sense that would be a good place to start.

"We have to stop," Deneaux said, catching her breath. "I need a cigarette. My nerves are shot."

"Bullshit. I've seen your nerves—you're as cool as they come. I can see you needing the cigarette, though. Either way, I want to get my bearings before we go charging up into something." Mike was checking out their location.

Trip had leaned his joint-fitted mouth close to Deneaux's flame. She was slowly pulling it farther from him and smiling as he leaned in closer to get at it. BT reached out and grabbed his shoulder before he fell completely over. Deneaux cackled softly and lit her cigarette.

"Trip?" BT asked.

"We almost at the show? I could really go for a funnel cake, corndog...maybe one of them giant pretzels slathered in mayonnaise and relish."

"And...he's gone," Deneaux said as she took a deep drag, resting her left elbow on the back of her right hand.

"Wonderful timing, Trip." BT was looking around. An ear piercing screech ripped through the relative bubble of calm that had settled around them. Mike was just swiveling his head upward to where the noise had come from. A white blur of teeth and claw had launched and was coming straight for BT. Deneaux dropped her right hand to her holster and pulled her pistol free before Mike could even turn to face the threat. Deneaux's first shot peeled back the top of the creature's skull, the second, which was not strictly needed, crashed into and through the row of barbed teeth.

"So much for that." Deneaux was much more concerned with the cigarette that had fallen and was now encompassed by a spreading pool of black blood.

"We should get out of here. I'm thinking that whatever that thing is, its friends will be drawn to the noise instead of repelled by it," Mike said. "You alright?" he asked a visibly shaken BT.

"Do I look alright? That thing wanted to give me a lethal hickey."

"Holy shit," Trip said as he bent to get a closer look at the fallen monster. "Is that a baby from *Tremors*?"

"No time to figure it out, Trip. Is there enough of you left inside of there to give us a clue about what we're supposed to do?" Mike asked.

"Do?" Trip asked. "I would think that would be an easy enough decision."

Mike sighed in relief that he might be on the verge of some answers.

"First we get away from pucker face there and then get some munchies, because even though I'm starving, I don't think I could eat while I'm looking at that mess. I mean, I'd try, because I hate to waste good snack cakes, but I wouldn't like it."

"This couldn't get any more unreal if it tried," BT sighed.

"Oh, I wouldn't call that thing unreal," Deneaux said as she stepped over the body.

"I just wanted a nebulizer. I should have stayed back and let you get it like you offered."

"I'm glad you're here, though, buddy," BT said.

"Brother, I am not."

As Mike spoke, a military helicopter flew past to their left, heading straight for the CDC.

"Only a half an hour before the fireworks begin!" Trip exclaimed excitedly.

"Fireworks?" Mike asked.

"Military fireworks," Trip answered.

"Does the simpleton mean ordinance?" Deneaux looked to Mike.

"How would he know that?" BT wanted to know.

"I don't think we can risk him not knowing something important. Let's get to the CDC, help out this Army grunt and doctor and head for the hills." They moved out.

"There goes our ride." Deneaux was pointing up to the retreating chopper.

"Beckham has boots on the ground. Guess we're up, though I don't have a clue what the hell we're going to do," Mike said.

"Oh, I think I have an idea." BT was pointing to a soccer field. Hundreds, if not thousands, of the infected creatures were pouring across it. Like a river of the damned, they flowed toward the CDC. Maybe subconsciously, and mistakenly, thinking there was a cure—or more likely that a meal had been dropped from the air. Sky fries? "They get to Beckham, he doesn't have a shot in hell."

"We engage them and we don't have a shot in hell," Mike replied.

"If dimwit here is right," Deneaux said as she pointed to Trip, who was busy shoveling beef sticks into his mouth, "then we don't have much of a chance anyway. Not if they're planning on bombing the city."

"How bad does it have to be before they'd bomb a U.S. city?" Mike wondered.

"That, at least, means it's not too late; they're trying to

contain it," Deneaux responded.

"Yeah, that's like trying to save a tree from a forest fire by cutting it down," Mike replied.

"Enough stalling. We need to do something," BT said.

"I'm stalling because I'm terrified," Mike said.

"Fair enough," BT shrugged.

"Okay, this seems simple enough that I should be able to explain it to you two geniuses," Deneaux piped in. "We just need to buy this Beckham fellow enough time to grab the good doctor and get away. That means we need to divert that horde. That building there looks like the perfect place to lay down some sniper fire."

It was a grand hall; looked more like something that belonged in Ancient Greece. Large white columns rose up to hold the overhanging roof in place. It had three floors, which would give them a perfect firing angle, but with all the doors and windows on the first floor, it was going to be impossible to keep the infected out for long.

"Death by fireball or by human leeches. Sounds like a win-win. Let's go," Mike said wryly. They went to the far side of the building, away from the soccer field. BT picked Mike up so the other man could see through a window that had been broken out. The office was covered in blood and Mike remarked that the cleaning staff must have called in sick that month, but otherwise it was free from the enemy. He broke out the remaining shards with his butt stock and climbed through, doing his best to avoid the pooling liquid. BT hefted Deneaux up; Mike helped her through. Trip was comparing how BT picked him up to his time in the Bolshevik Ballet.

"I was an incredible swan," he told Mike proudly.

"I'm sure you were. Now could you please be quiet?" Mike asked.

Trip did two nearly flawless pirouettes in the middle of the room.

"Please tell me he isn't doing ballet," BT said as he pulled himself up through the window. Mike handed him his rifle and they were quickly on the move heading to the top floor.

"We're not alone," Deneaux whispered as they entered the stairwell. The emergency lighting was lit but it did little to push back the dark shadows that nested on each level. When they got to the second level, BT nearly fell over a boot. He gagged when he realized the boot was attached to a leg that no longer had a body to go with it. Two stairs up was the matching boot and on the next landing was the headless torso.

"Is it possible to run so fast you leave your legs behind?" Trip asked. He was clearly nervous.

"And be so afraid you can lose your head?" Deneaux quietly crowed.

"That's not even funny," BT said as he stepped gingerly around the separated body parts. A screech echoed down the hallway from the floor above, then the sound of retreating footsteps as someone was making a run for it.

Mike, who had been trailing the others, pushed past Trip, Deneaux, and finally BT to get up to the third floor. He did not want to have to face the creature in the darkened stairwell; he thought he would be able to get a better shot off in the hallway. Mike burst through the door just as a frightened student dashed by, hardly sparing a glance for him. Mike was rethinking the wisdom of his actions as he saw three of the creatures at the far end of the long, but rapidly shrinking corridor. When the lead monster saw Mike raise his weapon, it bounded up the wall to its right, then somehow, incredibly, on its next bound forward, it was on the ceiling. One quick leap brought, it all the way to the opposite wall and then onto the floor where it surged towards them. It had done the impossible maneuver so quickly Mike had not even had a chance to change his aim point so by the time the monster was back on the floor, it met a triumphant trio of bullets. The first shattered its awkwardly bent elbow; the next two removed large chunks of skull and brain, spraying the two behind it in a thick detritus of organic material.

If the second thing had not slipped in the gore of its fallen brethren, Mike did not believe he would have been able to kill it before it would have had him. He knew he had completely lucked out when his three round burst smashed face-first into the being, caving in its gut-churning, puckering mouth and blood caked face.

It took the combined firing of BT and Mike before they were able to take the third one down. It had not helped either man's psyche that what they'd shot had up until very recently been a young girl of perhaps seven or eight. Her pale blue dress was now riddled with holes. Her Princess Jasmine bow fluttered to the ground, landing next to her outstretched arm.

"They're so fast." Mike looked to BT.

It was Deneaux who got them moving.

"What about the survivor?" BT asked pointing down the hall where the fleeing student had run.

"Not our mission." Mike tapped his shoulder to follow the older woman. It was a tough call, but there was nothing they could do. The city was about to become a fireball; all they could offer the kid was to die with others.

Deneaux had found a large room that was used for

conferences. An oversized oval table dominated. Three conference call telephones sat atop the piece of furniture and a small projection screen took up the far wall. She went around the chairs and to the first of the four windows. It was Trip who had the presence of mind to lock the door behind them. The other three took a moment to look at each other before they did what was cosmically expected of them.

"I'm not very altruistic," Deneaux said as she slid the window open.

"Is that supposed to be some sort of revelation?" BT asked. "That's like a politician saying they've lied from time to time."

"Good one," Mike told his friend.

"Or like Mike admitting he had absolutely no idea what the fuck he was doing right before he did something stupid."

"Really man? Now you've just gone too far. You want those to be your final words to me?" Mike replied.

BT was aiming down into the thick of the thundering herd that was heading away from them, but it was Deneaux's shot that rang out first. A creature stumbled and rolled twice before it stilled and was run over by those behind; not more than a couple took notice of the shooter and none had turned to go her way. BT was taking his time with well-aimed shots, though it would have been difficult to miss with so many targets overlapping each other. The louder crack of the 5.56 round attracted more attention, and some were attempting to swim against the monster current.

Mike wanted to give them a good reason to come at them; he leaned half his body out of the window, so much so that BT thought it prudent to grab him by the belt to make sure he didn't topple out. Mike was stringing together a litany of obscenities as he pulled the trigger. He was also cycling through rounds as fast as his handheld machine gun could fire.

"Come and get me you fucking misshapen monsters!" echoed across the area as his bolt slid open at the end of the expended magazine. Dozens of monsters lay dead or dying, but more importantly, the trio of shooters had been noticed by a significant portion of the mob. "Gone and fucking done it now." Mike was giving himself a hard time for actually accomplishing what he'd set out to do, he wasn't overly thrilled that they were coming and in droves.

"BT, help me with the table. We're going to have guests for dinner soon and I don't like what's being served," Deneaux said.

"Deneaux dropping some humor? We must be about to die," BT said as he peeled away from the window and grunted as he pushed the table up against the door. Trip was lying down on top of it, a plume of marijuana smoke encircling his head. "Don't move," BT said as he thumped the wall with the heavy piece of furniture.

"Wasn't planning on it," Trip replied, taking another hit.

"They heading in yet?" BT was aiming at the door, waiting for the assault to begin.

"Umm…some are, but I think we've got a problem," Mike said.

"Holy shit," Deneaux said as she pulled her window shut and stepped back from the opening.

"Don't think that's going to help," Mike replied. .

"What the hell is going on?" BT didn't want to spare a glance from his post.

"The fuckers can climb." Mike had shoved a new magazine into its well and released the bolt.

BT rushed across the room and poked his head out the window. "Thought you might be full of shit," he said, right before he started shooting.

"Yeah I picked this particular time and place to have a little fun." Mike moved to another window and leaned out to shoot at the monsters that were scurrying up the side of the wall. "Why can't they be slow, like sloths? Oakley! Going to need you over here!" Mike shouted to Deneaux, using the nickname referring to her Annie Oakley deadeye style of shooting.

"Tremor babes at the door!" Trip was singing to the tune of Frank Sinatra's "Got You Under My Skin".

"I've got them," Mike told Deneaux who had stopped midway across the room. "You're a better shot, and they're zigzagging all over the place."

BT was swiveling like he was mounted on ball bearings. Blasts echoed in the small room. The smell of expended rounds and smoke choked the air. The door vibrated as the first of the beings smacked into it. The stout oak had held on the initial assault, but Mike knew it was only a matter of time.

"Eight more minutes," Trip said gleefully. He had taken his shoes and socks off to show Mike how many toes that was.

"Eight minutes to what?" a clearly nervous Mike asked.

"Beckham catches his ride and then the fireworks begin!" he replied, clapping his hands together like an excited toddler.

Mike's train of thought was shaken as the door pounded again. This time, he was certain he'd seen light come in around the doorjamb. The assault paused; Mike considered Trip's words. "The bombing is in eight minutes?"

"The whole city is going to be one big fireball!" This time he didn't clap; his expression changed from confusion to escalating fear.

"Did he just say they were going to bomb Atlanta in eight minutes?" BT asked in between magazines.

"That's the government's answer to almost everything." Deneaux was shoving rounds into her revolver.

Mike figured he should be more nervous about the bombing than he was. He didn't figure they had anywhere near eight minutes left, though. "Behind you, BT!" Mike shouted just as he saw an impossibly clawed hand reach through the window followed by a fanged sucker mouth. Deneaux placed a shot in its face just as a relieved BT got back into position. He nodded his thanks to her and fired.

A resounding crack reverberated in the room as the door was split dead center and bowed inwards. Mike fired point blank at the creature that looked into the gash. There was a loud screech and wail as the others pressed towards the opening, realizing that their quarry was within reach. Mike removed a spare magazine and gripped it in his right forward hand. He wanted it as close as possible for when his present magazine was spent. He knew he'd never have enough time to pull it free and get it situated.

"Trip, walk over here with me," Mike said as he got to about the middle of the room. The door burst open and the screechers streamed in. Mike screamed a war cry as he fired off multiple rounds. Wood splintered, heads exploded, chests ruptured, and blood flew as brass was tossed into the air. The creatures danced like puppets as they were peppered with multiple rounds. *So many,* Mike thought as he kept firing. One had made it past the initial point of entry and was running along the wall, Mike followed it with a trail of bullets until he was finally able to put one in its side, blowing through its kidneys and severing its spine.

There was so much smoke in the room it was getting difficult for him to track targets. He thought his time had come when he felt something bump up into his side. It was BT, he'd been pushed away from the window. Deneaux was next. The three warriors stood with their backs together, continually shooting into the ever encroaching enemy.

BT roared a savage primal cry as he swung his rifle like a baseball bat, sending a mouthful of teeth flying across the room, the monster's jaw was shattered in a half dozen places. The smoke was so thick, all they could see was a whir of gnashing teeth and slashing claws, but still they fought on.

"Group hug!" Trip had somehow got into the middle of the trio.

Mike awoke in the cab of the truck with a start, fending off a claw that was determined to rip half his face free. "What the fuck!" He sat up.

"You alright man?" BT asked, he was driving.

"Where the fuck are we?" Mike asked.

"Huh? We're almost to the hospital, man, remember? I knew you were tired but I had no idea you were going to fall asleep the second I pulled away."

"We're not in Atlanta?"

"I knew I should have left your crazy ass at home." BT was looking sidelong at him.

"Bullshit. You telling me I was just sleeping?"

"That's what I'm saying."

"You looked exhausted," Mike told him. Then he looked to BT's ammo pouch. "Where are your magazines?"

"They're right here." BT put his hand to his side. When he came up empty he stopped the truck. "Must have fallen out."

"I'm out too," Deneaux said. "And my gun is hot."

"Everyone out!" BT was angry. "I'm going to find my damn bullets."

Mike found himself standing next to Trip who was smoking another joint. "He's not going to find anything is he?" Mike asked Trip.

"Doubt it." Trip exhaled.

"Did we accomplish our mission?" Mike asked.

"Yup." Trip was inhaling.

"So, now that the Master Sergeant and the Doc made it out, what happens to their world?" Mike asked.

"That's someone else's story to tell," Trip responded with a smile.

The Fall of Fort Bragg

by

Rachel Aukes

An Extinction Cycle Novella

$$— 1 —$$

@FortBragg: Unfolding situation outside the base. Shelter in place. More information will be released as it becomes available.

Sheila Horn paced the living room for the hundredth time that hour, pausing to reread the latest tweet from Fort Bragg's official account. God, how she wished her husband were home with her and their two girls. Instead, Parker Horn, a Delta Force operative, was somewhere outside the base and likely smack dab in the middle of this whole Hemorrhage Virus mess.

Not that Sheila was much safer.

The horrifying virus that began in Chicago had stretched out like a waking feline, spreading its claws into all major US cities within days—hours in several cases. Nowhere seemed immune to its relentless expanse. All the towns surrounding Fort Bragg proved to be no exception, and troops across the military base were working full twenty-four hour CQ—charge of quarters— to keep the virus from crossing the perimeter.

How bad had things got outside Fort Bragg? It was hard to tell from the television videos, which made the situation resemble Armageddon.

Every time she heard a Jeep's engine, her heart jumped with hope that Parker was coming home, but no Jeeps pulled into her driveway. She tried calling Parker to order him to stay alive and hurry home, but she always reached his voicemail. She told herself that his not answering didn't mean he'd been killed or was too injured to talk. On missions, he always went into radio silence. This time, he just happened to be offline longer than usual.

While he was out there—somewhere—she was stuck at home in the middle of the world's worst catastrophe. Alone and isolated with two girls, both under the age of ten.

Whenever she thought of Parker coming home, her emotions swung from wanting to strangle him for leaving her at a time like this to craving to hold him and never let go. Either way, she wanted him home, and soon.

Her phone chimed, signaling a new tweet had posted, and she nearly dropped her phone in her haste to check it.

@FortBragg: Base is on lockdown until further notice due to reports of infected outside the base. All personnel are directed to shelter in place. More info as it comes.

"Tell me something useful already," Sheila grumbled at the screen.

"Who are you talking to, Mommy?"

Sheila turned around to find her younger daughter standing at the edge of the hallway. "What are you doing up so early, Jenny?"

The five-year-old rubbed sleep from her eyes. "I'm hungry."

Her mother cocked her head. "How about I make you

some Mickey Mouse pancakes?"

Jenny's brows rose. "With blueberry eyes?"

Sheila smiled. "With blueberry eyes." She shooed her daughter away. "Now, go and change, and I'll get started on breakfast."

Jenny hustled back to her room, dragging her fuzzy green blanket behind her. Since school had been cancelled all week, her older sister would still be sound asleep.

As Sheila whisked pancake batter, she kept reading her Twitter feed as more and more updates posted.

@FortBragg: Ongoing incident with infected at base entrance. First responders are on scene. All personnel continue to shelter in place.

@FortBragg: First responders are on scene to secure the base. No personnel should leave their shelters.

Her screen froze, and she tapped the button to refresh her list of tweets. Nothing. She closed and reopened the app. Still nothing. She tapped buttons harder and shook her phone, as though either of those actions would do any good. Of course, nothing. When she noticed she had no Wi-Fi or cellular signal, she blew out a breath. "You've got to be kidding me."

She clutched her now-useless phone and felt suddenly and completely disconnected from the world. In a rush, she picked up the house's land line. "Oh, thank God," she said on a sigh when she heard a dial tone. She glanced at the sheet of paper pinned to the wall. It was the Fort Bragg family call tree, her lifeline to the base. Her name was midway down the list. Alickina "Alic" McGregor—

the name at the top of the list—had been initiating the call tree every three hours between sunrise and sunset. Even though the calls rarely brought new information, Sheila craved receiving them, if only to hear another voice. She glanced at the clock.

Two hours and thirty-eight minutes to go.

She grabbed the television remote, clicked on the TV, and flipped through the channels. Most were no longer on the air, and the remaining ones were replaying day-old news. By now, every city looked the same. Channel after channel showed videos of the violent infected, often scenes of them attacking people. The current video showed a police barricade across a street.

The images brought fear that nestled deep within Sheila's core. Even still, she couldn't take her gaze away. The camera zoomed in on a solitary officer who held his baton in defense against a half dozen or more infected. They shrieked before lunging forward as though they were heads of a single, massive hydra. The officer cried out and disappeared under the frenzy. Blood sprayed. The screams continued, but the camera never panned away.

Sheila cringed, but continued to watch the scene unfold. Nightmares had plagued her dreams ever since she'd seen the first graphic images a few days ago. Their primal screams and their suction-cup lips, jagged teeth, and bloodied faces were frightening enough. Their heavily jaundiced eyes… Eyes that were no longer in any way human, eyes that bore into her with the hungry stare of a fast-moving, irrational predator craving to destroy. What she couldn't get out of her head was knowing her husband was out there somewhere, surrounded by those hordes.

She made pancakes, watching the video clips in a daze.

"We get to watch TV this morning?" Jenny asked.

Sheila clicked off the set. "No, dear. I was just checking the weather."

Jenny shrugged before jogging down the hallway in pink polka dot pants and a purple striped shirt. The bright color combination was horrible, yet a perfect fit for the girl's personality.

Her daughter's obliviousness to the situation outside the base made Sheila worry even more. What could she possibly do to protect her girls from the horrors just outside their doorstep?

Jenny frowned. "Is everything okay, Mommy? You don't look happy."

Sheila forced a thin smile. "Just tired, sweetie. Now, show me your outfit." She motioned with a finger, and Jenny responded by twirling around with a wide smile and an extravagant flair.

Sheila put her hands on her hips. "Well, aren't you looking extra beautiful today."

Her daughter grinned as she took a seat at the table, her smile showcasing the gap where her two lower baby teeth had recently been.

Sheila sprinkled blueberries around the pancake and placed the dish in front of her daughter. "A big breakfast for my growing girl."

Jenny puffed out her chest for a bare moment before tearing into the fluffy pancake, not bothering with syrup. She took a too-large bite for her small mouth and struggled to chew with her mouth closed.

"Mom, my phone's not working," Tasha's voice came from Sheila's right, and she turned to watch her older daughter stare at her phone while lumbering down the hallway. If Parker had any idea how much time his older daughter spent on her phone, the veins would burst in his forehead.

"I think the network's down," Sheila replied before patting a chair. "Have a seat, sweetie, and I'll fix you a pancake."

"A Mickey Mouse one?" Tasha asked hopefully as she dropped her phone on the table, plopped into a chair, and lay her head on her arms.

"Absolutely," Sheila said, before adding, "Now sit up, sleepyhead. We don't slouch at the table."

The eight-year-old mumbled something under her breath, but obeyed her mother.

While making breakfast, Sheila glanced at the table to watch her daughters. Tasha stole a bite from Jenny's breakfast and received a slap on the hand in return. Sheila shook her head with a smile. Some days, like today, they were her little girls. Other days, she swore her older daughter was eight going on fourteen, and her younger wasn't far behind. They were growing up *way* too fast.

Sheila glanced out the window, to the street filled with carloads of soldiers heading in for duty. She didn't like the idea of her daughters growing up so fast, but she was downright terrified of the idea of her daughters not getting the chance to grow up at all.

— 2 —

SHELTER IN PLACE.

Fayetteville and the surrounding area have fallen to the infected, but Fort Bragg is secure! All military personnel are responding to any threats to the base, and all inactive military personnel on base have been called to active duty.

All non-military personnel are to continue to shelter in place. A second distribution of rations will be made on Friday. Phone lines and power lines are down, with no estimated time of repair. Do not leave your home unless you must relocate to one of the base's emergency shelters.

In national news, interim president Nathan Mitchell has authorized Operation Reaper, which he's called a "fight to save the country." The initiative is focused on eradicating the infected in the largest US cities. We expect Operation Reaper will make a tremendous impact on the current levels of violence and help clear the congestion of infected outside Fort Bragg. More details will be provided as information becomes available.

As a reminder, shelter in place. FORT BRAGG IS SAFE!

The letters were typed in a big and bold font on the flyer left on Sheila's doorstep.

A couple of hours after the power went out, Sheila had heard a knock on her door. By the time she'd answered, Alic McGregor—along with two armed soldiers—were already halfway down the block. Sheila had called out, but Alic had kept jogging, a thick stack of paper in her arms.

Alic, who must've had one of the few house generators on the base to run her computer and printer, had delivered a new flyer every day since. Unlike the other two flyers, today's paper brought new information. Sheila reread the paragraph about Operation Reaper several times, confused. She'd assumed the military had been focused all along on killing the infected, but according to the flyer, they were only now going in hard.

Understanding of what Operation Reaper was all about dawned, and her eyes widened. "Oh, hell."

Jenny gasped. "You swore!"

"Sorry, honey," she absent-mindedly waved off her daughter. She reread the flyer one more time, focusing on one word: *eradicating*. The only way to take out all the infected in a city in one fell swoop was to bomb it. Either the military no longer cared about the uninfected, or there weren't enough left to matter.

Goosebumps popped up across her skin. The United States was going to bomb its own cities. In a daze, she crumpled the paper and stared out the window. She saw Kelli standing in front of the large bay window in her house across the street, gripping a matching sheet of paper. The two women shared a knowing, somber glance before Sheila turned away to continue pacing her living room.

The base had been in a stalemate against the virus for two weeks now. Yet, she knew every day the base was losing troops while the numbers of infected grew outside the perimeter. Base commanders had already brought the perimeters in, cordoning off a two-mile radius of the most central parts of the base. Homes outside the safe area had been evacuated to emergency shelters set up in the barracks.

Sheila shook her head. At the rate the base was retreating inward, how long could they hold off the infected? She feared it might already be too late for Operation Reaper to do much good.

"Did the paper say we can go outside yet?" Tasha asked.

"Yeah, can we?" Jenny tacked on.

Sheila gave her daughters a melancholy expression. "Unfortunately, not yet, girls. It says there are still sick people out there."

Tasha dramatically plopped down on the sofa. "I haven't been to Briley's house in ages."

"I'm bored," Jenny added.

Sheila sighed. "I'm sure it won't be too much longer. They just want to make sure no one else gets sick. Staying inside keeps us safe."

"This sucks," Tasha said. "We're going to be bored *to death*."

Sheila pursed her lips. "Now, now, it's not that bad."

Tasha jumped up. "Yes, it is! I can't use my phone. I can't see Briley. I can't watch TV. I can't do *anything*."

Sheila thought for a moment, then she spun on her heel, walked into the kitchen, and returned with a jar of peanut butter and three spoons. She set down the jar on the coffee table and held out a spoon to each girl. Jenny's eyes widened before she grinned, grabbed one, and scooped directly from the jar. Tasha's stern expression softened, and she took a spoon. All three sat on the floor around the small table and took turns dipping into the jar.

As Sheila licked peanut butter from her spoon, she fought back the exhaustion that had made a home deep within her bones. Keeping children locked up in a house was like keeping a herd of wild hyenas in a cage. She knew bribing her daughters with sweets wouldn't work forever, and she'd eventually have to get more creative. *Damn it, Parker. Come home!*

Fortunately, the base still had running water. Without that, she would've been forced to leave the house and check in at one of the base's shelters. As it was, the quarantine frayed her nerves. The lack of electricity took away the comforts Sheila had grown used to. Her food pantry was as empty as her emotional reserves felt. At least more food was coming on Friday. Unfortunately, her energy wasn't so easily replenished.

A knock caused Sheila to jump, and she sprang to the door. When she opened it, she tried to hide the disappointment when she saw it was her neighbor and not Alic McGregor delivering good news. Sheila threw a hand to her hip. "Kelli Rasmussen, you just about gave me a heart attack."

Kelli gave her a dramatic pout. "Sorry, Shelly. I had to get out. I am going insane cooped up inside that tiny house day after day."

Sheila winced at the nickname Kelli gave her when they first met over a year ago. Behind her, she heard her daughters chatter and snicker, no doubt mimicking Kelli's squeaky voice.

Kelli continued. "It's different for you. You have your girls…" She motioned to Tasha and Jenny, who were currently half-painted in peanut butter. The corner of Kelli's lip curled downward in disapproval, and Sheila's eyes narrowed, ready to defend her daughters if her neighbor was uncouth enough to say anything.

"I'm stuck over there all alone," Kelli finished.

"Well, you have Michael," Sheila began.

Kelli rolled her eyes. "Who's always on duty anymore."

Sheila sighed. "I know it's hard, but we were ordered to stay inside. It's only temporary. The virus—"

Kelli waved her off. "Oh, that's just Alic playing the overly protective mother hen like usual. Michael said that they have everything under control and that we're completely safe inside the fence. I mean, look around you. The only thing to worry about outside is the weeds taking over my flower beds."

Even though Kelli was Sheila's least favorite neighbor, Sheila found it a comforting sensation to be interacting with another adult after so many days of being around only children. "Why don't you come in and sit for a spell?" Sheila offered finally.

Kelli beamed and strode inside. "Why, I'd love to. I was about to go out of my mind over there. I'm living on saltines and tap water. It's worse than a state penitentiary."

Sheila frowned. "Don't you have enough food to get by until Friday?"

"Probably not," she said in a singsong voice. She pouted, then pinched an invisible inch of fat on her perfectly flat abs. "I suppose I could stand to lose a few pounds."

"Nonsense," Sheila replied. "Now, take a seat and let me see what I can pull together for you."

"Oh, you don't need to bother. You have the girls to feed."

"Hush," Sheila said. "I would never be able to sleep at night knowing you're going hungry across the street. Girls, how about you visit with our guest, and I'll be back in a jiffy."

As Sheila headed to the kitchen, she heard Tasha's sigh before the girl exclaimed, "It's so nice to see you, Mrs. Rasmussen."

Inside the kitchen, Sheila slumped. She nibbled her lip as she stared into her pantry. A half-empty box of spaghetti, a can of green beans, a can of peaches, peanut butter, and a bag of rice and a couple cups of flour was all that sat on the shelves. The way it was, Sheila was scrounging to get by until Friday. She had nothing to spare. Ire rose like bile in her throat at Kelli's poor planning.

Before she let anger and self-pity make war in her chest, Sheila filled a baggie with rice, grabbed the can of green beans—since the girls hated them anyway—and marched the food out of the kitchen. She presented her gift to Kelli…who eyed the food as though it could be contaminated. Her neighbor accepted the offering with a patronizing smile. "Well, bless your heart. You've brought me beans and—?"

"Rice," Sheila finished, growing impatient. "I know it's not much, but if you don't want them—"

Kelli snapped the food to her chest. "I want it. Thank you. I mean it." Kelli batted her eyes. "It's just that I remember you had a lovely wine cellar the last time I was here. I thought maybe you'd have one or two bottles to spare."

Sheila glanced up at the ceiling. *I will not kill her. I will not kill her.* When she spoke, she enunciated every word. "We're in the middle of an epidemic, Kelli. This is not a garden party. Do you understand what I'm saying?"

"Oh, well, I didn't mean to step on your toes. Look at the time; I'd better get going," Kelli said in a rush as she hustled to the door. "Thank you, Shelly. Much appreciated."

Sheila watched as Kelli crossed the street and disappeared inside her house, only to reemerge seconds later. Sheila shook her head as she watched Kelli stroll down the sidewalk, stopping at the next neighbor's house. "That woman is a darned fool." When she turned around, she found both girls raptly watching her.

"I don't like Mrs. Rasmussen, either," Tasha said. "She's not very nice to us."

"I know, sweeties. She doesn't always show the best manners around people," she said, instead of saying *she's a spoiled brat* as she really wanted to.

"I'm glad you didn't give her the peaches," Jenny said.

Sheila put her hands on her hips, pretending affront. "Jenny Lynn Horn, don't you think for a second that I've forgotten that peaches are your favorite fruit in the whole wide world. I'd never give away our peaches. In fact, how does peaches for breakfast sound?"

Jenny beamed. "Sounds yummy."

Sheila took a seat in between her daughters and wrapped her arms around them. After a lengthy pause, she spoke. "Things will get better. Just you wait and see."

If only Sheila could convince herself of the lie she just told.

Being cut off from the rest of humanity did strange things to a mind, and she found herself in a constant battle against worst-case scenario paranoia. She had to remind herself that home was the safest place to be. More importantly, home would be the place Parker would come first to find them.

Assuming he was still alive.

— 3 —

A scream shattered Sheila's dreams. She tumbled out of bed and leapt to the window. She could've sworn the yell had happened right outside her house, yet she saw nothing in her yard or on the street. Nights were darker without electricity, and it was more difficult to differentiate shrubs from things that were far more dangerous. Trees created eerie, dancing shadows in the moonlit breeze.

Movement near Kelli's house caught her eye, and she snapped away from the window. Terrified she'd been seen, she stood frozen behind the curtain for a long moment. It wasn't until long after her heartbeat slowed that she looked back outside. No monsters, no sign of anything out of the ordinary. Relief filled her.

She squinted at where she'd sworn she'd seen movement at Kelli's house, but knew her eyes had been playing tricks on her. They were safe here. The infected couldn't get past the perimeters. After all, Alic McGregor's flyers promised that the sirens would sound if the base were breached.

She turned to find a shadow standing in her doorway. She shrieked and grabbed her chest. When the shape morphed into a lanky, five-foot-tall person, she relaxed and leaned on her mattress. "Oh, sweet baby Jesus, Tasha, you scared me half to death."

"Sorry, Mom," Tasha said. "I thought I heard something."

Sheila hugged her daughter. "It was nothing. How about you head on back to bed?"

"But, what if someone sick got on the base?"

Sheila mustered confidence she didn't have. "They can't, sweetie. Soldiers like Daddy won't let them come through."

Tasha's eyes widened. "You mean Dad's out there with all the sickies?"

Sheila winced. "You know his missions are always secret, but I'm sure he's far away from the sickies."

"How can you be sure?"

Sheila rubbed her daughter's back. "Because he left *before* people started getting sick, so his mission must be for something else. You have to have faith. Daddy is the very best at what he does. I know he'll come home safe and sound as soon as he can."

"But, what if he doesn't?"

Sheila cocked her head. "Didn't he promise you he'd come back home?"

"Yeah, I guess."

"And has he ever broken a promise?"

"No."

"There you have it." Sheila's voice softened. "I know it's hard, but try not to worry. Daddy will be home before you know it, and everything will be just fine. My guess is that he has to stay away until the sick people are all gone and it's safe for him to come home."

Tasha sniffled. "I miss him, Mom."

She hugged her daughter. "I do, too, sweetie. I do, too."

A round of automatic gunfire sounded, and its proximity was unmistakable.

"Mom, that sounded really close," Tasha exclaimed.

Sheila released her daughter and peered outside. "Yes, it did," she murmured as she closed and locked the window. She strode over to her dresser and rummaged through her underwear drawer until she found the black lockbox. She punched in a four-digit code, and the box unlocked with an audible click. She pulled out the Glock 19.

"Whoa. I didn't know you had a gun."

"I've had one for a while," Sheila spoke as she slid rounds into the empty mag. She'd never loaded her gun in the dark before. In fact, she hadn't loaded her gun in well over a year. Her husband's best friend, Reed, had taken her to the gun store to buy the pistol after she tried to convince Parker she needed a gun.

"Does Dad know?"

Sheila smirked. "He knows."

Parker had been adamant that a gun would serve Sheila no good if she didn't go out and practice regularly. She had practiced a bit for the first year. Then, her trips to the range became less and less frequent until she stopped going altogether. Though, she told Parker she still practiced.

He never seemed to understand that she'd bought the gun to *have*, not to *use*.

After she bought it, he told her he didn't think she could pull the trigger against another person. She vocally disagreed with him at the time, but deep down, she knew he was right. Not that she'd ever admit that to him.

Lately, she was becoming more and more afraid she may have to use the gun. Still, she slept better at night knowing she had a powerful weapon to protect herself and her girls.

"Tasha dear, I need you to go to Jenny's room and stay with her while I look around. Okay?"

"I can come with you."

"No." She shoved the mag into place, swept back the slide, and turned to Tasha. "I'm just going to check all the windows and doors. I'd feel much better knowing that you're looking after your younger sister. Okay?"

Tasha nodded, the small movement nearly imperceptible in the darkness.

As her older daughter padded off to Jenny's room, Sheila held the gun to her chest, closed her eyes, and prayed. After taking a deep breath, she went to Jenny's room. Inside, Tasha sat on a beanbag chair, while Jenny breathed slowly and deeply like a girl in a sound slumber. Sheila and Parker had often joked that a freight train could run through the house, and Jenny would sleep right through it. Sheila wasn't sure about a freight train, but automatic high-caliber gunfire nearby clearly wasn't enough to wake the little girl.

She shut and locked the bedroom window and closed the blinds, shrouding the room in blackness. The only light now came from the hallway, where moonlight crept in through other windows. She caught a glimpse of Tasha's silhouette as the girl bolted from the room.

"Tasha! Get back here!" she whispered and stomped to follow. The pair collided in the doorway, and Sheila had to grab her daughter to keep from knocking her down.

Tasha held up a well-worn doll—a baby made of cloth

and stuffing, whose soft black curls had morphed through eight years of Tasha's cherishing into a horrible case of bedhead. "I was just grabbing Blinky. That's all." She nestled into Jenny's beanbag chair again, this time hugging her doll.

Sheila whispered, "You need to stay in here. I'm going to close the door. If Jenny wakes, the dark will scare her. Don't let her use a flashlight. I'll come back as soon as I've had a look around."

"Okay, Mom," Tasha got out through a yawn.

Sheila closed the bedroom door behind her with a gentle click, then moved into fast action, shutting and locking every window and closing all the blinds. It was late April, and hints of summer had saturated the house with humid, warm air. She didn't look forward to having the windows closed.

Confident the house was secure, she set the gun down, poured herself a glass of water, and leaned against the kitchen counter, gazing out at her back lawn that was in desperate need of a mow. Her small backyard was enclosed in a wood privacy fence, and had always been her private oasis. The girls' swing set beckoned for play, and her hammock swung lazily in the breeze. She yearned for the long afternoons she'd spent reading books while the girls played outside.

She let out a wistful sigh. "Parker Horn, I sure could use you around here right about now," she said to herself before taking a long drink.

A shout outside caused her to splash water on her pajamas. She jerked around and searched in the direction of the sound. She slapped the glass down, grabbed the gun, and rushed to the living room windows to find two men running down the middle of the street. At first she thought they were running together, until the second man howled and tackled the first. Her eyes widened as the pair wrestled in a battle of life and death.

Chills flitted across her skin as she regarded the gun in her hand. After a furtive glance back down the hallway where her daughters slept, she made up her mind. She wiped sweat from her face and forced herself to take the few short steps to the front door. She looked through the peephole one more time before unlocking the deadbolt.

Sheila found herself fumbling with the handle, her nerves making her fidgety. Every cell in her body screamed at her to run into the girls' bedroom and cower. Her daughters needed her to protect them.

The man outside also needed her.

She swallowed and pressed the front door open with the barrel of the gun.

One of the soldiers climbed to his feet. He stood, as though searching for something. In the moonlight, she noticed the patch on the shoulder of his ACUs.

Her lips parted. "Parker?"

The man spun around to face her.

She gasped. He growled.

Blood dripped from his mouth, not that his mouth appeared human in any way. What she'd mistaken to be Parker's tight haircut was a bald head covered in dark blotches. His eyes glistened in the moonlight—yellow slits that made her imagine a cobra about to strike.

Which he did.

He—more of an *it*, really—screamed before it dove at her and closed the distance in inhumanly fast strides that resembled more of a leopard's leap than a two-legged sprint.

She fired without thinking. The gun bucked in her

hand with every shot, but she hit the infected at least once, and it tumbled to the ground.

Someone gasped behind her, and Sheila spun around to find Tasha staring wide-eyed at the infected Sheila had just shot.

"Get back to Jenny's room and lock the door!"

Her daughter didn't move. Instead, her mouth opened in a silent scream.

Sheila turned.

The infected soldier grunted as it pushed itself from the ground. Its gaze moved to Tasha, and it seemed to smile, as though mocking them. A sadistic snarl came from that O-shaped mouth the instant before it pounced.

"No!" Sheila shoved Tasha inside and yanked the door shut, barely closing it before the infected slammed into it. Wood cracked. She braced herself against the door to hold it. "Run!"

Tasha took off at a sprint down the hallway just before the infected hit the door again. Automatic gunfire blasted Sheila's ears, and she flung herself to the floor, covering her head.

When the gunfire ended, a loud ringing in Sheila's ears remained. The world around her was muted, yet her senses somehow seemed heightened. The floor was cool on her bare skin, yet it felt like a raft holding her afloat on a rough sea. She smelled gun smoke and something else—a sour tang of blood and rot. She looked up to see bullet holes riddling her front door. She jumped to her feet and checked herself for wounds and sobbed in relief to find nothing.

"Mom? What's going on?" Tasha yelled out.

"Stay there! I'll be right there as soon as I know it's safe!"

Her door opened, and she swung around to shoot.

"Whoa!" A soldier yanked her gun from of her hand, nearly knocking her down. They stood there a moment—she shivered while he watched her. She couldn't make out his features. He wore NVGs—night vision goggles—just like the ones Parker had let her try on before, so she knew he could see her better than she could see him.

"Did it touch you?" he asked.

Calm English sounded incompatible with the gruesome chaos she just bore witness to, and it took her a moment before the words unjumbled in her mind. She shook her head. "No."

"Ah, hell," another voice called out from behind him. "It got Singh."

Sheila peered over the soldier's shoulder to see several other men—all wearing NVGs—encircling the fallen man. She watched as a soldier lifted his rifle, aimed at the man on the ground, and fired a single shot, the muzzle flash lighting up like a single, angry firefly.

"You need to stay inside," the soldier standing before her said.

She looked up at him. Fear rose in her gut. She mentally willed her hands to stop shaking, to no avail. "How many are inside the base?"

The NVGs hid any expression. "Don't worry. We have things under control."

She motioned to the dead soldier in the street. "You call that under control?"

"Listen, lady," he snapped. "We're having a rough go at it, but don't bet against us yet. We're going to whip those things."

"I know," she stammered before lifting her chin. "Tell me what I can do."

He stared at her for a long moment, then sighed. He handed her gun to her. "The best thing you can do is stay inside."

She reluctantly claimed the gun.

He continued. "Your first instinct should be to stay quiet and stay hidden. If you find yourself cornered, then shoot. Go for the head, the heart, anything that would stop someone fast. The key is to kill them before they can heal." He nodded to her house. "When's your husband get home?"

She shook her head. "He's off base."

After a long pause, he spoke. "I'll tell you what, my house is just a couple of blocks west of here. I'll stop by when I can. Okay?"

"Okay," she quietly said, before adding, "I'd like that."

"It's settled then." He held out his hand. "Private Nicholas Vadreen at your service."

She took his hand with a smile. "Nice to meet you, Private Vadreen. I'm Sheila Horn."

A Humvee zoomed down the street with its lights off. It cranked to a stop near the bodies, and the troops began to pile into it. Vadreen nodded to the window. "You'd better get inside. Stay quiet and don't be seen, got it?"

Sheila nodded. Before heading inside, she turned. "Oh, and Private?"

He turned.

"Thank you."

She headed inside and locked the door. Tonight, she'd console her daughters. Tomorrow, they'd prepare to fight.

— 4 —

In the morning, the Horn family ate the bland flatbread Sheila had concocted out of flour, water, and salt, and grilled on the small camping stove she'd found in the basement. The girls dutifully ate their breakfast, dipping the warm bread first in oil and then in sugar and cinnamon.

Sheila skipped the sugar for her own bread because she knew that once the small bowl was empty, there would be no more. Instead, she added sprinkles of cayenne pepper, which helped to make the barely edible cardboard more palatable.

Outside, gunfire had become a constant backdrop, like an album of percussionist music stuck on repeat. The noise jabbed at their nerves, and Sheila often noticed her girls flinching at loud explosions, or gunfire that was far too close to home.

A large Army vehicle rattled the windows as it drove by. Sheila had gotten quite good at discerning the sounds of various engines. Most that passed her house were personal vehicles—soldiers reporting to duty and later returning home—and she suspected a few were fleeing the front lines to be with their families. Over the past couple of days, she noticed fewer and fewer vehicles drove by. *They're just working longer CQs... I hope.*

As soon as the girls forced down the last bites of their bread, Sheila grinned and pulled out the can from behind her back.

Jenny's eyes grew wide. "Peaches!"

Tasha slapped her sister's arm. "Be quiet, you dummy."

"Tasha," Sheila scolded. "You do not hit your sister, and we don't call people names."

"Sorry, Mom," her older daughter mumbled, lowering her eyes.

Jenny sulked as she rubbed the skin her sister had smacked. "I didn't mean to say it so loud. I thought you forgot about your promise."

"It's okay," Sheila said. "Just try to keep your voice down." She spooned the peaches into two bowls, using her finger to scoop out every last drop of juice. Her mouth watered for a taste, but she pushed a bowl in front of each girl. "I'd never forget a promise. I just wanted to make sure you girls ate a full breakfast this morning. Now, take your time and enjoy your dessert."

Sheila watched them as they ate, pure joy on their faces. Instead of joy, she felt a heavy weight had settled onto her chest. Last night had been a wake-up call. There'd be no more peaches. No more electricity. No more school. The infected hordes had staked their claim to the world outside the base, and the remaining uninfected were sorely outmatched.

The non-stop gunfire also meant that the numbers of infected had grown outside the perimeters. The soldiers were fighting the good fight, but she'd begun to fear they were also fighting a losing fight.

Since last night, Sheila carried the Glock on her. She'd taken one of Parker's holsters and an ammo pouch and strung both onto her belt. The bulky weight at her hip felt strange, and she found herself continually readjusting, trying to find a more convenient placement.

"Mom, do you want one?" Tasha asked, holding out a peach slice on her spoon.

Sheila shook her head. "No, thank you, sweetie. I'm full."

Tasha tutted. "Have it, Mom. *Please*."

She smiled gently. "Okay." She plucked the peach from the spoon and plopped the whole slice into her mouth. A tiny shot of juice sprayed from her mouth and onto Tasha's arm.

Both girls giggled in response. Before long, their giggle fits had all three dribbling juice from their lips. For a brief moment, Sheila felt normal.

A distant explosion so big that it knocked a glass onto the floor shattered the moment.

"Mommy!" Jenny cried out.

Sheila grabbed each of her daughters' hands. "It's okay, sweeties. It sounds a lot closer than it really is."

"It sounds really close," Tasha said.

"I know it does," her mother added on with soft words. She let go, bent down, and picked up the broken glass while fighting back the tears that came with emotional exhaustion.

After the hearty breakfast, they played hide-and-go-seek. While Sheila tried to make it fun, all three knew it was no game. The girls understood why they needed to hide, and Sheila's heart ached at seeing how hard each girl worked to do a good job. She didn't relent until she found Jenny asleep under the sink three hours after they began the game.

While the girls took their afternoon naps, Sheila watched the street from her living room windows. All that remained of last night's violence was the dark stain in the middle of the street, but she knew another stain marred the steps outside her front door. She didn't see or hear any infected, but she kept watching. When hardly any soldiers returned home, Sheila began to worry even more. She watched until the bright sun gave her a headache and the girls woke.

Sheila and the girls spent the remaining daylight setting up a shelter in the attic. The girls called it their treehouse—after all, they'd always wanted a treehouse—but it would be so much more than that. Sheila set out every container she could find in the house and filled it with water. She stored most of the water in the attic, but she also set containers in the "official" hiding spots around the house, such as behind the furnace and in the pantry.

Three sleeping bags were lined up on the floor. The attic was stuffy and hot, so they only spent the nights up there, but Sheila slept better in the attic than she had for weeks in her bedroom.

Up here, they were invisible.

Three mornings later, Sheila found herself pacing the living room and watching Kelli's house. The girls hadn't eaten in over a day, and their crabbiness was turning into lethargy—and that terrified Sheila. She knew that if anyone knew where extra food could be gotten, it would be Kelli Rasmussen.

She grabbed a bottle of wine and placed it in a tote. She double-checked to make sure her gun was loaded. "Sweeties, I'm going to run across the street to Mrs.

Rasmussen's. I won't be gone for more than five minutes. How about you go up to the attic until I get back?"

Both girls' eyes grew wide.

"You're going *outside*?" Tasha asked.

"You can't!" Jenny exclaimed, finding a hidden wellspring of energy. "The sick people—"

"I have to, girls. I promise I'll be right back. Now, you'd better be ready for the word." She paused before whispering out the code word with enthusiasm. "Supergirl!"

The girls scrambled to the attic stairs, but not before Tasha threw a hard look over her shoulder.

Leaving her girls alone tore her up inside, but she had no other choice. Friday had come and gone, and no trucks had delivered rations. If she didn't find food and find it soon, they'd starve.

She slung the tote over her shoulder and strode to the front door. After scanning the area for a long moment, she unlocked the deadbolt and twisted the handle. She half-expected to be attacked as soon as she cracked the door open, but the only thing that had changed from when she was safely ensconced within her home was that the sounds of fighting were louder outside. She took a step over the threshold and felt her courage falter.

The noise of engines sent her jumping back inside and closing the door. Through the peephole, she watched a car zoom past, followed by an SUV. She watched them disappear in the distance. *Do you know something I don't know?*

When all she could hear was the usual sounds of battle in the distance, she tiptoed down her front steps and jumped over the dark stain as though she were a skittish deer during hunting season. She glanced up at the clouds in a silent plea for rain to wash the stains away. When no torrents of water fell, she inhaled and continued. She held the Glock steady before her with both hands as she hustled across the street, giving the second stain a wide berth, and up the sidewalk to Kelli's front door.

When she reached the door, she leaned against the wood and let out a deep breath. She rapped, the noise sounding as loud as the gunfire around her. When Kelli didn't answer, Sheila frowned and knocked again. After endless seconds and still no answer, she tried the door. Locked. All the windows were open, and the breeze lightly blew the curtains. She tried to peer through gaps in the fabric but saw nothing out of the ordinary.

She threw a furtive glance around her. No signs of movement. She looked at the living room window and when she saw no heads peeking out, she was infused with the confidence she needed. She hustled around Kelli's house and under the lean-to where an SUV sat covered in a layer of dust.

Sheila hopped up the single step to the side door and knocked on the glass. The window on the door was half covered by a curtain, and she peered inside to the kitchen. The table was set with fancy placemats as though it were about to be included in a photo shoot for *Better Homes and Gardens*.

Sheila tried the door handle and found it unlocked. She stepped inside. "Kelli?" Sheila called out softly. "It's Sheila. Kelli? Are you here?"

Sheila shook her head. Kelli must've been on one of her daily strolls, no doubt still on the prowl for alcohol. Venturing out was going to get her neighbor killed. She glanced down at her tote and chuckled drily. *That's the pot calling the kettle black.*

"Kelli? Yoo hoo." When she received no response, she glanced into the living room, the floor plan a mirror image of Sheila's house. Accepting that she was alone in the house, Sheila returned to the kitchen. She stood for a long moment, debating whether she should wait or come back another time. The girls would begin to worry soon, and Sheila couldn't risk them coming to look for her.

Sheila headed toward the door, grabbed the handle, and paused. She turned around and cocked her head. *Just a little peek won't hurt anyone.*

She opened a cabinet door. Rows of glasses. Sheila scrunched her nose and opened the next cupboard. Plates. She opened the third and closed it in a rush, feeling like she'd been caught doing something wrong. She frowned, then slowly peered inside again. Boxes of prepackaged rations lined the shelves. As she checked the remaining cabinets, she found them filled with the same. There was enough food to feed a family for months. Kelli's husband must've been sneaking home extra C-RATS every chance he had for the past year.

Kelli had had the gall to ask Sheila for food. "That bitch."

Her teeth clenched. She unslung the tote, set it on the table, and holstered her gun. She took out the bottle of wine and filled the bag with the rations. She made damn sure she squeezed every package she could into the tote. When the bag was stuffed, she glanced at the bottle that sat on the table, next to the silk floral centerpiece. She smiled. "I'd call that an even trade."

She gave another glance down the hall. "What else has Michael been sneaking home to his princess, I wonder?" she murmured.

Sheila slung the food over her shoulder as she walked

casually down the hallway. In the bathroom, she found a stack of medical kits. She took one for herself. Then, she continued to the master bedroom. When she opened the door, she brought her hand up to her mouth, and the kit fell to the floor with a thud.

The room looked like it had been painted in blood. Bed sheets were shredded. A broken lamp lay on the floor. Body parts lay on the bed and on the floor. Bits of flesh and gore were sprinkled across the bed and on the wall. Clumps of blonde hair peeked out from the edge of the bed. A broken screen lay on the floor by the window left wide open.

Sheila ran.

— 5 —

Sheila couldn't sleep. Visions of blood colored her thoughts. Her mind imagined a hundred different ways Kelli had met her doom. The image that flitted through her mind the most was a mental video of Kelli's agony as she was torn apart piece by small piece. She imagined a monster scratching through Kelli's abdomen, laughing while it ripped out her organs.

Sheila shivered. Every muscle in her body was taut, and she craved to toss and turn. Instead, she lay rock-still in her sleeping bag as if any movement would draw a monster to her.

Tasha and Jenny were sound asleep, despite the stifling heat in the attic. After returning from Kelli's house, Sheila had reinforced the windows by stringing up of silverware and trinkets on twine cord behind every curtain. That way, if anything moved a window in even the slightest way, the homemade alarm system would alert Sheila and the girls.

A North Carolina house closed up in late springtime leaves a stale mugginess that saturates clothes, hair, and skin. The attic was nearly unbearable. Cold showers twice a day helped with the sweat and grime, but they were always sweaty again ten minutes later.

A heavy vehicle zoomed down the street, and artillery rocked the earth soon after. Dust flitted down from the insulation and wood frame above their heads.

Jenny shot up. "Mommy!"

"Sh, sh," Sheila said, tugging her younger daughter into her arm. Distant, inhuman screams floated through the attic. *God, it sounds like they're right outside. Please, God, don't let them find us!*

Tasha pressed against Sheila. "Mom, I'm scared."

Sheila pulled Tasha into her other arm and held both her daughters. "It's okay, sweeties. I have you. Everything's going to be all right."

Despite the heat, they clung to one another. Her daughters relaxed in her embrace and eventually dozed off. She stared into the dark, listening to the gunfire and screams coming from all directions.

Deep in her gut, she knew it had finally happened.

They'd lost to the Hemorrhage Virus.

***

The Horns didn't leave the attic for two days, with the sounds of violence always just outside. After dark on the second day, massive airplanes flew over.

It's Operation Reaper. They're going to bomb us now, too. Just like they did the cities.

She clutched her daughters, waiting for the fiery blast.

The bombs never came.

She had no idea what the planes had done, but over the next few hours, the sounds of artillery and gunfire and screams became less and less until silence reclaimed the base. It was odd to hear no sounds of battle—Sheila had grown accustomed to living in a war zone. She crept on her hands and knees to the attic entrance.

"Mom, what are you doing?" Tasha whispered harshly.

"I'm going to check on things. I'll be right back."

Jenny sat up straight. "But—"

Sheila held her forefinger to her lips. "Remember, why are we in the attic?"

"Because we're invisible up here," Jenny replied.

Sheila nodded. "Good girl." She glanced to Tasha, who was clutching her doll. "You two stay quiet, and I'll be back in two shakes of a lamb's tail."

Tasha's bottom lip quivered, and Sheila turned away against the guilt for leaving her girls alone. Jenny was young enough that she couldn't fully comprehend the dangers that awaited them outside. Conversely, the understanding was clear in Tasha's eyes, and Sheila hated knowing that at least one of her daughters would be forever scarred and changed by memories of this catastrophe.

Sheila extended the ladder as quietly as she could, but gravity took over and the legs dropped to the floor with a solid thud. She cringed before frantically scanning the hallway for trouble. When nothing came at her, she let out the breath she'd been holding and climbed down the steps.

She pulled out her gun and searched the house. She found no signs of anything being disturbed. She checked the doors and windows and found them all still secure. She leaned against the wall and sighed.

A knock on the front door sent her nearly clawing onto the ceiling. She scrambled to make sure she had a round in the chamber and rushed forward. When she peered through the peephole, a tide of relief washed over her. She hustled to open the door. "You don't know how good it is to see you, Private Vadreen."

His eyes lit up. "You're okay."

She nodded. "We've been hiding in the attic."

"Smart thinking," he said, and added in a low tone. "A lot more folks should've been that smart."

She frowned. "Tell me, how bad is it?"

He mirrored her frown. "It's bad."

After an uneasy silence, she tugged the sweaty shirt out from her chest. "I'm sorry. I imagine I'm a bit ripe."

He smirked. "You're a far sight better than any of the guys I've been around lately."

She blushed and motioned him inside. "Would you like to come in? I'm afraid I don't have much to offer in the way of food or drinks. Well, I have nothing to offer except wine, but you're more than welcome to a bottle."

He waved her off. "Thank you, but I'm just passing through. I need to get back to the barracks."

"You're not going home?"

His brow furrowed. He looked down and gave his head a slow shake.

"Oh, I'm so sorry," she said.

When he finally met her gaze, he shrugged. "We won. That's what matters."

She leaned against the door frame. "For a while there, I must admit, I thought we were on the losing side."

"Didn't we all," he added. "We took one hell of a beating, but we whooped their asses. Sorry for my language. President Mitchell sent out every C130 the flyboys had, they filled them up with some kind of magic dust, and everyone released their payload. I'm not sure how it worked, but evidently it poisoned anyone who'd been infected, wiping them out."

Goosebumps covered Sheila's sweaty skin. "They're all gone?"

"Every last one of them. Well, it's still working its magic. Most have scampered off to die in dark corners, but yeah, it seems to have worked. We'll be in the clear in no time."

She clasped her hands together and closed her eyes. *We're safe.* Parker would be home soon. Everything would be fine, just like she'd promised her girls.

An animalistic scream in the distance was echoed by gunfire.

Sheila snapped her eyes open. Private Vadreen twisted around, grabbing for his rifle. The gunfire continued, followed by a grenade blast. When he turned back to her, his expression had sobered. "You'd better stay inside."

— 6 —

As things turned out, the infected hadn't all died. Only *most* of them died. The ones who survived seemed angrier than ever. Sheila remained in the attic with her girls, coming down only once when Private Vadreen dropped off a couple jugs of water and rations when the water quit running two days earlier.

Sheila had drilled dozens of peepholes through the attic walls, both to let in fresh air and so she could have a visual connection with the outside world. Without the peepholes, she'd go crazy. If the sounds of the screams, shouts, and gunfire were any indication, Fort Bragg was making its final stand.

The three females stayed plastered to their tiny windows. A good mother would hide her daughters from the horrors taking place outside. A good mother wouldn't let them see the infected hunt down the soldiers in the streets and tear into them. By the third day, Sheila no longer had the energy to keep scolding them to get away from the peepholes when they had nothing else to look at in the barren attic.

Army trucks plowed down some of the infected, and soldiers laid down automatic fire on those still standing, but still too many escaped. As Sheila watched, she tried to find weaknesses in the infected, but the truth was, she couldn't.

She'd watched one take several gunshots, and it still managed to take down a soldier before it finally died. She assumed the soldier died since he didn't move, but he must've only been injured, because then she watched as he morphed into one of *them*. The transformation of flesh and bones was something right out of a horror movie.

She hated horror movies.

Those infected killed indiscriminately—anyone and everyone was fair game. She couldn't understand why they enjoyed killing so much. It was as though the virus made them into bloodthirsty hunters. They seemed to find glee in death and dismemberment.

Right now, she watched a trio of infected skulk down the empty street. The group moved erratically, their joints and bones making odd cracking and popping sounds. One would make a guttural moan before running up to a house and sniffing it out for signs of life. They moved forward with purpose, like military scouts—albeit alien scouts—as they laid claim to Sheila's block.

One ran up to Kelli's house but then bypassed it as if it already knew no life waited for them inside. When another let out a primal scream and ran toward Sheila's house, she held her breath. She couldn't see the creature once it got close, and she prayed it would move as swiftly past her house as the other had Kelli's.

The other two in the street stopped and turned as one to face Sheila's house. *No, no, no. What are they doing?*

The peephole was suddenly covered by a yellow eyeball less than an inch from her own and Sheila tumbled back, landing on the floor with a thud.

The infected just outside her peephole screamed. Sheila bit back a scream of her own.

"Mommy?" Jenny whispered.

Sheila furtively waved her hands before pressing a forefinger to her lips.

Her daughter's lips scrunched together as though it was a struggle to keep silent.

Sheila's heart pounded. How in the world did it climbed the house?

Glass shattered downstairs. Sheila whimpered and Tasha gasped. Both her daughters' eyes grew wide.

Jenny took off at a frantic scuttle over to Sheila, making a *swish-swish* noise across the floor. She crawled onto her mother's lap, and Sheila clutched on to her. The sound of claws scratching at the ceiling beneath them sent goosebumps across Sheila's skin. She motioned to Tasha, who moved far more quietly but just as quickly as her younger sister had, and wrapped an arm around her as well.

When something scraped against the attic door, Sheila wanted to cry out for help. Instead, she disengaged herself from her daughters as carefully as possible, though both struggled to cling to her. With them tucked behind her, she pulled out the Glock and aimed it at the only way in or out of the attic. The scratching grew relentless, and Sheila craved to yell at it to go away, to cry for help, or just to shout out every profanity she knew.

She remained silent, and her two girls remained diminutive statues behind her. She chewed on her bottom lip, praying for the infected to grow bored and leave them alone.

Instead, its impatience and agitation seemed to grow because the scratching increased. The infected were supposed to be dumb, their brains fried by fever. Yet, the attic door moved as though the infected knew where its prey hid.

Sheila leapt forward, jumping on the door and slamming it closed just as the infected tried to press it open. An angry scream reverberated through the floor. A second later, the door flung upward and Sheila was tossed to the side. The infected popped up from below and its gaze settled on her daughters, who were cowering in the corner.

Sheila rolled and fired several shots point blank at the back of its head. It fell and landed on the floor below with a thud. She leaned over the edge, aimed, and fired the remaining rounds at its chest.

It didn't move, but she couldn't tell if she'd killed it. A small part of her wondered who it'd been. Private Vadreen? Reed? *Parker?*

She slammed the attic door closed as she hurriedly reloaded her gun. She looked at her daughters. "Are you okay?"

Jenny sniffled and nodded.

Tasha swallowed. "Yeah. Did you see that thing?"

It was then Sheila noticed the bullet hole just above where her girls were sitting. She glanced down at the gun she held and tapped it against her forehead. *Idiot! Parker would never make that kind of stupid mistake*, she scolded herself.

Damn it, where are you, Parker?

She'd nearly shot her own daughters. She hadn't even considered what was on the other side of the infected when she'd fired.

Tasha shuffled to one of the peepholes. "I don't see the other monsters, Mom. I think they left."

Filled with doubt, Sheila crawled over to look outside. Sure enough, she could see no infected, but she wasn't taking any chances. This time, she sat right in front of the attic door—between the door and her girls—and aimed.

When the door lifted, Sheila fired, but the infected dodged her shot with uncanny speed. Her eyes widened in shock, and she took aim again. An explosion tore through the attic. Sheila felt herself thrown like she was tumbling beneath a waterfall. For the briefest instant, she felt a blissful weightlessness before she crashed. The impact knocked the breath from her, and her vision went black.

When she came to, she heard the *rat-tat-tat* of gunfire, but it sounded warbled, like she was underwater. A peaceful silence followed until she noticed a strange sensation, as though she was being shaken.

"Miss?" a distant voice asked.

Her eyelids seemed to fight against her as she pried them open, forcing herself to consciousness. A soldier in full battle gear was kneeling over her, grabbing her shoulder.

"Are you injured?"

She frowned, then shoved his hand off her. "You blew up my house."

"I saved your life," he corrected.

My life. The web in her mind morphed eventually into a straight line of coherence. She looked up toward the attic to find a large hole where much of the attic had been. "My girls."

"Excuse me?" he asked.

She lunged to her feet, only to collapse in a dizzy spell to the floor. She reached out with her hands. "Tasha! Jenny!"

"Mom!" came Tasha's voice from the attic. "We're up here!"

The soldier, realizing Sheila wasn't alone, rushed over to stand beneath the hole where two other soldiers stood. "Come on, girls. Jump on down. It's not safe up there."

Sheila pushed herself up, more slowly this time. Her vision tunneled, but she didn't black out. When she saw the two soot-covered girls peer over the edge, she cried out. "Oh, sweeties!"

The soldiers reached up. Tasha helped her younger sister down before letting herself fall into another soldier's arms.

Sheila let out a sob, rushed forward, and got down on her knees, hugging each girl as she was lowered to the floor. After a precious moment, she pulled back and brushed hair from their faces. "Are you okay? Do you hurt anywhere?"

"My ears hurt," Tasha said.

Jenny lifted her elbow to reveal a minor floor burn.

Sheila let out a sob of relief.

"How those kids survived that blast is a goddamned miracle," one of the soldiers said.

"Watch your language," Sheila scolded, and returned her focus to her girls.

"Sorry," the man said.

When she remembered why the soldiers were there in the first place, she looked around her and found the remains of two infected on the floor. An amputated hand lay mere inches from her knee.

She stepped back, pulling her daughters with her.

"Don't worry," one of the men said. "This pair's days of scaring little girls are over."

Sheila shook her head. "There were three of them."

The man who'd first approached Sheila spoke. "It's probably long gone by now, looking for more of its friends. They're sneaky like that."

"Sometimes, I swear they're hunting us as much as we're hunting them," another said.

She protectively held her girls tighter.

The man shrugged. "Now, the noise is likely to draw in more, so we need to get a move on. Fort Bragg has transferred headquarters and shelters to the tunnels. Grab whatever you need, and we'll bring you there. It's the only safe place for you and your girls."

Sheila frowned. She'd seen the tunnels before. "Impossible. They're not big enough to hold everyone."

The soldier grimaced. "They're plenty big enough."

Sheila froze and watched the man for a moment before turning robotically to her daughters. "I need you to run to your rooms and grab your bags." She paused to glance at two of the soldiers. "These men will go with you."

The men gave small nods. "You need to hurry. We're not going to wait for anyone," one of them said.

When both girls continued to watch her, she shooed them away. "Grab your bags, just like we talked about. Hurry."

Jenny, with tear-filled eyes, took off at a run to her room, sliding flat against the wall to stay far from the bodies, and a soldier jogged to catch up to her. Tasha, with her jaw set hard, took tentative steps alongside the soldier serving as her guard as they stepped over the bodies.

"Ma'am," the third soldier said. "Is there anything you need?"

Sheila gave a tight nod. Bile rose in her throat as she

stepped over the first mutilated corpse. It no longer had a face, and its chest was a mishmash of tattered organs. Still, she feared that it would reach out and grab her at any moment. She refused to look at the second.

When she reached her bedroom, she grabbed Parker's Texas Tech cap hanging behind the door and slipped it on over her greasy hair. She felt odd having a strange man in her and Parker's bedroom, but he didn't enter, as though sensing she needed the space. She grabbed the duffle bag she'd already packed with a couple outfits and extra cash. She opened the underwear drawer and ruffled through the underwear, socks, and ties. Some folks would find it odd how many ties Parker had for never needing one for work, and memories of their times together brought out a smile.

Her humor faded as quickly as it came, and she grabbed the extra boxes of ammo for her Glock and dropped them in the bag. She turned. "I'm ready."

The soldier nodded, and they headed down the hall.

She stopped at Tasha's room, where her older daughter was standing in the middle of the room, holding a purple T-shirt in her hands.

"Hurry up, dear. We need to get moving," Sheila said.

Tasha sighed and held up the shirt. "But, my dinosaur shirt hasn't been washed."

"It's okay, sweetie."

"But, it has a stain."

"Just grab it. We'll wash it when we get to the tunnels."

Tasha frowned at her mother before stuffing the shirt into her bright backpack. Strapped to the front of the pack was Blinky.

Sheila turned to check on Jenny, who was already

wearing her little backpack and holding her favorite fuzzy green blanket. Sheila frowned when she saw Jenny's limp bag. "Are you sure you're all packed?"

"I'm all ready," she said in a hurry, her eyes flitting around the room.

Sheila stepped forward and motioned for her daughter to turn around. "Let me see."

She twisted away. "I'm ready, Mommy, really."

That piqued Sheila's curiosity. "Stand still, beanpole." She held her daughter and unzipped her pack to find it empty except for a very large Colt .45 pistol.

Sheila's eyes widened, and she glanced back at the soldier who seemed just as surprised. She yanked out the gun. "How did you get this, Jennifer Lynn?"

Jenny fidgeted. "It's Daddy's."

"I know full well it's Daddy's. I asked, *how did you get this?*"

"I-I found the key to Daddy's gun case, but I wasn't stealing it, I swear! It's his favorite. I just wanted to give it to him."

Sheila gave a weak smile. "What do you say I hold on to it for now? You can give it to him when you see him. Now, how about you put everything back into your bag?"

Jenny nodded and ran over to her bed where the bag's original contents sat in piles. She stuffed an armful into her bag. Sheila helped her with the zipper, and Jenny marched to the door.

The soldier standing in her room grabbed the blanket left on the bed. "Hey, squirt. Aren't you forgetting something?"

She turned and saw her blanket, and she rushed back for it. She grabbed it and then tugged his hand. "Pick me up."

"Jenny, you're too big—" Sheila began.

The soldier picked up the small girl in a swift movement, and Jenny giggled.

"Looks like someone had a visit from the tooth fairy recently," he said.

She pulled her lips back farther to showcase her missing teeth and held up two fingers.

"Wow, that's impressive," he replied.

Sheila smiled. "You're good with kids. I'm guessing you have some of your own."

He nodded. "Three. Ages six, nine, and twelve. They're already in the tunnels, so you can meet them when you get there."

When all six reached the living room, Sheila looked across the men's faces. "Thank you."

The soldier shrugged. "Just doing our job, ma'am." He motioned outside. "Let's load up and head in. It's been a long day."

Before they headed out the front door, Sheila paused. "Oh, just one second. I have to leave a note for my husband."

The soldier nodded and motioned the others to the Humvee parked on her front yard.

Sheila ran to the kitchen, grabbed a piece of chalk and wrote on the chalkboard wall:

Parker – Went to tunnels for shelter. Love you! Sheila

Satisfied, she set the chalk down.

Gunshots erupted outside.

Her gaze shot up. "No!" She ran from the kitchen and out the front door. The three soldiers were fighting with a single infected. She searched for her daughters, but couldn't find them anywhere.

She pulled out her pistol and ran toward the fray. By the time she reached them, the infected was down, along with two of the soldiers. The third began to pace, cussing up a storm.

Sheila gave the infected lying on the ground a wide berth. "Where are my girls?"

The man ignored her.

She looked at the Humvee and yanked open the door to find her daughters hiding in the back seat on the floor. "Oh, thank God," she muttered. "Are you both okay?"

They looked up and nodded.

Jenny began to cry. "Mommy, I want the monsters to go away!"

Sheila rubbed her daughter's head. "They will, sweetie." She gave Tasha a reassuring squeeze as well. "We just have to be strong for a little bit longer." She'd almost said *until Daddy gets home*, but she realized that in all likelihood, Parker Horn was already dead.

"No, no, no, no, no," the remaining soldier continually repeated to himself.

Sheila glanced back at her daughters. "Wait here," she ordered before turning to the man pacing the ground. "We need to get to the tunnels."

Still, he ignored her.

She grabbed his shoulder.

He swung his rifle around at her, and she jumped back. "Hey!"

She noticed the blood streaming from his neck, and she covered her mouth. "You're hurt."

"I'm bit," he said in a monotone voice. His stressed features morphed into robotic movements as though he were on autopilot. Then, he turned his rifle on himself and pulled the trigger.

Sheila cried out and found herself doing a three-sixty to regain her bearings. She stumbled to the Humvee and climbed into the driver's seat.

"Mom, there's blood on your face," Tasha said from behind her.

Sheila looked at herself in the mirror, finding blood splatter across her cheeks and forehead. Terror climbed her spine, and she used the bottom of her shirt to scrub the blood away. Would the soldier's blood be infectious already? Could she get sick that easily?

"What do we do now?" Tasha asked.

Sheila numbly looked around the interior. The only access to the tunnels that she knew about was over ten blocks from her house. Ten blocks was an impossible feat when they couldn't make it twenty yards outside the house without being attacked. She looked at the steering wheel. Worse, she didn't have a driver's license.

She sucked in a deep breath and turned to face her daughters. "I'm going to get us to the tunnels."

— 7 —

Sheila Horn had been behind the wheel of a car before. After all, driver's education was a required course in her high school. She understood all the fundamentals of driving, but when it came to putting them all together, she had the coordination of a drunk giraffe. The D+ she got in that class was the lowest grade she ever got in her life. Her dad had said it best when he told her on her sixteenth birthday, "Some people can't play the piano; some people can't sing. You, pumpkin, sure can't drive a car."

She started the vehicle and popped the Humvee into gear. She stepped on the gas and they lurched forward. She slammed on the brakes and they slammed to a stop.

"Mom, I don't think you're doing it right," Tasha offered.

"Yeah, it doesn't do that when Dad drives," Jenny added.

"Thank you for your helpfulness, girls," Sheila replied drily before adding, "This is a very big vehicle. It doesn't drive like Daddy's car."

She tried again. This time, she was able to keep the speed slow enough for her to maintain control, and—

rather than making a U-turn, which she deemed was logistically impossible—she decided to drive around the block to get turned in the right direction.

In a way, she was lucky that there were no other vehicles on the road, because she would've driven right through them. She tried to keep the Humvee straight, but every time she moved the wheel, she overcorrected and ended up jumping curves—on either side of the road. By the time she'd taken out the third mailbox, she felt like she was finally getting a handle on the driving thing.

"How much farther?" Jenny asked.

"A bit farther," Sheila answered.

"Do you want me to drive?" Tasha asked. "It doesn't look that hard."

"I've got it under control," Sheila snapped. "I need you two to stay down back there."

She drove for over a block before she saw the first sign of life: a shadow that disappeared behind a curtain. The shredded bodies scattered across the ground served as a warning for her to not stop. In this neighborhood, the houses were larger, homes of general and flag officers, and she wondered if they'd had more soldiers to protect the families. Not that it looked like it had done any good.

Movement out of the corner of her eye caused her to swerve. She lost control and slammed on the brakes.

The shape turned out to be a middle-aged woman who stopped in front of the Humvee, loosely gripping a shotgun over her chest. The woman's T-shirt hung on her, and strands of her greasy hair draped her face while most was pulled back into a loose ponytail. She looked like she hadn't showered in a week. More importantly, the woman seemed uninjured and—especially—uninfected.

The woman's features were undeniably familiar, but

Sheila gaped at her for a couple of long seconds before she recognized the woman. Sheila's eyes widened, and she hurriedly rolled down her window and stuck her head out. "Alic? Is that you?"

Alic McGregor's ramrod-straight form relaxed, and she rushed over to stand at Sheila's door. "Sheila? Oh, thank God. I couldn't see you through that grimy windshield."

"Hi, Mrs. McGregor," Tasha said.

"Hi, Mrs. McGregor," Jenny echoed.

Alic smiled warmly. "Hello, girls. You don't know how good it is to see your faces."

"What are you doing out here?" Sheila asked. "It's too dangerous to be outside."

Alic held up a roll of papers.

"Are you crazy?" Sheila motioned around her. "You can't be still trying to deliver newsletters."

The other woman lifted her chin. "There are people still in hiding. They need to know that the tunnels are safe."

She unrolled the papers so Sheila could see the page. Written in bold black marker was:

Fort Bragg has fallen.
Seek shelter in the tunnels. You'll be safe there.
ALL ARE WELCOME.

Below the words was a hastily drawn map of the barracks area of Fort Bragg, with a large X marking the tunnel's main entrance.

"People need to know," Alic said simply.

Feeling deflated, Sheila self-consciously tucked a loose clump of hair under her cap. "We're headed to the tunnels now. Why don't you come with us? We can post the flyers along the way."

Alic let out a deep sigh. "I'd like that very much." She jogged around and climbed in the front seat. "Today hasn't been going well. I lost my security detail before I had a chance to post any flyers."

Sheila stepped on the gas pedal, and the vehicle hit the bumper of a car.

Alic gave an incredulous stare. "You can drive, can't you?"

Sheila shot her an indignant glare. "I haven't gotten around to getting my license yet."

"How about I drive?" Alic offered.

Sheila didn't hesitate to manhandle the shifter into park. "Be my guest."

Alic hopped out and walked around the front of the Humvee. Sheila looked outside and chose instead to shimmy ungracefully across the front seats. Alic climbed behind the wheel and smoothly shifted gears.

That Sheila couldn't smell Alic was a sign of how badly they all needed showers. She discreetly sniffed her armpits and grimaced. *Hopefully, the tunnels have running water.*

Alic covered the next couple of blocks in half the time it had taken Sheila to cover the first block. Alic swerved frequently to give wide berth to vehicles parked along the sides and to avoid running over debris.

"You drive like Daddy, Mrs. McGregor," Jenny said, leaning as close to the front seat as she could get.

Alic's brow rose. "Is that good?"

"Dad's a great driver," Tasha answered.

"He's the best," Jenny added, beaming.

Alic's face softened, and she threw a glance in Sheila's

direction. "Any news on your husband? His name's Parker, right?"

Sheila swallowed and nodded. "He was off base before they locked everything down."

"Oh." Alic veered around a car stalled in the middle of the road. "Well, Roy has spoken highly of him. If anyone can make it out there, an ACE man can."

"Thanks," Sheila replied. "How's Roy?" She'd always known Alic's husband only as Colonel McGregor, and using his name felt foreign on her lips.

"Roy is in the tunnels waiting for me. Or, at least, he'd better be in the tunnels. Can you believe that fool was going to send an entire squad to pick me up?"

Sheila shrugged as if she'd expect nothing different.

"Humph," Alic added. "I already feel awful about what happened to Jemison and Rafter. I told him I'd divorce him if he risked the lives of any more of his men for me."

"I bet he wasn't too happy about that."

"Not one bit. Nonetheless, he knew I was right. If he sent a team for me, then he should be sending teams for every family left out here. If he did that, there'd be no one left to hold off the Variants."

"Variants?"

"That's what they're calling the ones that survived the poison."

"Oh," Sheila said without really listening, as she was too focused on scanning the landscape before them from left to right and back again. She expected to see yellow eyes watching her from behind every parked car and from within every house. Instead, it seemed as though the neighborhoods were devoid of any life.

"Everyone's gone," she said under her breath.

"What?" Alic asked.

"Oh, nothing," she quickly replied. "Just talking to myself."

Where everyone went was something Sheila didn't really want to know. She'd seen what had happened to Kelli and what had nearly happened to her and the girls. She suspected the Variants were picking off families one house at a time because there weren't enough infected to make a full-out assault.

Sunlight glistened off metal, and Sheila pointed. "Watch out. It looks like a lot of shrapnel straight ahead." As soon as she said the word "shrapnel," she frowned. Since when had shrapnel become a part of her daily vocabulary?

Alic leaned forward. "I see it. My God, this whole base has become a war zone."

She turned to the left and brought the Humvee onto the sidewalk to avoid the twisted metal that looked like it had come off a military vehicle but was now blackened chunks.

"If we didn't have this Humvee," Alic said, "we'd likely have blown tires by now and would be walking the rest of the way to the tunnels."

Sheila shivered at the thought.

"Mom, can we get up now?" Tasha asked from behind Sheila's seat.

"Not yet," Sheila answered. "The tunnels aren't much farther."

"How did you get a hold of a working Humvee?" Alic asked.

Sheila thought about the troops who'd come to her rescue, and her heart became leaden. "A couple of the Variants broke in and found us hiding in the attic." She shivered. "Lucky for us, there were troops in the area who heard my gunshots. They took out the Variants and were going to take us to the tunnels, but…"

"But something happened," Alic finished for her. "I know. *Something* always happens as long as those Variants survive. Roy said that whatever they sprayed across the cities was supposed to kill them all, but there seem to be plenty that proved immune. Roy said the ones that are left have changed. They're more aggressive."

Sheila chuckled drily. "How could they possibly get any meaner?"

Alic shrugged. "He also said they're getting smarter."

Sheila sobered. "Let's hope he's wrong."

"Let's hope," Alic echoed before pointing at the clubhouse. "Let's post the flyers here."

Alic pulled the Humvee off the street and weaved it through the parking lot until she reached the bulletin board where folks posted flyers on events, lost-and-found items, and ads. She stopped with the bumper a few feet from the board and looked around. "I don't see anything. You?"

"Nothing," Sheila said.

Alic grabbed the flyers, and Sheila grabbed her hand. "I'll do it. You stay behind the wheel in case we need to make a run for it."

After a moment of thought, Alic nodded. "Okay. Be careful."

Sheila glanced back at her girls, who were both watching her with saucer-sized gazes.

"Don't worry, sweeties. I'm just hanging something on the board and will right be back. You can watch."

"Be careful," Tasha said. "I'll watch out for the monsters."

"Yeah. Me, too," Jenny said.

Sheila smiled. Then, she turned, took a deep breath, grabbed the flyers and staple gun, and stepped outside. She did a full three-sixty first, smelling the air but noticing nothing but grass and trees. She then jogged over to the board and began to staple flyers over the other pages, making no attempt to have them lined up properly.

Every staple pounding into the board seemed like thunder to Sheila, and she felt her heartbeat crescendo in response. Movement at the tree sent Sheila racing back into the Humvee. "In the tree! Go, go, go!"

Alic snapped the vehicle into gear, and Tasha started laughing. "Mom, it's a squirrel!"

"Squirrel!" Jenny belted out a laugh. "Mommy's scared of a squirrel!"

Rather than accelerating, Alic kept her foot on the brake. She looked to where Sheila was pointing, then looked back at Sheila before bursting out laughing.

Sheila looked back at the tree to find the squirrel flicking its tail. "Well, it was a really big squirrel." She started laughing. The Humvee filled with the pleasant sounds.

Alic sighed after she caught her breath. "Oh, thank you. I needed that."

Sheila shot one more glance back at the squirrel. This time, the squirrel had disappeared. In its place clung a yellow-eyed Variant, and it seemed to be mouthing something intelligible to her. Her smile dropped. "Step on it, Alic! Not joking this time!"

The Humvee sprung forward, throwing everyone back in their seats. Sheila reached for her gun and readied it. The Variant gave chase, and Sheila watched it gain on them through the side mirror.

She snapped around to check on her daughters. "Stay down back there and hold on!"

Alic tore around corners and zigzagged down the street. The Variant hopped over cars to close the distance. When it was several car lengths behind them, it stopped cold and turned toward a house.

It was then Sheila saw the woman standing behind the large bay window. Sheila didn't recognize her, but that made the punch to her gut no less painful. "Oh, no," she said breathlessly. Sheila watched the Variant scream before crashing through the window.

Sheila clenched her eyes shut and turned away.

"I feel very sorry for whatever drew its attention away from us, but I'm thankful it gave up," Alic said, her voice sounding hollow. She slammed her hand against the steering wheel. "Damn it!"

No one had anything to say after that.

The tension in the Humvee rose when Alic turned the corner. Before them stood haphazard rows of military vehicles, cars, trucks, and anything else that could congest a road.

A full-out traffic jam.

"It just keeps getting better and better," Alic said drily.

"Maybe there's another way," Sheila offered.

"I've lived at Fort Bragg for over twenty years," Alic said. "There's no other way."

The Humvee slowed to a crawl. Alic pressed against a car bumper. As she moved it out of the way, it complained with a metallic shriek.

"It's too loud," Sheila said. "You'll draw attention to us."

Alic scowled. "Everyone must've made a mad rush for the tunnels as soon as it was announced. Since your husband is off base, you wouldn't have been notified. There must be hundreds of people who haven't been notified yet."

"How much farther to the tunnels?" Sheila asked.

Alic's lips thinned. "About three blocks, give or take."

Sheila thought of the Variant that had chased them, and felt the warmth drain from her face. "That's a long distance."

"We can't stay here. We're basically dinner in a can for the Variants as long as we're sitting still. We can't drive, because everything's too jammed together down there for the Humvee to get through."

Sheila took in a deep inhalation before turning to face her daughters. "Jenny, Tasha, we're going to go for a walk."

"But, I don't want to go outside," Jenny complained.

"We have to, sweetie. We can't stay here anymore," Sheila said, then swallowed as she looked over both her girls. "Now, I want you to hold each other's hands and don't let go, no matter what."

— 8 —

Leaving the relative security of the Humvee was the second hardest thing Sheila had done that day. Once outside, Tasha and Sheila each took one of Jenny's hands, while Sheila held the pistol in her free hand. Alic and Sheila shared a knowing look. The older woman took the lead, holding her shotgun level before her.

The street looked blocked all the way to the barracks. Cars, trucks, and military vehicles were slammed together, left in the exact positions where they'd collided. They were strewn on the street, sidewalks, and lawns. Car doors had been left open. Broken glass lay on the concrete. Blood splattered windshields. When she saw a butchered body lying on the hood of a car, Sheila sucked in a breath and turned away.

"Don't look at the cars," she ordered her girls. "Just keep your eyes on the path straight ahead."

Except there was no path. They had to weave through the vehicles, sometimes climbing over one to make forward progress. Sheila was surprised they hadn't seen more Variants by now. The infected prowled the night in greater forces, but perhaps that was because the uninfected were at a disadvantage during those dark hours. Regardless, they seemed to have little deterrence to hunting in the broad daylight as well.

Maybe she imagined the hair-raising feeling of predatory gazes upon her, but that didn't make the feeling any less real. She threw quick glances at the surrounding buildings. They stood like tireless ghosts in the harsh sunlight. Every shattered window seemed to hide a specter in its darkness.

She shivered.

"Ouch, Mom," Tasha said in a loud whisper, trying to yank away. "You're squeezing too hard."

Sheila looked down to her wincing daughter, then to her hand, realizing her fingers had formed a vise around her daughter's. She forced herself to relax. "Oh, sorry, sweetie."

A feral shriek shattered the air, and Sheila spun around to seek out the source while raising her gun. A Variant crouched on the hood of a nearby truck. It peered down at the four females. It howled again, echoed by a dozen more howls encircling them.

Sheila's blood froze. "Oh, God, no. They're everywhere."

Alic fired her shotgun. The crouching Variant leapt to another vehicle with inhuman speed, effortlessly dodging the blast.

Alic yanked around. "Go! I'll cover!"

Sheila gave Alic an incredulous look.

"I'll catch up. Now, go!"

Sheila jumped into action and then tugged Tasha's arm. "Don't let go!"

Sheila led her daughters past Alic as the woman fired another shot. The two women made eye contact just long enough for Sheila to see the resolution in Alic's eyes. Sheila hoped the other woman had seen the raw gratitude in hers.

Sheila fought against the urge to call for Alic. Instead, she ran, pulling her girls along as quickly as they could keep up. Tasha kept pace with her mother, but they'd made it only a few dozen feet before Jenny's short legs began to lag behind.

The howls grew louder, and Sheila caught movement out of the corner of her eye. "Faster!"

They were proving nowhere near fast enough to escape the Variants.

Jenny tripped. "Mommy!" Tasha pulled her sister's arm, and Sheila switched positions to carry her younger daughter. She picked up Jenny, but froze before she took a step. Sprinting directly at them was a Variant.

"Mom!" Tasha screamed.

Sheila dropped Jenny and tucked both girls behind her. She raised her gun and fired off shot after shot. The Variant dodged to the left and right, missing the bullets. When she fired her last round, she could've sworn the Variant was grinning with its horrifying mouth filled with shard-like teeth.

Gunfire erupted. The Variant screeched and twisted before lobbing off to disappear behind a tree.

"Head to your two o'clock. Get a move on!" a male voice shouted.

Sheila found the soldier waving at her from the front door two buildings down. She dropped the gun and grabbed Jenny and Tasha's hands. She pulled them with her as she ran. A soldier stood scowling on the rooftop and laid down cover fire once she reached the building.

It was a small office building with shattered windows.

She jumped first through the open doorway, dragging her girls behind her. She slipped. Her feet went flying out from under her, and her head slammed against the floor. She felt a thud, then saw stars. The pain followed immediately. Stings shot through her body from where she'd hit the floor hardest—her head, elbow, and butt. She forced herself to her feet, fighting to stand straight through the dizziness.

She then noticed why she fell. Fresh blood marks scraped the floors as though whatever had been attacked here had been dragged off into the darkness. Neither girl had fallen, and she reclaimed their hands to lead them down the hallway. Jenny was gasping for air, and Tasha had pink cheeks.

"You're doing great, girls. Just a little bit farther," Sheila said in between breaths.

A shape moved in front them, and Sheila froze. She reached for her gun, realizing she no longer had it on her.

"This way," the shape spoke—a soldier wearing full impact armor and gas mask. He motioned Sheila and her daughters to the bottom of a stairwell, where he pointed to the stairs.

Sheila looked over her shoulder. "Wait. Alic is still out there."

He shook his head. "No time."

Sheila tensed. "But—"

"You know how many of those things were on your tail? Move it!"

Sheila bit back any further complaint. Instead, she gave a tight nod and pressed her girls forward. "We're almost there, sweeties."

He yanked the door shut behind them and then followed.

"Shouldn't we brace something against it?" Sheila asked.

"Wouldn't do any good. Besides, the bastards seem to prefer climbing walls over taking stairs."

"Oh."

They ran up the stairs where the sounds of gunfire became louder and louder.

On the roof, she found one soldier on his stomach, firing down to the street below. A second soldier stood nearby, covering the first.

"Reloading," the first said.

"I'm in." The second soldier dropped to a knee and began firing.

Sheila clutched her daughters to her and stood with them against the wall that led to the stairwell After a minute, the gunfire stopped.

"Looks like they're bugging out."

"Until they get bored again, anyway," the second answered.

Sheila cupped Jenny's face. "How are you doing?"

Her younger daughter was still panting, her face flush. Her bottom lip quivered. "I want to go home." Then, she burst out sobbing.

"Oh, sweetie." Sheila hugged her, realizing just how strong her little girls had been so far. "I know you do. We will as soon as we can. First, we get to have a sleepover in the tunnels. It'll be fun."

Jenny sniffled. "No, it won't."

Sheila tucked a tuft of loose hair behind Jenny's ear before turning to Tasha. Her older daughter had dark circles under her eyes, and her rosy cheeks glistened with sweat. Even so, there was a quiet strength in her eyes—she had the same resolute gaze as her father. She winced.

"My ears still hurt," she said sheepishly as if she felt bad complaining about something.

Sheila gently checked Tasha's ears before hugging her. "You just have to hang in there for a little bit longer, sweetie."

"Are any of you injured? Bit? Scratched? Cut?"

Sheila turned her attention to find the soldier who'd led them up the stairs standing near them. She shook her head. "We're okay."

Sheila looked over to the two soldiers who were surveying the street below.

"How about Alic? She's still down there," Sheila called out. "Do you see her?"

One of the soldiers spoke without turning her way. "She's not coming."

Sheila heaved and nearly threw up. She slid down the wall to sit on the roof. Alic had to have known that to remain out there was suicide, that she'd been lying when she'd said, "I'll catch up."

Sheila knew that what Alic had done hadn't been for Sheila's benefit. It'd been the same reason Alic had put her own safety at risk to distribute flyers. She'd always been the one to help new families acclimate to military life, and she'd been the one in on domestic disputes and such. Alic had just kept doing what she'd always done, and it'd gotten her killed.

Sheila felt anger that Alic had stayed behind to hold off the Variants, but the truth was that if Alic hadn't been foolishly valiant, Sheila, Tasha, and Jenny would all be dead right now. Alic McGregor had given her life to save them.

"The base is crawling with the suck-faces now," the other soldier said. "Wherever they slinked off to after the killer rain, they're back. And, they brought friends."

One of the soldiers near the roof edge came walking over. He reached into his Velcro pocket and pulled out a candy bar. He broke the candy bar in half and held it out between the girls. "I only have one, so you'll have to share it."

Both girls eyed it hungrily. Jenny reached out, but Tasha slapped her hand away. "Ow!"

"We don't take things from strangers," Tasha said.

"Is that right?" the man said. He held out an open hand. "Well, I'm Jinx. It's nice to meet you."

Tasha shot a pleading glance to her mother, who smiled and nodded. She shook his hand first, then Jenny did. When he held out the candy bar halves again, the girls ripped the candy from Jinx's hands in a flash and tore into them like the rabid children they were.

Sheila forced herself back to her feet, and she shook Jinx's hand. "I'm Sheila Horn. These are my daughters, Tasha and Jenny. I can't thank you enough for the help back there."

Jinx's brows furrowed. "Horn, as in Big Horn's wife?"

She nodded.

"Well, I'll be damned. We've been on several missions with Big Horn and Team Ghost before," the other soldier at the rooftop waved, taking a toothpick out of his mouth. "I'm Chow. Jinx and I are with Team Titanium. That guy that brought you up is Rosie from the 802nd."

The third soldier shook her hand. "The name's Collin Rosenstein."

"But, we just call him Rosie," Jinx said.

"Stay frosty," Chow said. "I see movement. Get back into position and keep your eyes and ears open."

"On my way," Rosie said and headed back down the stairs.

Jinx began to patrol the other three lines of the roof.

As the soldiers maintained the perimeter, Sheila pulled out the Colt she'd taken from Jenny. She'd seen Parker handle that gun at least a hundred times. It was an antique, a gift from his grandfather. She remembered watching how lovingly he'd clean the gun and the pride in his eyes when he'd shown it to her the first time.

God, how she wished Parker were here right now.

Except he wasn't here. All she had of him was a heavy, oversized pistol that was empty. She should've left it behind, but somehow it felt like the last physical tether she had to Parker.

Chow whistled. "Now, that's a pretty hand cannon."

Sheila looked up to see Chow eying the Colt as he walked the roofline.

"It's Parker's," she said and slid the gun back through her belt loop. "But it's empty."

"Contact." Jinx motioned, breaking into their conversation. "Looks like our ugly friends are coming from the south this time." He lifted his rifle and fired off a series of shots.

Chow ran over to Jinx and joined in.

Sheila's daughters clung to their mother as the gunfire echoed around them. Jenny clapped her hands over her ears.

"I'm out!" Jinx called out. "Reloading."

More gunfire erupted downstairs. Sheila jumped to her feet and pulled her daughters away from the doorway.

Jinx frowned and turned to the closed door. He tapped Chow's shoulder and make a quick hand signal before running over to the stairwell. "Stay here," he ordered before opening the door and heading into the unknown battle taking place beneath them.

She searched the roof to find a better place for her and her girls. Several feet away, the building's air conditioning unit stood on metal legs that held it about a foot above the surface. She pressed her daughters toward it. "I want you to tuck in under that, okay? *Supergirl!*"

Neither girl hesitated. Jenny rolled under the unit first, followed by Tasha. Sheila made eye contact with each fearful girl before she herself sat down in front of them as a last line of defense.

She clasped her hands together. *Please, God. Don't let them find my little girls.*

Jinx quit firing. He walked the roofline before turning to face her.

Sheila took a deep breath. "Are they gone?"

"For now," he said. "But, they'll be back. They always come back."

"Like a bad girlfriend," Chow added.

Sheila snapped to see the other soldier emerge from the stairwell. "Thank God you're okay." Her relief disappeared when she realized Chow was carrying Rosie.

"The bastards came at us from two directions this time," Chow said as he helped Rosie down.

Sheila ran over. Rosie's face was wrenched in pain. He held a hand against his neck, and red blood flowed between his fingers.

Her eyebrows tightened. "Oh, Rosie."

"Those things are fast," Rosie gritted out.

Jinx pulled out a first aid kit and knelt beside Rosie.

Chow grimaced. "They're toying with us. Every time, they come at us from a different angle, making us burn through our ammo. If these guys played chess," he looked down shook his head, "they'd have us at one move short of checkmate right now."

"We've got to get off this roof," Jinx said. "We're sitting ducks up here. We know it and they know it."

He patched Rosie's neck, and the wounded man hissed. "How about you treat me to dinner before you start on the rough play?"

Jinx smirked and slapped Rosie's knee. "You're lucky. It's just a scratch."

Rosie's expression fell, and he pointed to his neck. "You know damn well what it is."

Jinx's lips thinned. He glanced at Chow, whose expression was unreadable to Sheila.

Jinx shrugged. "Who knows? Maybe the pixie dust they dropped changed things, and they're no longer infectious."

"Yeah, maybe," Rosie said, not sounding like he believed the words.

Sheila forced a placating smile and squeezed Rosie's hand, and the rooftop fell into a silent routine of patrol, wait, shoot, and repeat.

"Hang in there," she told her daughters as she cupped both their cheeks. "We'll be to the tunnels soon."

"Promise?" Jenny said.

Sheila smiled and ran her fingers over her chest. "Cross my heart."

"Pinky swear?" Tasha asked.

Sheila held out her pinky and her daughter latched on to it.

"Now, get some sleep."

She dusted off her pants, walked over, and checked on Rosie to find him sleeping fitfully. His face was a sheen of sweat and his eyebrows tight as though he was fighting through a nightmare. She rubbed his arm, and his features calmed. She stood and walked over to where Jinx stood, patrolling the east and north sides of the rooftop.

"How's he doing?" he asked when she approached.

"How do you think? He's infected, and he knows it." She closed her eyes and sighed. "I'm sorry. I don't mean to be short. It's just—"

"I get it. You're a civvie and not used to all this." He chuckled and motioned around them. "Shit, I've made it through five tours, and this scares the living crap out of me."

He watched her for a moment. "I'll tell you what you can do. We have a few C-RATS stashed over there. How about you fix us up some dinner?"

She guffawed.

"What?"

She started to walk to where he pointed. "If you knew me, you'd know better than to ask me to cook anything."

He shrugged. "They're C-RATS. They can't get any worse."

She smirked. "I bet they can."

A few minutes later, everyone ate while Tasha and Jenny slept soundly. Chow and Jinx continued to pace the roof edges, taking brief pauses to shovel bites of their prepared meals into their mouths.

"I never thought it was possible for C-RATS to be made worse, but you have a gift," Jinx said. "What made you think it would be a good idea to mix lasagna with stroganoff?"

"Don't say I didn't warn you." Sheila leaned back. "So, what's the plan for getting off this roof?"

Chow's response was a blank stare.

She pursed her lips together. "Don't tell me that Team

Titanium can't come up with a plan for getting to the tunnels. I can practically see them from here."

"We have plans," Jinx said. "Plan A is to hold position until rescue arrives."

"The problem with Plan A is that we can't raise anyone on the radios."

Sheila's brow rose. "What about Plan B?"

Jinx swallowed. "We have a Plan B, but it didn't quite pan out as expected the first time we tried it."

"Jinx..." Chow cautioned.

"You were Plan B," Rosie said from behind her.

She turned. "What do you mean?"

When neither man spoke, Rosie continued. "Come on guys, don't want to own up to your own plan now?"

Chow sighed. "The Variants are watching the roof like a bull after a red flag, so we can't make a move without them on our backs. There's not enough of them down there for a frontal assault, so we've been biding our time."

"Yet," Jinx added. "There's not enough of them *yet*, but that's changing. They're forming into packs. There are more of them every time they attack. It's just a matter of time which runs out first—our ammo or them. We're down to four ammo clips, so the odds aren't in our favor."

"We have to leave the roof," Chow said. "Without reinforcements, we need a diversion to do that."

"Plan B," Rosie said.

"Unfortunately, there seems to be only one thing that draws their attention away from us."

Sheila's lips parted. The single word came out a whisper. "People."

Jinx winced. "Yeah."

Her jaw tightened as she connected the dots. "My girls

and I were your Plan B."

Chow held up his hand. "The plan sounded better in concept than it worked in execution. We had no idea a couple of women and two little girls would come running down that street. We were banking on it being some asshole from ISIS to be strolling by."

Her fists clenched. "I can't believe you were using people as sacrificial lambs."

"Listen," Jinx held up his hand. "We could've made it, but we stayed behind to help you."

"You *intended* to leave us to get torn apart," she said.

"But we didn't," Chow countered. "Plan B had some flaws to it. We realize that now."

"Tell me you didn't do the same thing with your friend Alic back there," Jinx said. "Tell me you didn't use her as a diversion for you to escape."

Sheila's eyes widened and her jaw dropped. In spite of her anger, she clamped her jaw shut rather than snapping back with a sharp retort. They were right. She knew it and they knew it, and shame filled her. She took a deep breath and closed her eyes. When she opened them, she shot Jinx a scathing look. "Alic volunteered. It was her choice. She sacrificed herself for my girls. She's a hero, and I won't tarnish that by calling her a diversion. Not now, not ever."

Jinx watched for her a moment, then gave a tight nod.

She cocked her head. "So, Plan B is waiting for a diversion. Our lives are depending on luck?"

Chow's lips thinned, and he glanced over Sheila's shoulder. She turned to find Rosie watching them all intently. His eyebrows furrowed in concentration— though it could've also been in pain—and after a moment, his entire body seemed to relax.

"What the hell," he said, sounding utterly defeated. "Looks like you guys got yourselves a diversion."

— 9 —

Sheila glanced at Jinx, whose face bore a hard expression, but said nothing. She looked across the roof to see that Chow also stood still, his gaze fully on Rosie.

Her jaw slackened. "Rosie. You can't—"

Rosie cut her off with a wave of his hand. "We all know the situation. We need a diversion, and we're fresh out of grenades. We're not going to make it through the night up here. Either way, I'm not going to make it through the night."

"You don't know that," she said. "Someone may pass through. We can get you help."

He shook his head and winced at the movement. "I can *feel* it. It's the virus. I can feel it eating through my blood like termites. I'm already seeing things that I know aren't real. I don't know how much longer I'll be able hold it off. I'm running out of time. I can help you get off this roof and to tunnels."

"We're all running out of time," Jinx said, the words barely above a whisper.

She swallowed, finding wise words impossible. Instead, she turned to her sleeping daughters. Even with dirt smudges on their faces and their clothes wrinkled, they looked innocent, even peaceful, in their slumber. So help her, God, she'd do anything for them.

Her nails dug into her palms. She hated that her heart had leapt the instant Rosie volunteered. She hated that she found hope when another person would have to die. When she turned back to Rosie, she said the only thing she could. "Thank you."

His features softened. "I want to do it."

Chow broke the silence. "It's going to be dark in a couple of hours. You'd better wake your girls."

Fifteen minutes later, Sheila hugged Rosie and watched as Chow helped him down the stairs. She followed with her girls behind her and Jinx covering their backs.

We're going to die.

She hated the thought that was on auto-play in her mind, threatening to freeze up her muscles.

Shut up, shut up, shut up, she scolded herself.

Once they reached the bottom of the stairs, Chow released Rosie. "Run like a bat out of hell for the HEMTT in the alley behind the medical center. It wasn't blocked in when we left it, and it's ready to go. You get in there, and you drive. As fast and hard as you can. Plow through the suck-faces."

Rosie gave no sign of hearing him.

Chow patted the wounded man's soldier. "You can do this."

Rosie cocked his head slightly but then didn't look back. Instead, he clenched his rifle and took a tentative step forward, then another. Sheila imagined the soldier was fighting against every survival instinct in his body.

Chow turned to them. "Ready?"

Sheila swallowed and nodded.

We're going to die.

Chow motioned for Tasha. She walked over and he picked her up, and Jinx picked up Jenny. Sheila felt helpless, carrying nothing while the soldiers were carrying both her girls and their rifles. A few minutes earlier, the three men had pooled their ammo, which gave a full clip to Jinx and Chow each and one and a half clips to Rosie. She hated to admit that she was disappointed that Jinx and Chow hadn't kept more ammo for themselves.

Sheila walked, sandwiched between the two men, knowing that they had positioned her there to protect her. She realized how much harder she and her girls made the soldiers' journey to the tunnels, and she wondered if either man had considered leaving them behind.

They stood at the back entrance and waited. It felt like minutes had passed since Rosie had disappeared out the front door. The silence was long and stifling.

"Maybe they're gone," she offered in a whisper.

Chow gave his head a slow shake from side to side.

"Nah. They're still out there. There's more of them out there than ticks on a deer," Jinx whispered back.

Gunfire erupted behind them, and Sheila jumped.

Chow motioned forward, and he strode out the back entrance. They walked side by side, and Sheila had to jog to keep up due to her much shorter legs. Every footstep of hers sounded like a sledgehammer pounding the ground while the men, even carrying all the extra weight, were far quieter. The only louder sound was Rosie's gunfire.

Chow's head was constantly turning left to right as he scanned the landscape, and Tasha seemed to be doing the same. Jenny watched her mother over Jinx's shoulder, and Sheila never took her eyes off her except to make quick glances at Tasha.

When the rooftop was a block behind them, hope surged. Rosie had done it!

Then everything went quiet.

Chow and Jinx began to jog, and Sheila ran. Her heart pounded. Did Rosie make it? Were they far enough away that the Variants wouldn't find them? How much farther to the tunnels?

As the men picked up speed, Sheila found she could no longer keep up. They weaved around shrubs as they ran across the open lawn at the edge of the barracks. Some windows were shattered, but she didn't slow down to search for shapes that might be moving around inside.

She noticed both soldiers began to slow their pace for her. And she realized that she putting her girls' safety at risk.

"Go. I'll keep up," she whispered harshly between puffed breaths.

"Come on. One block to go," Chow said, and his words gave her strength.

She pushed herself to run faster, but her legs refused to pump harder.

"Contact!" Jinx called out and fired off a quick succession of shots to Sheila's right. Jenny screamed and clasped her hands over her ears.

Chow fired off shots in another direction.

When she saw the pack of a dozen Variants running toward them, terror rose within her.

"I'm empty," Jinx yelled.

A few seconds later. "I'm empty," Chow said.

She could see the tunnel entrance. *Too far.*

She studied the men to each side of her. Both wore hard looks, holding on to her daughters while switching to knives with their other hands. They were strong and fast, maybe fast enough to make it.

The knowledge of what needed to be done sent a sob racking through her body. She took off her cap and slid it onto Tasha's head.

"Tasha, I need you to look after Jenny. Girls, remember the Supergirl game."

Her daughter frowned, not understanding what Sheila was about to do.

Chow looked at her with full understanding written all over his face. He shook his head. "Don't even think about it."

She turned to see the pack gaining on them.

No time!

"Get my girls to the tunnels!" she yelled and spun on her heels.

"Damn it, Sheila," Jinx called back to her.

"Mommy!" Jenny screamed.

Sheila stood firm, but looked over her shoulder. "I'll see you in the tunnels, sweeties." She found the lie rolled off her tongue easily.

"No, Mom!" Tasha cried out.

"Go!"

Jinx scowled, but Chow gave her a nod, and they sprinted away with her daughters. Tears welled in her eyes, and she turned away so they wouldn't see her cry.

We're going to die no longer floated through her mind. Now, a new thought emerged, and it soothed her. It gave her strength she needed. She wiped tears from her cheeks as a sense of tranquility smothered her terror.

She looked up and held her arms out to the Variants as though welcoming them into a mother's embrace.

My girls are going to be okay.

— 10 —

Chow's first instinct had been to knock out Big Horn's wife, throw her over his shoulder, and run to the tunnels. The problem was that even running at a full sprint, they didn't stand a chance of making it to the tunnels before the super freaks reached them. If the kids' mother could buy them a few seconds then, maybe—just maybe—they had a snowball's chance in hell to survive this day.

He counted two seconds. The pack would be reaching her about now.

A .50 cal rattled the ground, and he spun around to see the pack get torn apart. Variants twisted in a ghastly, bloody dance as bullets shredded them. In the middle of the pack, he could still see the woman in the arms of a Variant, as though it were trying to protect her against the onslaught. He knew the truth was far more sinister.

The scene was over within a few seconds. When the echoes of gunfire faded, all the Variants lay on the ground. Nothing moved.

Chow fell to his knees, still clutching the girl to him. If the .50 cal had erupted only a few seconds earlier... *Just a few seconds.*

"Mom!" Tasha fought his hold, but he held her tightly.

She hit him. "Let me go! Mom!"

He clamped his eyes shut and ignored her pleas. How could he tell Sheila's daughters that her death was for nothing? That if help arrived just a few seconds earlier, their mother would still be alive? When he opened his eyes, he turned to Jinx whose expression bore the same raw torture Chow was experiencing.

"Pick up the pace! The noise will draw in more."

Chow looked up to see troops waving down from the .50 cal set up above the tunnel entrance, mostly hidden by the shrubs. Smoke emanated from its hot barrel.

His jaw tightened. He stood and handed Tasha over to Jinx. "Get them to the tunnel."

Fists clenched, he strode toward to the gunner. "You were too late!"

The soldier frowned. "I fired as soon as I saw them coming."

"Hey, get back here, pipsqueak!" Jinx hollered from behind Chow.

Chow turned back.

"That one's a slippery little kid," Jinx called out to him, while he held a sobbing Tasha in his arms.

Chow shot a final glare at the gunner before he turned, ran, and caught the surprisingly fast little girl. "Whoa there, Jenny."

"But, Mommy..." she began.

"She's—" What the hell was a guy supposed to say to a little kid who'd just lost her mother? "We need you to go to the tunnel. Okay, kid?"

Jenny frowned, then she rummaged in her backpack and tugged out a small green blanket. She held it out to Chow. "Mommy gets cold. She'll need this."

"Oh." Chow realized the little girl didn't yet

comprehend what had happened to her mother. He pressed the blanket back toward her. "How about you hold on to it for now?"

She stomped her foot. "No. Mommy will be cold when she wakes up."

He held out his hands in surrender. "Okay, okay. I'll leave it with her, but I need you to go with Jinx right now. Deal?"

The girl held on to the blanket for a moment as though she were considering her options. She stuck out her chin, gave a single nod, and then handed him the blanket.

He forced a smile, took the blanket, and motioned toward Jinx and her older sister. "Now, hurry to the tunnels."

"Okay," she said and then started running toward Jinx.

Chow turned and headed toward the girls' mother. His boots grew heavier with each step and felt like they'd been filled with concrete by the time he reached her body. Sheila Horn lay on the ground, a dead Variant sprawled across her, and blood pooling around her. In a surge of anger, he snarled and kicked the Variant off her.

He went to cover her body. He paused and frowned. Her body was intact, with only a few tears in her skin from the attack. She almost seemed peaceful as she lay there. He scowled. But she was still dead. If he had ammo, he would've made sure she remained at peace. Instead, he gave a small prayer that maybe the powers to be could show a little mercy for once and keep her from turning.

His lips thinned when he saw the ring on her left hand, knowing he'd be the one to break the news to Big Horn...assuming the guy was even still alive. With how bad things were at Fort Bragg, survival outside the base had to be impossible.

He knelt and tugged the wedding ring off her finger. Then, he shook the small blanket out and lay it across her torso.

"Get a move on. Tunnel door's closing!" Jinx yelled back.

Chow glanced back to find safety waiting for them. When he shed a final glance at Sheila Horn, a glint of sunlight caught his eye. He bent down one last time and tugged the empty Colt out from her belt. He'd make damn sure that peacemaker would kill another Variant or two.

Then, he took off at a run toward the two girls he'd give his life to protect.

Epilogue

She woke up in the middle of the night. Her mind, at first fogged with jumbled memories of little girls and a man in a green uniform of some kind, became clearer with each passing breath. Soon, everything in her mind faded to leave a clean, simple slate. She sat up, and the small blanket that had been covering her slid off.

Everything looked different, smelled different, though she could no longer recall what the world had been like before. Her palms seemed to stick to the concrete, and she looked down at her hands. The longer fingers seemed foreign to her, yet very much felt *right*.

Joints popped and clicked as she pushed to her feet. Hair flitted to the ground around her. She cracked her jaw and cut her lip. She touched the jagged tooth, then ignored it. She eyed the blanket. She bent over and picked it up. It smelled familiar and tugged at an emotion she could no longer place. She sniffed it and felt a yearning…but more so, she felt a craving.

She craved to destroy.

A shrill scream called out to her, and she cocked her head. She reached out with her new and improved senses and found the one watching her from a nearby tree. She could feel him as much as she could smell, hear, and see him. He understood her. He was kindred and called to her to join him.

She gave a primal scream and ran to him.

Together, they would hunt and kill.

Continue reading the main storyline with

EXTINCTION HORIZON

book 1 of the Extinction Cycle saga

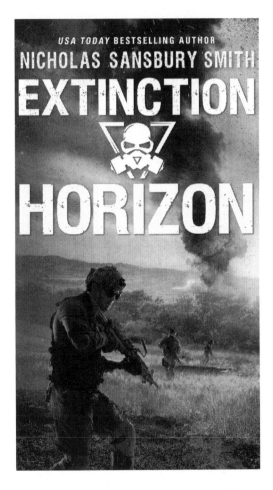

Available wherever books are sold.

About the Authors

Extinction Cycle Creator Nicholas Sansbury Smith

Nicholas Sansbury Smith is the New York Times and USA Today bestselling author of the Hell Divers series. His other work includes the Extinction Cycle series, the Trackers series, and the Orbs series. He worked for Iowa Homeland Security and Emergency Management in disaster planning and mitigation before switching careers to focus on his one true passion—writing. When he isn't writing or daydreaming about the apocalypse, he enjoys running, biking, spending time with his family, and traveling the world. He is an Ironman triathlete and lives in Iowa with his wife, their dogs, and a house full of books.

Learn more at NicholasSansburySmith.com

About Anthony J Melchiorri

Anthony J Melchiorri is a scientist with a PhD in bioengineering. Originally from the Midwest, he now lives in Texas. By day, he develops cellular therapies and 3D-printable artificial organs. By night, he writes apocalyptic, medical, and science-fiction thrillers that blend real-world research with other-worldly possibility. When he isn't in the lab or at the keyboard, he spends his time running, reading, hiking, and traveling in search of new story ideas.

Learn more at AnthonyJMelchiorri.com

About Rachel Aukes

Rachel Aukes is the award-winning author of 100 Days in Deadland, which made the Best of the Year list by Suspense Magazine. Her current series are the Fringe Series (space adventure). Her other series include the Deadland Saga and the Colliding Worlds Trilogy.

Over the past twenty years, she's consulted across the corporate world and taught at a local university, warping the minds of both today's and tomorrow's generations. A licensed pilot, she can be found flying old airplanes over the Midwest countryside with her husband and an incredibly spoiled, fifty-pound lapdog. She lives near Ames, Iowa.

Learn more at RachelAukes.com

About Russell Blake

Featured in The Wall Street Journal, The Times, and The Chicago Tribune, Russell Blake is The NY Times, WSJ, and USA Today bestselling author of dozens of action/adventure and mystery novels, including Fatal Exchange, Fatal Deception, The Geronimo Breach, Zero Sum, The Assassin series, The Delphi Chronicle trilogy, The Voynich Cypher, Silver Justice, the JET series, bio-thriller Upon A Pale Horse, the BLACK series, Ramsey's Gold, Emerald Buddha, The Goddess Legacy, Deadly Calm, Extinction: Thailand, A Girl Apart, A Girl Betrayed, techno-thriller Quantum Synapse, and The Day After Never series.

Non-fiction includes the international bestseller An Angel With Fur (animal biography) and How To Sell A

Gazillion eBooks In No Time.

Blake is co-author of The Eye of Heaven and The Solomon Curse with legendary author Clive Cussler.

Blake also writes under the moniker R.E. Blake in the NA/YA/Contemporary Romance genres. Novels include Less Than Nothing, More Than Anything, and Best Of Everything.

Having resided in Mexico for fifteen years, Blake enjoys his dogs, fishing, boating, tequila and writing, while battling world domination by clowns. His thoughts, such as they are, can be found at his blog:

Learn more at RussellBlake.com

About Jeff Olah

Jeff Olah is the author and creator of the best-selling series The Dead Years, The Last Outbreak, and The Next World. He writes for all those readers who love good post-apocalyptic, supernatural horror, and dystopian/science fiction.

His thirst for detailed story lines and shocking plot twists has been fueled over the years by stories from Cormac McCarthy, Ray Bradbury, and Stephen King. He also has a difficult time tearing himself away from character driven dramas like The Walking Dead, Breaking Bad, and LOST.

Jeff is addicted to lifting weights, running hills, and chocolate protein shakes. He lives in Southern California with his wife, daughter, and seven-year-old Chihuahua.

Learn more at JeffOlah.com

About Mark Tufo

Mark Tufo was born in Boston Massachusetts. He attended UMASS Amherst where he obtained a BA and later joined the US Marine Corp. He was stationed in Parris Island SC, Twenty Nine Palms CA and Kaneohe Bay Hawaii. After his tour he went into the Human Resources field with a worldwide financial institution and has gone back to college at CTU to complete his masters.

He has written the Indian Hill trilogy with the first Indian Hill – Encounters being published for the Amazon Kindle in July 2009. He has since written the Zombie Fallout series and is working on a new zombie book.

He lives in Maine with his wife, three kids and two English bulldogs.

Learn more at MarkTufo.com

Made in the USA
San Bernardino, CA
09 February 2019